MW00852613

PAGES OF PAIN

Troy Denning

PAGES OF PAIN

Random House and its affiliate companies have worldwide distribution rights in the book trade for English language products of TSR, Inc.

Distributed to the book and hobby trade in the United Kingdom by TSR Ltd.

Distributed to the toy and hobby trade by regional distributors.

Cover art by Robh Ruppel. Interior art by Diesel.

First Printing: September 1996
Printed in the United States of America.
Library of Congress Catalog Card Number: 95-62250

9 8 7 6 5 4 3 2 1

ISBN: 0-7869-0508-5
2627XXX1501

TSR, Inc.
201 Sheridan Springs Road
Lake Geneva, WI 53147
U.S.A.

TSR Ltd.
120 Church End, Cherry Hinton
Cambridge CB1 3LB
United Kingdom

The BLOOD WARS™ Trilogy
J. Robert King

Blood Hostages

Abyssal Warriors

Planar Powers
December 1996

ACKNOWLEDGMENTS

The opening and closing epigraphs and all stanzas of poetry used in the story are from the poem "Dolores" by Algernon Charles Swinburne.

I would also like to thank the following people for their contributions to *Pages of Pain:*

My editors, Brian and Phil, for their comments, their encouragement, and especially their patience—without which the Lady might have done the Thrasson *real* harm.

My fellow Alliterates, for letting me inflict some of Her Serenity's more cutting passages on them.

Dave "Zeb" Cook and the others who created the Cage and gave the Lady of Pain her edge.

My instructor, Master Lloyd Holden of the AKF Martial Arts Academy in Janesville, WI, for his remarks on the relevant portions of the manuscript.

And, as always, Andria, for support and patience well beyond the call

For my brother Bill,
The Last Do-Gooder in Sigil

PAINS OF THE MIND

Black hair and ebony eyes, a cleft chin and sun-bronzed skin, he is no denizen of mine. He shoves his way through the teeming lanes of the Lower Ward, both arms wrapped around that enormous amphora he carries and no hand free for his sword. He wears the bronze armor of Thrassos, with no cape to protect against the acid haze that always hangs in this part of the city. From his belt dangles a purse, fat and naked, just daring some fingersmith to ply his trade. The gray-swaddled crowd swirls around him with scarcely a stare; with Abyssal fiends and celestial seraphim walking the streets, they have better things to heed than wide-eyed pilgrims too naive to hide their coin.

A clever disguise, but I know that Thrasson for a Hunter.

Those ebony eyes can see through my thickest granite walls, and that long aquiline nose can smell a drop of blood at a hundred paces. Those ears—small and shaped like shells, in the human fashion—those ugly little ears can hear a hiss of pain in the next ward. He has one of those long forked tongues that can taste the fear of those who have looked upon my face. And if the Thrasson presses his hands to the cobblestones, he can feel the coldness of my passing. I know he can.

In Sigil, the Lady of Pain *always* knows. I hear all the lies whispered into all the tepid ears in the dark bedchambers of all the great manors. I see every hand that slips into an open pocket on every bustling street, and I feel the dagger that burns in the belly of every trusting fool who ever followed a glitter girl into a dark alley. No longer can I tell where Sigil begins and I end; no longer can I separate what I perceive from what the city is. I *am* Sigil.

(In a dreary room where sick men slake their secret fevers, a yellow-bruised girl climbs naked from the zombie pit. She opens her palm and walks the aisles and does not cringe when the hot hands caress her thighs. She lives the best way she can; in Sigil, the noblest act is to survive.)

I open my eyes, and the Lady of Pain is there—not just watching, but stalking the Hunter up the teeming street, with the clamor of forge hammers ringing in my ears and the stink of hot slag scorching my nostrils. She is tall and serene, a statuesque beauty of classic features, with sulfurous eyes and a cold, callous air. A halo of many-styled blades surrounds her head, some notched and pitted, others silver and gleaming, but all keen-edged and tainted with blood. The hem of her brocaded gown sweeps along the grimy cobblestones, but never soils.

My gray-swaddled denizens bustle by, blissfully unaware that she—no, I—that *I* walk among them. Only if my feet break touch with the ground will they notice me, and I am careful to keep my shoes on the street. Better for them to see the Lady of Pain when they have offended me, when they feel the fear eating their bellies and hear the death gods calling their names.

Whenever my denizens brush against me, tiny white welts rise on their skin. Before my eyes, these blisters swell into thumb-shaped pods. They begin to grow more slowly, then sprout dozens of hooked spines. As the crowd mills about, the barbs catch hold of anything they touch, and the husks pass to fresh carriers. They continue to enlarge and soon latch onto someone new, then someone else after that, and it is not long before a sea of bulging pods is spreading steadily outward around me.

My denizens continue to bustle about their business. They cannot see the pods, nor feel the extra weight, nor even smell the fetid reek that clings to their bodies. Only I perceive the husks, slowly swelling and turning emerald and gold and ruby and jet;

only I see them oozing yellow ichor and starting to throb like hearts.

Thus are the four Pains spread through the multiverse—agony, anguish, misery, and despair—to ripen and burst and bring low the mighty and the meek alike. From whence they come, I do not remember. It may be that I create them myself, or that they rise from some hidden place deeper and blacker than the bottom layer of the Abyss, where smoke hangs thick as rock and death is the sweetest memory. I can only say there is a void in my chest where I once had a heart, and from this emptiness springs all the suffering in the multiverse.

At first, the Pains are like a kiss, hot and breathy and welcome. They reach out with long cajoling fingers and make my bones hum with delight. I warm to the touch and, though I know what must follow, yearn for more. My flesh tingles and flushes and shudders, and the more my ecstasy builds, the more the void pours forth. It fills me to glutting, sates me with honeyed rapture until bliss rolls half a turn and becomes sweet agony. Then my body nettles with a blistering itch no ointment can heal. And the greater my woe, the more scalding the anguish that seethes from the empty well inside. I boil in my own sick regret, and I cannot staunch the flow. It billows up in white plumes and blanches my bones with sorrow; I burn with the shame of a thousand evils I cannot recall, and still the well pours forth. It fills me as fire fills a forge, until I must burst or scour myself clean on the swarming streets of Sigil.

They are a gift, these Pains.

(A bottle of Arborea's best in one hand and a chain of Ossan pearls in the other, a jolly merchant home early flings open his door to see his young wife lying cold and blue on the floor, her child clinging to her breast and wailing for a reason. There is no reason; only life and suffering and then a terrible lingering emptiness, and, hard as I try, I cannot see beyond that.)

Pain can force fathers to forsake their daughters and heroes to betray their kingdoms. It can change the hearts of tyrants, or subdue the lands of proud and vicious warriors. It is pain that makes wives hate husbands and immortals beg for death, and only pain that can shackle whole planes to the will of a single lord.

And so the gods send their Hunters; they thirst for the Pains as flames thirst for tinder. The wicked ones would make a weapon of suffering; they would spread it among their enemies and brandish it over the heads of their comrades. And worse would the good ones do; they would drive torment from the multiverse altogether—destroy misery if they could—and end forever all suffering and despair.

Frauds and fools, every one—and the good ones more than the bad. Like quicksilver, pain slips from the hand that would grasp it and divides before the blow that would cleave it. Without the Pains, the multiverse can endure no more than wind can blow without the air. Suffering breeds strength from weakness, it heralds new births, it guides all beings through life. The dead soar to oblivion on black wings of anguish, and even pleasure springs from the same well as agony. To shun pain is to lie stillborn forever.

(A child, wishing he could swim once more in brown waters, lies slick with sweat and speckled in pink, his stiff legs withering to useless sticks. I have hugged him to my breast; the Pains have rooted and sprouted unseen and unfelt, and now they have burst. It is not right, and it is not wrong; it is life.)

At a crossroads, the Hunter stops and turns his head right, then left. He is looking through walls with those ebony eyes, searching for what has already found him. I take him in my arms and press myself close. A hundred blisters sprout beneath his armor, and still I hold the Thrasson tight as a lover; I hold him tight so the pods will root deep, deep down in his soul and not rub off.

His body tenses.

That huge amphora slips through his arms and nearly crashes to the street. He cries out and drops to his heels. He catches it, and gives out a long breathy sigh, as though smashing that jar would be worse than dying.

Perhaps it would. There is a golden net inside, god-enchanted just to catch me.

The Thrasson balances the amphora on the street and slowly

turns, his free hand on his sword and his eyes narrowed. It may be that he felt a chill beneath his armor, as though a ghost had embraced him, but he cannot be certain. So sudden and fleeting was the touch that even now he wonders if he imagined it. The crowd swirls past, cursing him for a fool or a madman and keeping a watchful eye on his weapon hand. Though I stand less than a pace away, of course he cannot see me. Soon enough, he decides it was nothing more than a sudden case of armor itch. He takes up the amphora again and bulls his way back into the crowd. Already, I see a thousand hooked spines stabbing through his backplate.

Do not call it revenge—never revenge. Even the gods deserve their pain, and the Thrasson shall bear it to them.

HALL OF MARBLE

After so many hours harrowing Sigil's teeming lanes, what does the Thrasson think when at last he plows through the crowd and sees the Blue Hall looming ahead? I know. The Lady of Pain always knows, and she will tell you:

The Hall of Information looked exactly as twenty or more peevish direction-givers had said it would: an imposing monolith of pale blue marble, with a roof of black slate and three massive columns straddling a pair of gray entrance ramps. Inscribed on the capitals of the three pillars were the words "Cooperation," "Compliance," and "Control," an oddly ominous motto for what was purported to be a service bureau. A web of fracture lines laced the "Cooperation" post, which, despite a supporting cage of steel braces, appeared on the verge of collapse.

Clutching his amphora in both arms and pushing through a torrent of drab-cloaked beings—human and otherwise—the Thrasson angled across Crystal Dew Avenue toward the ramp between "Compliance" and "Control." The nearer he approached the hall, the less he agreed with the churls who had called it "an edifice of stately grandeur." Even a simple man of action could see that the building suffered from a clumsy attempt to substitute opulence for taste. The stark bands of the onyx corner boards made a mockery of the marble facade's soft swirls, while the turquoise window casings looked like the painted eyes of a common harlot. The door guards, with their crimson breastplates and rusty shoulder spikes, added just the splash of blood to make a vulgar mess of the whole thing.

Jewel of the Infinite Planes indeed! Sigil so far had been a bitter disappointment to the Thrasson. So thick was the ginger air that it dragged over his face like cobwebs; just breathing the awful stuff filled his throat with a burning, acrid grit. In some wards, the avenues ran ankle-deep with swill, and in others, a man could hardly shove his way through the throngs that packed the streets. Everywhere, the constant drizzle stained the dreary building facades with runnels of yellow sulfur. Upon each sweltering breeze came a stench more rancid than the last, and nowhere did the clamor ebb for even a moment.

The Thrasson had heard that Sigil was shaped like the inside of a floating wheel, and that if he looked straight up, he would see the roofs of distant buildings instead of sky. So far, he had seen nothing but a sick, brown haze. It was said that the city was the hub of the multiverse, that somewhere in its bounds lay a portal to each world in the infinite planes; to the Thrasson, it seemed that every one of those portals was the wrong end of a garbage chute. He wanted nothing more than to complete his task and be gone from the place.

The Thrasson climbed the ramp and crossed the portico, unabashedly returning the stern glower of the guards. He would have welcomed a challenge, so anxious was he to vent his frustration. In addition to the difficulties of delivering the amphora, no one in the city seemed to know of him. He did not expect them to recognize him by sight, or anything so foolish, but it did seem reasonable to assume that by now his deeds would have been sung in even the lowliest gutter house of Sigil. Yet, when he introduced himself, he still had to recount his entire list of feats—

at least those he could remember—and even after he described the felling of the Acherian Giant, most people simply turned away in indifference. The only ones interested in him were the thieves eyeing his heavy purse and the guides who, hearing the name of the one he wished to find, scurried away without naming a price.

As the Thrasson neared the entrance, the sentries reached over and pushed open the doors. They gave no salutation or comment, and their faces betrayed no hint of either respect or disdain. They were simply holding the doors for a man burdened with a heavy amphora.

That anonymous courtesy made the Thrasson's belly burn with indignity. Still, as it was the burden of fame to suffer ignorance in good grace, he paused long enough to utter a few sentences of thanks.

"Bar that, pal," answered the tallest guard, a square-chinned fellow with a two-day growth of beard on his cheeks. "We'd do the same for any blood. Now get on with it." He jerked his head toward the entrance. "Madame Mok don't like us letting in drafts."

The Thrasson stepped into a murky foyer of blue marble, where he found himself standing at the end of a serpentine visitors' queue. The line switched back and forth a dozen times until it finally stopped before a high, looming counter of black marble. The massive desk stood directly beneath a glowing chandelier of blue-green beryl crystals. It was flanked by a pair of silver, hand-shaped braziers, from which rose two plumes of pink, apple-sweet incense smoke.

Behind the lofty counter sat a single bespectacled clerk, hunched over the bench and using quill and ink to scratch notes into a parchment ledger. From the wooly nap atop his head rose the double-curled horns of a bariaur, a sort of goatlike centaur that roamed many of the multiverse's planes. The Thrasson had already been surprised by the hundreds of bariaur pushing through Sigil's packed streets; in his own plane, Arborea, the bariaur were an unsettled, carefree race who would sooner leap into a cesspool than enter a city. He found it difficult to believe that any of them actually abided in Sigil, much less worked inside a gloomy building like the Hall of Information.

The Thrasson considered the line only a moment before deciding it was beneath him to wait. Scattered among the humans were frog-faced slaadi, dwarves both bearded and bald, a svelte trio of elves, even a lizardlike khaasta warrior, but he saw no sign of anyone who matched his own stature. Had he seen the shimmering feathers of an astral deva's seraphic wings, perhaps, or the smoking horns of a great baatezu lord, he might have waited. As matters stood, however, it seemed apparent that his business took precedence over that of anyone else in the foyer.

The Thrasson pushed straight through the looped line, issuing stern yet polite commands for those ahead to stand aside. The humans obeyed, of course, though it surprised him to note how many of them looked taken aback. Even in Sigil, it should have been obvious from his bearing and fine armor that he was a man of renown, beloved of the gods and deserving of all respect.

When the Thrasson reached the khaasta, the reptilian suddenly raised its tail to block the way and craned its sinuous neck around to glare. The warrior's head was typically lacertilian: a flat wedge that was mostly snout, with a long, stupid grin and beady slit-pupiled eyes that betrayed no emotion at all.

"You wait like the ressst of ussssss, berk."

The Thrasson regarded the tail. The thickness of a human leg, it was armored in leathery scales and braided with the rippling sinews of a race not far removed from the brute. The appendage was no match for the star-forged blade in the Thrasson's scabbard, but he had no wish to punish the khaasta so severely. He threw one leg over the tail, then forced the scaly appendage downward until he had it trapped between his knees.

"You would be wise to defer to your better."

The khaasta's head began to bob in that angry lizard way, then its scaly hand dropped toward a broad manskin belt.

The Thrasson snapped his hips forward, trapping the tail behind one knee and before the other, then scissored his legs. With a sharp pop, the appendage kinked and went limp. The reptilian roared and produced a stiletto from its belt sheath, but with its broken tail still trapped between the Thrasson's legs, it was helpless to spin and attack.

At the head of the line, the old bariaur scowled and looked up from his ledger. "Here now! What's all this?" He peered over his spectacles at the growling khaasta. "People are working. If you can't be quiet, I'll ask you to leave."

The khaasta quickly slipped his dagger out of sight. "Assssk *me* to leave?" He pointed a single yellow talon at the Thrasson, who released his tail and continued to push toward the counter. "That berk'sss the one who'sss shoving ahead!"

The bariaur studied the disheveled line, then turned his glower upon the advancing Thrasson. "We have procedures in this hall. You'll have to stand in line like everyone else."

"Do you not know me, old sir?" The Thrasson hipped aside a scowling dwarf and continued forward. "Have you not heard of the slayer of the Hydra of Thrassos, the tamer of the Hebron Crocodile, the bane of Abudrian Dragons the savior of the Virgins of Marmara . . ."

He reached the counter, and the bariaur leaned over his desk to scowl down at the Thrasson, who continued to list his feats: ". . . the champion of Ilyrian Kings, the killer of the Chalcedon Lion—"

"No, I have not heard of you," the bariaur interrupted, "nor do I much care what you've done. If you can't comply with the rules, I'll have you removed."

The clerk cast a meaningful glance toward the door. The two sentries now stood inside the foyer, glaring at the Thrasson as though they had expected trouble from him all along.

"What'ssss of me tail?" complained the khaasta. "There'sss lawsss againssst the breaking of tailssss, there issss!"

The sentries nodded, more to each other than the khaasta, then snapped their glaives to the advance guard and started forward. The crowd parted to let them through, and the bariaur scowled down at the Thrasson.

"Is this true? Did you assault the reptilian?"

"I caused him no serious injury." The Thrasson's tone was sharp, for it had been the khaasta who had wronged him. "He dared block my path, and even you must see that my concerns take precedence here."

The bariaur arched his brow, then raised a hand to stop the two sentries. "Are you declaring an Emergency Priority?"

"If it means I am entitled not to wait, then yes."

The bariaur licked his lips, then clasped his hands on his desk and leaned on his elbows. "The proper procedure is to announce the Emergency Priority to the door guards, who will then certify that you have the proper funds and escort you to the front of the line, so as to create minimal disturbance and avoid unpleasant incidents such as the breaking of tails." The clerk made a sour face and glanced at the khaasta, then looked back to the Thrasson. "However, since you have already reached the counter, we will skip certification and proceed directly to collection. You may now present the fee."

"Fee?"

"Ten gold pieces." The bariaur's eyes grew large and menacing behind his spectacles. "Otherwise, every sod who came through those doors would declare an Emergency Priority, would he not?"

When the Thrasson did not immediately produce the fee, the guards began to advance again. "By order of the Hall of Speakers, false declaiming is a crime against the Lady's Order," said the tallest one, who had spoken to the Thrasson before. "Crimes against the Lady's Order are punishable by a sentence of not less than—"

"I have the fee!"

The Thrasson placed the amphora on the floor and balanced it against the counter with his leg, then opened his purse and counted out the gold. Ten gold coins would buy a lot of wine, but he could always get free wine back in Thrassos. He passed the coins up to the bariaur, who confirmed the count, entered the amount in his ledger, and dropped the coins into a slot on the surface of his bench.

"Do you want a receipt?"

"No. I want—"

The bariaur raised a finger to silence the Thrasson, then produced a large iron bell from behind his bench. He rang it six times. Though the tolling was not particularly loud, it reverberated through the cavernous hall as clearly as birdsong. By the time the last knell had died away, a gentle murmur had arisen to fill the entire structure. A trio of human youths, all dressed in pale blue uniforms with ugly red shoulder sashes, rounded a corner and stood at attention beside the counter. Around the opposite corner came another six guards, all wearing the same red plate armor as the door sentries. These men positioned themselves between the crowd and the counter, holding their glaives at port arms. From somewhere in the depths of the building echoed the measured clatter of four hooves clacking upon the marble floor.

The bariaur dipped his quill in the ink, then poised it over his ledger and peered down at the Thrasson.

"Name?"

The Thrasson hesitated, loathe to admit his one weakness in public. An impatient murmur rustled through the lobby, and the guards began to push the crowd back.

"*Name?*"

"I–er–uh, why is my name important?"

The bariaur's eye twitched. "We have our procedures, berk. Name?"

"You dare call *me*–" The Thrasson bit his tongue, reminding himself that he needed the bariaur's cooperation to keep the promise he had made. "I–uh–I can't tell you my name."

Deep in the building, the steady clacking of hooves grew louder, and the two door sentries stepped to the Thrasson's flanks. "Can't, or won't, berk?"

"I cannot." Though hardly intimidated by the guards, the Thrasson forced himself to answer politely. His task did not call for the shedding of blood, and it was the hallmark of a true champion never to cause unnecessary harm. "I don't know my name. I recall nothing before awakening on the shore near Thrassos, where the citizens were kind enough to care for me until I could repay their hospitality by slaying the great hydra. Not long after, I heard of the mighty crocodile menacing the fishermen of the river Hebrus, so I journeyed–"

"Yes, yes, I have heard all that," the bariaur snorted. "But what am I to put in the ledger? He who slew the Hydra of Thrassos, then tamed the Hebron Crocodile, and on and on? I only have one line."

The Thrasson thought for a moment, and while he thought, the clacking of hooves deep in the building continued to grow louder. At last, he looked up. "The people of Thrassos call me the Amnesian Hero. That should fit on one line."

The bariaur nodded sagely. "The Amnesian Hero it is, then." He scrawled in his ledger, then dipped his quill again. "And may I put down Thrassos, Layer the First, Arborea, as your home?"

The Amnesian Hero nodded. "That is the only home I know."

The bariaur wrote this as well, then peered down at the Thrasson. "I'll grant that not knowing your own name is serious, but it hardly seems an Emergency Priority." He dipped his quill and, almost sympathetically, said, "Still, you paid the fee and I can't get it back for you. Who would you like to see first? The Bureau of Human Affairs, or perhaps the Nonplanar Races Commission? By the Emergency Priorities Edict of the Hall of Speakers, you have a maximum of ten appointments to answer a single question."

The Amnesian Hero felt an unexpected flutter in his stomach. "You can tell me who I am?"

The bariaur smacked his lips. "I'm not authorized to dispense that information." His quill remained poised over the ledger. "My duties are limited strictly to the scheduling of appointments. Now, whom do you wish to see?"

The Amnesian Hero came close to requesting the Bureau of Human Affairs, but at the last moment found the strength to resist the temptation. Whoever he was, he was certainly a man of renown, and men of renown did not put their personal needs above their promises.

"If you don't know who you wish to see, I am authorized to give you a list."

The clacking of hooves deeper in the building grew so loud that the Thrasson expected to see an enormous bariaur rounding the counter at any moment. Voices in the impatient crowd began shouting suggestions, some more polite than others. The guards yelled back, bellowing warnings about staying in control and complying with the rules. To make his answer heard above the clamor, the Amnesian Hero nearly had to shout.

"I'm not here about my name. I want to see the Lady of Pain!"

The old bariaur yanked off his spectacles, and, save for the mounting echoes of hooves on marble, the chamber abruptly fell silent. The clerk leaned out over the counter and, bushy white brows half-arched, peered down at the Amnesian Hero.

"Pardon me. Did you say, the Lady of Pain?"

The Amnesian Hero nodded. "I did." He gestured at the large amphora he was still balancing against the counter. "I have a gift for her."

Nervous laughter rustled through the crowd, drawing several stern threats from the guards. On the other side of the counter, the steady clacking of the hooves suddenly ceased. The bariaur's face turned a deep shade of crimson.

"This is no time for jokes, berk! You're the one who declared an information emergency!"

"I am not joking," the Amnesian Hero replied. "I came to deliver a gift to the Lady of Pain. My question is: where do I find her palace?"

A brief clatter sounded from the rear of the counter, then a second bariaur appeared beside the clerk. She was by far the largest the Amnesian Hero had ever seen—at least that he remembered seeing—looming a full head above her associate. In fact, she was so large that the silk-draped swell of her broad, goatlike forequarters was visible over the lip of the counter. Her face was gaunt and amazingly flat, save for a long narrow nose hanging like a bartizan over her gash of a mouth. Her hair was dyed the same pale blue as the hall's marble walls, and she wore it in a long, unruly mop that could not quite conceal the two golden horns curling back from her temples.

The Amnesian Hero felt his mouth gaping open. He promptly clamped it shut and averted his gaze. Horns were something of a deformity on female bariaur, and it would be unseemly to stare.

The female took a moment to glower over the crowd, then turned her glare upon the clerk. "You rang the emergency bell, Earlick?"

Though she pronounced it "Earlick," Erlik was a common enough name for the Thrasson to suspect she was being intentionally insulting.

Without looking the female in the eyes, Erlik nodded. "I did, Madame Mok." The clerk squinted at his ledger and laid a finger on the appropriate line. "A human, one Amnesian Hero of Thrassos, Arborea, Layer the First, declared an Emergency Priority and paid the fee."

Madame Mok glared down at the Amnesian Hero, her sour face now absolutely curdled. "And this Amnesian Hero, has he no real name, *Earlick?*"

"None that I can recall." The Amnesian Hero was tired of being treated as though he were not there. "I remember nothing before awakening on the shore near Thrassos, where the kind citizens cared for me until I grew strong enough to repay them by slaying a hydra that had–"

"Silence, berk!" Madame Mok snapped. "We have our procedures in this hall. . . ."

The Amnesian Hero bristled under the rebuff, but inclined his head politely and allowed Erlik to answer for him.

Erlik swallowed, then licked his lips. "The Amnesian Hero cannot recall his name."

"I see. And has a Mercykiller confirmed his claim? Or could this be another attempt by the Hall of Records to embarrass us?"

The color drained from Erlik's face. "I d-don't have the auth-th-thority to auth-th-thorize–"

"Of course you don't." Madame Mok turned to the Amnesian Hero, then pointed at one of the door sentries standing beside him. "You will look into the Mercykiller's eyes and repeat your name."

Growing more perturbed with each passing moment, the Amnesian Hero turned to the guard. Though there were not many Mercykillers in Arborea, the Thrasson had heard the name before. They were a group of fanatics who dispensed "justice" to the "guilty"–though no one in Arborea seemed to have a clear idea of who the guilty were or what justice they received.

The Amnesian Hero met the Mercykiller's gaze, and the sentry's pupils suddenly seemed as glimmering and dark as cavern pools. The Thrasson felt a gentle tingle behind his brow and realized the fellow was looking someplace beyond his eyes. It did not matter to the Amnesian Hero; the best thing that could happen to him would be for the guard to discover that he *did* know his name.

"I cannot remember my name," said the Thrasson. "I recall nothing before awakening on—"

"That's enough—I don't need your whole life history." The Mercykiller turned to Madame Mok and nodded. "He's telling the truth."

She smiled rather wickedly. "Now that we have established who you are—or, rather, who you are *not*—what do you want from the Hall of Information? I believe I overheard something about a gift?"

"For the Lady of Pain." The Amnesian Hero rested a hand on his amphora. "My question is: where do I find her palace?"

Again, a nervous chuckle rose from the crowd. Even Madame Mok sneered in amusement. "And this gift, it is from you?"

The Amnesian Hero scowled. "Am I not the one who paid good gold to have his question answered?"

"You paid to have your appointments expedited—as they have been," Madame Mok corrected. "But I am in control here. If you wish to have your question answered, you must comply with my procedures."

The Amnesian Hero ground his teeth and said nothing.

"Is the gift your own?" demanded Madame Mok.

"No, I am only the bearer. The gift comes from Poseidon, King of Seas and Cleaver of Lands."

Madame Mok's face turned as pale as alabaster. An astonished drone buzzed through the foyer, and people who had been waiting in line all day long began to scramble for the exits. The guards turned away from the crowd and formed a ring around the Amnesian Hero, who, though surprised by the reaction, was glad to be at last accorded the proper respect.

"Poseidon?" Madame Mok asked. "The *god* Poseidon?"

"Of course. What mortal would dare send a gift to the ruler of Sigil?"

Madame Mok fixed the Amnesian Hero with her harshest stare. The Thrasson stood proudly while she scrutinized his patrician features, the rich red tint of his bronze armor, the silver-gilded hilt of his star-forged sword, even the polished leather of his sandal straps. When her gaze finally returned to his face, her expression had changed from imperious to suspicious. She slipped back from the counter's front edge.

"You're a proxy, then?"

"Hardly. A proxy is a servant. I am a man of renown, beloved of the people and favored of the gods, as befits the bearer of a gift from the King of Seas."

The color began to return to Madame Mok's face. "Then you are not invested with Poseidon's power?"

"I have might enough of my own." The Amnesian Hero glanced contemptuously at the ring of glaive blades leveled at his chest. "Now, if you will direct me to the Lady's palace, I will deliver the gift and be gone from this swarming city."

"And this gift, what is it?" Madame Mok leaned over the counter to peer down at the amphora. "Some of that rancid pine sap you Thrassons call wine?"

"I suspect not." Poseidon had told the Amnesian Hero only that the jar contained a treasure that the Lady of Pain had lost before the founding of Sigil. "However, since the Cleaver of Lands bade me never to remove the stopper, I cannot say what the amphora holds—nor would I, if I knew. What passes between Poseidon and the Lady of Pain is no business of mine—or yours."

Madame Mok's face grew pinched and red. "In this hall, I decide what is my business and what is not!"

"Then *you* remove the stopper." The Amnesian Hero waved at the amphora. "If the contents are truly the concern of the Hall of Information, it will not trouble the Lady that you opened her gift."

The Thrasson's mocking manner drew none of the expected sniggers from the guards. Instead, Madame Mok studied him with narrowed eyes for several moments, until finally the shadow of a smile crept across her lips.

She shrugged. "As you wish. The amphora's contents are no concern of mine. I was only trying to do you a favor, Thrasson."

"I am sure you intend to tell me how."

Madame Mok nodded, accepting the sarcasm with surprising humility. "Tell me, how much do you recall about the Lady of Pain?"

"I know only what the King of Seas told me," the Amnesian Hero admitted. "She is the winsome ruler of Sigil, alone and aloof, and very sad."

"All that is true, of course, but she is also quick to anger. If she dislikes the gift, she will certainly slay you."

"I thank you for the warning, Madame Mok." The Amnesian Hero believed at least this much of what she said. Conditions in Sigil certainly suggested the city's ruler was callous and cruel. Still, the Thrasson had every intention of delivering the amphora. Poseidon had promised to restore his memory once the Lady of Pain received her gift. "We men of renown must accept such risks, so I would be grateful if you would direct me to the Lady of Pain's palace."

Madame Mok gave him an acid smile. "Certainly. It will be a pleasure to get you out of my hall. I trust that heavy purse of yours contains five more gold pieces?"

Though the Thrasson would gladly have parted with the coins just to learn the location and be on his way, a Mercykiller stepped to the counter and aimed a glaive at Madame Mok's breast.

"By edict of the Hall of Speakers: bribery, or the solicitation thereof, is punishable by—"

Madame Mok slapped the glaive aside. "Buckle your bone-box! I'm not hunting a garnish." She turned back to the Amnesian Hero. "Do you have it or not?"

The Thrasson opened his purse and withdrew five yellow coins, then raised a hand toward the counter. Madame Mok shook her head and pointed at the square-chinned Mercykiller who had accused her of soliciting a bribe.

"Give it to Cwalno."

The Amnesian Hero passed the money to the guard, who held the coins at arm's length and grimaced as though clutching a handful of scorpions.

"What am *I* to do with these?"

Madame Mok pointed at the door. "Go outside and hire eight lantern boys and a sedan chair for the Amnesian Hero."

"A sedan chair?"

"Of course. He'll need to show the proper dignity when he goes to see the Lady." Madame Mok looked down at the Amnesian Hero, then glanced at his open purse and sneered. "In fact, I'm sure he has coin for each of you Mercykillers as well. Why don't you give him a full escort and make sure he arrives at the Gatehouse in style?"

"Are you sure that will do?" The Amnesian Hero shoved his hand into his purse. "I have more gold. Perhaps you want to come too?"

Madame Mok smirked and shook her head. "That isn't necessary. Eight Mercykillers should be enough—even for you, Thrasson."

BLEAK HOUSE

How squalid the Amnesian Hero must find the Hive as he rides down Whisper Way in his elegant sedan chair, borne over the muck and the sludge on the hulking shoulders of four white-tusked ogres, four lantern boys leading the way and four more bringing up the rear, four Mercykillers to the left and four more to the right. How he must despise the grimy bloodblades who slip along the mud brick tenements, shadowing his chair, balancing the heft of his purse against the swiftness of his guards' bare blades. How he must abhor the droning black flies that hang in the air as thick as drops during a rainfall, feeding upon the stink of a street knee-deep in carrion and offal. How he must pity the gray armies of children, with their wooden forks and their starving eyes and their rat-hunt scramble.

How the Thrasson curses the wickedness of callous, foul Sigil, until he comes at last to the Marble District, where the buildings are tall and stony and black with soot. His bearers turn down Bedlam Run toward the Lady's palace, and how he gasps at its sprawling, begrimed majesty.

The Gatehouse looks like no palace the Amnesian Hero has ever seen. Large enough to house the Cleaver of Lands himself, its shape, that of an immense battle crown with a long, blocky wing spreading outward from each side. The walls were as drab as mudstone and as high as cliffs, their faces striped by three mundane rows of small square windows. The most striking feature was the central gate tower, an immense helmlike turret crested by six curving spires that arched inward toward a central minaret so high the apex was lost in Sigil's brown fog. The gate itself was an impossibly huge portcullis, with bars the size of Arborean cypress trees and spaces through which a titan could have passed.

A long string of gray flecks stretched from this entrance halfway down Bedlam Way. So dwarfed by the Gatehouse's immensity were these specks that the Amnesian Hero did not recognize them as people for several minutes, until his bearers had carried him close enough to make out the shapes of their heads sitting atop their hunched shoulders. The column packed the street completely, leaving only enough room for area residents to squeeze along the tenement fronts on the way to and from their homes. The Thrasson groaned, realizing that this was a line of petitioners, waiting to see the Lady of Pain.

"Lock that bone-box, berk!" hissed Cwalno, who was marching along outside the chair box. "In this part of town, sniveling draws bloodblades like flashing gold draws glitter girls."

"I do not snivel. As for your bloodblades, let them come. I would welcome the fight." The Amnesian Hero glared at the supplicants ahead, wondering how many coins it would cost to declare an Emergency Priority to bypass them. "Is no place in Sigil free of these monstrous lines?"

Cwalno squinted at the wretched column. "Bar that. If you wait, I wait—and I'm not staying down here a minute longer than I need to."

The assertion seemed bold for a mere guard, but the Amnesian Hero would be glad to avoid paying more bribes. He was running low on gold, and he hated nothing more than relying on the good will of others for his wine.

As the Thrasson's procession approached the line of supplicants, the four Mercykillers moved forward to shove people out of the way. The petitioners grudgingly yielded to the rough treatment, pressing aside just far enough to let the sedan chair pass. Most were humans, but the Amnesian Hero also saw bariaur, elves, dwarves, ogres, khaasta, githzerai, and a few other races he had never before encountered—at least that he could recall. All had gaunt, haunted faces wearied by hunger and despair, and the soiled rags hanging from their bony shoulders hardly resembled the bejeweled foppery of most royal supplicants.

The Thrasson saw teary-eyed women supporting drooling elders whose glassy eyes were looking somewhere far beyond. He saw lonely naked orphans with swollen bellies and skin hanging loose on their crooked bones. He saw burly guards holding the leashes of wild-faced men with shackled hands, he saw coughing, quivering women trembling with age and flushed with fever, but nowhere did he see anyone arrayed in what Madame Mok called "the proper style." Aside from his own, there were no sedan chairs, no lantern boys or guards, not even a single figure dressed in a cloak decent enough to hang in a shepherd's hut.

Cwalno reached up to draw the chair curtain closed.

The Thrasson grabbed the cloth and held it open. "What do you hope to hide, Cwalno? I've already seen that those poor wretches hardly look like royal supplicants."

Cwalno appeared vaguely uncomfortable, but chuckled grimly. "Who else would they be?" He shoved aside a babbling madman whose handler had dropped the leash. "You can't think a sane man would—er, sorry. That must be why Poseidon sent *you*."

The Amnesian Hero locked gazes with the Mercykiller. "I hope you are not trying to say that I am demented."

Cwalno sneered, while at the same time hastening to shake his head as though he had been terribly misunderstood. "A cutter like yourself? 'Course not!" There was a mocking tone to his voice. "I'm only talking about your condition. Poseidon wouldn't send no blood with a memory to deliver his present.

Any berk who can remember half what he's heard about the Lady of Pain would sooner jump into the Abyss than stand face-to-face with her."

The Amnesian Hero sat back and nodded thoughtfully. Despite Cwalno's condescending manner, there was truth in what he said. The King of Seas was by nature a selfish god, hardly the type to restore a mortal's lost memories in return for a simple errand like delivering a gift. Since accepting the amphora, the Thrasson had been expecting to run into some such trouble. Now that he finally had some idea of its nature, he was almost relieved.

"If the Lady is so terrible to face, why are all these people waiting to see her?" As the Amnesian Hero studied the throng of dismal supplicants, it occurred to him they all had an abundance of one thing. "Do the wretches not fear the Lady because of the gifts they bring her?"

Cwalno eyed the derelicts with a disdainful smirk. "And what could the Lady want from these sods?"

"Their suffering, of course! That's why she is called the Lady of Pain, is it not?"

Cwalno sneered, but was careful to neither nod his head nor shake it. "You'll see soon enough, Thrasson."

The Mercykiller pointed forward, where his three crowd-breaking companions had just pushed through into a large open square. A dozen men in cloaks of bright, spangled colors were cavorting in the space, leaping and tumbling and springing off their hands both forward and backward, all the while voicing a dismal, deep-throated dirge with no words the Amnesian Hero could identify.

On the far side of the square stood the yawning mouth of the Gatehouse's central tower. There were no guards in the area other than the strange acrobats, yet the crowd made no effort to creep forward. They seemed entirely resigned to their wait. From them, even the frantic energy of the tumblers drew no more than gray, disinterested stares.

The scene kindled a feeling of sad inevitability in the Amnesian Hero. The sensation had a vague familiarity that he sometimes experienced in moments of empathy, as though sensing the emotions of others could trigger the sentimental dregs of his own lost history. The Thrasson made no effort to call forth the memory which stirred the emotion; a thousand times he had tried to fish his past from such residues, and never did he draw up more than frustration and biting despair.

The Mercykillers led the procession straight across the square, marching through the acrobats' performance without a word of apology. The intrusion bothered no one, least of all the tumblers, who incorporated it into their act by doing handsprings between the armored guards and somersaults under the chair box. One exceptionally lithe performer leaped high over the forward bearers to come down, light as a feather, on the support shafts before the chair box. He squatted there like a frog with red mad eyes, glaring at the Thrasson and singing in a high, jittery voice:

"O tower not of ivory, but builded
By hands that reach heaven from hell;
O mystical rose of the mire,
O house not of gold but of gain,
O house of unquenchable fire,
Our Lady of Pain!"

The Amnesian Hero leaned forward, carefully considering the words of the mad-eyed acrobat. In the Thrasson's experience, the accomplishment of any great feat required the solving of a riddle, and the fellow's strange words were nothing if not an enigma. He weighed each element of the song: a tower built by hands that stretched from the Lower Planes to the Upper, a magic rose growing in slime, a house of gain and unquenchable fire.

"Of course!" The Thrasson peered past the acrobat, noting the overall shape of the Gatehouse. The central tower was clearly a crowned head. The side wings could be taken for arms, while the corner towers bore a superficial resemblance to closed fists. "The Gatehouse *is* the Lady of Pain!"

The acrobat cackled and bobbed his head, singing:

"I have passed from the outermost portal
To the shrine where a sin is a prayer;
What care though the service be mortal?
O our Lady of Torture, what care?
All thine the last wine that I pour is,
The last in the chalice we drain."

This riddle was even simpler than the last, divided as it was into two-line sections, and the Amnesian Hero was almost disappointed in the answer.

"Often have I been warned to abandon hope before entering some dank place. Many times has someone assured me I would find only anguish inside, or warned me the place's terrible occupant would pour my lifeblood upon the stones. Yet, it is always I that return to the light, and it is always my sword that is smeared with steaming black gore." The Thrasson glanced past the acrobat and saw that they had nearly reached the looming bars of the portcullis. "You must do better than that to frighten the Amnesian Hero."

The acrobat smiled grimly and opened his mouth to speak again—then the shaft of Cwalno's glaive caught him in the head and sent him flying.

"That's enough blather, addle-cove!" The Mercykiller rolled his eyes and turned to the Amnesian Hero. "Pay him no attention. They do that to every poor sod we bring down here. It means nothing."

Quietly seething at his guard for interrupting the third riddle, the Amnesian Hero watched the acrobat gather himself up. "Everything means something."

"Not down here it don't."

The Amnesian Hero looked forward and saw that they had reached the jaws of the great gate tower. He expected the Mercykillers to stop at the threshold and send him into the bleak place alone, but they did not hesitate to escort him inside. The Thrasson found himself in a circular courtyard surrounded by high, gloomy walls. An enormous mosaic of gray-shaded basalt covered the floor, so large that the Thrasson could determine only that the pattern represented some twisted conglomeration of bones. A handful of brightly-cloaked attendants and despairing supplicants stood scattered along the curving walls, their voices filling the area with a gentle murmur of sobbing and softly uttered words of comfort.

Halfway across the circle, the huge portcullis divided the courtyard in two. The bars looked more enormous than ever, descending from a vaulted half-ceiling high overhead to rest inside a set of immense lock wells. The Thrasson could not imagine the creature the gate was meant to keep out, but it seemed clear enough that the present occupants never raised the portcullis. The lock wells were so full of rust and corrosion that a halo of orange crust covered the floor around the base of each bar.

The Amnesian Hero's procession passed through the gate without having to tighten its formation. The back half of the courtyard, covered as it was by a second half-ceiling, was even gloomier than the front. The square eyes of dozens of candle-lit windows peered out from the depths of the citadel, barely illuminating dozens of brown stains that trailed down the walls from a leaky roof. The steady drone of solemn voices, frequently punctuated by an echoing scream from some place deeper in the building, filled the air with a grating hum.

As the eyes of the Amnesian Hero adjusted to the dim light, he saw that this area was far more crowded than the front half of the courtyard. To his left, a long line of petitioners waited before an iron door, patiently allowing a colorfully dressed attendant to sprinkle powder over their filthy heads. In the back of the enclave, a spangle-cloaked dwarf kneeled before another iron door. He was wailing madly and, despite the efforts of two escorts to restrain him, beating himself fiercely about the head. A short distance away, another pair of burly attendants had the arms of a lithe, black-caped woman stretched taut between them. She seemed to be glaring at a gentle-looking elf who stood a safe distance away, addressing her in a voice of honey and holding his palms spread open. Behind him, a third iron door led deeper into the palace.

Cwalno led the Amnesian Hero's procession past this group, then stopped. Fifteen paces ahead, before yet another iron door, stood a second elf who bore a brotherly resemblance to the first one. Along with a small group of brightly cloaked attendants, he was studying a dazed man with the tip of a tongue showing at the corner of his mouth.

Cwalno turned to the Amnesian Hero. "I'll arrange an audience with the Lady of Pain. You wait here."

After the Amnesian Hero nodded his assent, Cwalno marched over to the second elf's group and shouldered past the brightly cloaked attendants. The Thrasson watched until the Mercykiller began to whisper into the elf's ear, then turned his gaze upon the black-caped woman being restrained near his sedan chair.

It is a ploy, of course. While he watches the woman, the Amnesian Hero is listening to every word Cwalno says. The Mercykiller does not realize this; only I know that the Thrasson is a Hunter, gifted by the gods with those ugly little ears that can hear the spider in the corner sighing.

"Madame Mok's sent a special barmy for you, Tyvold." The Mercykiller points at the sedan chair, but the Amnesian Hero, cunning as always, pretends not to notice. He continues to stare at the black-caped woman, as though he finds her more interesting than any discussion about his fate. "Sod claims he can't remember his own name."

Tyvold sneers and does not look toward the Amnesian Hero. "Did he wait in the Salvation Line?"

"What do you think? I'm going to camp down here twenty days?"

Tyvold shrugs. "That is your choice, of course." He turns away from Cwalno. "This isn't the Prison, you know. Mercykillers have to wait like everyone else."

"That so?" Cwalno demands. "And maybe Factol Lhar wants to show me permits for those Bleak Cabal soup houses springing up all over the city? If every letter ain't just right, you can be sure *he* won't have to wait in line at *our* place."

Tyvold's kindly features stiffen into a mask of anger. He knows it is a sign of inner deficiency for a high-up in the Bleak Cabal to show irritation–it suggests that he himself is nearing readiness for the Grim Retreat–but the elf cannot help it. The Mercykillers, with their blind devotion to "justice" and "order," are the worst of the Deluded. Not only do they think the multiverse has meaning, they are convinced it is their duty to impose that meaning on everyone else.

Of course, the fact is that *nothing* has meaning, especially the multiverse. But try telling that to a Mercykiller, and you'll spend the next ten years on the Racks of Enlightenment with a self-renewing charge of Mockery. By the time you come out, you'll be as mad as Cwalno and his kind. Better not to argue. Quarreling implies meaning, and, as Factor of the Redeemable Wing of the Gatehouse's Asylum, Tyvold has seen enough madmen to know what comes of allowing meaning to creep into one's mind. The elf waves the barmy before him into the care of two assistants, then turns to the Mercykiller.

"Very well, Cwalno. Describe your ward's condition. By itself, a simple memory lapse hardly entitles him to a cell in the Asylum."

"Don't you worry. He's barmy enough. To start with, he's looking for the Lady of Pain. Says he's got a gift for her from Poseidon."

"Truly? That *is* interesting." For the first time, the Factor of the Redeemable looks in the newcomer's direction. "Do continue."

There can be no doubt that the Amnesian Hero finds it difficult to hide his rage as Cwalno, hardly able to stifle his laughter, describes how Madame Mok tricked the Thrasson into seeking the Lady of Pain at the Gatehouse. Even when the Mercykiller snickers out an account of how she convinced him to hire a sedan chair and a full escort for the journey, the Amnesian Hero shows no sign of the fury so surely eating at his stomach. He is too clever for that. Instead, as Cwalno chuckles at how his captive suggested the wretches outside have come to offer their suffering to the Lady of Pain, the Thrasson betrays no hint that he is listening with his ugly little ears. He rests his chin on his hand and continues to stare at the black-caped woman, and so complete is his control that his cheeks do not even flush with anger.

From what the Amnesian Hero could see of her shadowy face, the woman's features were slender and winsome, not quite sharp enough to be those of an elf. She had left her black hair hanging loose and long over her shoulders, like a rippling black penumbra that might have flowed from the Abyss itself. With huge dark eyes and a button nose over a cupid's bow mouth, she was possessed of a dusky beauty that seemed to mock cuteness more than celebrate it.

When the woman's gaze swung toward the Amnesian Hero, the darkness that masked her face seemed to move with her head. Whatever was casting the shadow, the Thrasson realized, it was not anything in Sigil. The woman was probably a tiefling, a child borne to a human and—well, to something else; even in Arborea, the Amnesian Hero had learned better than to ask. Although no two tieflings were alike, they were all quick to anger and rather touchy about their heritage.

"What do you look at, pretty boy? You want to make kiss with me?" The woman puckered her lips and made smacking sounds. "Last chance before they lock us up, yes?"

The tiefling's keeper stepped closer to her. "Jayk, that's enough. Isn't this what landed you here in the first place?"

Jayk shrugged indifferently, but kept her huge eyes fixed on the Amnesian Hero. "What matter if I make kiss with him, Tessali? He is dead already, yes?"

"Were I you," said the Thrasson, "I would not be so certain."

The Amnesian Hero sprang from his sedan chair and landed light as a cinder on the gray floor, then started toward the tiefling. His Mercykiller escorts moved to block his way, but he pushed past them with hardly a glance. In the performance of any great feat, the champion always had to face some trial of character or intellect, and there was much about Jayk's manner to suggest she embodied such a test.

"I have fought the Hydra of Thrassos and wrestled the Hebron Crocodile and harried the Abudrian Dragons and battled many more foes too numerous to name, and always have I been the one who departs the bloody fray standing and alive."

"Or so thought you." Jayk gave him a coy smile, then ran her dark gaze down his armored body. "Pity for a man like you to think he is alive." She turned to Tessali and asked, "A sad, sad delusion, is it not?"

The Amnesian Hero frowned, but continued toward the tiefling. Arborea was a place of passion and vigor, where life was an eternal celebration and death its inevitable but loathsome end. He had never met someone who called living a sad delusion, and he could not decide whether she belonged to some strange faction of death worshipers or was only suffering from some planetouched dementia.

The tiefling's keeper, Tessali, grasped the Thrasson's arm. "You mustn't get too near. She's one of the—"

The Amnesian Hero shook free of the elf's hand. "If life is a delusion, then it is not a sad one." He continued to stare at Jayk. "And, if you will be kind enough to repeat the Third Riddle of the Gatehouse, I hope to remain deluded even after I have seen the Lady of Pain."

Jayk threw back her head and laughed, a bony, fiendish rattle that drew a chill up the Thrasson's spine. He did not flinch or back away.

"The Third Riddle of the Gatehouse?" Jayk cackled. "The dead go in and the dead go out, and still they are as barmy as you! Now we make kiss, yes?"

The Amnesian Hero realized instantly the tiefling's riddle, lacking the poetic form of the first two, was not the one he sought. Still, he hesitated before replying, trying to decide whether the test was to show his courage by kissing Jayk, or demonstrate his resolve by resisting the temptation.

Taking advantage of the pause, Tessali slipped between the Amnesian Hero and the tiefling. "Stay back! She's one of the Menacing Mad."

"Me?" Jayk scoffed. "It is you who clings to delusion like his mother's teat!"

With that, Jayk's head shot forward, the pupils of her dark eyes taking the shape of two elongated diamonds. The Amnesian Hero thought he glimpsed a pair of needlelike fangs folding down from the roof of the tiefling's mouth, but her mouth closed abruptly when her burly handlers jerked her back. Tessali stepped away and turned around, rubbing his neck as though he could still feel her hot breath upon his skin.

Jayk switched her gaze to the Thrasson, the pupils of her dark eyes slowly returning to the round. She gave him a provocative smile, then ran her tongue over her damson lips.

"Come to me. It will be a long time before you make kiss with a woman, no?"

"No." It seemed clear enough now that the test had been one of resolve. "There are women enough in Thrassos, and I will have my pick of them after my audience with the Lady of Pain."

Again, Jayk threw her head back and gave that bony laugh. "You have not solved the Third Riddle, no? The Lady of Pain, you will not find her here! This is the House of Barmies, do you understand? And you and I, we are their prisoners!"

The Amnesian Hero scowled. "Now it is you who are deluded. I have solved the First Riddle, and the second as well, and I have seen the Lady's vassals waiting with their gifts of pain—"

"The Stumbling Dead, yes, hoping for a bed of straw and a bowl of gruel, fighting against their next stage, the fools!" Jayk went limp, leaving her body to dangle by her outstretched arms. "I wish I were one of them, and you as well—but we are here, prisoners of the Bleak Cabal, to be locked away until we become as barmy as they, yes?"

The Amnesian Hero shook his head. "No! This is the Lady of Pain's palace!"

" 'Course it is!" growled Cwalno. The Mercykiller was approaching with Tyvold at his side and a dozen wide-eyed assistants at his back. "Do I look the sort to disobey orders? You heard Madame Mok say to take you to the Lady of Pain."

The Amnesian Hero eyed the Mercykiller warily and said nothing, and Cwalno tensed in his stance. Yet, so perfectly had the Thrasson played his role to that moment that even Tyvold—who has lured a thousand madmen cunning as fiends into the dark warrens beyond the iron door—failed to guess that his ward had long ago learned the lie. The elf only stepped forward, raising a gray canvas cloak that an assistant had fetched for him from the depths of his asylum.

"This is the Ceremonial Robe of Pain." Tyvold gave it a shake, unfurling a dozen straps, chains, and belts attached to the sleeves and waist. "Before you see Her Serenity, you must remove your armor and put on this instead."

Cwalno motioned to the other Mercykillers. They inched toward the Amnesian Hero, their knuckles growing white around the shafts of their glaives. The Thrasson's eyes widened. He swung his gaze toward the tiefling, who winked and gave him a crooked smile.

"Maybe you make kiss with me now, eh?"

The Amnesian Hero's hand dropped toward his sword.

The Mercykillers lowered their glaives, but Tyvold motioned them sharply back, then inched toward the Thrasson.

"What about the Third Riddle?" the elf asked. "Don't you want to hear it?"

The Amnesian Hero paused short of touching his sword. "I do, if you can tell it."

"And then you will change your armor for the Ceremonial Robe?"

"Of course." The Amnesian Hero glanced at the Mercykillers, almost sneering at the confidence in their stances. "If the riddle is a good one."

Tyvold screwed his face up in thought, and though the Amnesian Hero must have known that the elf did not have the Third Riddle, he was too cunning to give up his pretense even then. He waited a moment longer, then gripped the hilt of his sword.

"Do you know the Third Riddle or not?"

"Of course," Tyvold blurted. "I walk upon four legs in the morning, two at noon, and three at night!"

So common was the riddle, and so well known the solution, that the Amnesian Hero did not bother to answer. He simply drew his sword and, before the Mercykillers could stop him, pressed the tip to Cwalno's throat.

"I paid my gold to the Hall of Information, and I expect to see the Lady of Pain! Take me to her now!"

Showing no concern for their comrade's safety, Cwalno's companions stepped forward, slashing at the Thrasson's throat or trying to drive their hard steel through the soft bronze that covered his torso. Of course, the attacks failed. The Amnesian Hero's armor had been forged by the god Hephaestus himself. While he wore it, no weapon could harm him; the blades aimed at his neck dipped and broke upon his pauldrons, and those striking at his chest simply shattered against his breastplate.

The Amnesian Hero whirled on his attackers, slipping between the shafts of the closest pair's useless glaives. He tapped his sword against one man's armored midriff, then flipped his wrist and caught the other on the backswing. The star-forged blade cut through their armor as though it were cloth, leaving a deep gash in each warrior's flank. The two men screamed and dropped to their knees, blood spilling from the rents in their breastplates.

The Amnesian Hero was already past them and behind their comrades. The Thrasson lowered his blade and drew it lightly across the thighs of two more Mercykillers. Again, the star-born steel cut through armor as easily as silk, and the Mercykillers hurled themselves to the floor, screaming more in terror than pain.

The Thrasson barely had time to lift his blade before Cwalno and three more guards were upon him, hurling themselves forward in a wall of armored flesh. The Amnesian Hero did not resist the charge. Rather, he dropped to the floor and slid toward their feet, bringing his sword across the front of his body in a sharp arc that cut deep into the shins of two of his foes. He rolled onto his stomach and sprang up behind the last pair of attackers, denting the helmet of the closest with his sword pommel and dropping the fellow on the spot.

Cwalno turned, a belt axe in his grasp.

The Thrasson lopped off the offending hand, then sent the Mercykiller flying with a thrust-kick to the chest. Cwalno's wound was the most severe the Amnesian Hero had inflicted, but he refused to let that trouble him. The oaf had been instrumental in deceiving him. In the future, perhaps Cwalno would think better of helping Madame Mok ridicule those who came to her for help.

The Amnesian Hero took a moment to look the Mercykillers over. Although none were in danger of dying, they seemed too awed by the speed of their demise to cause him any further trouble. The Thrasson turned his attention to Tyvold, who was staring, gape-mouthed, at the mayhem on the floor.

"Now I have a riddle for you, elf:

"Cold eyelids that hide like a jewel
Hard eyes that grow soft for an hour;
The heavy white limbs, and the cruel
Red mouth like a venomous flower–"

"You didn't say he was one of the Menacing!" Tyvold screeched, glaring down at Cwalno's groaning figure. The elf backed away, clutching the Ceremonial Robe of Pain as though it were a shield, and looked toward Tessali. "He's one for your wing, brother."

Tessali shot his brother an angry look, but quickly ordered, "Clear the area!"

The elves and their attendants began to cautiously retreat toward the iron doors that led deeper into the asylum's wings. Jayk's handlers also began to withdraw, dragging their squirming charge along.

"Wait!" the Amnesian Hero called. "All I want is my answer!"

Ignoring him, Tessali reached the iron door and yanked it open. "Fetch the netflingers and sleepcasters!" His voice echoed off the stones of a long, murky corridor. "And be quick! We've got an armed Menace out here, and he knows how to use his weapon!"

The hollow echoes of alarm cries began to spill through the doorway, drawing an angry curse from the Amnesian Hero. "By the bolt of Zeus, what's wrong with you people? Just tell me how to find the Lady of Pain, and I'll be gone!"

"I help you, yes?" called Jayk. "You have only to take me with you!"

"Quiet!" One of the tiefling's guards slapped his palm over her mouth, then dragged her through the iron door.

They were only halfway across the threshold when the Amnesian Hero noticed a certain narrowing in the pupils of Jayk's eyes. The man screamed and jerked his hand away. The appendage was bleeding profusely and already beginning to swell. He opened his mouth to say something, then his eyes rolled back in his head. He fell dead on the floor, his vacant gaze fixed on the gloom above.

Jayk whirled on her second captor, her mouth open to reveal the needlelike fangs that had folded down from the roof of her mouth. The guard wisely released his grip and hurled himself to the floor. The tiefling laughed, then blew him a kiss and, leaving Tessali to quiver behind his iron door, slunk across the floor to the Amnesian Hero.

"Come, you and I, we leave here together." Her pupils were still slender and diamondlike, and she had two runnels of dark blood dribbling down her chin. "Then I show you how to find the Lady of Pain, yes?"

The Amnesian Hero did not answer immediately. Instead, he cleaned and sheathed his sword, at the same time studying the carnage around him. Why would so many men elect to do battle with him rather than answer a simple question about the Lady of Pain? When he could think of no reasonable answer, he reluctantly looked back to Jayk and nodded.

"As you will; we have a bargain." He picked up his amphora, which his nervous chair-bearers had been wise enough to leave lying upon the floor, then turned toward the exit. "It appears I have need of a guide."

DUSTMEN

How Jayk got that blood-bubbling slash across her thigh, I do not know. Nor can I relate how she and the Thrasson came to be panting for breath in a crooked dead-end alley, surrounded by black tangles of razorvine and cornered by seven armored githyanki. I can only say that as they fled the Gatehouse, the tiefling's body flared with a silver aura of delight, and the sight of a denizen's joy is more than I can bear. There is a flash behind my eyes, then a raw, scintillating light—a sparkling torment like an axe blade in my brain—and then I see nothing but bright-winking stars. It is my weakness, this bedazzled blindness. It is a false fire, a brilliant burning apparition that flashes and fades and leaves in its place a silhouette all the blacker for its passing, and so it was that I lost for a time the Amnesian Hero and his guide.

When my vision cleared, I found them in this cul-de-sac, gasping for air and searching the hard walls for escape routes that were nowhere to be found. Every barricaded door and bricked-over window hung hidden behind thick snarls of razorvine that even the Amnesian Hero knew better than to think of climbing. Beneath the glossy black leaves lay fluted stalks with ridges as sharp as swords, and so dense were the coils that anyone scaling them would find himself hopelessly tangled. There was only one way out of the trap. The Thrasson lay the amphora on the ground, then drew his star-forged blade and faced the githyanki.

They had the look of elves gone bad. Their faces were slender and delicate, marked by sharp angles and warped features, with gritty yellow skin and eyes that gleamed like polished coal. They kept their gray lips raised in snaky, fang-toothed snarls, and their flat noses were so small they looked almost absent. All seven were armored in dark, baroque plate and tall cone-shaped helmets, and each carried a two-handed sword with a saw-toothed blade. Wherever they could find a lobe or a fold of skin to pierce hung chains of gold finery, a sure sign that they were both more vicious and more capable than the many bloodblades who would gladly have taken the jewelry from their dead bodies.

"We have no . . . quarrel with you." The Amnesian Hero was still winded by the long run from the Gatehouse. "Stand aside, and I won't hurt . . . any of you."

"Tessali said you two was barmy," sneered the tallest githyanki. "Come along quiet. You're worth more alive than dead."

The Amnesian Hero gnashed his teeth at the speaker's insolence, but held his temper and tried to think of a quiet way to dispose of his seven enemies. The sound of clashing steel would certainly draw the attention of the many search parties scouring the streets of the Hive for him and Jayk, and then there would be even more bloodletting.

The Amnesian Hero sighed heavily. "Very well. It seems we are captured." He flipped his sword around and laid the hilt over his free arm, then stepped forward. "I have no wish to fight."

The githyanki slipped back. "That's far enough, berk." He pointed at the ground. "Drop your sticker there."

"As you wish." The Amnesian Hero stopped and gently tossed his sword into the dirt. Though it grated on the Thrasson to treat his weapon so badly, he hoped the act would quell the githyanki's suspicions. If he could make a hostage of the leader, perhaps he could end the confrontation without shedding blood or creating a clamor. "We surrender."

"Surrender?" scoffed Jayk. She was standing behind the Amnesian Hero, and he could not see what she was doing. "Never!"

"Magic!" Three githyanki cried the word at once, then lunged for the tiefling together.

Cursing Jayk's impatience, the Amnesian Hero pivoted on his heel and slammed a spinning thrust kick into the first warrior's flank. The fellow's breastplate spared him any shattered ribs, but the blow sent him crashing into the next githyanki, who was knocked deep into a vicious snarl of razorvine. The third one charged past, his saw-toothed sword already arcing down at the tiefling. The Thrasson thrust a hand out and caught him by the collar, then yanked him off his feet.

The githyanki's helmet hit the ground first, striking with a deep, metallic toll. Two paces beyond the fellow's feet, Jayk was tossing a gob of rough wool into the air and uttering the dark-sounding syllables of a spell. Before the Amnesian Hero could turn to face his remaining foes, four huge swords slammed into his back. The blades shattered against his god-forged armor, but that did not prevent the impact from driving him off his feet. He landed face first and tasted mordant Sigil dirt.

The battle clamor grew abruptly distant and muffled. The Amnesian Hero feared, for only the briefest instant, that a foe's blade had actually rent Hephaestus's magic and struck his head. When he did not fall unconscious or feel his skull erupting into pain, however, he quickly realized that could not be so and sprang to his feet. He found himself facing four astonished githyanki holding four broken swords. They appeared to be shouting at each other, but the only sound in the alley was a faint, uneven drone no louder than a fly's buzzing—apparently a result of the spell Jayk had cast.

Resisting the temptation to glance at his sword, which still lay upon the ground behind his four enemies, the Amnesian Hero hurled himself forward. The leader shoved his fellows into the fray and retreated. The three githyanki flailed at the Thrasson, but their broken swords always shattered against a pauldron or glanced off a vambrace. The Thrasson slammed his elbow up under a chin, and one foe fell; he grabbed a throat and pinched off the carotid arteries, and another dropped; he trapped a wild swing, then popped a shoulder out of its socket. The last attacker fell to the ground, the scream that came from his gaping mouth silenced by Jayk's magic.

As fast as the Amnesian Hero disposed of his enemies, he was not quick enough to reach his sword; the githyanki leader had already snatched it off the ground. This time, the Thrasson did not rush to the attack, as even his god-made armor was no defense against that star-forged blade. Instead, he glanced in Jayk's direction and found her atop the warrior he had kicked earlier, clawing at his eyes and doing something bloody with a dagger. Not three paces from her, one githyanki was thrashing about in the razorvine, growing more tangled by the instant and bleeding from all the places not covered by his dark armor. Another fellow, the one whose helmet had made such a toll when the Thrasson jerked him to the ground, was shaking his head and slowly rising to his knees.

The Amnesian Hero took a flying leap at this githyanki, kicking him in the helmet with enough force to smash his face back to the ground. When the warrior's body fell instantly limp, the Thrasson snatched up his sword and whirled around, automatically bringing the weapon up to slap aside a slashing blade that was not there.

The githyanki leader, more cautious with his own safety than that of his underlings, had not leapt to the attack. He stood three paces away, frantically trying to rouse his fallen warriors by kicking them in the helmets. The Amnesian Hero raised his borrowed sword to column guard and advanced. The githyanki retreated a few paces, then stopped and sank into a battle stance. Though the star-forged sword in his hands was as light as a feather, the brute held it with both hands, a sure sign that he was more accustomed to fighting with force than finesse.

The Amnesian Hero stopped two paces from his foe, pretending not to notice that he was standing among the fallen githyanki.

He smiled, then dipped his heavy sword in salute. The leader leapt forward, trying to catch his prey at a disadvantage. The Thrasson wrenched his heavy sword up into a high block, deliberately allowing his attacker time to close. The gold-draped warrior sneered and threw his weight into a vicious downstroke.

The Amnesian Hero held his position until the blades clashed, then deftly danced aside as his star-forged sword sliced through the clumsy weapon he now held. The surprised leader lurched forward, stumbling over a fallen underling and landing on his knees. The Thrasson sprang on him instantly, bringing the pommel of his broken sword down on the unarmored base of the fellow's neck. The githyanki collapsed in a heap.

The Amnesian Hero retrieved his sword, then glimpsed Jayk out of the corner of his eye. He turned to find her stooping over a fallen githyanki, one foot atop his dislocated shoulder to keep him pinned to the ground while she pulled his head up by a topknot of coarse hair. Before the Thrasson could fully grasp the situation, she slipped her free hand around the warrior's neck and calmly drew a dagger across her victim's throat.

"Jayk!" the Amnesian Hero screamed. "What are you doing?"

The Thrasson's words were barely audible, of course. Jayk's spell had not yet lapsed, so all sounds in the alley remained muted. The tiefling stepped over to another of the unconscious githyanki and pulled his head up.

The Amnesian Hero rushed over and caught her dagger arm. Jayk whirled on him so quickly he thought she might be attacking, but she only tipped her head and gave him an innocent smile. A cold shudder ran down his spine. He pointed at the bloody blade and shook his head to indicate there was no need to slay their foes. The tiefling thrust her bottom lip out, then stuck her knife into her belt without cleaning off the blood.

The Thrasson released her, then saw that she had already slashed the throats of four warriors. A fifth hung motionless in the razorvine, the hilt of a baroque throwing knife lodged between his eyes. Sickened by the needless killing, the Amnesian Hero cleaned his blade and thrust it into his scabbard, then retrieved his amphora and turned to leave.

The Thrasson found the tiefling in front of him, using the stump of a broken githyanki sword to hack through the leader's neck. This one was the last to die; she had already decapitated the other survivor.

The sight stunned the Amnesian Hero so badly that he could not quite believe what he was seeing. The other attacks could be excused by the heat of battle; it was not unreasonable to slay disabled foes to prevent them from rejoining the fray later–but this was murder. The Thrasson lay the amphora aside, then caught Jayk's arm and wrenched the bloody sword from her grasp.

"You're a maniac!"

The only sound to pass between the Thrasson and the tiefling was a muted drone. Jayk ran her red-stained fingers through the flickering motions of a counterspell, at the same time raising her gaze to meet that of the Amnesian Hero. Her black eyes were large and round, and her mouth was shaped into a small, astonished **O**. On her shadowy face, the expression seemed more a parody of innocence than one of innocence itself, but neither did she show any sign of guilt or remorse.

The tiefling gestured at the fallen githyanki. "You think I kill them, yes?"

"You *did* kill them." The Amnesian Hero's stomach began to churn, and he had the sick feeling that taking Jayk as his guide had been a terrible mistake. "Tessali was right. You belong in a locked cell."

The tiefling's face grew even darker. "Me? I do not think the Lady of Pain lives in a barmyhouse, huh?" She spun on her heel and started toward the back of the alley, limping because of a slashed thigh she had suffered when the githyanki first ambushed them. "You know nothing!"

The Amnesian Hero glanced over the dead githyanki. "I know that I had disabled these warriors." His voice was hard with reproach. "There was no reason to kill them."

"There was reason–good reason." Jayk stopped at the back of the alley and flashed a smile. "Besides, life, she is only an illusion."

"Illusion or not, there's no glory in killing helpless foes." The Amnesian Hero fixed her with a stony glare. "It's better to let them live, so they can describe the battle and sing your fame."

"Pah! Fame is delusion."

"To those who lack it, perhaps." The Thrasson picked up his amphora and gestured up the alley. "Let's go. You promised to show me to the Lady of Pain."

"No. It is better to hide here." She waved at the back of the alley, where the razorvine was so dense it hid the walls of the surrounding buildings. "If someone comes because of the fighting, they will not look for us in there."

The Thrasson scowled. "There's no use stalling. If you lied to me–"

Jayk raised a hand. "I do not stall." She motioned at the githyanki. "We should not show ourselves. The bounty hunters, they already look for us in all the streets and alleys of the Hive, yes? But they do not expect to find us here. It is much better to wait, you will see–but hurry!"

Deciding that the murderous tiefling was bound to be more experienced in such matters than he, the Amnesian Hero reluctantly nodded. While he cut a swath through the razorvine, she used a saw-toothed githyanki sword to drag the severed stems aside. It took only a moment to clear their cubby hole, then they took the amphora inside and pulled the stalks back over the entrance. The hollow was just large enough for them to squat side-by-side without brushing against the surrounding vines, and the light filtering in from outside was dim and spotty. The Thrasson knew the hiding place would not stand up to a close inspection, but he had also seen enough of Sigil to realize its residents instinctively shied away from razorvine; if someone came to investigate the fighting, the last place they would search for victors was among the black-leaved tangles.

The Amnesian Hero used his sword to clear a small viewing hole. "I trust you know what you're doing, Jayk."

"I cannot walk far with this." Jayk gestured at her wounded thigh. "And if you were to help me, people would notice and call Tessali's netflingers, yes?"

The Thrasson nodded. "I suppose so."

The netflingers had attacked as they struggled to push their way through the Salvation Line outside the Gatehouse. The steel mesh nets were surprisingly effective; as soon as they settled over a victim's torso, the flinger pulled a draw cord that tightened the outer loop and pinned the captive's arms to his ribs. Despite his enchanted armor, the Amnesian Hero had been temporarily caught in one. He would have been dragged back to Tessali, had Jayk not saved him by creating a cloud of stinking magic gas that had sickened his attacker and sent the entire Salvation Line scurrying for cover. The two escapees had joined the resulting stampede and fled the Marble District, then ducked into the back alleys to avoid Gatehouse search parties. Had they not stumbled into the githyanki bounty hunters, they might well have escaped the Hive entirely undetected.

Noticing that Jayk had made no move to stanch her bleeding, the Amnesian Hero gestured at her wound. "Aren't you going to do anything about that?"

Jayk kept her dark gaze fixed on her leg, watching with a peculiar fascination as the blood bubbled from the slash. "Why?"

The Amnesian Hero rolled his eyes. "So you don't bleed to death before I see the Lady of Pain."

He pulled his dagger and cut her trousers away from her wound. As he worked, the murmur of soft voices began to rustle down the alley. The Amnesian Hero peered through the viewing hole he had cut and saw a pack of wild-haired urchins pulling a wobble-wheeled cart around the corner. None of them looked to be more than eight or nine years old, though they were so scrawny and sunken-eyed that it was difficult to tell.

When they saw the dead githyanki, the eldest, or at least the largest, raised a hand to stop the procession. He performed a cursory scan of the area, then sent a single sentry up the alley to keep watch. The rest, he led forward to the corpses.

As they approached, the Amnesian Hero saw no sign of shock or fear on the faces of the children, or even of distaste. The youngest, a soot-faced waif no taller than the Thrasson's sword, was smiling and strutting proudly along at the leader's side.

"See, Spider?" Only after he heard her voice could the Amnesian Hero tell that she was a girl. "I telled ya they ran down here.

I heard a clank!"

"Aye, you did well, Sally." Spider ran a wary eye back up the alley, pausing to study each bricked-over window and vine-choked doorway. "But I'd like to know what happened to that tiefling and her blood. They might not like us scraggin' their kill."

Disgusted by the thought of children robbing the dead, the Amnesian Hero started to rise. Jayk caught his arm and shook her head. The Thrasson reluctantly remained were he was and continued to watch. When no one appeared to chase them off, Spider waved the other children to the corpses.

"Let's nick 'em! And be sure to check their teeth."

The leader and another boy used a githyanki sword to drag free the warrior in the razorvine, then the entire pack set to work stripping the bodies. They took the corpses' armor and weapons, then their boots, purses, and underclothes as well. They ripped rings from earlobes and fingers, they tore studs from noses, lips, and tongues, they knocked out teeth and cracked them for the fillings, they harvested the githyankis' coarse topknots for rope-making; young Sally even cut the tattoo of a snake from the leader's arm, claiming to her disgusted comrades that she could sell it for two coppers. By the time the urchins had packed their cart, taking care to secure the best treasures in secret pockets inside their rags, the bodies lay naked and even more mangled than before.

Stomach churning with both revulsion and pity, the Amnesian Hero watched the waifs until their cart wheeled around the corner.

"What place is this?" He whirled on Jayk, searching for some hint of emotion in the delicate features of her shadowed face. "Did I wander through a portal and fall into the Abyss?"

"Do not be so silly." Jayk slipped her hand into the crook of his elbow and gave him a beguiling half-smile. "You would know it if you were in the Abyss. This is still Sigil."

"That is what I feared." The Amnesian Hero shook his head, then started to push open their door of vines. "I can wait in this place no longer. Take me to the Lady of Pain."

Jayk pulled him back to his knees. "Be patient. Those bodies, they are worth seven coppers. The children will report them, and our ride will come soon. While we wait, you can tell me about yourself, yes? Who you are, and why you wish to fight the Lady of Pain?"

"Who said I want to fight her?"

The tiefling shrugged. "It does not matter. You will lose anyway."

"I'm only trying to deliver a gift." The Thrasson gestured at the amphora. "Why should that offend her?"

"Who is to say it will?" Jayk asked. "Now, tell me about yourself. If I am prepared, things will go faster at the Mortuary."

"Mortuary?"

"Did you not say you wanted to see the Lady of Pain?"

"Of course, but—"

"Then I must know more about you."

The Amnesian Hero frowned. "You *can* take me to the Lady of Pain? If you're another of Sigil's tricksters—"

"I will show you how to find the Lady! But first, we make the preparations, yes? Tell me who you are."

The Amnesian Hero hesitated, then forced himself to lift his chin proudly. "I am the slayer of the Hydra of Thrassos, the tamer of the Hebron Crocodile, the bane of Abudrian Dragons, the savior of the Virgins of Marmara, the champion of the Ilyrian Kings, the killer of the Chalcedon Lion—"

Jayk grasped his forearm. "I am already impressed with your swordsmanship. Only your name, yes?"

The Thrasson's gaze dropped. "I don't know it."

Jayk's shadowy face rippled with confusion. "How can that be? Your mother, she could not speak?"

"Of course she could!" The Amnesian Hero flushed, then amended, "At least I assume she could. I can't remember."

Jayk's dark eyes widened. She stared at the Thrasson and said nothing.

"I awoke on the shore near Thrassos, on the first layer of Arborea. I recall nothing before that."

Jayk seemed unable to take her dark eyes off him. "You have

no link to your past?"

The Amnesian Hero looked away. "Sometimes I glimpse the face of a woman I think I once knew, but she always disappears before I can speak with her." He did not add that he was usually drinking at the time. "But I am sure I am a man of renown. That much is obvious from my bearing."

"And your skill with a sword, yes?"

"Yes." The Thrasson smiled, warming to the tiefling. "I must have lost my memory battling one of Poseidon's sea monsters. That would explain why I was found on the shore of an Arborean sea, and why he promised to restore my memories in return for delivering this."

He thumped the amphora.

Jayk's jaw dropped. "You want your memories back? But you are halfway to the next stage!"

"Stage?"

"Of death! To remember is to go backward! You are like the zombie." She pronounced it *zoombee*. "He cannot recall the light at his back, yet he is afraid to face the dark truth ahead."

"Jayk, the light is still real for me. I am no zombie."

"You are, my dear. That is what I shall call you, yes?"

"No!"

"Zoombee! It sounds so nice, so . . . enticing."

Jayk's face drifted toward his, her dark lips parting ever so slightly. The Amnesian Hero had tasted the mouths of many Arborean women, of course, but he could feel something more powerful, far deeper and brutally primal, drawing his head toward hers. Men of renown were not expected to forgo the pleasures of the flesh—some of their greatest feats came from yielding to such temptations—but the Thrasson could not forget how the tiefling's pupils had a habit of narrowing to black diamonds, nor the fangs that he had seen folding down from the roof of her mouth.

"Later." He abruptly pulled back. "Perhaps when the light isn't so bright."

Jayk inclined her head, her eyelids lowered too far for the Thrasson to see whether her pupils were shaped like circles or diamonds.

"Whenever you are ready, Zoombee." She gave him a knowing smile. "I will be ready too."

The Amnesian Hero—Zoombee—swallowed nervously, then turned away. "You are beautiful, Jayk, but I do not think it is our destiny to . . . make kisses."

"But why not, Zoombee? Because I am tiefling?"

"You must not think that." The Thrasson looked back to Jayk and found her lips bowed into a coy grin. He felt himself flush, angry at being mocked. "Because you are a murderess—and because I must think of other business. Remember the Lady of Pain?"

The tiefling's face drooped into an insincere sulk. "Soon, Zoombee. I think that is our ride coming now."

The Amnesian Hero looked through his viewing hole. He saw only the dead bounty hunters, but he did notice a foul odor building in the alley. At first, he thought the stink was coming from the githyanki corpses, but as the fetor grew stronger, he realized that could not be so. Even in Sigil, seven bodies could not rot fast enough to emit such a stench so soon. The Thrasson rubbed his hand in the mordant dirt, then covered his mouth and nose to mask the awful reek.

Jayk yanked his hand away from his face. "It is better to grow accustomed to the smell now. If you retch later, someone will hear you, yes?"

A pattern of slow, rhythmic creaks began to echo off the tenement walls, underscored by the rising drone of an insect cloud. The Amnesian Hero did his best to breathe through his mouth and keep his nostrils closed, but the effort was doomed to failure. Every time he inhaled, he found himself fighting to hold his gorge down, and every time he exhaled, he begged Apollo to keep him from drawing another breath. His prayer went unanswered, for this is Sigil, and the gods have no power here. The Thrasson continued to breathe the rancid air. He began to feel hot and queasy; he grew sicker with every lungful, and soon his legs trembled with weakness.

A cloud of black flies drifted around the corner, swirling over what appeared to be a jumbled, floating mountain of corpses. The

Amnesian Hero gasped at the sight and, gagging on the stench, wished he hadn't. Then he noticed a pair of high sideboards holding the pile in check and realized the bodies lay heaped on the bed of a mighty barrow. So enormous was the wagon that it brushed the tenements on both sides of the alley, dragging long tangles of razorvine free of the mud brick walls.

Standing high atop the hill of rotting flesh, his shape blurred by the haze of flies whirling around him, was a single figure in a black cape similar to Jayk's. He glanced over his shoulder and called something to the driver. A huge, creaking wheel rolled into sight, and the wagon began to swing around. The back corner pushed through a tangle of razorvine and crunched against the building beneath, then the guide snapped a sharp command. The barrow lurched to a halt.

"This is our ride?" The Amnesian Hero did his best to sound more curious than repulsed; this simple errand was becoming something of a feat, and during feats, true men of renown accepted even the most loathsome events with good grace. "I notice the man wears a cape similar to yours."

"Yes, we are both Dustmen." Jayk leaned close and peered through the viewing hole as the guide and driver scrambled down to retrieve the githyanki. "But we must not let him see us when we climb aboard."

The Amnesian Hero scowled. "How will we do that? Won't he notice us . . . sitting on . . . the . . ." The Thrasson let the question trail off, barely managing to keep from retching as he realized where they would be riding. "We can find a disguise for me somewhere in that mess. I'd much rather ride in front."

"That is not possible, dear Zoombee. You must be strong and ride with me, yes?"

"Surely, they'll let you ride in front! Perhaps one of them is a friend of yours."

"Friendship is a delusion!" Jayk hissed the words, never taking her dark eyes off the two Dustmen, who were already dragging the second pair of githyanki back to the wagon. "Besides, we must think of the Mercykillers. If the driver does not know about us, it is easier for him to lie, yes?"

"Yes." The Amnesian Hero sighed, remembering how the Mercykiller guard at the Hall of Information had invaded his mind to verify his statements. "I trust I'll have a chance to wash the stink off before my audience with the Lady of Pain?"

"But why, Zoombee? She will like the smell of death!"

They watched the Dustmen throw the last of the githyanki onto the wagon. Then, as the pair climbed over the heap toward the front of the huge barrow, the Amnesian Hero used the amphora to push the razorvine out of their way. By the time he and Jayk had crawled from their hiding place, the crack of the driver's whip was echoing down the alley. The Thrasson threw the amphora onto his shoulder, then, trying to ignore the indignity of what he was doing, ran for the death wagon.

RIVERGATE

They had entered the Mortuary District, the Amnesian Hero could tell. He knew by the steady trundle of the death wagon, by how it no longer veered down every side street in search of unclaimed corpses, by the way its axles groaned under its burden of spent lives. The barrow was overloaded, bodies heaped higher than the side slats, and the driver was heading for home. Through a tangle of arms and necks and dead, bulging eyes, the Thrasson could see a long file of somber monuments drifting past the wagon: granite balls clutched in rusty iron claws, soaring obelisks of white marble, black walls etched with a thousand names, a hundred worthless stones erected to the memories of someone whom someone else had once thought worth remembering. Jayk lay next to him, breathing fast and shallow and hot; his own heart was beating like a sword against a shield. Soon, the wagon would enter the Mortuary proper, the true palace of the Lady of Pain, and he would present her with Poseidon's amphora.

The wagon lumbered past another dozen monuments, then the

driver suddenly drew rein. The Amnesian Hero thought they were slowing to pass through the Mortuary's gate, until a gruff voice barked "Halt!"

As the barrow creaked to a stop, Jayk cursed softly and began to fumble through her pockets. The Amnesian Hero pushed his hand through the tangle of slimy bodies to clutch her arm, then squeezed until she stopped moving. Unless the unpredictable tiefling did something to attract attention, they would avoid detection. They were buried under several layers of corpses and had already escaped notice many times as the Dustmen clambered over the pile above.

The wagon rocked, and through the jumble of bodies, the Amnesian Hero glimpsed a stern-jawed man peering over the side slats. His helmet was orange instead of crimson, but his brown eyes were every bit as stony as those of the Mercykillers who had escorted the Thrasson to the Gatehouse. Jayk must have been able to see the man also, for she tried to twist her arm free. The Amnesian Hero held her fast. The guard could not see them buried so deeply in the shadowy tangle of bodies, and the Thrasson would not let the tiefling cause another bloodletting.

From the front of the wagon came a familiar voice. "We had an escape at the Gatehouse today." It was the elf, Tessali. "I assume you know Jayk the Snake?"

"Of course." The driver's tone was flat and uninterested. "Everyone in the Mortuary knows her."

"We think she'll come back for her spellbook."

The Amnesian Hero's stomach turned, and he found himself gagging on the rancid closeness of the corpses. The skin of the cadavers felt cold and slimy against his own, the fly drone grew dizzying in its volume, and he found himself considering the possibility that Jayk had brought him here solely to recover her lost property.

Tessali continued, "She'll be with another barmy, a Menace in bronze armor." As the elf spoke, the guard peering over the side slats probed the pile of corpses with a steel-tipped spear. "Her companion is tall and swarthy, and more dangerous than she."

"Danger is an illusion." It was the assistant Dustman who

answered, and he sounded as apathetic as the driver. "But we haven't seen them."

"That so?" growled another voice. "Look at me and say that."

"That won't be necessary, Raq," said Tessali. "He has no reason to lie."

"Everyone has reason to lie," growled the Mercykiller.

"Not about this. Secretary Trevant had her committed in the first place."

A burning feeling welled up inside the Amnesian Hero, and he found himself squeezing Jayk's willowy arm so hard he thought it would break. Any doubt about the tiefling's motives vanished; given her thirst for blood, it seemed clear enough that she was more interested in taking vengeance on Secretary Trevant than helping him find the Lady of Pain. Had it not been for the likelihood of landing in the Gatehouse alongside her, the Thrasson would have reported Jayk himself.

The orange-helmeted guard used his spear to push a githyanki off the pile over their heads, then thrust the tip down through the tangle of bodies. The point struck the Amnesian Hero's forearm and chipped against his vambrace. The guard stirred his weapon around, catching some of Jayk's shadowy hair and twining it about the shaft.

"Have you found anything, Mateus?" called Tessali.

The guard shook his head. "Worms and stink." He withdrew his weapon, ripping a tress of hair from Jayk's head. The Amnesian Hero felt her arm tense, but the tiefling did not cry out. "If your barmies are in there, they're as dead as everyone else."

"We'll let this one go, then." To the Dustmen, Tessali said, "I apologize for wasting your time."

"The dead need no apologies." The driver cracked his whip, and the wheels began to creak. "And time is an illusion."

Mateus jumped off the wagon, a lock of shadowy hair waving from the head of his spear. The Amnesian Hero released the tiefling's arm and quietly struggled toward the surface, kicking and pushing to free himself of the bodies. He could not be certain Tessali would recognize the tress as Jayk's, but he wanted to be ready.

"What are you doing, Zoombee?" Jayk hissed. "They hear you!"

The Amnesian Hero ignored the tiefling and pushed past a decomposing bariaur, smearing his bronze armor with some sort of brown ichor that might once have been skin. He came up amidst a cloud of whirring flies, then craned his neck toward the wagon's tailgate. Through the droning black haze, he saw Tessali's slender figure standing in the middle street, pulling a strand of shadow off the head of Mateus's spear. The elf was surrounded by two more of the orange-helmeted guards, another pair of men armored in Mercykiller crimson, and a spangle-robed Bleaker with a bucket of sand in her hands.

The Thrasson reached down and pulled Jayk up through the heap of bodies. "Prepare your magic—but don't kill anyone, or I'll throw you to the elf!"

"If you do that, how will you find—"

"I know why you brought me to the Mortuary, tiefling!" The Amnesian Hero worked his arms to the top of the pile. "Don't insult me further, or I'll throw you out now!"

Jayk pushed out her dark lip. "You misjudge me, Zoombee. Just because I get what I want—"

The tiefling was interrupted by Tessali's cry. "Wait! Stop the wagon!"

The Amnesian Hero pulled himself free and spun toward the front of the barrow. The assistant Dustman was peering over the mound of bodies toward Tessali, but his gaze quickly fell on the Thrasson. The fellow's drab eyes lit with surprise, then he dropped out of sight and began to jabber about what was rising from the dead.

The Amnesian Hero jumped to his feet and clambered up the body heap, slipping and sliding on the glairy flesh underfoot. With each step, the flies rose around him in geysers. They felt like chiffon against his face and tickled his eyes with the beating of their tiny wings. He cringed and breathed through clenched teeth to avoid swallowing any of the gruesome creatures, and he suffered one of those vague sensations of familiarity that sometimes troubled him. The Thrasson shuddered to think of where he might have done this before; short of Hades's realm, he could not imagine another place where he might have climbed a mountain of decaying corpses.

The wagon lurched to a stop. Behind the Amnesian Hero, a growing clamor heralded the pursuit of Tessali and his guards. Whatever Jayk was doing, she was not casting a spell. The Thrasson could hear a muffled thumping as she kicked at a side slat somewhere back near the tailgate.

The Amnesian Hero crested the pile to find the two Dustmen waiting in the driver's box. The assistant held a simple wooden club, while the driver was armed with a long, coiled whip.

"S-stand fast, you barmy." The driver raised his whip toward the Thrasson. "We are n-not afraid of you."

Deciding that the Dustman was lying, the Amnesian Hero sprang into the driver's box. The assistant leapt off the wagon without bothering to raise his club. The driver was a little more courageous, at once sidestepping the attack and striking at his foe's unarmored face. The Thrasson caught the blow on his forearm. He hooked a hand over the whip handle and jerked it free, then shoved the Dustman off the high barrow.

A loud crunch sounded from the rear of the wagon. Jayk cursed and hissed a wicked-sounding incantation. Several men shrieked in fear, and Tessali barked, "Don't stand in the street dancing! Cut their heads off!"

Taking no time to look back and see what Jayk had done, the Amnesian Hero cracked his newfound whip over the four haggard dray horses. The beasts leaned into their harnesses and raised their hooves as though to step forward, but the barrow did not budge. They snorted in irritation and calmly placed their feet back on the street.

"Hey, Zoombee! Do you think a few snakes will stop these sods for long?" The muffled thumping resumed at the back of the wagon. "If you don't want me to hurt them, then we go, yes?"

The Thrasson took a moment to examine the driver's box and found the reins wrapped around a tall wooden lever rising alongside the footboard. He pulled the straps free, then jerked the shaft back. Something clunked down near the wheels. The horses snorted wearily and started to pull without being urged.

The Amnesian Hero cracked the whip over their heads, then cracked it again. The startled beasts whinnied in surprise and broke into a full walk.

"Run, you poor beasts!" The Thrasson snapped the rump of a horse in front, then did the same to the animal's partner. "Run as though across the Elysian Fields!"

The horses broke into a ragged trot. The Amnesian Hero continued to pop the whip frantically, urging them into an awkward canter. Knowing better than to think the haggard beasts could pull the heavy barrow any faster, or for very long, he tossed the whip aside. He took up the reins and, shouting for the pedestrians ahead to clear the way, did what he could to guide the rumbling wagon down the center of the street.

The avenue ahead was broad but crowded, with a long row of somber stone monuments standing along each side. Behind each rank of memorials ran a narrow gallery crowded with shabby stalls selling dried flowers, small flasks of inebriants, boiled rats, and other offerings for the dead. These markets were bordered by the district's drab, onion-domed tenements, most with thick growths of razorvine covering their roofs. A hundred paces down the lane, the street ran under a high arch of ragged stone, then ended in the courtyard of a low, menacing dome surrounded by a cluster of windowless towers. Despite the lack of a sign, the gloomy aura of the place left no doubt that it was the Mortuary.

"Turn right!" Jayk's voice was barely audible over the rumble and groan of the careening wagon. "Turn sharp!"

The Amnesian Hero scanned the right side of the avenue, looking for a large street. He found nothing wider than an alley. Under the best of conditions, guiding the wagon into the narrow lane would have been a harrowing task. With the barrow thundering along faster than most men could sprint and the malnourished horses already beginning to stumble, his chances of wrecking seemed far greater than those of making the corner.

"Turn now, Zoombee!" Jayk yelled. "The elf, he is too fast!"

The Amnesian Hero scowled, but began to ease the wagon

toward the alley's fast-approaching mouth. "How is turning—"

"Do it, or I help Tessali to the next stage!"

The Amnesian Hero cursed, then braced himself and pulled hard on the reins. The inside horses turned almost gracefully, but the outside lead could not keep up. He stumbled and would have gone down, had the others not pulled him along by his harness. The team angled toward the only possible opening, the dark-shadowed alley the Thrasson had been watching.

The front wheels turned, then the barrow's momentum seemed to catch up all at once. The Amnesian Hero felt the bench tilting beneath him and dropped the reins to grab for the high side. A tremendous splintering sounded from the rear of the wagon, followed by the soft rumble of shifting bodies and Jayk's wild, exhilarated scream. The Thrasson found himself holding onto the edge of the seat and pulling himself upward, praying that somehow his small mass would be enough to keep the barrow from tipping. Corpses began to tumble out, lightening the high side and shifting more weight to the low.

The wagon flashed past a gray obelisk, striking it with a wheel. There was a tremendous clunk, then the barrow rocked away. The Amnesian Hero thought they were going over, but the horses, feeling their impending doom, screamed and bolted forward. The wagon accelerated through the turn and into the narrow alley, two wheels still spinning in the air.

A deafening crash shook the alley. The Thrasson felt his hands lose their hold on the seat, then he bounced off the footboard and tumbled down through the reins and harness lines to land on the hauling rod. The horses were shrieking in panic, their whinnies echoing off the walls like the voices of so many banshees. The wagon was trembling with their efforts to drag it forward, but it had gotten lodged between the tenement walls and would not budge.

The Amnesian Hero disentangled his body, then pulled himself back into the driver's box. Ahead of him, the horses stood scraping at the dirt in the dark alley, forced by the hauling rod to lean against each other at a cockeyed angle. On the high side of the wagon, the wheels were braced against a tenement wall; on the low side, one of posts to which the side-slats were fastened had become lodged in a narrow doorway, preventing the barrow from moving forward. The cargo bed was two-thirds empty; most of the corpses lay scattered at the mouth of the alley behind them, piled four and five bodies deep. Tessali was in the street beyond, just starting to pick his way through the tangle, with his crew rushing up behind him.

"You call that driving a wagon, Zoombee?" In the wagon's rear corner, near the broken side-slats she had kicked out, Jayk pushed her head up between two corpses. "I know skeletons who do better!"

"And I wish you good luck with them—after we part." The Amnesian Hero climbed into the cargo bed and began to kick corpses about. "Where is my amphora—or did you dump that over the side as well?"

"No, of course. I know you need it to see the Lady of Pain, yes?" Jayk rose and tugged the neck of the jar into view. "I hold it very tight for you."

"Then I thank you for that much, at least."

The Amnesian Hero clambered back to take the amphora, but Jayk let it slip back into the bodies.

"Worry about your jar later, Zoombee." She pointed at the slat-post lodged in the doorway. "Now you must cut us free. I will slow our pursuers."

Jayk plucked the finger off a decomposing corpse. She turned and casually tossed it in Tessali's direction, belting out a wicked-sounding incantation. The elf cringed and raised an arm as though to ward off a blow, but no black bolts of lightning or noxious clouds of gas appeared to strike him down. Nothing happened except that a cadaver's arm flopped across his feet.

Tessali wiped his brow and lifted a foot to start forward again—then fell to his face as the corpse's hand clutched at his ankle. Several assistants rushed into the tangle of bodies to help him up and met the same fate when the limbs of other cadavers began to flail at their feet. Only the woman in the spangled robe was wise enough to stand her ground and avoid the gruesome mess.

"Come on, Zoombee, cut us free!" Jayk clambered forward to

take the wagon's reins. "I thought you wanted to see the Lady of Pain!"

The Amnesian Hero had his doubts about Jayk's true intentions—he was beginning to wonder if even she knew how to find the Lady—but at least the tiefling had a plan for escaping Tessali. He drew his sword and hacked off the offending post with a single blow. As the wagon lurched forward, he took the precaution of cutting off the other slat-posts as well. Jayk turned the horses toward the barrow's low side, and the wagon began to right itself.

The Thrasson waded forward and grabbed hold of the driver's box, but stopped short of climbing over when a female voice began to echo down the alley behind them. Jayk slapped the reins, urging the exhausted dray horses into a trot. The Amnesian Hero dropped into a crouch and spun around, expecting to find a ball of fire or bolt of lighting arcing through the air. Instead, he saw the spangle-cloaked woman, still standing outside the alley, reaching into her sand bucket. Tessali and his assistants were still struggling to crawl free of the corpse field.

"There's no need to worry," the Amnesian Hero reported. "Tessali and his men have yet to escape the corpses, and the woman—"

"You mustn't look, Zoombee!" Jayk cried. "She's a—"

The tiefling's warning came too late. Tessali's sleepcaster had already pulled her hand from the sand bucket and flung it in the Thrasson's direction. Something stung his eyes. The creaking of the wagon's wheels grew distant, then his vision narrowed and became dim. He yawned and felt his legs melting beneath him. A dark fog filled his head, and, as he sank into oblivion, he found himself hoping no one would mistake him for a corpse and steal his god-forged armor.

The Thrasson dreams of mazes, of the many kinds of mazes.

Out of the darkness skips a column of soot-faced urchins, holding hands and chanting a dismal, deep-voiced dirge. As the line weaves past, it suddenly breaks, and two hands reach out to take his. He finds himself between Spider and Sally, the body robbers from the alley. Their faces have the somber, expressionless aspect of Dustmen, their hands the glairy feel of dead flesh.

The line follows, he sees, a pattern traced in the dust. The path meanders back and forth past itself, sometimes running for long stretches before reversing course and sometimes not, but always bending inward, following the curve of a bordering circle. The air grows thick and hot. The dirge builds to a roar; Sally's hand trembles in his, and he knows they are dancing toward a grim center of darkness and loss and despair. The Thrasson, ever the hero, rubs his foot across the boundary in the dust, then steps across and drags the children after him.

A pair of distant, anguished wails sound behind him, then he finds himself holding hands with the stumps of two small arms. He spins in horror and discovers that he is alone, standing upon a black mirror that reflects all the stars in the heavens. The flickering pinpoints are connected by twinkling threads of silver that light the way to any place in the multiverse. He still hears the shrieking of the children, bemoaning their lost arms. He tries to follow one of the silver strands to them. With each step, their voices change position and grow more distant. He turns toward them and steps across the line.

Now he stands between two hedges of razorvine, and he can no longer hear the urchins at all. The Thrasson calls after them. There is a long silence. After a time, a deep growl rumbles down the pathway. He has yet to meet the monster he cannot kill, so he drops the children's severed arms and draws his sword. Only then does he recognize his own voice in the rumbling thunder, calling the names of Spider and Sally.

A riddle player and an untangler of enigmas and a man of no small wit, the Thrasson grasps at once what he has become: orphan torturer and stealer of arms. A true monster. He bellows in rage and slashes at the razorvine with that star-forged sword of his, chopping and slicing and pulling aside the severed stalks with no regard for his bloodied flesh. When at last he hacks through the hedge, he finds that he has come to a cave darkly. He stands alone in hollow gloom, with the sound of his own breath whispering down unseen passages ahead and behind and to both sides, wondering how he stumbled into this blackest of all labyrinths.

He entered by choice. We all do. Whether we are mapping the heavens or skulking the lanes of the underworld, whether we are hunting the imprisoned fiend or have ourselves become the monster, whether we are searching for what is lost or hiding what must never be found, we all round that first corner by choice—and by then, we are lost.

You too. You must decide what is false and what is true, and what is true for me but not for you. We are wandering the mazes, all of us, and we cannot hope to escape until we learn to tell between what is real and what is real for someone else. There lies the madness, and the truth as well.

But now the dream is done. It ended back in the cavern, when the Amnesian Hero slammed down on a bed of hard cobblestones and awoke to find himself crumpled at the base of a squalid hut of unmortared stones. His body was still covered by his bronze armor, and he felt remarkably refreshed, as though he had just awakened from a long and profound sleep. For a moment, the unexpected vigor confused him. He thought that perhaps his whole miserable trip to Sigil—better yet, his life since awakening on the shores of Thrassos—had been an unpleasant dream.

The horrid stench of decay quickly dashed his hopes, however, as did the fading rumble of the death wagon. The Thrasson pushed himself upright and saw that he was in a district of shabby gray huts similar to the one at his back. A few stooped forms were scurrying along from one shadow to the next, bare blades flashing in their hands. Otherwise, the street was largely deserted. Jayk the Snake stood a few steps away, cracking the long driver's whip over the heads of the stumbling dray horses.

"Wait!" The Amnesian Hero leapt to his feet and started after the wagon. "The amphora!"

Jayk caught his arm. "I have it, Zoombee!"

The tiefling gestured toward the squalid hut's entryway, where the shadows were too deep to reveal what might be leaning against the wall. As she turned, the Amnesian Hero glimpsed the familiar pearly flash of an abalone comb in her hair. He dropped a hand to his belt and discovered that his coin purse was gone.

"And my coin sack?"

"That, too."

If the tiefling was disappointed that he had noticed, her tone did not betray it. She reached under her cape and produced the purse, now heavily soiled by blood and ichor. He snatched it from her and opened it to peer inside. He still saw plenty of gold, but three other items were missing.

"You are such a berk, Zoombee! The sack, it fell off in the wagon. I do not covet your gold. It is nothing but an illusion."

Jayk turned toward the entryway, but the Amnesian Hero caught her by the arm. He gestured at the comb in her hair.

"Give it back."

The tiefling rolled her eyes, but reluctantly removed the comb and returned it.

"The thread and the mirror, too," he said.

"These are women's things, yes?" Despite her objection, Jayk reached into her robe, producing the silver palm mirror and the spool of golden thread she had taken from his purse. "Why does a man like you carry them?"

"I don't know." The Amnesian Hero returned the objects to his purse and drew it closed. "They were all I had when I awoke on the shores of Thrassos."

Jayk considered this a moment, then said, "So they have no meaning to you. It would have been better to let me keep them."

With that, she stepped through the entrance and instantly disappeared into the shadows. The Amnesian Hero paused long enough to tie his purse onto his belt with a double knot.

"Are you coming, Zoombee? Or do you wait for Tessali and his sleepcaster? You like that mindrest, yes?"

Before he could reply, a door creaked open, spilling a sliver of dark purple light into the doorway, barely illuminating the amphora leaning against the wall. The Thrasson grabbed the jar and followed the tiefling into a windowless chamber that was lit—barely—by three damson-flamed tapers. Unable to see anything except the flickering candles, the Amnesian Hero stood in the doorway, listening as the clatter of a slovenly feast rattled to a stop. The room reeked of charred meat, sulfur-burning pipes, and some rancid swill that smelled like moldy copper.

"What you got there, Jayk?"

The speaker seemed to be somewhere ahead and to one side of the doorway, though it was impossible to be certain. The fellow's voice was so deep and raspy that it croaked out of the darkness from all directions.

"Two silver's the best I'll go," the speaker croaked. "Maybe one more, if you throw in all his goods."

"You think me clueless?" Jayk started forward, vanishing into the purple darkness like a ghost. "Even without his goods, this one goes two gold at least!"

Cursing the tiefling's treachery, the Amnesian Hero reached for his sword, at the same time stooping down to put the amphora on the floor. From the darkness ahead came the sound of chair legs scraping across wet wood.

"Sit, my friends." Jayk's tone was amused. "This one, he would be more trouble than he is worth. I keep him for myself."

The Amnesian Hero felt more than heard the sigh that rustled through the room. A few chairs clattered, and, growing more accustomed to the darkness, he glimpsed a dozen dark shapes returning to their seats. They had high, pointy heads and humped backs, and several seemed to be holding large bone clubs in their gnarled hands. Although many of them sat facing each other at the same tables, not a word passed among the entire group.

The voice that had welcomed Jayk chuckled merrily, then asked, "You got jink?"

"But of course, Brill."

From the darkness ahead came the chime of a thumbnail striking metal, then the Thrasson saw a flash of gold arcing through the darkness. There was a sharp crack, and the coin disappeared in midair. The Amnesian Hero saw a black tendril curling back toward the wall, where a hulking, round-headed silhouette stood behind a chest-high curtain of darkness that was probably a serving counter.

The round-headed figure, presumably Brill, spat the gold into a small spindly-fingered hand. He stowed the coin—the Thrasson's, no doubt—somewhere under his counter.

"Your friend got a name?"

"Zoombee. And we have trouble close behind."

" 'Course," Brill grumbled. "Why else come around when you got jink?"

With a great groan, the silhouette heaved his bulk up and lumbered along to one of the purple tapers. He fumbled beneath his counter a moment, then held a second candle to the damson flame. The wick caught fire, flooding the chamber with a flickering yellow light that gave the Amnesian Hero his first good look at Brill and the room's other occupants.

He nearly dropped the amphora.

Brill was a slaad, one of the massive, froglike beings reputed to scavenge the battlefields of the Lower Planes. The Amnesian Hero had never before seen one in the flesh—at least that he could recall—but he had heard many accounts of their taste for blood. This one was a Green, with a flat pate, scalloped brows jutting over wide-set eyes, and a mouth large enough to swallow a swine.

The Amnesian Hero could not identify the race of Brill's customers, but they were uglier than the tavern keeper himself. They did not bother to cover their leathery nakedness, perhaps because of their sparse covering of wiry bristles, which would have torn most garments to shreds. The shape of their bodies bore a remote semblance to that of a human, though too skeletal, somehow twisted. They had waspish waists showing ugly grates of ribs, knobby-jointed limbs much too long for their bodies, and gnarled, yellow-taloned fingers that looked as though they could dig a bear from its cave. The tables before them were piled high with charred haunches and shoulders, many of which looked human.

As one, the customers swung their gray eyes toward the Amnesian Hero and burst into fits of hissing, as though laughing at some joke he had not heard.

"What manner of place is this?" the Thrasson gasped, wondering again if perhaps he had not lost his way and tumbled into the Abyss. He turned to Jayk. "Where have you taken me?"

It was Brill who answered. "I call the place Rivergate." The slaad passed the candle in his hand to Jayk, then said, "You know where to hide."

The tiefling nodded, then stretched over the counter and brought her mouth close to Brill's. To the Thrasson's surprise, the slaad let her kiss him upon the lips long and hard. They remained coupled for several moments. When she finally drew back, her pupils remained round, and there was no sign that her fangs had dropped. The Amnesian Hero could not help thinking of their own near kiss and wondering if he, too, would have been spared her bite.

"Zoombee, don't be jealous," Jayk chided. "You won't make kiss with me."

Brill placed a dusty jug and two black mugs on the counter. "Go on, then—before your trouble walks in the door. You know what a mess these rutterkin make when they get to killing."

Jayk filled both mugs, then corked the jug and tucked it under her arm. Leaving one cup on the counter, she moved deeper into the tavern, joking and flirting as she danced past the tables of rutterkin. Though they never made any reply the Amnesian Hero could hear, twice she pinched long-lobed ears and threw back her head to laugh. The Thrasson followed without picking up the cup she had left for him. He loved wine as much as the next man—perhaps even a bit more—but he had no stomach for the coppery vinegar he smelled in this place.

The Amnesian Hero had barely worked his way past the first table when something snapped his backplate and jerked him onto his heels. Shifting the amphora's weight to one arm, he spun around to see a long, slender tongue curling back toward Brill's mouth.

The slaad gestured at the mug on the counter. "Forgot your drink."

The Amnesian Hero tried not to make a distasteful face. "I'm, uh . . . not thirsty."

Brill croaked what seemed to be a laugh. "I wouldn't waste blood port on no human, but I expect you'd rather have Arborean ruby anyway. Take it and drink up, or you'll have reason to wish you had."

Deciding to accept Brill's threat as the price of a good hiding place, the Amnesian Hero retrieved his mug and joined Jayk at the back of the room, where wisps of black mist were pouring through the cracks of a badly warped door. The tiefling shouldered the portal open and stepped through, already quaffing down the contents of her mug. The Thrasson started to follow, still holding his cup in hand.

"Drink, Zoombee!" Jayk urged. "Otherwise, you find yourself swimming in the River Styx."

The Amnesian Hero paused with one foot over the threshold. "This is a portal?"

"Yes. If you step through without drinking, then splash," she explained. "The key is backwards. That is why it is a good place to hide, you see?"

The Thrasson did not see, but he was too proud to admit it. He raised his mug and stepped into the room. The wine proved to be somewhat tangier and more fruity than his Arborean favorites, but it was at least palatable. He drained the entire cup in a single gulp, then licked his lips clean.

"I had no idea how thirsty I had become."

He thrust the cup at Jayk to be refilled, then found a safe corner in which to place the amphora. The storeroom stank of mildew and sour coppery wine, which, from all appearances, was the rutterkins' preference in drink. Casks and boxes stood against every wall, stacked to the ceiling and more often than not barely visible behind silky veils of spider webs. In the center of the room sat several stools and a barrel with a set of knucklebones etched for gambling.

The Amnesian Hero closed the door and pulled a stool over, then sat down and pressed his eye to a crack. Without Jayk's candle, the main room had again grown gloomy and purple. Brill and the rutterkin were no more than vague black shapes, more imagined than seen unless they happened to be silhouetted against a taper's damson flame. Save for the constant sound of gnawing and an occasional sniggering hiss, the tavern remained quiet.

Jayk placed the Thrasson's cup in his hand. "When Tessali comes, you must tell me so I can put out the candle. Otherwise, he sees the light through the cracks, yes?"

The Amnesian Hero did not bother to ask why she thought Tessali would look for them in Rivergate. The Thrasson had met enough elves in Arborea to know that tracking ran in their blood. He took a long swallow from his mug, then smacked his lips and took another one.

"What is to prevent Tessali from tracking us from Rivergate's door into this storeroom? I worry that he'll have us cornered."

"There is no need for that." Jayk sounded amused. "Brill and the rutterkin have a certain, how do I say . . . *fondness* for elves and humans. Tessali and his guards will not linger."

"As long as there is no killing. They may be chasing us, but the misunderstanding is more our fault than theirs." The Amnesian Hero did not add that in Jayk's case, the pursuit was entirely justified. "They don't deserve to land on a rutterkin's plate."

"Why do you fret so much about this 'killing' all the time?" Jayk demanded. "Even if you believe life is genuine, why does it make you so envious to see others advance toward the One Death?"

"It does not make me envious!" He turned away from his peephole and looked at the tiefling, who sat on a stool, absently rolling the knucklebones between her fingers. "But murder, and especially senseless murder, is the enemy of civilization. Even your Dustmen understand that, or I doubt they would have committed you to the Gatehouse."

"My work had nothing to do with it!" Jayk hurled the knucklebones into a web-filled corner. "That was Komosahl Trevant! He's jealous of my gifts."

"Your gifts?"

Jayk's eyes grew narrow and sly. "I know you have seen them, Zoombee. That's why you won't make kiss with me, yes?"

"You mean your fangs?" He hid his expression by draining his mug, but as he drank, he kept a wary eye on the tiefling's shadowy face. "And the way your pupils change into diamonds?"

"Of course." Jayk smiled, then came over and pulled his empty mug from his mouth. "It only happens when I am excited. Frightened or angry, you know, but especially when I am amorous, Zoombee."

The Thrasson's mouth grew dry. "And you c-call this a gift?"

"But yes!" Jayk took his empty mug and returned to the center of the room. "My destiny, it is to help people reach the One Death. But Trevant, he does not understand this. He says I have too much excitement to be a Dustman."

Jayk whirled back toward the Thrasson, sloshing wine as she poured. "I ask you, how can I have too much excitement? That is how I help others, is it not?"

"Well—"

"But Trevant is a coward. He says the other factions will drive the Dustmen from the city if I give so much help." She thrust the wine back into the Thrasson's hand. "I say he is a fraud. How can he claim to know the One Death and fear anything? It is impossible!"

"And that's the real reason you were taking me to the Mortuary," the Amnesian Hero surmised. "You wanted me to avenge Trevant's betrayal."

"You will do that, Zoombee?" The tiefling dropped beside his stool and, resting her arms in his lap, gazed up at him. She did not quite flutter her eyelashes. "For me?"

"Maybe—er, *no!*" Always vulnerable to adoration, the Amnesian Hero barely caught himself. "Weren't you supposed to be taking me to the Lady of Pain?"

Jayk rose and backed away, her dark eyes now as cold and hard as obsidian. "I mean to do both, Zoombee. We can summon her whenever we like." Her lips curled into a cunning smile, then she shrugged. "So what is the harm if we do it in Secretary Trevant's office?"

The Amnesian Hero scowled. "I don't see how that avenges you."

Jayk raised her mug to her lips and took a long swallow, staring at him over the rim.

"I'm sure others can tell me how to summon her," the Thrasson warned.

"But will they? You have wondered why everyone thinks you are barmy for wanting to see her?" Jayk sat her mug on the barrel and met the Thrasson's gaze. "The Lady, she does not deal kindly with those who summon her—or those who help. That is why you need me. Only I will show you. I ask—no, I demand—one thing in return: Komosahl Trevant must be near, yes?"

"We struck our bargain in the Gatehouse." The Amnesian Hero turned back to his peephole, already beginning to feel the wine. "You said nothing about Trevant then."

"Exactly."

Though he could not quite figure out why, the Thrasson had the unpleasant feeling Jayk had just declared herself winner of the argument. He swallowed another mouthful of wine and silently cursed Rivergate's darkness. Staring into the murky room gave him an uneasy feeling, as though he were spying upon the realm of Hades itself and might be caught at any moment.

An irritating creak sounded across the room, then a beam of gray light shot through the purple murk. Squinting against its unexpected brilliance, the Amnesian Hero saw the blocky shape of an armored man silhouetted in the doorway. The warrior glanced back over his shoulder.

"We'll need the torches." The voice was that of Mateus.

The Amnesian Hero glanced in Jayk's direction, whispering, "Put out the candle. They're here."

By the time he looked back through his peephole, Mateus was leading the rest of the party into Rivergate. A Mercykiller followed close behind with a lit torch, then came Tessali, the sleep-caster, and the other guards.

They advanced just far enough so that the torch lit the dark corners of the room. Tessali braced his hands on his hips and, being careful to avoid looking at what lay piled on the tables, stood in the heart of the light.

"We're pursuing a tiefling sorceress and a bronze-armored warrior."

A rutterkin stood, ripping a hunk of meat from a haunch of flesh that looked slender enough to be elven, and glared directly into Tessali's eyes. There was no other response.

"If you'll tell us where they are, we'll retrieve them and be gone," Tessali said. "They're barmies, both of them, and quite dangerous."

This drew a chorus of wispy teeters. One of the Mercykillers drew his sword and stepped in front of Tessali, pressing the blade to the throat of the rutterkin who had risen to mock the elf.

"The Factor asked you a question, berk."

The rutterkin calmly raised a misshaped arm and placed his bare hand over the blade. "Uh . . . et ur . . . mood air . . . ut brey . . . feast."

The rutterkin's words were so slow and thick that it took the Amnesian Hero a moment to puzzle them out. By the time the Mercykiller had done likewise, Tessali had pulled the fellow away and pushed him back toward the door.

"We're here for everyone's good," the elf said. "We are not looking for a fight."

"Then leave," croaked Brill.

Mateus whirled on the slaad. "At first glance, some of that meat seems human. You wouldn't want me to take a closer look, would you?"

Brill squared his massive shoulders. "Imported. Scavenge it from the Blood War myself."

"And I suppose you have the permits to prove that?"

Brill's gulp was audible even through the storeroom door. His beady eyes darted toward the tiny chamber. Mateus took the torch and began to lead the procession toward the storeroom.

The Amnesian Hero hissed a quiet curse.

"What is it?" Jayk whispered.

"Brill betrayed us," the Thrasson whispered. "Get ready."

He reached for his sword and felt Jayk's hand on his arm. "Brill did not turn stag. It is part of the bob."

The tiefling pulled him through the darkness to the back corner of the room, guiding him into a hiding place between two large casks. In the next instant, the warped door flew open and Mateus, with one of the Mercykillers close behind, charged across the threshold.

Their torch hissed and went out at once. The Amnesian Hero heard a brief purl of water, then two splashes and a pair of gurgling screams. A musky river smell filled the storeroom, but even that faded almost before the Thrasson had identified it.

"What happened?" It was Tessali. "Light!"

The sleepcaster uttered a brief incantation, then the tavern was flooded with a brilliant sapphire light that shone from the blade of her dagger. It was difficult to say whether Tessali or the Amnesian Hero was more surprised to find the rutterkin surrounding what remained of the elf's party.

"Lut . . . toe . . . bite!"

A rutterkin snatched the glowing dagger from the sleepcaster's hand, then tossed it into the storeroom. This time, the doorway filled briefly with swirling black currents, and again the purl and musky smell of a river suffused the air.

"Time for you to leave, elf," croaked Brill.

The Amnesian Hero peered over a cask and saw the murky outlines of the rutterkin stepping aside to let Tessali pass. The elf led his party back to the door, then managed to garner his courage and stop. His face was barely visible in the purple candlelight.

"I know they came in here–a human and a tiefling. I'm not leaving until I know what happened to them."

Brill's arm arced through the dim light, swinging toward the storeroom. "They went through that door, just like your guards." He croaked several times, chuckling. "Go ahead. Take a look."

A wave of sibilant snickers rustled through the tavern.

"Your humor is not appreciated." Despite his words, the elf turned a thoughtful eye toward the storeroom. "And you may be assured the Harmonium will return to inspect your licenses."

"There is no reason for that." The voice, that of a human female, triggered one of those vague sensations of familiarity that sometimes troubled the Amnesian Hero. A chair scraped in a dark corner, then the woman continued, "I have been sitting here for several hours, and I can assure you that the ones you seek are not here."

Tessali turned toward the voice, which seemed to be approaching the counter. "And who are you, milady?"

"A woman alone and in distress."

A tall, statuesque beauty clothed in a simple white gown walked into the dim light. With glistening olive skin, high cheeks, and proud emerald eyes, her face was as regal as it was stunning–and it was one the Amnesian Hero knew as well as he knew his own.

"Perhaps you would be kind enough to escort me to a safer part of the city?" The woman glanced around the dark room as though surprised to find herself in such a place. "I seem to have lost my way."

The Amnesian Hero slipped from his hiding place and crept forward, barely able to hold his tongue. Jayk grabbed his arm and pulled him back, then gently closed the storeroom door.

"Zoombee, what has happened to you?" she hissed. "We're almost safe!"

The Thrasson pressed his eye to the peephole. "It's her! The woman who appears–" He almost whispered 'when I drink wine,' but caught himself and said instead, "The one I know from before!"

"Pah! That cannot be."

In the main room, Tessali was rubbing his chin and studying the woman with a thoughtful air. "This is a bad district for a woman of your . . . appearances. How did you come to be here?"

The woman shook her head, her expression dazed. "I cannot–I honestly don't know. I was at home, then this."

"Yes, perhaps you *should* come with me." Tessali wrapped an arm around her shoulder, then glanced at Brill. "Is her account settled?"

Even the slaad could not think quickly enough to make a profit from her unexpected appearance. He only shook his head, croaking, "Didn't know she was here."

"Good." Tessali motioned for his remaining guard to open the door. "We'll be going."

"No," gasped the Amnesian Hero.

He tried to pull the door open, but found it blocked by Jayk.

"Zoombee, don't be a fool!"

"I can't let him take her!" the Thrasson whispered. "She knows who I am!"

"What is she doing here? How did she find you?" Jayk demanded. "This woman, she must be a sleepcaster's trick."

"Out of my way!"

The Thrasson pushed Jayk away, then remembered the portal and fumbled around in the darkness until he found the wine. He returned to the door and jerked it open, but by then Tessali had already taken the woman and left. The Amnesian Hero raised the jug to his lips, then rushed across the threshold, leaving both the amphora and his tiefling guide behind.

DABUS

Dim has fallen over the city. It would be wrong to call it dusk; there are no rays of sunlight fanning up from the skyline, no silverlit clouds hanging low over the horizon, no deepening hues of blue spreading across the heavenly vault. There is only the waxing gray gloom, spilling from the alcoves and niches of the city's hundred-thousand hovels, spreading over the scum-coated cobblestones, rising like a ground fog to fill the avenues with a thickening ashen murk. In Sigil, we have no twilights before the dawns, no endings presaging fresh beginnings, no deaths begetting new births; we have only that eternal ashen instant that follows what was and precedes what will be, that wavering gray span that separates the dying and the death.

Once the Amnesian Hero has dodged past the rutterkin tables and dashed by Brill's gloomy counter and burst from Rivergate's doors, it is into this gray eventide that he stumbles. Already has the street filled with the scuttling denizens of the night: bustling, dark-cloaked figures who melt into the shadows as suddenly as they emerge. Already has the throng swallowed Tessali and the white-gowned beauty, carried them into the ashen gloom and swept clean their trail. Already has the Thrasson lost his quarry and his good sense as well; he will go after the woman, search her out in winding lanes he has never walked.

Still clutching the jug of Rivergate wine and watching for a flash of white dress in the dimness ahead, the Amnesian Hero raced down the street. When he found only skulking figures camouflaged in night-gray cloaks or armored in spiked plate, he turned and rushed in the opposite direction. The cobblestones rattled with the sound of claws on stone, and the air stank of acrid, lower-planar sweat. Sporadic screams of anguish rose and fell in the distant darkness; the clamor of clashing steel grew common, and the din of growling voices became a constant rumble. Twilight had fallen in the district of blood.

Realizing that he was in danger of losing his way back to Rivergate, the Thrasson ceased his running. "Tessali!"

Had the elf actually answered, the Amnesian Hero might have come to his senses and given some thought to his actions. What would he do? Try to explain that he was not "barmy," then demand the return of a woman whose name he could not recall? As it was, the Thrasson's voice merely vanished into the general roar. He found himself standing alone and ignored in a street bustling with brutish beings, his mind still clouded by Rivergate's powerful libation, not quite able to comprehend how he had again lost the one woman who could possibly tell him his name.

The Amnesian Hero fixed a wary gaze on the dark figures streaming past. Had he seen one of the ghastly brutes skulking the streets of Thrassos, he would have drawn his sword on the spot and driven it from the city. Now, he found himself in need of their aid and ready to ask it. Wondering how he had fallen so low, he took another swig from his jug and stepped into the path of an ember-eyed shadow.

"If you would be kind enough to offer your indulgence–"

"Out the way, bubber!" As the creature spoke, its lips were illuminated by a faint, fiery glow deep in its gullet. "I'll scorch ya!"

It sidestepped the Thrasson, buffeting him with a murky wing that suddenly unfolded from its back. The Amnesian Hero accepted the indignity with atypical restraint, more interested in finding his white-gowned woman than teaching proper manners. He grabbed the next figure in line, a lanky slope-shouldered brute in scale armor, and dragged him to a stop.

"A moment of your–"

Something long and snaky lashed over the fellow's shoulder and pinged off the Amnesian Hero's bronze armor. The Thrasson glimpsed the form of a thick scaly tail arcing away, then felt the tip of a dagger pressed up beneath his jaw.

"Le'go-n-step'way, berk." The voice was raspy, the breath foul. "Maybe I don' killya."

The Amnesian Hero calmly released the brute's arm and grabbed his knife hand instead. With a quick twist against the joint, the Thrasson turned the dagger away and, in the same motion, forced his adversary to his knees. He found himself looking down at a gaunt, scaled face with sunken eyes, an arrow-shaped nose, and a row of tiny tusks rising from behind a pouting lower lip. The fellow was one of the barbazu, a race of minor fiends the Thrasson had encountered when Apollo sent him to deliver a message to the Lord of the Stinking Mire.

"You have no cause for alarm." The Amnesian Hero twisted the barbazu's wrist until the dagger came free and clattered onto the cobblestones. "Nor do you have need of weapons."

The crowd parted and continued to scurry past, giving wide berth to the confrontation. Any human that could drop a barbazu to his knees was not to be bothered–especially in this part of Sigil, where strength was the only law.

The Amnesian Hero said, "I only want to ask about Tessali."

"Who?" The fiend's tail appeared above his shoulder, but hovered there and did not strike; there would have been no purpose, as the bony end-barb had broken off the first time it hit the Thrasson's armor. "D'ya think I know every–"

"An elf. He has a human with him, a beautiful woman."

The barbazu's gaze flickered to the wine jug, which the Amnesian Hero still held in his free hand, then over the rest of the Thrasson's body.

"The elf's armor red?" The fiend's speech was still raspy, but less urgent now.

"I fear not." The Thrasson was disappointed; there could not be many elves in this squalid district, and it was just his luck the barbazu had seen the wrong one. "He was wearing a spangled cloak. The woman was in white."

"Oh yeah, a tasty scrap." The barbazu glanced over his shoulder. "I seen 'em. Hangin' all over that elf, she was."

"Where?" The Thrasson peered past the fiend into the deepening gloom. "How long ago?"

"Five gold," the barbazu replied. "Worth 'at much jink, by the look o'er."

"The question is a simple one." The Amnesian Hero wrenched his captive's wrist further and pivoted away, forcing the fiend facedown on the cobblestones. "Answer it, and I won't break your wrist. That should be payment enough."

The barbazu bobbed his head. "Two alleys back, on the right." His voice grew spiteful. "Lookin' for a place to do him. Hope she does."

The Amnesian Hero pivoted away from the barbazu, at the same time savagely twisting the fellow's wrist around. The brute had no choice but to start rolling. The Thrasson could easily have broken his captive's arm, but he settled instead for smashing his wine jug over the fiend's thick skull.

"You should be more cordial in what you wish for others." The Thrasson placed one hand on the hilt of his sword, then, wondering at the depth of his rage, cautiously backed away. "In the future, I suggest you curb your tongue."

"Pike it, bubber." The barbazu gathered himself up and, just as cautiously as the Thrasson, backed away in the opposite direction. "You already got yours. That tasty morsel, she ain't never going back to no vinegar-swillin' sod like you."

With that, the fiend melted into the crowd and was gone. The Amnesian Hero turned toward the alley, convinced by his strong emotions that the woman had indeed been someone special to him. When he found her—and liberated her from Tessali's tender care—he would certainly find his past. Unfortunately, he would still be honor-bound to deliver the amphora. No matter how badly Poseidon had understated the errand's difficulty, for a man of renown to renege on a promise to the Cleaver of Lands would be as unfitting as it would be foolish.

The Thrasson reached the mouth of the second alley and paused to get his bearings. Although he remembered which way to turn, finding Rivergate again would be difficult. He could not tell the difference between any of the huts in the district. They were all windowless heaps of stone, unmortared and accessible only by tunnel-like entryways. After he rescued the mysterious woman, he would need to ask directions, which meant he would need to incapacitate his pursuers, at least temporarily.

Hoping he would not be forced to kill anyone, the Amnesian Hero drew his sword and started down the murky passage. Like many of Sigil's back lanes, this one appeared quiet and deserted; most people avoided such places as a matter of course, and those who did not preferred leaving or hiding to being noticed. The alley was littered with flat stones that had fallen from the tumbledown walls that formed its looming sides. The musty smell of clay hung heavy in the moist air. A few paces ahead, a large mud puddle glimmered faintly in the gray gloom.

Thinking to pick up a trail of wet footprints on the far side, the Amnesian Hero dashed forward and leapt over the muck hole. Though his god-forged armor weighed little more than a leather jerkin, the puddle was a large one; his rear foot fell a little short, sinking into the slime with a long slurp. Before he could pull free, the mud compressed around his ankle and clamped it in place. He lost his balance and fell flat. The Thrasson cursed his clumsiness and tried to bring his leg forward.

He found himself sliding back toward the puddle. Digging the fingertips of his free hand deep into the dirt, the Amnesian Hero pulled forward and tugged harder on his leg. He felt warm mud slithering up his calf. An unfamiliar pounding erupted in his ears; could he actually be *frightened?* The Thrasson craned his neck to look over his shoulder, found that he could see nothing, then peered beneath his arm and decided he had good reason to be alarmed. A snaky tendril of mud had engulfed his foot, and even now it was stretching out of the puddle, writhing like an eel and steadily working its mouth up his leg.

The Amnesian Hero pushed his torso up, then swung his sword around to attack. To his horror, he could barely touch the strange creature. His leg seemed to be stretching toward the puddle, and, at least where it was not covered by bronze armor, his flesh was turning as gray as the muck itself. He could no longer see the difference between the tendril and his own knee; the mud had already claimed everything below that, and he had a dead, tingling feeling in his toes.

The Thrasson thrust the tip of his sword, all that could reach, into the muck. The star-forged steel cut through the tendril easily enough, but the mud simply oozed back behind the blade. He rolled onto his side, then curled toward his feet and attacked the base of the appendage. The blow severed it cleanly, but his foot remained bound to the puddle by a curtain of mud dribbling from his shin. By the time he cut through this, the base of the tentacle had reattached itself.

The Amnesian Hero could no longer feel his toes. His thigh had turned as gray as pearls, and his knee had become an amorphous mass of muck. He could not believe that a simple mud puddle would accomplish what the Hydra of Thrassos and the Acherian Giant had not.

The Thrasson looked down the dark alley, straining to see his quarry. "Help! Tessali!"

No answer.

"Tessali, this is the Amnesian Hero! I won't harm you. Perhaps I will even surrender!"

Nothing stirred in the darkness. The Thrasson felt himself sliding back toward the puddle, and that was when he realized he had seen no footprints in the dirt before him.

The puddle had swallowed Tessali's party, too.

The Amnesian Hero wedged his sword between the stones of the alley wall, anchoring himself in place. Any normal weapon would have snapped, but it would take a far greater strain to break—or even bend—his star-forged blade.

The mud reached the hem of the Thrasson's loin tasset. He felt as though his ankle, all he could still sense of his foot, lay twice a leg's length from his hip. He might save himself by using his star-forged blade to cut off his own leg, but he refused to consider such a cowardly act. Who had ever heard of a one-legged man of renown? Better to suffer an ignoble death now.

The Amnesian Hero turned his face groundward. "How have I offended you, O Great and Wicked Hades, that you treat me thus? I deserve a death more glorious than this!"

"But Zoombee, I have told you—you are dead already."

"Jayk?" The Amnesian Hero craned his neck around to see the tiefling carrying his amphora down the alley. "Truly, the gods are watching out for me."

"You must not be so absurd, Zoombee!" Jayk scoffed. "I heard you when you called to Tessali."

The Thrasson flushed. "You do realize I had no true intention of surrendering?"

"But of course, Zoombee." Jayk smirked, then leaned the heavy amphora against a nearby wall. "Who would surrender when he can let an ooze portal suck him into a Paraelemental Plane?"

One of the stones anchoring the Thrasson in place popped free. He resumed his steady slide toward the puddle. "Jayk, will you please free me from this mud?"

"I will try, Zoombee." The tiefling reached under her cape. "It can be very difficult. Perhaps my magic works better if you help me with Trevant, yes?"

The Thrasson felt his free foot brush the puddle's surface. He tried to lift it free, but he was too late; a long cord of mud rose with his toes.

The Amnesian Hero returned his gaze to the tiefling. "If you think I'll buy my own life at the expense of an innocent—"

"How can you say Trevant is innocent? He betrayed me!"

"Be that as it may, I won't help you." Caught by both legs now, the Amnesian Hero began to slide more rapidly toward the puddle. He stared into the mud. "Will you help me or not?"

"I suppose I must." Jayk's voice was both sharp and resigned. "You are too handsome to become one with Ooze."

The tiefling threw a small sliver of glass into the mud, at the same time speaking the words of a simple incantation. The ooze started to stiffen, the writhing of the tendrils slowed, and a glassy sheen spread over the surface of the puddle. A deep, penetrating cold pierced the Thrasson's leg, then he ceased sliding.

"Why do you wait, Zoombee? Cut yourself free!"

With both legs caught, the Amnesian Hero found it much more difficult to reach the mud. When he did slice into the icy muck, however, it stayed cut, and he soon freed the newly caught foot. After that, it was a simple matter to hack a large block from the puddle. Dragging a leg twice its normal length behind him, he crawled a short distance down the alley and began to hammer at the frozen sludge.

A few blows later, he had knocked the worst of the icy mud off his legs. In the dim light, he could not tell how quickly the color was returning to his chilly flesh. He felt a slight, aching burn as his elongated leg resumed its normal proportions, then his skin began to nettle as it does after being extremely cold. He still had no feeling below the ankle, and the foot itself gleamed with the same faint glow he had earlier observed on the surface of the mud.

The Thrasson rose and limped along the edge of the puddle, both testing his legs and searching for clues as to the fate of Tessali and the white-gowned woman.

"Zoombee, what are you looking for?"

"Signs of Tessali and the woman we saw in Rivergate. They were supposed to have come down this alley."

"Who tells you a thing like that?"

The Amnesian Hero stopped and looked up. "A barbazu."

"And you believe him? I see Tessali in the street–searching for that glitter girl in white." Jayk shook her head sadly. "Poor Zoombee, he even trusts fiends."

The Thrasson flushed again, feeling foolish for allowing his enthusiasm to overcome his judgment. "I did have him at a disadvantage." Still, he sheathed his sword and, seeing no other way back to Jayk, went to the edge of the ooze portal. "Can I walk on this?"

"Until it thaws."

The Amnesian Hero limped across the ice, then stopped at Jayk's side. "I am in your debt. Perhaps I can help you recover your spellbooks, but I won't—"

"Harm Trevant, I know. That is fine. You must live by the rules of your delusions." Jayk looked at his sandaled foot, then added, "Now we must go. We must find a healer before your foot thaws."

The Thrasson scowled at his glimmering foot. "What happens then?"

"It probably does not matter, if you still wish to see the Lady of Pain." Jayk turned toward the mouth of the alley. "But you were in the ooze too long; it has taken your foot. If a healer does not restore it before the mud thaws, the portal will finish its work."

The Amnesian Hero cast an uneasy glance at his glimmering foot, then picked up the amphora and turned to limp after Jayk.

Two paces away, the tiefling had stopped to stare at four slender figures with clouds of white hair piled high atop their heads. They had small coin-shaped noses, deep-set eyes, and squat brows with two sets of horns—one pair straight and one pair curled. All four beings were calmly stacking stones across the mouth of the alley, an activity strangely at odds with their flowing, elaborately embroidered robes.

Jayk raised a hand to her mouth and retreated, backing into the Amnesian Hero. She stopped, but did not turn around or speak.

"What's happening here?" the Thrasson asked. "Why are you so afraid?"

"Dabus!"

When Jayk offered no further explanation, the Amnesian Hero pushed the amphora into her arms. Placing one hand on the hilt of his sword, he stepped forward and pointed at the wall.

"What are you doing here?"

In unison, the dabus stooped over as though to pick up something. Although the Amnesian Hero could see no loose stones on the ground, when they rose again, each held a flat rock in his hands. They placed the stones on the wall, then bent down to get another.

"Answer me."

The Thrasson stepped forward and thrust his heel against the wall, kicking a small gap open. Normally, he would never have been so rude, but he was alarmed by Jayk's reaction. The dabus merely picked up the dislodged stones and returned them to their places.

The Amnesian Hero kicked the stones again. "Answer me."

The dabus stopped working and, still ignoring the Thrasson, turned to each other. Their mouths began to work, spewing long streams of symbols into the air. There were no sounds, merely strange combinations of pictures and signs that hung about their heads like hummingbirds.

After a brief consultation, two dabus bent down and retrieved a pair of war-axes from the same mysterious place they fetched the stones. As they stepped over the wall, the Amnesian Hero noticed for the first time that their feet—if the dabus had any beneath the hems of their long robes—did not touch the street.

The Thrasson stepped back and drew his sword.

Jayk was at his side instantly. "No, Zoombee! You mustn't strike them!" She thrust the amphora into his arms, precluding any chance that he would. "We are in enough trouble!"

"Trouble?"

"They are building a maze. You should summon the Lady of Pain now, while you still can."

The Amnesian Hero ran his gaze around the alley. "Then she's near?"

"The Lady is always near," Jayk replied. "All you need do is pray to her."

"Pray?"

"Yes. She always appears to those who pray to her."

"And then what?"

Jayk's face paled to a pearly gray. "Then she flays us—alive, yes?"

"No, not us." The Amnesian Hero did not bother to ask why the Lady would want to flay them. Having explained many times that he had only come to deliver a gift, he was beginning to realize that Sigil's residents did not understand their queen. "There's no reason for you to be here. I'll pray alone. This armor was forged by Hephaestus himself, and even Apollo's arrows cannot pierce it. I doubt the Lady of Pain's wrath will rend it."

The shadow returned to Jayk's face, but she made no move to leave. "It is better to accept our pain here than to be trapped in the mazes forever."

"Phah! In Arborea, we play mazes for fun." The Thrasson leaned the amphora against the alley wall. "And there is no reason for you to stay. This is not your doing."

Jayk smiled and glanced toward the mouth of the alley, where the dabus had already raised their wall to waist height. She shook her head. "That is not for you to decide."

"Perhaps not, but the Lady already intends to imprison me. What do I have to lose by forcing her dabus to release you?"

The Thrasson strode forward and faced the two armed dabus. He gestured at Jayk with his sword. "She has no part in this. As men—er, beings—of honor, I ask you to release her."

The dabus held their axes at port arms and watched him carefully, but made no other response. The Amnesian Hero waved Jayk forward. When the expressions of the Lady's servants did not change, he sheathed his sword and turned his back on them.

"Wait for me outside." The Amnesian Hero leaned close to embrace Jayk, at the same time slipping the golden thread from his purse. He pressed it into her palm and whispered, "When you hear me praying, hold the end and throw the spool over the wall. It will not be long before I return to help you retrieve your spellbooks."

"Zoombee!"

Jayk pulled away and tipped her chin back, her lips barely parted. Tempted as he was, the Amnesian Hero did not accept the invitation. The tiefling's eyes were closed, and her mouth was not open far enough to see whether her fangs had descended. He grabbed her by the waist and spun her toward the wall, lifting her over in one swift motion. Without breaking rhythm, one of the dabus builders took her from the Thrasson and set her on the ground.

The Amnesian Hero sighed in relief. Before undertaking a feat so perilous as summoning the Lady of Pain, true men of renown always saw their beautiful maidens to safety. He retrieved the amphora, then went to the center of the alley and kneeled in meditation, trying to think of a proper prayer for Sigil's ruler.

Because he knew so little about her, the task was a difficult one. Beseeching her for mercy was out of the question, of course, as was singing the praises of pain; in his experience, the worst kind of supplication was an insincere one.

By the time he recalled the strange riddles from the Gatehouse and realized what to say, the dabus had raised their wall to chest height. The Amnesian Hero laid the amphora on the ground before him, carefully arranging it so that it lay exactly parallel to the walls, then sat back on his haunches and crossed his arms over his chest.

By the hunger of change and emotion,
By the thirst of unbearable things,
By despair, the twin-born of devotion,
By the pleasure that winces and stings,
The delight that consumes the desire,
The desire that outruns the delight,
By the cruelty deaf as a fire
And blind as the night,

By the ravenous teeth that have smitten
Through the kisses that blossom and bud,
By the lips intertwisted and bitten
Till the foam has a savor of blood,
By the pulse as it rises and falters,
By the hands as they slacken and strain,
I adjure thee, respond from thine altars,
Our Lady of Pain.

The prayer is, I think, the most beautiful ever uttered in Sigil. How it speaks to me! Of reckless yearnings pursued unto misery, of secret lusts that are themselves unbearable torments. Pleasure and pain, they are one; hope nurtures despair, love breeds loss, joy begets sorrow—this Thrasson, he knows me for the thing I am.

His fine words I would forgive, if I could.

But this is Sigil. Here, no god may enter—and if the Thrasson prays to me, what do I become but a god?

It must not be. The doors would open; the city itself would crumble, and there I would stand, one alone against all the gods of the multiverse. With chains of starlight and axes of fire, they would come for me, the bad and the good, and make a war to sunder the planes themselves.

What then? With Pain caged in the deepest Abyss and bound to the will of Demogorgon or Diinkarazan or some other god of wickedness, what then? I will tell you: tyranny and cowardice, darkness in every plane, and fear in every breath; a single foul ruler himself ruled by hungers foul beyond imagining, all the multiverse his to pillage and to ravish as he desires.

And worse still, if good prevails: endless worlds of endless ease, with no suffering to build strength, no anguish to breed courage, no fear to foster cunning; a multiverse of middling passions and bland hungers, where nothing is ventured because nothing can be lost, where no anger is consuming, no love passionate, and no life worth living.

I have no choice in the matter. For the good of the multiverse, I must punish the Thrasson—but do not think I have forgotten the tiefling. She taught him to pray, and for that I will be avenged.

I open my eyes, and the Lady of Pain is there before him, her feet still touching the dirt so he cannot see her. He waits with his arms crossed over his chest and that amphora lying on the ground before him. He is a clever one, this Hunter. If I forgive his prayer—still the most beautiful ever spoken in Sigil—his master will be the first to storm my doors; yet, the instant I punish him, he will open his jar and release that enchanted net it carries.

But he has forgotten my children. I have but to desire and the dabus perform. Already, the two axe-bearers have drifted forward to remove the amphora. They stop beside it.

"Leave that be!" The Amnesian Hero's eyes grow as round as coins. "Poseidon sent it for the Lady of Pain!"

My children honor him with a reply, but if the Thrasson can read their rebuses, he does not care that they are acting on my wishes. He stands and reaches for his sword. One dabus picks up the amphora, and the other raises his axe to do battle. I lift one foot off the ground, then the other, and–

–suddenly the Lady of Pain was there. Like the dabus, she hung a little in the air, the hem of her long, brocaded gown hovering just inches above the dirt. The Amnesian Hero forgot about his sword–and the dabus and his amphora as well–and let his jaw drop. The Lady was a striking beauty, tall and slender, with classic features and an aura of inviolable serenity. She had a halo of steel blades instead of hair, lips as black as kohl, and unflinching yellow eyes that kindled a sick, feverish fear in the Thrasson's breast.

Still kneeling, the Amnesian Hero placed his hands on his thighs and bowed deeply. His palms felt hot and wet against his bronze cuisses.

"Greetings. I am the Amnesian Hero of Thrassos, bearing a gift from the god Poseidon, K-king of Seas and C-cleaver of Lands." He gestured behind him, where the dabus had retreated to the wall with the amphora. "With your p-permission–"

The Lady raised her hand, and the Amnesian Hero stopped talking. She fixed her sulfurous gaze on him and, for the first time, truly seemed to see him. Thinking she was about to speak, the Thrasson held his bow. Though he remained absolutely motionless, he kept his toes bent, so that he could spring to his feet quickly. If she attacked, as everyone seemed to believe she would, he had every intention of defending himself.

The Lady curled her fingers into a black-nailed claw, which she dragged downward through the air. A loud, metallic squeal arose behind the Thrasson, and something shoved his face toward the ground. He caught himself on his hands, then glanced over his shoulder. There was no one behind him save the dabus guards, standing several paces away, as motionless as statues and still holding the amphora. Their two companions had nearly completed the wall; the crest stood only a row short of a man's height.

The Amnesian Hero felt several ridges of bronze pressing into his back, then realized that his god-forged armor had actually been dented. He looked back to the Lady of Pain. Several of her fingernails were broken, and her brow was raised ever so slightly. It occurred to the Thrasson that he had just survived an assault by Sigil's fearsome ruler. To his surprise, he found that he was less terrified than confused about what to do next.

As the Lady showed no sign of continuing her attack, he elected to turn his palms up and spread them wide to show he meant no harm. "Please, milady, do not fear me."

The shadow of a smirk flashed across her mouth. She extended a single finger.

"I come in peace." Again, the Thrasson gestured at the amphora. "I only want to deliver this gift from Poseidon."

The Lady drew her finger through the air, and again the creak of folding metal rang off the alley walls. The Thrasson rocked backward, giving way to a terrific pressure against his chest. He looked down to see a long groove running the length of his breastplate, as though some enchanted weapon had struck him a mighty blow. Despite the amicable nature of his mission, a seething anger began to build in his stomach.

"Until now, I have tried to comport myself peacefully." The Thrasson sprang to his feet, dropping a hand to the hilt of his star-forged sword. "But I warn you, this armor was made by Hephaestus himself. I will suffer no further damage to it."

The Lady slightly narrowed her eyes, then curled her hand into a fist. The screech of crumpling metal rang in the Thrasson's ears. His chest filled with shooting pains, and he looked down to see his corselet reshaping itself into the figure of an hourglass. Only the anguish in his body convinced him that he was seeing something real. No foe had ever dented his god-forged armor, and he could scarcely believe the Lady of Pain was crushing it without so much as a blow.

The Thrasson's body believed. His aching ribs made soft popping sounds, and his breath left him and would not return. Hurting too much to scream, he dropped to his knees and fumbled his dagger from its sheath. He jammed the tip beneath the first buckle and cut the strap. His lungs filled with air, but the crushing anguish in his stomach deepened. Not worrying that the blade might slip and cut him, the Amnesian Hero shoved the knife down the crooked seam and severed the other two straps. The armor fell away, clanging softly into the dirt.

Even before the pain began to recede, the Amnesian Hero was on his feet and reaching for his sword. He would win no combats against the Lady of Pain—or anyone who, like the gods themselves, used magic without casting spells—but Hades had heard his prayer for a glorious death, and the Thrasson would not squander the honor by dying poorly. In fact, he found himself looking forward to the battle; a valiant effort would secure his name—or rather his legend—a place in the songs of bards throughout the multiverse.

It was not to be. His sword had not even cleared its scabbard before a loud clatter erupted from the far side of the wall.

"Zoombee!" The golden thread came arcing into the alley, unspooling as it flew, then the stones in the dabus' wall began to tremble.

The Lady of Pain pivoted her blade-haloed head toward the sound. The Thrasson drew his sword, but resisted the urge to attack. Despite appearances, he was quite certain that his powerful foe had not forgotten about him.

Jayk pulled her torso atop the wall, then froze in shock as she found herself looking down at the Lady of Pain. "By the One Death!"

The Lady raised a hand, as though to help the tiefling over.

Jayk's face went as pale as pearls, then the stones resumed their trembling. She glanced behind her and frowned, then grunted and began to flail her legs at something.

"Don't fight me!" The voice was Tessali's. "This is for your own—huh!"

Jayk landed a kick, then hoisted herself entirely onto the wall and, like a rope-dancer, ran along the crest. The long-fingered hand of an elf caught her ankle, and she pitched headlong off the wall, crashing down upon the two dabus guards. The amphora came free of their grasp and thudded to the ground, rolling clear as a tangled heap of tiefling and dabus crashed down behind it.

The Amnesian Hero rushed over to the jar, silently thanking

Apollo for not letting it shatter—then he noticed the crack in its neck. A loop of fine golden thread had pushed through the tiny fissure and seemed to be writhing out. The Thrasson kneeled down and clamped his free hand over the crevice. The filament pushed its way between his fingers and continued to work free.

"I fear your gift has been damaged." Still holding his sword, he turned to the Lady of Pain. "Whatever your intentions for me, perhaps you should open it now."

The hem of the Lady's gown billowed outward, as though she were walking forward. She seemed to step downward, then her dress fluttered again, and she vanished from sight.

"Milady?"

Another clatter sounded from the wall, then Tessali's voice called, "I need another net. They're both here!"

The Amnesian Hero turned to see a barmy net spinning through the air toward his head. He reached up and caught several strands in his hand, then, before Tessali could pull the draw cord, yanked his attacker from the wall. The elf had barely hit the ground before the Thrasson's sword was slashing back and forth through the net, cutting it to pieces.

By the time he turned back to the amphora, the golden thread had worked completely free of the crack. It rose into the air and began to circle.

PAINS OF THE FLESH

Against that golden strand, there is no slip.

Still as stone, I stand before the Amnesian Hero, both feet smooth upon the ground. The Thrasson and his ilk call me gone, but not so that flaxen thread. Like a worm to a corpse, it comes to me and scribes its circle.

There is time yet, I think. I steal forward, feet as soft as feathers upon the haze-brown sky. The Thrasson's supplication, those divine lines, cannot stand: he must recant. He must disavow, he must renounce, he must curse my name and sob, wail, and beg for death. He must suffer for what he has done; for the good of the multiverse, he must rue the hour he uttered that beautiful prayer.

I do not reach him.

Once more the filament circles me, and something–I cannot say what–stirs in that void where I once had a heart. It is nothing I have ever felt before: a fluttering, a feeling as gentle and lonely as a mourning dove's lament; it is like a lover's hand: warm, comforting, and somehow familiar, so very inviting and so very dangerous.

Daedalus himself, most cunning of men, spun that golden fiber. It is sturdier than any chain Hephaestus ever forged. To pull against that filament is to make it stronger; to cut it is to braid it double, to untwine it is to spread it in an inescapable mesh. The Thrasson has cast Poseidon's net, if a single strand can a net make, and I dare not give it the touch.

I close my eyes, and when the thread circles the third time, no fiber drags across my skin, no filament tightens around my throat, no string binds my wrists. The Lady has gone from that dim alley.

The Thrasson stands unrepentant, the tiefling unpunished beside him. A key has turned, a lock has clicked; a door hangs unlatched and the treasure sits unguarded. I could go into the mazes after them, but there are dark things in the labyrinth, and corridors innumerable, branching and twisting and feeding into themselves in an irreducible tangle. In those passages all wanderers perish, by bloody claw or upon tottering legs, but always with the certain knowledge that the exit lay just beyond the next corner. Perhaps that is punishment enough.

And, in truth, I dare not allow the Thrasson to open the amphora and cast at me more strands from Poseidon's net. Already, the first has found me again. I feel a growing surge in that void where I once had a heart, a rhythmic roar that builds and fades, then rises again more powerful than before. The smell of brine and the salt sea pervades the air, and a stiff breeze whispers across the water. Hard as I try, I cannot shut off the sounds or ignore the scents; they are inside, like nightmares gushing from that dark well in my chest.

Standing above white-crested waves I see the Lady of Pain, gowned in white cloud and belted in golden light, her lips the same turquoise as the Arborean Sea. A string of pearls, black and lustrous like succubi tears, hangs around her neck. About her head flashes a diadem of blue lightning, while in place of her red-stained blade halo waves a flyaway mane of yellow hair. The strands vanish into the air and have no ends; they are a hundred thousand golden threads that lead to a hundred thousand of the multiverse's infinite planes.

In the air beside her—me?—hangs a ghostly visage made of the wind itself and as huge as the sun: the Elemental Queen of Air. Though her features are as translucent and shifting as a breeze, I see something in the shape of her face, in the angle of her oval eyes, and in the set of her high cheeks: a certain motherly semblance to the Lady of Pain.

On my other side stands a trident-wielding giant, waist-deep in waves, reeking of kelp and salt air, sea-foam for hair, sparkling skin like moonlight on water. Upon his lips, a father's miserly smile. He is stretching an upturned palm toward me and looking out to sea.

This cannot be! If I had parents, I would remember. This memory—this illusion—is some trick of Poseidon's, a ruse to win my trust and nothing more.

A black-sailed dhow approaches, steered by a single black-hooded helmsman. On the deck rest four black coffers, the bride price mighty Poseidon demands for the heart of his golden-haired daughter. The boxes hold agony, anguish, misery, and despair—the four Pains that rule the multiverse—but how I know, I do not know; that is as dark to me as the face beneath the hood.

And now the tide turns; the surf roars more softly each time it rises, the smell of brine grows sour and distant, the face of the Elemental Queen vanishes in a shimmer of still, hot air. Poseidon sinks beneath the waves; the whitecaps subside, the sea calms to a turquoise mirror and the air spills from the dhow's black sail. The helmsman turns his hooded face toward me, and a whirlpool opens beneath his vessel; down he is drawn, down into that void in my chest he whirls, this night-cloaked stranger who paid the bride's price for my heart.

CITY OF IRON

The Amnesian Hero stood in the charcoal dimness, cautiously awaiting the pleasure of the Lady of Pain. Although she had disappeared a moment earlier, a certain disturbing stillness continued to hang in the air. The alley had suddenly grown hot and muggy, and the musty smell of clay seemed stronger, perhaps because Sigil's other fetid odors had vanished. Even the murky light looked somehow deeper—not darker, but heavier and more enduring. From the wall behind him came a frightened gasp and the rasp of boot heels kicking for purchase in the dirt. Thinking the Lady of Pain had finally shown herself, the Thrasson raised his sword and spun.

He found Jayk stooped over Tessali, trying to dodge past the elf's kicking legs and catch hold of a flailing arm. The Thrasson stepped over, grabbing the tiefling's collar and throwing her against a hut wall. Her pupils were diamonds and her fangs were folded completely down.

"Have I not warned you about this, Jayk?"

Before Jayk could answer, Tessali was on his feet and climbing the wall. "Over here! Help!"

One-handed, the Amnesian Hero jerked the elf down and pushed him to the ground. "You, be silent!"

Tessali's eyes darted to the crest of the wall, then half closed in disappointment. "What's taking so long?" he yelled. "I'm all alone with these bar–*arrrgh!*"

The complaint came to an abrupt end as the Amnesian Hero placed his foot across Tessali's throat. The Thrasson glanced toward the wall, but saw no sign of anyone coming to aid the elf.

Jayk gathered herself up, still staring at Tessali through her diamond-shaped pupils. "I make kiss with him, yes? When he reaches the next stage, he is not so much trouble."

"No," the Amnesian Hero said. "We need him alive, to trade for my wine woman."

"Wine woman?" Tessali asked.

"The one in white." The Amnesian Hero did not explain that he called her wine woman because she only appeared when he drank wine. "She approached you in Rivergate."

Tessali knitted his brows. "You *were* there!"

"She will be your ransom." The Thrasson did not bother to confirm the elf's deduction.

"But Zoombee! Did you not hear me? I told you he was looking for this 'wine woman'!"

Tessali nodded. "That's right. We lost her."

"Lost her? How?" The Thrasson put a little more weight on the elf's throat. "If something happened to her. . . ."

"I can't say what became of her," gasped Tessali. "We were barely a dozen paces out the door when she escape–er, when she disappeared."

The Amnesian Hero had no need to ask for details. The same thing had happened to him a dozen times; he would be crossing a room toward the woman, or perhaps pursuing her down a crowded lane, when his view was blocked by a pillar or a corner. In that instant, she always vanished.

"I'm sorry," Tessali said, seeming to sense the Thrasson's disappointment. "But if she's important to you, come back to the Gatehouse. Sooner or later, we will—"

"You will not catch her," said the Amnesian Hero. "No matter how hard you search, you will not even see her."

"Then the elf, he is worthless." Jayk started toward Tessali, the tips of her needlelike fangs showing beneath her cupid's bow lip. "I make kiss with him, yes?"

"No." The Amnesian Hero started to rebuke the tiefling, then thought better of it and glared down at Tessali. He removed his foot from the prisoner's throat, then said, "Your life rests in your own hands. If you make any more trouble, I'll let her do as she pleases."

Tessali paled, then glanced in the tiefling's direction. She gave him a coy smile, but the Amnesian Hero resisted the urge to warn her against being too hasty in judgment. For now at least, the more frightened the elf was, the less likely he would be to cause trouble.

The Amnesian Hero stepped away from Tessali and positioned himself near the middle of the newly erected wall. He could not see into the murky corners where it connected to the huts, but there was enough light to spy anyone clambering over the top. No one came. The street on the other side had fallen ominously silent, and the ground had ceased to reverberate beneath the endless file of feet. The Thrasson sheathed his sword.

"We appear to be alone."

Jayk groaned. "Yes. The wall, it is finished. Now we are trapped."

"Trapped?" Keeping a wary eye on the tiefling, Tessali rose. "That can't be!"

A shadowy sneer creased Jayk's lips. "Why not? The Lady, she never sends Bleakers to the mazes?"

Tessali scowled. "Of course she does." He studied the stone wall, as though considering what lay on the other side. His face suddenly seemed to light, then he said, "In fact, I've been in the mazes several times myself."

The Amnesian Hero raised his brow. "The Bleakers play at mazes?"

"Not play." Tessali's expression was guarded. "But people

sometimes find themselves caught in a labyrinth through no fault of their own. The Bleak Cabal tries to help them find their way."

"And the Bleak Cabal does not become lost?" the Thrasson demanded.

Tessali shook his head. "We have freed our minds of delusion; we are not fooled by false paths." The elf's expression was smug. "If you will let me, I will guide you out of the mazes."

"And straight into one of your cells, no?"

Tessali received Jayk's skepticism with a smile. "Surely, that is better than remaining lost in the mazes?" He gestured at the dim walls around them. "And your constraint would not be permanent. You will be released when we have freed you of delusion."

"When we are barmy as you, yes?" Jayk shook her head violently, flinging golden drops of venom from her fang tips. "You do not even know when you have hit the blinds. You are such a berk!"

Tessali received this insult with a look of infinite patience. He turned to the Amnesian Hero, spreading his hands in entreaty.

"You two are the ones who have hit the blinds. Won't you let me show you the way out?"

The Amnesian Hero pointed at the wall the dabus had built. "That looks real to me."

"It is real, but not every wall is a maze wall. Some are just walls."

"Why would the dabus build a new wall here?" The Thrasson asked.

Tessali pulled a stone loose and tossed it on the ground. "This wall does not look so new to me."

"It is. The dabus built it as I tried to present Poseidon's gift to the Lady of Pain."

Tessali's brow arched in compassion. "There were no dabus."

"I saw them." The Amnesian Hero pointed at Jayk. "As did she."

The elf shook his head sadly. "But I didn't. When two troubled people spend time together, they often feed off each other's delusions."

The Amnesian Hero cast a questioning glance at Jayk, who was quick to explain, "He did not see the dabus. They were gone before he came."

Tessali gave her a patronizing smile. "You can fashion an explanation for everything. That is the nature of delusions."

The Amnesian Hero pointed at his crumpled corselet. "What of that? Did I imagine the Lady of Pain crushing that, too?"

The elf glanced at the armor, but his smug expression wavered only slightly. "Bronze does not make the sturdiest armor. In this district, there are any number of denizens who could crush it."

"Not that armor, Tessali. You are the one who is fashioning explanations." The Thrasson kneeled beside the cracked amphora. "You can lead us nowhere but into more trouble."

"Tessali was trying to trick us." Jayk slipped to the elf's side. "Now I make kiss with him, yes?"

"No. Let him go." The Amnesian Hero picked up a piece of slashed barmy net. "If Tessali can find his helpers, then we should go with him."

Tessali's jaw dropped, but he was quick to start up the wall. "I shall hold you to that, you know."

The Amnesian Hero did not even look up. "I am a man of my word, Tessali."

The Thrasson cut a length of rope from the barmy net and wrapped it around the amphora neck, then used the rest of the mesh to fashion a sling so he could carry the jar on his back. Even in the simplest maze, it was wise to keep both hands free.

By the time the Amnesian Hero finished, Tessali was sitting atop the stone wall, staring in gape-mouthed astonishment at whatever lay on the other side.

"What say you, elf?" The Amnesian Hero grinned at Jayk, who had recovered the spool of golden thread and was busy untangling the slack. "Will we be going back to a nice warm cell in your Gatehouse?"

Tessali's head slowly turned toward them. "Sigil's gone! There's nothing there, not even the ground!"

"Then we would be wise to stay within the boundaries of the maze, would we not?" The Amnesian Hero slipped the amphora sling over his shoulder. "If you can't see anything, come down from there and stop wasting time."

The elf made no move to obey. "What have you done?" His eyes were wild with fear. "Your madness has doomed us all!"

"By the One Death, be quiet or I silence you myself!" Jayk's threat was an idle one, for her fangs had finally folded into the top of her mouth. "Zoombee will get us out."

"Get us out?" Tessali screeched. "These are the Lady's mazes! Nobody can get us out!"

"Zoombee can." Jayk placed the spool in the hands of the Amnesian Hero. Save for a single strand leading into a dark corner, the golden thread was neatly coiled about its barrel. "Zoombee has a plan."

Ignoring Tessali, the Amnesian Hero turned his full attention to Jayk. "You anchored the other end outside?" He had little doubt that she had, but he thought it wise to be certain. "It is tied securely?"

"But of course, Zoombee." Jayk's reply was light-hearted and merry, as though being lost in the Lady's mazes was little more than an afternoon diversion. "I run it down the seam between the wall and the hut, where nobody sees it, yes? Then I tie it twice around a stone in the bottom."

"You did well. We should be back in Sigil in no time." The Thrasson waved Tessali down from the wall. "Come along. We won't hurt you, and you can tell me about the Lady of Pain. I'd like to know more about her before I present Poseidon's gift again."

Tessali's wild-eyed fear gave way to gape-mouthed incredulity. "You're barmy as a dretch in Cania." He climbed down from the wall, shaking his head slowly. "And I must be an addle-cove for keeping your company."

Rewinding as he walked, the Amnesian Hero followed the thread into the dim corner. As he and his companions moved, the darkness seemed to thin ahead and swallow everything behind. It took only a few steps to reach the corner and discover that the wall no longer abutted the hut. Instead, a long narrow passage had opened between the two. The golden thread ran straight down this corridor and disappeared into the silent gloom ahead.

"This can't be right," Tessali whispered. "There should be a busy street here."

"There should be a wall." Jayk was standing beside the hut, looking down a gloomy side passage that ran along what had once been the front of the building. Now it was simply a long wall of unmortared stone, similar to the one down which the golden thread ran. She kneeled and began scraping at a stone with her fingers. "This is where I tied the thread."

"That is the trick of mazes," the Amnesian Hero said. "You cannot trust what you remember. You must place your faith in the thread, no matter how strange its course may seem."

Tessali shook his head emphatically. "I climbed over only one wall before I found you, and it was no thicker than my foot is long. We must be going in the wrong direction."

"By that thinking, when you climbed the wall, you would have seen the street on the other side." The Amnesian Hero continued to rewind the thread. "Did you?"

"I saw nothing but . . . nothing."

"Then trust to the thread. This place makes no sense, and only the thread can lead us back to the world we know."

With that advice, the Amnesian Hero started down the passage, his frozen foot clumping bluntly on the rock-hard ground. He had forgotten all about it during his audience with the Lady of Pain, but now he recalled that he needed to find a healer before it thawed. He redoubled his pace, wrapping the thread around the spool so furiously that his wrist began to tire. They passed several more side passages before following the thread down one, then began a zigzagging course through the murky corridors. The Thrasson did not ask Jayk how long her spell would last; even if he had truly wanted to know, the knowledge was no use to him. Aside from walking faster, he could do little to speed their escape.

Hoping to keep his thoughts off his foot, the Thrasson waved Tessali to his side. "You may tell me about the Lady of Pain."

"What do you want to know?"

The elf had no trouble keeping pace with the Amnesian Hero. Even at his best, the Thrasson could not rewind the spool faster than his companions could walk. If his foot started to thaw, he would have to give up rewinding the thread and simply follow it to the exit, but he was loath to abandon one of the few possessions linking him to his past.

"I need to know everything about the Lady," said the Amnesian Hero. "Who is she?"

Tessali scowled. "What kind of question is that?"

"An honest one, but of course," said Jayk. "There are so many things Zoombee does not know. He has lost his memory."

Tessali arched one of his peaked eyebrows. "Truly? That *is* interesting." He rubbed his chin, then looked back to the Thrasson. "With a little work, we can discover what you're trying to forget."

"I am not trying to forget anything."

Tessali looked doubtful. "How would you know that without knowing what you've forgotten? In these cases, by far the most are caused by a simple lack of mental strength—"

"My mind is as strong as my arm." The Amnesian Hero glared down at the elf. "Just tell me how I can get the Lady of Pain to accept Poseidon's gift. I'll be fine."

Tessali rolled his eyes. "You see, this is exactly what I'm talking about. If you'll just let me help you, you won't need to ask such addle-headed questions. You'll *know* why that can't be done."

The Amnesian Hero almost stopped to face the elf, then thought of his frozen foot and followed the thread around a dark corner. The hard-packed ground gave way to cobblestones, while the stones in the corridor walls were now held in place by generous amounts of mortar. The Thrasson might have been tempted to accept Tessali's offer of help, had he not suspected the elf would insist on a stay in the Gatehouse after they escaped the mazes.

"Just tell me about the Lady of Pain," commanded the Amnesian Hero. "Poseidon has promised to restore my memories after I deliver this amphora to her."

"He'll never be forced to keep that promise, which you would know, were it not for your unfortunate—and most likely curable—condition."

Tessali, the Amnesian Hero realized, was insidiously clever. Even as he dodged the questions about the Lady of Pain, the elf was deftly trying to bait the Thrasson into accepting help.

"I should warn you, Tessali, that I regard the dodging of my questions the same as making trouble." Without slowing his pace, the Amnesian Hero cast a meaningful glance in Jayk's direction. "I suggest you start answering."

"Let me have him now, Zoombee." As she spoke, Jayk slipped up close behind Tessali and pushed her head over his shoulder. "Already, he has dodged many questions, yes?"

"No!" Tessali skipped forward, then gazed over his shoulder at the Amnesian Hero. "I was only suggesting how I might help you remember for yourself."

The Amnesian Hero motioned Jayk back to her place, then spoke to the elf. "For now, Tessali, I prefer that you tell me what I wish to know."

"Why don't you ask me, Zoombee?" Jayk's tone was hurt. "Any Dustman knows more about the Lady than this dagger-eared leatherhead."

The Amnesian Hero noticed a certain narrowing of the tiefling's pupils. Unless he did something to assuage her jealousy, the elf would soon fall to her venom.

"Asking Tessali doesn't mean I trust him, Jayk." The Thrasson felt a salty bead roll down his brow, then noticed that Tessali was also perspiring heavily. Only Jayk did not appear to be sweating, though her skin was so shadowy that it was difficult to be certain. "I have my reasons for wanting to hear what he says."

"Yes?"

The truth was that the Amnesian Hero thought Tessali's account more likely to be coherent and reliable, but he did not dare say that to Jayk. The Thrasson looked forward to the elf, who was walking half-backward, at once keeping a sharp watch on the tiefling and trying not to stumble over the passage's uneven floor.

"I want to see if Tessali can be trusted." The Thrasson was thinking fast. "I'm counting on you to tell me if he leaves anything out, or says anything untrue."

"That would be difficult to do." Tessali appeared even more anxious than the Amnesian Hero to move the conversation forward. "The Lady of Pain is an enigma even to the citizens of her city."

"That is not what Zoombee asked," warned Jayk.

An expression of relief flashed across Tessali's face. "Right you are." Now that he was confident the tiefling was not going to jump him from behind, he began to watch where he was walking. "To start with, nobody knows who the Lady of Pain is, but I can tell you she doesn't like the gods. They're always trying to break into the city, and . . ."

Much of what Tessali says is mistaken, of course. Sigil's denizens understand me only slightly less than they comprehend the true nature of the multiverse, and that is little enough. Still, with only occasional prompting from Jayk, the elf tells what he knows, which I do not intend to share for fear of seeming deliberately misleading–whether or not I am–and soon the Thrasson understands me no better than those who abide in my crowded warrens.

All the while, they continue to walk, following that golden thread–a clever idea, that–deeper into the mazes. They pass a hundred dark passages, any one of which would lead them to the same place they are going, and round a hundred corners. Sometimes, they make a dozen turns in the same direction. They cannot understand how they fail to cross their own path, but never does that golden thread intersect itself, and always the confident Thrasson tells them they cannot trust their own senses–in that much, at least, he understands me better than any who call my twisting streets home.

Even now, I could peel the skin from his bones, make him repent for that beautiful prayer he spoke. Even now, I could deny the tiefling her One Death, bestow upon her an endless, aching immortality as miserable as my own. Even now, I could turn Tessali's gaze inward, show him the same darkness in his heart that he seeks so diligently in those of others. Even now, I could free Poseidon's net, pull back the hood of that black-cloaked helmsman and look into the eyes of the dark one who bought my bride's dark heart.

The time will come when I must. But now the walls have turned to iron around the Thrasson and his companions. The floors have changed to brick, the air has grown hot as forge smoke, and an orange glow has lit the dimness. Their throats have been filled with scorching ash, and each rasping breath has begun to scratch like crushed glass.

Off the main corridor opened a dozen dark passages, every one fresh with a damp, cool breeze, and still the thread did not turn. It ran straight down the lane between two scorching walls of orange-glowing iron. The Amnesian Hero stumbled forward at a trot, choking on each breath of blistering air and twining the golden thread around his own arm because that was the only way to take up line as fast as they were moving. The soft, squashing sound that came with every other step left no doubt that his foot was beginning to thaw, and he found himself wondering if he would be thirsty in the Paraelemental Plane of Ooze. He would have gladly given all the gold in his purse for that jug of wine he had smashed over the barbazu's head.

A tremendous rumble shook the corridor, crashing down from above with such force that the Amnesian Hero found himself lying facedown on the scorching bricks before he realized he had fallen. He pushed himself to his knees, then raised his eyes toward the heavens and saw a sheet of icy, pearl-colored marbles pouring out of the darkness. The balls struck with all the suddenness of an Abudrian Dragon's wing, slamming him back to the ground and drawing a pair of astonished outcries from his two companions.

The Thrasson bent an arm around to feel for the amphora. When he found it in one piece, he fought through the pounding hail and rose to his feet. The ice was falling at a steep angle, hammering at the walls ahead, turning to steam the instant it touched the hot iron and filling the air with a deafening, hissing roar. Even the pellets that struck the floor bounced once and melted before they came down again. A rusty, mordant-smelling fog was creeping upward, growing steadily redder and thicker.

The Amnesian Hero looked down to inspect his frozen foot. Already, the orange fog was so thick he could not see his own ankle, but he did notice tendrils of silver steam rising from the vicinity of his toes.

"We must keep moving!" He started forward again, calling over his shoulder as he ran. "Are you still with me, Jayk?"

"But of course, Zoombee! Just keep shouting, so I do not lose you."

"Tessali?"

A slender hand grasped the Thrasson's shoulder.

"Stop!" Tessali jerked the Amnesian Hero to a halt. "We must . . . turn back!"

The Thrasson glanced over his shoulder and saw that the storm was much less severe behind them. "No."

He started forward again, only to feel the elf dragging on the amphora sling.

"This is madness!" Tessali jerked the Thrasson around. They could barely see each other through the battering white curtain. "You have . . . no idea where we're going. We've been walking for hours!"

"So it would seem, but time means nothing in a maze." The Thrasson had to yell to make himself heard over the roar of the storm. "We must trust to the thread."

"Trust to the thread!" Tessali pointed at the massive tangle covering the Thrasson's left arm. "You have two leagues there. How much more thread could your spool hold?"

"As much as we need," the Amnesian Hero replied. "It has never run out."

Tessali shook his head. "That can't be. Don't you see? It's an illusion! One of the Lady's torments."

"Believe what you will. I have had this thread since long before I entered Sigil."

"You think you have, but it's a delusion." Although he too was yelling, Tessali's tone was patronizing and overly patient. "Please try to understand."

Jayk jerked the elf's hand away from the Thrasson. "No, you understand! You are in the land of barmies now, so you do what we say, not us as you say. Yes?"

To Tessali's credit, he managed to avoid flinching when he met the tiefling's diamond-eyed gaze. "I'm trying to help us all."

"You may turn back if you wish." As he spoke, the Amnesian Hero glanced at his feet. The orange fog was already waist-deep, but he still saw thick plumes of silver steam rising from his toes. "But trouble us no more. I haven't time to discuss the matter."

"Your foot, Zoombee?" Jayk shouldered past the elf, her shoulders hunched against the barrage of hailstones. "I can refreeze it."

The Amnesian Hero shook his head. "In this heat, I fear it would not be worth the trouble."

Tessali glanced at the silver steam rising from the Thrasson's toes. "I've noticed your limp. What's wrong?"

"I stepped in something called an ooze portal, and now my leg is turning to mud."

The elf furrowed his brow. "But if you escaped, you should be recovering—"

"Zoombee's foot was caught a very long time," Jayk said. "It had already changed when I froze the puddle."

"Why didn't you tell me?" Tessali dropped to all fours and disappeared into the orange fog, then began tugging at the Amnesian Hero's leg.

The Thrasson jerked his foot away. "What are you doing?"

Tessali raised his head. "I *am* a healer."

"You are a tangler of minds!" Jayk corrected. She looked to the Amnesian Hero. "Don't trust him, Zoombee. He'll steal your thoughts."

"If I were going to do that, Jayk, wouldn't I want to work on the other end?" Tessali's face betrayed the pain of exposing the flat of his back to the hail, but he made no move to stand and escape the barrage. He looked back at the Amnesian Hero. "I'm only trying to stop the ooze. That way, we can make our decision without worrying about your foot."

"You cannot convince me to turn back, if that is the price of your help." The Amnesian Hero moved to step around the elf. "I would rather turn to mud than lose my way in these mazes."

Tessali raised a hand to stop the Thrasson. "It is not the way of the Bleak Cabal to place conditions on its help. We'll trust to the thread. Just let me do what I can."

The Amnesian Hero nodded, more than a little relieved by the elf's generosity. He looked around for someplace to escape the storm. Finding none, he retreated down the corridor to where the hail was not so heavy, unwinding the golden thread as he went. He braced a hand on Jayk's shoulder, then Tessali squatted down and lifted the Thrasson's foot out of the orange fog. A thin veil of steam was rising from the thawing flesh—but not thickly enough to hide its slimy, claylike texture.

Tessali pulled his dagger from its sheath, drawing a suspicious glare from Jayk.

"I warn you, mindtangler, if you try any of your tricks—"

"You'll see that I regret it, I know." Tessali did not even look up as he spoke. "Jayk, I'm well aware that the Amnesian Hero is all that stands between you and my death. The last thing I'm going to do is cause him harm."

With that, Tessali began to probe the thawing flesh. To the relief of the Amnesian Hero, nowhere did the dagger tip sink more than a coin's thickness into the pearly ooze that covered his foot.

Tessali nodded in approval. "Good. It's thawing from the outside. There's no chance of the ooze working its way into your bones." He cleaned his dagger blade on the ground, then returned the weapon to its sheath. "I can't restore your foot to normal—that would require a better healer than I—but I can keep the ooze from consuming the rest of your body."

The Amnesian Hero narrowed his eyes. "You do not mean to cut it off. . . ."

Tessali smiled and shook his head. "No, nothing like that." He felt around on the ground for a moment, then came up with the jagged corner of a broken brick. "This should do nicely."

"To do what?" Jayk demanded, ever suspicious.

"Turn his foot to stone—or brick, in this case," Tessali explained. "When a patient shows an unusual talent for escaping, we are occasionally forced to use such a spell to keep him restrained."

The Thrasson scowled. "I am not fond of being restrained."

"You won't be," Tessali assured him. "You, I'm not going to mortar to the floor."

"I still dislike this idea," the Amnesian Hero said. "Can't you do something else? If we run into trouble, a brick foot will slow me down."

"Not as much as turning into a puddle of ooze," Tessali countered. "I'm sorry, but this is all I can do. Besides, you're already lame. The only difference you'll notice is that your foot seems heavier. And I'll change it back the instant we find someone to restore it."

The Amnesian Hero stared at his thawing flesh for several moments, then finally nodded. The elf pressed the stone into the slimy flesh, but jerked his hands away when a deep, rumbling bellow rolled over the passage.

The roar was not nearly so loud or sudden as the thunderclap that had preceded the hailstorm. Rather, it built more gradually, seeming to echo out of all the side corridors at once.

Jayk's big eyes darted from one side passage to another, then settled on Tessali. "You make this sound!"

Only the Amnesian Hero's firm grasp kept her from lunging at the elf. "Leave him alone. Tessali has nothing to do with it."

The bellow sounded again, a little louder than before, then died away. Jayk craned her neck to look back down the passage.

"Zoombee, if Tessali is not causing the sound, who is?"

"The monster of the labyrinth, of course." Continuing to hold his foot above the fog, the Amnesian Hero gestured for Tessali to continue. "I was starting to worry there wasn't one."

Tessali pushed the brick shard into the Thrasson's soft foot. "I'd think it wiser to worry because there *is* one."

"Despite what you claimed earlier, Tessali, you have not played many mazes, have you?" The Amnesian Hero did not wait for the elf to respond. "If there is a monster, he must be fed. And since he must be fed, there must be some way to put food into the maze. Is all this not true?"

"Of course."

The Amnesian Hero raised his left hand, which was all but hidden beneath the unruly tangle of golden filament. "I think the thread is leading us to that place now."

Tessali frowned, puzzled, then suddenly paled. "You mean *we* are the food!"

The Thrasson nodded and drew his sword. "I suggest you hurry, Tessali. In my experience, the monster seldom strays far from the food gate."

SIGN OF ONE

Again, the bellow rumbled through the labyrinth's thousand passages, overwhelming even the roar of the wall-pounding hail. As before, the sound came from all directions at once, left and right and front and back; the dark sky crackled with its fury, and the brick-paved ground trembled at its might. The Amnesian Hero bent forward, as though that would help his gaze pierce the fog's turbid density. He saw nothing but cascades of white hail vaporizing against orange-glowing iron.

"That one sounded louder," whispered Tessali. To prevent the group from becoming separated in the thick fog, both he and the tiefling were holding onto the Thrasson's amphora sling. "It's getting closer."

"Good." The scalding air had reduced the Amnesian Hero's voice to a croak; each time they rounded a corner, the iron walls seemed to glow more brightly with their orange heat. "We must be nearing the exit."

The Amnesian Hero continued to clump ahead, half-lifting,

half-dragging his lame foot. Despite Tessali's assurances, the brick was proving more awkward to walk upon than had the frozen ooze. The Thrasson could never quite tell when the dead thing was resting on the ground, and, after hoisting its heavy bulk so many countless times, his entire leg was burning with fatigue. When they finally met the monster, he would need to kill it quickly; if the creature tried to carry off one of his companions, the Thrasson would be helpless to give chase.

The Amnesian Hero stopped and looked over his shoulder. "Perhaps I should go on alone to hunt the beast down and kill it. I'll leave a loop of thread so we can find each other again."

"No!" Tessali and Jayk spoke at the same time.

"At last we agree on something, Jayk." The scorching heat had reduced Tessali's voice to a raw rasp. "We all stand a better chance if we stay together."

"I will not part from you, Zoombee. Not for a minute."

"As you wish. But stay close. If the monster takes one of you, I won't be able to catch it." The Amnesian Hero scowled in Tessali's direction, then added, "This brick foot is somewhat less than nimble."

"I can cut it off any time you like," replied Tessali.

Refusing to dignify the elf's offer with a response, the Amnesian Hero clumped into the hail. As he moved, he slowly twirled his left wrist ahead of him, winding the thread onto his arm while leaving his other hand free for his sword. Already, the spool had grown so thick that he could not have scratched his ear. If they did not come upon the exit in the next league, his arm would become too bulky to move.

They followed the thread down a series of short, dogleg turns, then found themselves in a region of broad, black-paved passages. The iron walls seemed to loom higher than ever, and the hail fell harder. Through the orange-glowing fog, the Amnesian Hero occasionally saw a dark, windowlike square set high on a wall's iron face, but the shapes were always too distant to investigate more carefully. Every now and then, what might have been a tongue of flame licked out of one of these portals. The Thrasson tried to stay in the middle of the avenue, preferring to let the black forms remain a mystery—if that was possible.

They advanced perhaps a thousand paces into this strange region before the Amnesian Hero felt a soft tug on his left arm. So gentle was the pull that he thought he had imagined it, then it happened again.

The Thrasson said nothing and continued forward, trying to convince himself that the sensation was a result of his own weariness. He had, after all, been twirling his arm for untold hours, gathering an ever-increasing burden. Sooner or later, the repetition was bound to take its toll. The tug came again. It was difficult to be certain in the hail and the fog, but this time it seemed to him the thread had bobbed.

The Amnesian Hero felt his heart drop into his stomach. He knew at once the monster had found their thread, but he did not say anything to his companions. From the start, Tessali had despaired of finding a way out of the mazes, and even Jayk had fallen ominously silent over the last several hours. If he told them what had happened before he thought of a way to counter the misfortune, they would lose heart and surrender to despondency.

"Zoombee, what is happening to the thread?"

"What do you mean?" The Thrasson silently cursed Jayk's watchfulness.

"I see it, too!" Tessali added. "There. It's bobbing."

The Amnesian Hero clumped forward, trying to think fast. "The spool is getting difficult to wind." He raised his hand to display the massive tangle, then cringed as the thread snapped taut and gave a sharp twang. "And, every now and then, a hailstone bounces off the line."

"Zoombee, I don't like it when you lie to me," warned Jayk. "Something pulls on the thread, yes?"

Sensing it would be useless to try hiding the truth, the Amnesian Hero sighed and stopped walking. "Yes, but don't despair. We can still find the exit."

"How?" Jayk demanded.

"I, uh . . . we know the general direction—"

"We can worry about that later." Tessali, sounding surprisingly resilient in the face of their disaster, spoke with an air of authority. "If something's following that thread, I'm guessing it's the monster. Cut yourself loose, and we'll flee."

"Cut the golden thread? Never!" The Amnesian Hero was appalled at the elf's cowardice. "We'll set an ambush and deal with this monster properly. I will be the bait, of course. The beast will follow the thread straight into my arms."

"And then we attack it from behind!" concluded Jayk.

"If that should prove necessary." The Thrasson's throat, already tender from breathing the hot air, ached from so much talking. "After slaying the Hydra of Thrassos, I think I can kill a single labyrinth monster."

The Amnesian Hero clumped over to a wall and began to retreat, allowing the golden line to spiral off his arm as he moved. Jayk and Tessali walked at his sides, still holding onto the amphora sling and peering over their shoulders, as though they actually expected to see the monster coming. The fog remained thick as a blanket, and the hail continued to hiss and roar as it battered the labyrinth. As they passed beneath one of the windowlike shapes high on the wall, a tongue of yellow flame shot out to crackle above them, laving their heads with blistering heat and filling the air with an acrid, ashy smell.

They moved a little away from the wall. The thread continued to jerk at regular intervals, and again the monster's bellow rumbled through the labyrinth. The roar sounded even louder than before, but no one commented on it. Tessali's expression remained one of grim fear; Jayk's shadowy face seemed more angry than frightened. The Thrasson imagined that she was less afraid of dying than of remaining trapped in the mazes and never reaping her vengeance on Komosahl Trevant.

After a time, they reached the mouth of a side corridor. Although it looked to be as broad as the one in which they had been traveling, the Amnesian Hero thought it would do for their ambush. He sent his companions down the passage, having them count out each step until they could no longer see each other. It required only five paces before their figures were completely obscured by hail and fog.

"Stop!" He had to yell to make himself heard above the thundering hailstones, further abusing his scorched throat. "Wait there until I call. Do you understand?"

The reply came in the form of a barely discernible croak that the Amnesian Hero took to mean yes. He retreated five steps into the intersection and stopped to await his foe. The hail beat a brisk, broken cadence against what remained of his armor, but he doubted the monster would hear it over the roar of the storm. He pushed his sword into its scabbard and caught a few hailstones in his palm, then slipped them into his mouth to quench his thirst. The icy balls tasted like fish, but he let them melt and forced himself to swallow the foul water. If the fight happened to last more than a few moments, he did not want his breathing troubled by a dry throat.

The thread continued to tug at his left arm. The monster was winding the line up, suggesting it was a creature of foresight. Would the brute pause at the corner to check for an ambush? The Amnesian Hero caught another handful of hail and slipped it into his mouth, then drew his sword again. If he felt a sudden change in the tugging of the line, he would rush—or, rather, hobble—forward to attack. The Thrasson reminded himself to be careful; now that his torso armor had been crushed, his most vulnerable area would be open to a counterstrike. His first priority would be to destroy whatever weapon his foe would be carrying. The next attack would be a crippling blow to a leg, both to put the monster on an even footing with himself and to prevent it from carrying off one of his companions. The third strike would be the killing one.

The Amnesian Hero's planning came to an abrupt end as a tall, manlike silhouette appeared in the fog. Cowering against the battering hail, the figure looked distinctly unmonsterlike. It had a bulky head with a rather squarish crown, a slender hunch-shouldered build, and a pair of skinny, goatlike legs. The creature kept its gaze fixed firmly on the ground as it twined the golden thread around the shaft of a long lance, apparently oblivious to the possibility of ambush.

A monster of ploys and deception, the Amnesian Hero decided;

they were the most dangerous kind. He leapt forward, landing brick-foot forward to present his armored flank to the beast, then struck the lance off midway down the shaft. The creature croaked out a hoarse cry of astonishment and suddenly rose into the air, safely lifting its knobby legs over the Thrasson's slashing sword.

A pair of stone-hard hooves slammed one after the other into the Amnesian Hero's shoulder pauldron, driving him back before he could reverse his blade for an upstroke. Unable to bring his brick foot around quickly enough to catch his balance, the Thrasson stumbled and fell on the scorching bricks.

He found himself looking at the underside of what appeared to be a rearing goat. "A bariaur?" he gasped.

The "monster" dropped its forehooves to the bricks, and the Thrasson saw that it was, indeed, a bariaur–and an ancient one at that. Chipped and colorless as they were, the fellow's horns had two full curls. His eyes were rheumy, and a gray, mossy beard covered everything from his cheeks to his chest. His woolly pelt had grown into such a bushy mat of snarls and tangles that the shabby saddlebags laid across his back were barely visible.

The Amnesian Hero brought his sword into a guarding position, but made no move to rise off the hot bricks. "I beg your forgiveness. In this fog, I mistook you for the monster of the labyrinth."

The bariaur's gaze went to the golden spool wound around the Thrasson's arm, then he sighed in disappointment. "It can't be." His voice was brittle with age. "I won't allow it."

"I apologize for my mistake." The Thrasson gathered himself up, moving slowly to avoid alarming the old bariaur. "But you have heard the roars? When I felt the tugging on my line–"

"No! Be strong, you fool!"

The Amnesian Hero froze in a half-crouch. "Please. I mean you no harm–"

"No harm!" The words were something between a snort and a laugh. "He must go away!"

The bariaur lifted the butt of his broken lance. The Amnesian Hero raised his guard and started to pivot away, but there was no need. The old fellow closed his baggy eyelids and brought the shaft down between his horns, striking himself soundly on his own pate.

"He must go away!"

Confused, the Amnesian Hero thought it best to do nothing. The bariaur remained motionless a moment, then opened his rheumy eyes.

"Still there." The bariaur closed his eyes and hit himself.

"What are you doing?"

The bariaur struck another blow against his brow, this time without opening his eyes.

"Stop! You'll hurt yourself."

The bariaur brought the shaft down once for each word, at the same time muttering, "He must go away. Must go away."

Realizing that speaking would only make matters worse, the Amnesian Hero shoved his sword into its scabbard and clumped forward to restrain the mad bariaur. After suffering an inadvertent blow as the club hit him on a backstroke, the Thrasson caught hold of the shaft and wrenched it from the old fellow's grasp.

"I'll hold this for you." The last thing the Amnesian Hero wanted was for the bariaur to knock himself senseless—at least until the old fellow led the way to where he had found his end of the golden thread. "Beating yourself will not make me vanish."

The bariaur slapped his hands over his ears and, without opening his eyes, spun toward the side corridor, where Jayk and Tessali were just emerging from the fog. Both had their daggers in hand.

"Don't harm him!" the Amnesian Hero warned.

The pair stopped two paces short of the bariaur, who continued to cover his ears and keep his eyes closed.

"What are you doing here?" asked the Thrasson. "I didn't call for you."

"We hear yelling." Jayk flicked a hand skyward. "With all this noise, we think it is you, yes?"

"It wasn't me; it was our monster." The Amnesian Hero gestured at the bariaur. "I think he's what you call barmy. The old fellow keeps beating himself and saying that I must go away."

Tessali raised an eyebrow, then turned his gaze upon the cowering bariaur. After a moment, the elf pursed his lips and nodded grimly.

The Thrasson retrieved the severed lance and displayed the golden thread wrapped around its shaft. "If you convince him to show us where he started collecting this, we can find the exit."

The elf held his finger to his lips, then sheathed his dagger. The three companions waited silently in the battering hail. At last the bariaur took his hands from his ears and looked up. When he saw Tessali and Jayk standing before him, the old fellow wailed in despair and dropped to his foreknees.

"Silverwind, you old fool!" he cried.

Silverwind began to slap himself between the horns again. The Amnesian Hero moved to restrain him, but Tessali motioned the Thrasson back.

"You were almost out, and now you've lost control again," Silverwind complained.

He ran his rheumy gaze over the unexpected company, then he pitched forward into the fog. There was a sharp crack, then the bariaur's head rose briefly into view and disappeared again. Another crack followed, then another, and the Thrasson realized Silverwind was butting his horns against the ground. So powerful were the blows that pieces of brick began to fly whenever the old fellow raised his head. Still, Tessali refused to let the Amnesian Hero intervene. Finally, after the flying brick shards had given way to powder, the old fellow stopped. He left his head beneath the fog and, despite the smell of singed fur beginning to fill the air around his forequarters, made no move to return to his feet.

Tessali squatted on his haunches and waited patiently. When Silverwind finally looked up, the elf touched his fingertips to his own chest. "I am Tessali." He gestured at Jayk, then the Thrasson. "My friends—"

"Do not presume!" hissed Jayk. "I am no friend of yours."

The elf accepted the interruption without changing expressions, then continued, "My . . . companions are Jayk the Snake, and the Amnesian Hero." He extended a hand to the bariaur. "Why don't you stand? Your fur is beginning to scorch."

Silverwind glanced toward his knees, then allowed the elf to help him up.

"You were saying that we must go away," Tessali said. "Why is that?"

"Because I don't want you here." Silverwind's reply was meek. "You're in my way."

"In the way of what?" Tessali asked.

Silverwind turned half away, regarding the elf out of the corner of his eye. "They're not here." He closed his baggy eyelids. "Be strong, Silverwind."

"You can keep your eyes closed as long as you like, Silverwind. We'll still be here when you open them."

Silverwind covered his ears again.

Realizing that this might take some time, the Thrasson began to twine the thread off his arm onto the head of the bariaur's spear. If he wanted to avoid cutting it, working the golden strand onto its proper spool was going to be a major task.

After a moment, Tessali reached up and gently pulled one of the bariaur's hands down. Silverwind gasped and recoiled from the touch, then stared at Tessali as though the elf were a pit fiend.

"You see?" said Tessali. "We're still here. You can't make us go away."

With astonishing quickness for a bariaur his age, Silverwind dropped his head and butted Tessali in the chest. The blow drove the elf straight to the ground, where he landed with a loud groan. The Amnesian Hero rushed to restrain the bariaur, but, with his brick foot, he was not nearly so quick as Jayk. Before the Thrasson had taken his second step, the tiefling was at Silverwind's side, pushing her dagger up toward the bariaur's throat.

"Jayk, no!"

The tiefling stopped, her arm half-extended above her head and the tip of her knife pressing against the ropy outline of the bariaur's jugular. Her fangs were folded down and her pupils were shaped like diamonds. Silverwind stood motionless as a statue, his astonished gaze fixed upon the top of her head.

"But he attacked us, Zoombee!" Jayk complained.

The Amnesian Hero knew better than to appeal to her compassion. He raised the lance head, displaying the spool of thread the bariaur had gathered.

"We don't know where Silverwind started this. If you advance him to the next stage, how will we find the exit? How will you avenge yourself on Trevant?"

Jayk rolled her dark eyes. "You don't need to sweet talk me, Zoombee. If you say don't cut him, I don't cut him."

"Then be good enough to step back." Tessali rose, rubbing his chest but otherwise looking little worse for wear. "I'm sure Silverwind realizes by now that he won't be rid of us by attacking."

Jayk ignored Tessali and did not step away until the Amnesian Hero nodded. Once the knife was pulled away from Silverwind's throat, the bariaur closed his eyes and shook his head sadly.

"You were so close. So close."

"So close to what?" asked Tessali. "Tell me, Silverwind."

The bariaur opened his eyes and glared at the elf. He looked past Tessali at Jayk, then he turned to stare at the Amnesian Hero. "Why did you have to imagine them, old fool? You were so near escape; you had the golden thread. You would have made the exit soon."

"Wonderful," Jayk growled. "A Signer."

"Signer?" the Amnesian Hero echoed.

"Sign of One." Tessali rubbed his chin, continuing to focus on Silverwind. "They consider themselves to be the center of the multiverse and claim to create everything in it through the power of their minds. Silverwind's isolation seems to have convinced him that he is the only *real* being in the maze—or even in the entire multiverse."

Silverwind snatched the head of his severed lance from the hands of the Amnesian Hero, then turned to walk away. Tessali shook his head sharply, then pointed at the bariaur's arm and cupped his hand as though grasping something. The Thrasson nodded and grabbed the old fellow's shoulders.

"Silverwind, you should know better," said Tessali. "You cannot walk away from the creations of your own mind, anymore than you can walk away from this hailstorm you imagined. If you want to be rid of us, you must treat with us first."

The bariaur's shoulders sagged. "I suppose I must." He turned to face them. "Very well. Tell me your names again."

The elf smiled. "You will be glad of your decision. Call me Tessali."

A fierce bellow rumbled through the labyrinth, so deep and loud that it shook the bricks under the Thrasson's feet. The orange fog swirled around the company's hips, as though stirred by a wind they could not feel, and, for an instant, it seemed that even the hailstones paused in their battering.

"I thought *he* was the monster," Jayk complained.

"I–I am." Silverwind's hands were shaking, his bushy brow raised in fear. "What you hear is my dark self."

"Then tell it to be–"

Jayk's command came to a sudden halt as a massive gray paw emerged from the hailstorm to cover her face. The Thrasson glimpsed the shaggy silhouette of a huge, bearlike figure in the fog behind the tiefling, then the creature pulled her away and disappeared into the storm.

"Jayk!"

The Amnesian Hero grabbed Silverwind's broken lance and hurled it after the vanished beast, then reached for his sword and clumped after the monster as fast as he could. Tessali's figure dashed past, and there was a horrid scream. The elf's gray silhouette rose high in the hazy air and came down, striking the ground with a muffled crunch. Only a step and a half later did the Thrasson glimpse the monster again.

The beast was much larger than a bear, with a high, pointy head, a flat face, and a circular maw lined all around by stubby, sharp-peaked teeth. Long mats of ice-gray fur dangled from its entire body, lending it an indistinct shape that made it even more difficult to distinguish from the driving hail. Jayk's legs, kicking wildly, protruded from a particularly large snarl of fur. That was all the Thrasson saw of her before the creature vanished into the hailstorm.

The Amnesian Hero heard Tessali groaning on the ground and barely managed to lift his brick foot in time to step over the fallen elf. The Thrasson noticed that the golden thread was not winding off his arm, but trailing down toward the ground; Silverwind's lance had not lodged in the monster. He had no way to follow the creature, and, judging by the speed with which it had disappeared, less than no chance of overtaking it.

A clatter of hooves sounded at the Amnesian Hero's side, then Silverwind streaked past at a full gallop. The old bariaur lowered his head and disappeared into the storm.

In the next instant, there was a dull thud, a deafening bellow, and a muffled crash. Silverwind cried out, then Jayk shrieked in anger. The Amnesian Hero clumped another step forward and saw the back side of the monster three paces ahead, rising out of the ground fog as though it were struggling to its hands and knees. The Thrasson saw no sign of either bariaur or tiefling until the beast roared and raised its arm.

Jayk was clinging to its wrist, her face buried deep in its tangled fur. The monster bellowed sharply, then snapped its hand toward the wall. When the hairy arm reached the end of its arc, the tiefling seemed to hang on the creature's wrist for just an instant before coming loose and slamming into the hot iron wall.

The Amnesian Hero reached the monster and brought his sword down on the hairy arm that had just flung off Jayk. So tough was the beast's flesh that even that star-forged blade of his barely sliced its sinews; had the blow not landed exactly in the joint, the limb would have been saved. As it was, the Thrasson's strike, well-placed as always, cleaved off the great arm at the shoulder.

No geysers of red blood sprayed from the wound. The creature did not bellow in anguish or collapse in shock. Instead, a substance like black sap oozed from the wound, and the monster twisted around to look at its attacker. The Thrasson raised his sword and saw a gray blur arcing at him out of the fog. He pivoted into the blow, shielding himself behind his shoulder.

The strike landed full on his pauldron, slamming the Amnesian Hero into the creature's hip with such force that, had he not taken the blow on god-forged bronze, he would surely have perished. The Thrasson merely groaned, then, finding himself pinned against the monster, swung at its exposed midsection.

Again, his star-forged blade bit deep, but not deep enough to slice the great creature in half. The beast slammed a boulder-sized fist into the Thrasson's shoulder pauldron, with no more effect than before.

The Amnesian Hero tried to clump forward to attack again, only to discover himself stuck to the monster's side. He attempted to jerk his sword back and found it caught fast in the beast's black-oozing belly wound.

The creature opened its hand, extending a long yellow talon at the end of each finger. Had the Amnesian Hero not stared into the eyes of death a dozen times before—and sometimes more closely than this—he might have panicked or despaired. But he well knew that salvation often comes at that last instant, when the vicious attacker, sensing victory, grows reckless and moves in for the kill too quickly.

As the monster reached for him, the Thrasson switched his grip and shoved the hilt of his sword forward. The blade pivoted on the edge of the wound, driving the tip deep into the creature's belly.

The Amnesian Hero did not hear the monster's bellow in his ears; he felt it in his shuddering sword. He grasped the hilt with all his strength, then hunched down between his shoulder pauldrons and tried not to scream as the beast's claws closed around his abdomen.

With a sound like tearing sailcloth, the monster ripped the Thrasson away from its hip. The Amnesian Hero felt his sword slipping from his grasp and redoubled his efforts to keep hold of the hilt. For a moment, he seemed stuck, then, with a long, sticky slurp, the blade came free.

The Amnesian Hero found himself sailing backward through the hail and realized that whether he hit the wall or the ground, the amphora would break his fall. He flung his feet up over his head, turning a half-somersault in the air, then smashed face first into the hot iron wall. The searing pain came an instant before the aching agony, and both came before he fell headfirst to the ground.

As he landed in a crumpled heap, the Thrasson managed to twist onto his side and keep his full weight from landing on the amphora. Nevertheless, he heard the tiny rasp of the cracked neck's two halves grating against each other. He could not tell whether his skin hurt more from its brief contact with the scorching iron or his bones ached more from the impact, but there was no time to contemplate the matter.

The Amnesian Hero scrambled to his feet, then spun toward the center of the passage to see Silverwind trotting up to him. The bariaur held Tessali's groaning figure in his arms. The elf's cloak was shredded and bloody. Though one knee was bent at an impossible angle and his eyes were glazed with pain, he remained conscious and alert.

"By my name, I am glad I imagined you!" Silverwind exclaimed, stopping at the Thrasson's side. "All the same, I wish it hadn't been at the other end of my golden thread."

"*My* golden thread." The Amnesian Hero stepped around the bariaur, peering through the hailstorm in an unsuccessful attempt to locate the monster of the labyrinth. "What happened to the beast?"

Silverwind grinned proudly. "I imagined it out of existence."

"I suspect it will be harder to destroy than that." The Thrasson glanced along the wall, looking for Jayk. "Did you see what became of the tiefling?"

"Zoombee, I am here."

The Amnesian Hero turned to see Jayk a short distance away, rising out of the fog and holding her temples with both fingers. Her pupils were round and her fangs folded out of sight. The tiefling's shadowy complexion made it difficult to look for injury, but aside from her furrowed brow, the Thrasson saw no outward sign of harm.

"Are you hurt, Jayk?" asked the Amnesian Hero.

"My head, she feels like a shattered egg."

"But can you run?" asked Silverwind.

"I had thought I was advancing to the One Death," Jayk answered. "But I am not so lucky. I can run, as long as I can do it gently."

"Then I suggest we be on our way." The bariaur nodded toward the intersection. "I don't have much control over my dark self, I fear. It has a way of reasserting itself at the worst times."

ASH WINDS

Twining thread about his wrist as he hobbled along, the Amnesian Hero followed Silverwind back toward the intersection where they had met just a few minutes earlier. Despite the chance that the monster, wounded and furious, would be coming after them, the Thrasson had no intention of leaving a loose end of thread lying about the foggy maze; as one of his few connections to the past, the golden strand was far too precious for such carelessness.

After the tumult of battle, the roaring hail seemed almost quiet in his ears. The aching in his bones was already subsiding, but his seared chest still burned where it had touched the hot iron walls. The air seemed more scorching than ever. No number of foul-tasting hailstones could quench his thirst, and his parched throat felt ready to swell shut. He uttered a silent prayer to Hermes, begging the god of journeys to help the old bariaur retrace his steps quickly; if they did not escape the labyrinth soon, the Thrasson would perish of thirst.

At the Amnesian Hero's side walked Jayk. She kept her fingers pressed to her temples, as though trying to keep her brain from shaking inside her skull, and she seemed somewhat dazed. The Thrasson would have liked to stop and let the tiefling gather her scrambled thoughts, but that was out of the question until they found a safe place to rest. At least she was in better shape than Tessali, whose groans periodically overwhelmed even the battering hail.

As the Amnesian Hero approached the intersection, the angle at which the golden thread descended into the fog grew steadily steeper. Soon, it pointed almost straight down, and the Thrasson realized he had to be standing almost on top of the other end.

"Silverwind, wait a moment." The Amnesian Hero stopped and bent to retrieve the lance around which the bariaur had twined his end of the thread. "I don't want to lose you in this storm."

"Until I have treated with you, I don't see how that is possible." Silverwind turned around to see what the Amnesian Hero was doing. "But we really must–oh!"

The bariaur squinted down the corridor, then pinched his wrinkled face into a mask of self-reproach. "No, you old fool! Don't lose control now!"

Without rising, the Thrasson pivoted on his good foot. Through the curtain of hailstones, he saw a shaggy silhouette, barely perceptible, rising out of the fog. So efficient was the creature's camouflage that the Amnesian Hero could tell it was facing away from him only by the location of its missing arm.

"Zoombee, why is Silverwind leaving?" Jayk's voice was low and puzzled. The bariaur was fleeing. "You told him to wait. I'll make kiss with him, yes?"

"No! He's doing the right thing. I want you to go with him." The Thrasson pushed her toward the bariaur. "And don't bring your lips anywhere near him."

Jayk sighed, then groaned as she started after Silverwind.

Keeping his gaze fixed on the monster, the Amnesian Hero squatted on his heels and ran his hand over the fog-shrouded bricks. When he did not find the broken lance, he grabbed the thread and began to pull. The beast slowly turned toward him, holding its dismembered arm in its good hand. The creature pressed the base of the severed limb to its truncated shoulder and carefully held it there.

The Thrasson glanced behind him and saw Jayk following Silverwind into the hail. He gave the thread a rough jerk and felt it vibrate as the spool rolled across the bricks, but he did not find the lance itself.

The monster of the labyrinth took its hand away from its dismembered arm. Though the limb fell slack, it did not fall off.

"By Zeus, you *are* going to be difficult to kill." Even that quiet whisper hurt the Amnesian Hero's raw throat.

The beast gazed in Silverwind's direction and started shambling forward. The Amnesian Hero swept his hand over the bricks one last time and found nothing. He rose and clumped away, drawing his sword and keeping a careful watch over his shoulder.

The monster exhibited no particular hurry to catch up. Like the Amnesian Hero himself, it seemed to have concluded that this battle would be won by patience and providence, not ferocity or stealth. It would stalk its quarry at a distance, ready to spring when they finally grew distracted or collapsed from thirst.

The Amnesian Hero reached the intersection, where he found Silverwind waiting. The bariaur held Tessali's battered form in his arms, and Jayk was at his side.

"I don't see the monster." The bariaur sounded more relieved than was warranted.

The Amnesian Hero glanced back and saw that the beast had vanished into the storm. "The monster is there, be assured. You cannot imagine it away."

"Of course I can." Silverwind twisted around to scowl at the Thrasson, drawing a groan of agony from the elf in his arms.

Now that the Amnesian Hero was closer, he could see that the monster had opened a number of gashes in Tessali's side, in several places baring the elf's ribs.

"How does Tessali fare?"

"He needs my undivided attention, if he is not to fade away. I'll think on him when we find a sheltered place to stop."

"Let us go, then." The Amnesian Hero turned in the direction from which Silverwind had come, only to discover the bariaur facing the opposite way. "What are you doing? Show me to where you found the thread."

The bariaur shook his head. "I was following it in the opposite direction."

"That does not matter." As he spoke, the Thrasson pivoted on his brick foot, keeping a careful watch for the labyrinth monster. "The exit lies where you first found the string."

"That's ludicrous! Why would I imagine a golden thread leading *away* from the exit?"

The Amnesian Hero frowned, unsure of how to answer. Tessali seemed to have had the most success pretending to accept the mad bariaur's logic, but the Thrasson was not adept at such maneuvers.

"I cannot say why you would do such a thing. But when I appeared in the maze, I had the spool with me." The Amnesian Hero thought he saw a silhouette slipping through the hail behind Silverwind. He stepped around the bariaur and saw nothing, then displayed the tangle of thread wrapped around his hand. "The barrel is in my hand now, inside this tangle. If we had time, I would show it to you."

Jayk squinted at the Amnesian Hero, as though she were having trouble seeing him. "Perhaps you're hissh way . . ." The tiefling's words were slurred and slow. "Hissh way out."

Silverwind's eyes lit in sudden comprehension. "Yes, of course. *You* are my way out. Why didn't I see it before?"

"You must show me where you found the thread." The Amnesian Hero's voice was little more than a gravelly rasp. All this talking had left his throat as raw as a scuffed knee. "The exit is there, even if you did not notice it."

"How could I have, when I had not yet found you?"

With that, Silverwind danced around and started up the passage at a trot. Though the pace seemed gentle enough for the bariaur, it was all Jayk and the Amnesian Hero could do to keep up. The Thrasson clumped along beside the bariaur's rear quarters, one hand holding his sword and the other trailing the golden thread. He did his best to maintain a watch, but whenever he turned to look over his shoulder, he fell a step behind. His throat felt like it was growing smaller with every scorching breath, while the leg lifting his brick foot began to throb with a dull, deep ache.

Jayk did better than the Amnesian Hero, running alongside the bariaur with a steady, fluid stride. She complained frequently about her throbbing head, and also about how the constant jarring aggravated her pain. After a while, the tiefling stopped pumping her arms for balance so she could keep her fingers pressed to her temples. Not long after that, she started to stumble.

Still, their guide ran on through the storm. How Silverwind navigated all the twists and turns so confidently, the Amnesian Hero could not comprehend. He could barely see from the bariaur's rear quarters to his curling horns, yet the old fellow rushed through the hail and the fog as though he could see a hundred paces ahead. He would suddenly turn down a broad corridor masked by a curtain of gray hail, then dart toward a solid wall of iron, only to round a hidden buttress and rush into a network of narrow, twisting passages. Never did the old bariaur lead them into a dead-end blind, nor, as far as the Amnesian Hero could tell, circle back upon a path they had already taken.

The golden line dangling from the Thrasson's wrist always remained taut, but no matter how convoluted their course became, or how many corners they rounded, it never seemed to snag or drag. The Amnesian Hero took this to mean that he was dragging the broken lance along behind him, though he realized there might be other explanations. The thread was obviously magic, for instance, and perhaps that prevented it from tangling.

At last, the inevitable happened: Jayk stumbled and disappeared into the fog. There was a groan and two slaps, then the tiefling began to wail. Silverwind halted and turned around, and the Amnesian Hero kneeled at her side.

"Jayk, quiet!" The Thrasson feared her cries would draw the monster of the labyrinth. "I'm here."

"Zoombee! The spots, there are too many of them in my eyes!"

The Amnesian Hero pulled the tiefling to her feet. Her dark eyes remained unfocused and glassy, even when he poked his fingertips at them.

"She's lost her sight," said Silverwind. "I can carry her. Put her on my back."

The Thrasson made no move to do as the bariaur requested. "Her headache has been getting worse."

"Of course—she banged her skull," said Silverwind. "But I can't do anything about it here. When we get to a quiet place, I'll take care of it."

Jayk clutched the Amnesian Hero's arm and nodded. "I am strong enough to hold his waist, Zoombee. I only panicked because I felt lost. As long as I know you will not leave me in this place, I will be fine."

"Never! I promise, Jayk."

The tiefling managed a weak smile. "Then I am not worried."

The Thrasson helped her onto Silverwind's back, and the small company resumed its flight. The Amnesian Hero clumped along at the bariaur's flank, keeping a wary watch over his shoulder and expecting their guide to duck into some sheltered hiding place at any moment. Silverwind merely continued to trot along, picking his way through the corners and intersections with never a doubt.

After what seemed an eternity of running, the Amnesian Hero could take no more. His parched throat seemed in danger of bursting into flames with every breath, even his good leg was trembling with fatigue, and it was all he could do to drag his brick foot along behind him.

"Silverwind, stop!" The croaking words sounded more slaad than human. "I can't . . . keep this up."

The bariaur did not slow. "Only a little farther. I can almost picture the conjunction now."

The Thrasson tripped and fell. For a moment, he allowed himself to believe he was too tired to stand—then he felt a tug on the golden thread and thought of the monster of the labyrinth. If it was following, now would be the perfect time for it to attack. He drew a fiery breath into his aching lungs and, with a terrific growl, pushed himself to his feet.

Silverwind stood a few paces ahead, waiting impatiently. The

Amnesian Hero spun away from him, half-expecting to see the monster charging out of the storm.

There was nothing but hail.

Silverwind clopped to the Thrasson's side. Jayk sat slumped against the bariaur's back, eyes closed and winsome face entirely blank; only her arms, still locked about the bariaur's waist, suggested that she remained conscious. There could be no doubt about Tessali's wakefulness, however; the constant lament of pain that poured from his lips sent shivers down the Amnesian Hero's spine.

Silverwind shook his head in disappointment, at the same time eyeing the Thrasson. "Why do I always do this to myself? I almost have the conjunction in mind, and now I lose my concentration."

"Too . . . tired," the Amnesian Hero croaked. "Worried . . . about . . . the monster."

The bariaur peered into the hail, then snorted and shook his head. "Don't start imagining that again." Silverwind was speaking to himself, not the Thrasson. "The thing is out of mind."

"Stop . . . it!" The Amnesian Hero's patience was as exhausted as his body. "You are not imagining this! It's really happening to you–to *us!*"

Silverwind's bushy eyebrows came together. "Of course it's really happening. It's really happening because I'm really imagining it."

"No! Do you feel this?" The Amnesian Hero slapped the bariaur's leg with the flat of his blade. "I did it–not your imagination."

Silverwind's eyes grew watery. "It's happening to me again!" He dropped Tessali into the fog, drawing a howl of pain, then started beating himself about the head. "Why can't I control my own thoughts?"

"Because we are not your thoughts!"

The Amnesian Hero sheathed his sword, then reached down and helped Tessali stand. Silverwind continued to pummel himself.

Tessali leaned close to the Thrasson's ear. "Don't . . . confuse . . . issue." The elf winced with each rasping word. "You must . . .

accept what . . . Silverwind says."

The Amnesian Hero's jaw dropped. "You believe we're phantoms of his imagination?"

The elf's eyes grew stern. "His delus–ah–theory . . . is as sensible . . . as anything. If it . . . gets us out, I will accept . . . anything."

The Amnesian Hero rolled his eyes and looked back down the corridor. When he saw no shaggy silhouette skulking through the hail, he shrugged and looked back to Silverwind–and saw Jayk's limp form slipping from the bariaur's back. The tiefling hit the ground with no sound but a dull thud.

"Jayk?"

There was no answer. The Amnesian Hero slipped Tessali onto Silverwind's back, then stooped over and, rather awkwardly, scooped Jayk up in the crook of his arm. The tiefling's breath came slow and shallow. There was no sign of fresh injury, but the murky hair on the back of her head felt sticky with old blood.

The Amnesian Hero stepped closer to the bariaur, who was still pummeling himself about the head. "As you wish, Silverwind."

The bariaur stopped hitting himself. "What?"

"Don't be difficult. You have regained control of your mind." The Thrasson shoved Jayk toward the bariaur. "Now tend to your thoughts. I fear Jayk is in danger of fading."

Silverwind sighed and reached toward Jayk. Instead of taking her into his arms, he thumbed open her eyelids. Even the Thrasson could see that she was in poor shape. Her pupils were mere pinpricks, one a square and the other a triangle. An astonished blat slipped the bariaur's lips, then he reached around the back of her head and began muttering to himself as he worked his fingers through her blood-matted hair.

"How does she fare?" The Amnesian Hero's voice was sounding increasingly rough. "What happened to her?"

Silverwind continued muttering and did not answer.

Tessali, who was peering over the bariaur's shoulder, whispered, "Cracked skull . . . If Silverwind cannot save her . . . I might . . . but need . . . quiet. Try . . . not–" The elf scowled, his gaze shifting past the Amnesian Hero's shoulder.

Before Tessali could say more, the Thrasson thrust Jayk into Silverwind's arms. Yanking his sword from its scabbard as he moved, he spun around and saw nothing but gray hail.

"Where is it, Tessali?"

"Behind you . . . now," gasped the elf. "But don't worry . . . I saw something flapping . . . It's a black . . . ribbon."

"A ribbon?" The Amnesian Hero craned his neck and glimpsed a black tatter flapping in the hail. "What is it doing there?"

"Working . . . out of the amphora," said Tessali. "There's a crack—"

"In the neck of the jar. I know." The Amnesian Hero stepped to Silverwind's side, then turned around to present the amphora to Tessali. "Push the cloth back. I fear what might happen if that ribbon gets loose."

"Why?" Tessali grunted in pain, then the Thrasson felt him pushing against the amphora. "This looks like . . . common flax."

"Whatever it is, it is—" The words caught in the Thrasson's aching throat. He had to pause to work up enough saliva to coat his parched gullet, then continued, "It is Poseidon's gift to the Lady of Pain. I doubt there is anything common about it."

"By my curled horns!" Without warning, Silverwind turned to leave. "How feeble my mind has grown!"

The Amnesian Hero glimpsed a shaggy figure ambling through the hail, pulling up the golden thread and wadding it into a great tangled ball.

"Cut the thread!" Tessali's command came as Silverwind began to gallop away.

"I'd sooner cut you!" The Amnesian Hero clumped after his companions, wondering why, after staying to battle the monster earlier, Silverwind had suddenly decided to abandon him. "This thread is magical."

"Dead men have no use for magic!"

Already, Silverwind and his passengers were a silhouette in the hail. The Amnesian Hero looked back and saw the monster of the labyrinth following at a cautious distance. It was drawing the line up hand-over-hand, using both arms with equal ease. The Thrasson saw no hint of weakness, or even of lingering stiffness, in the limb that had been cut off. To his disappointment, the only sign of its earlier injury lay in its wariness; the creature was trailing him at the edge of visibility, discernible only because of the golden brightness of the thread ball in its hands.

As the Amnesian Hero turned to look forward again, he ran headlong into Silverwind's bulky saddlebags.

"This way."

The bariaur trotted around a salient of iron wall, leading the way into a section of narrow, zigzagging corridors with two branches at every turn. The Amnesian Hero's throat grew so dry that it seemed to stick shut between breaths. In the cramped passages, the hail echoed off the hot iron walls louder than ever, but it seemed that fewer of the icy balls could find their way down into the bottom of the tight confines. The storm waned to little more than a tempest. Visibility stretched to more than an arrow's flight, and the Thrasson saw that the walls were speckled both high and low with the same window-shaped squares he had noticed in the broader sections of the labyrinth.

Several times, gouts of flame spewed from one of dark openings to fill the narrow passage with roiling balls of fire. Silverwind seemed to have a sixth sense about these occurrences and never failed to stop or scurry ahead just in time to keep the company from being charred. Hoping to learn the old bariaur's secret, the Amnesian Hero often tried to peer into the depths of the black squares. He never saw anything except a barrier of inky blackness.

The monster of the labyrinth lagged far behind, lingering at the edge of visibility, often vanishing entirely as the Amnesian Hero and his companions rounded a corner. Whenever their pace slowed even slightly, however, the beast rushed them, bellowing its wall-shaking roar and driving the weary companions forward at a sprint. The thing was trying to run them to ground, the Thrasson knew, and it was succeeding. His tongue felt so swollen he could hardly draw breath. He had long ago sweated away the last of his water; now his blood was growing thick and gummy, and his heart had to pump like a forge bellows to force it through his veins.

The Amnesian Hero waited until they rounded the next corner, then caught Silverwind by the tail.

The bariaur danced around, his eyes flashing with irritation. "What now?"

The Thrasson tried to answer, but his tongue was too swollen to shape the words—or to let pass the air that would give them voice. He managed only a gurgled rasp, then pointed at his sword and gestured back down the way they had come.

"No, that won't do." Silverwind shook his head resolutely. "Slaying the dark self is impossible. It only comes back stronger than before."

The Thrasson wanted to retort that they had no choice, but could force no more than an angry croak from his throat.

Silverwind looked the Amnesian Hero up and down. "Well, I can't carry you, too. Not with the load I've already got." He hefted Jayk as though to illustrate, and the Thrasson saw that her complexion had faded to an alarming blue. "I suppose we'll have to hide."

The bariaur galloped a dozen paces down a branch corridor, then turned toward one of the windowlike squares on the wall. The Amnesian Hero half-expected Silverwind and his passengers to smash headlong into the inky blackness, but they simply passed through, as though they had stepped across the threshold of Rivergate's dark door. The Thrasson started to follow, then barely escaped being charred to cinder as a gout of flame shot from the square.

The Amnesian Hero first croaked in shock, then gurgled in anguish, despairing at how quickly death could come in the mazes.

In the next instant, Silverwind reappeared, still holding Tessali and Jayk. The bariaur and his passengers had not emerged from the black square so much as appeared beside it.

"Come along, Thrasson!" barked the bariaur. "If we let the dark self chase us through this conjunction, we'll be running for the next epoch."

Still in shock, the Amnesian Hero began to clump forward. He tried to ask about the gout of flame he had seen, but could not force the words from his throat.

"Cut . . . thread." Having ridden on Silverwind's back for the entire chase, Tessali had not yet lost his voice to thirst. "If beast follows . . . doomed."

Reluctantly, the Thrasson nodded and stopped beside another of the black squares. Intending to throw the thread through the conjunction and misdirect the monster, he wrapped a loop around the hilt of his dagger, then cut the golden filament with his star-forged sword.

The strand had hardly separated before the entire length of thread vanished, including the coil wrapped around his arm and the wooden spool in his hand. His stomach went hollow with loss, but he had no time to dwell on the feeling. A deafening bellow echoed through the labyrinth, followed by the distant, heavy thuds of the monster's pounding feet.

The Amnesian Hero rushed to Silverwind's side, then together they all leapt through the window of darkness.

There is a great roaring, and at first the Amnesian Hero thinks he is falling: the wind whips his hair, roars in his ears, nettles his scorched chest. Now the ash begins to scour his eyes; he sucks it in through his nose, he tastes it coating his swollen tongue, and he believes he has been incinerated by one of those flame gouts that spew from the black squares. Then his feet find purchase on something powdery but solid. He sees Silverwind standing before him, almost glowing in the strange, pearly light. Slowly the Thrasson's eyes begin to discern between the cloud of ash howling through the air and the river of ash swirling about his legs and the ramparts of ash flanking his shoulders, and he is delighted to realize he is still in the mazes.

The fool.

Yes, I am still watching. Even in the mazes, the Lady of Pain is always watching, as I am watching that scrap of black cloth that flutters from the Thrasson's cracked amphora. The ash wind has caught it, and soon the ash wind will pull it free, and what then?

Will it flutter through the mazes forever, always searching for what it can never find? Or will it rise up through that void in my chest where I once had a heart? I have not decided.

I have not decided.

I have not decided whether that strand of Poseidon's net caught me for good or ill, whether that one scrap of dream (I dare not call it memory) makes me weaker or stronger: better to know the source of the Pains, perhaps; better to know the reason for this emptiness in my chest, certainly–but what I know, I know only the half of.

And there lies the danger, does it not?

If ignorance is bliss and knowledge power, what has the King of Seas sent me? Half a truth, at best; half a memory, at worst; there is no help for it. I have seen what I have seen; a crack has opened, and I could not stop that black tatter from tearing free if I wanted to–and forgive me everyone everywhere–I do not want to!

"Do you want to mark our trail?" Silverwind grabbed the Amnesian Hero's arm and started to tug him down the passage, toward the dark mouth of a distant intersection. "Get away from that conjunction! Didn't you see how they torch up?"

The Thrasson, still unable to speak, scowled and peered over his shoulder. The conjunction appeared almost the same on this side as on the other: a black square, so flat and featureless it looked more like a painting than a doorway. Without any visible support, it hung motionless in the ash cloud, the only thing in the labyrinth that the howling wind seemed incapable of swaying. The iron-walled passages beyond the window remained cloaked beneath a veil of inky darkness; the monster of the labyrinth–or the Lady of Pain herself–could have been standing on the other side, and the Amnesian Hero would not have known it.

As the Thrasson studied the conjunction, the black ribbon flapping from the amphora's cracked neck finally came loose. He snatched at the scrap and missed, then tried again when the swirling ash wind changed direction and whipped the rag around his head. The tatter dodged his fingers as though it were alive, circling him two more times before it finally sailed past Silverwind. It floated about half the distance to the intersection and became caught in another whirlwind.

Hoping to catch the ribbon before it vanished altogether, the Amnesian Hero squeezed past his companions and went after it. He had no idea what to do even if he caught the scrap, but he knew miserly Poseidon would seize any excuse to withhold the promised payment. When the Thrasson returned to Arborea, he was determined that he would be able to report that the Lady of Pain had received the entire contents of the amphora.

As the Amnesian Hero clumped forward, he was relieved to see a black stripe flashing amidst the gray ash of the whirlwind. Then the stripe became a solid band, the band began to widen both up and down, and soon the entire swirling ash cloud had turned as black as shadow.

The whirlwind began to slow, shaping itself into the silhouette of a huge, barrel-chested giant. The Amnesian Hero's brick foot dropped like an anchor and brought him to a gape-mouthed stop. He felt as if the howling ash winds had stirred his thoughts into a muddle. He could not quite comprehend what had happened to the black tatter, or how he was going to recapture a shadow and feed it back into the amphora.

"Who wishes to pass this way?" So loud was the question that it shook tiny avalanches of ash off the passage walls.

"Aigggh!" cried Silverwind. "What has risen from the depths of your foul mind now, old fool?"

The giant took a single step forward, leaving his shadow behind and bringing himself belt-to-nose with the Amnesian Hero. The brute was as broad as the passage, with a pair of lice-ridden lion skins girding his loins and an iron club the size of a galley oar in his hand. His legs were big as trees, his skin as coarse as pumice stone, and his hairy belly so huge it bulged over the Thrasson's head like a billowing sail.

"Who wishes to travel the road of Periphetes?"

Coated as it was with ash, the Amnesian Hero's throat was much too dry to shape an answer—but he knew better than to think any answer would satisfy the giant. He had fought enough of the brutes to realize that Periphetes was about to demand a toll, and that the toll would be one they would not care to pay.

The Thrasson slammed the hilt of his sword into Periphetes's kneecap, then deftly leaned aside as the giant brought down a great palm to slap the irritation. Before the hand could rise again, the Amnesian Hero touched his blade to the middle knuckle, using just enough strength to inflict an admonishing prick and pin the great appendage in place—men of renown did not fell even the greediest of giants without first warning them to behave.

Periphetes lowered his head to peer over his enormous belly, showing a huge moon-shaped face with a grimy thatch of beard and a cavernous pug-nose. When the giant found his hand pinned to his own kneecap, he poised his great club over the Thrasson's head.

"Don't make me smash you, little man."

The Thrasson wagged a free finger at Periphetes, then gently pushed his sword forward. The star-forged blade sliced through the giant's thick hide until it drew blood, illustrating just how easily it could pierce hand and knee alike. The giant bellowed, but wisely refrained from bringing his club down.

"Stand . . . aside." Tessali's voice betrayed his pain, but somehow he found the strength to speak loudly enough to attract the giant's attention. "That sword . . . slices . . . steel."

"Is that so?"

Periphetes's face was too huge to conceal the flash of cunning that shot across it. His eyes darted from Tessali, who still sat astride Silverwind's back, to the Amnesian Hero and back again. When the giant's huge club began to move in the elf's direction, the Thrasson knew instantly that his adversary was hoping to make hostages of his three companions. He ducked between Periphetes's legs and rocked his sword across the back of the giant's hand. An index finger as thick as a lance shaft popped free and, trailing a cascade of dark blood, dropped into the ash.

Periphetes roared, and the club reversed direction.

The Amnesian Hero darted behind the giant's thigh, at the same time drawing his blade along inside his foe's huge knee. The star-forged steel sliced deep through tendon and sinew. Had the Thrasson not been crippled by a brick foot, he would have continued to dance around Periphetes, reducing the giant's leg to little more than a bloody post of bone. As it was, however, the Amnesian Hero had to settle for a single, vicious strike to the back of the knee.

The blade bit deep, then was nearly torn from the Thrasson's hands as Periphetes's leg jerked away. Knowing the giant would have to pivot backward to counterattack, the Thrasson ducked under the brute and assaulted the other leg with a vicious spinning slash. He heard the telltale pop of a separating tendon, then dived away before his foe's iron club could arc down to smash his skull.

The Amnesian Hero did not land upon the ground so much as he sank into a powdery bed of ash. His mouth filled with a sharp, metallic taste, then he found himself choking and sucking more dross into his swollen throat with each convulsion. Half-swimming and half-pushing, he raised himself out of the bitter stuff and spun toward Periphetes—or at least toward the place where he assumed the giant to be. So thickly did ash fill the air that no longer could the Thrasson see his foe.

Still choking for breath, the Amnesian Hero clumped out of the billowing ash cloud and found himself looking at Periphetes's flank. The giant was five paces away, kneeling on his savaged legs, holding his club high and sneering at the Thrasson. There was no time to dodge. The Amnesian Hero flipped his sword into a high block and held it with both hands, trying to pivot aside on his brick foot.

The blow landed with a tremendous clang.

Any other weapon would have shattered, but the Thrasson's star-forged blade held true. He felt his arms buckle beneath the impact, then his knees started to go, and he saw the iron club sliding past on the edge of his sword.

He could not let himself fall. If he fell, he would not have the strength to rise again until he could breathe, and by the time he cleared his throat, Periphetes would be striking again. The Amnesian Hero threw all his weight against the great bludgeon, at the same time circling his sword out from under it.

The giant's club landed in the soft ash, raising another gray cloud. The Thrasson hurled himself into the billowing dross, bringing his sword down in the place where he imagined Periphetes's wrist to be lying.

The blade hit with a sharp jolt, then continued to slice downward until it sank into the soft ash. A thick, coppery smell filled the Thrasson's nostrils, and he glimpsed the red stump of a log-sized wrist rising through the grayness of the cloud.

A great, racking cough boiled out of the depths of the Amnesian Hero's lungs, forcing a plume of spewing ash from his swollen throat. Ignoring his body's demand to stop for air, he pounded through the gray cloud and found Periphetes kneeling in the ash. The giant was clutching the stump of his wrist to his chest, a position that left his armpit well-protected against a flank attack.

With a quick kill out of the question, the Amnesian Hero flipped his sword around to try for the next best thing. Periphetes, stunned by the loss of his hand, did not turn to look until the blade was already slipping between his massive ribs. The Thrasson pushed into the stroke with all his strength, driving the weapon hilt-deep and stirring it around to enlarge the wound.

A long, breathy groan slipped from Periphetes's mouth. Then, almost in resignation, the giant lowered his elbow and smashed his attacker away from his flank. As the Thrasson flew through the air, his sword came free, and a single gout of frothy red blood shot from the wound. The Amnesian Hero hit the ashen wall without much force, then picked himself up and scrambled away as his foe's anguished gasps began to rumble down the passage.

Once he was safely out of reach, the Amnesian Hero dropped to his knees. His vision began to darken. He used his hand to clean the ash from his mouth and throat, but even then he could hardly suck down any air. His breath came fast and shallow and wheezy. He began to suffer a dry cough that dislodged no dross and added greatly to his misery, racking his chest with spasms as anguishing as they were uncontrollable.

As terrible as his agony was, the Thrasson knew Periphetes was suffering worse. Dying of a punctured lung was both a slow and painful way to pass to the next stage, and, if the Amnesian Hero had possessed the strength, he would gladly have spared the giant such a miserable death.

Silverwind padded up beside the Amnesian Hero, still holding Jayk in his arms. The Thrasson was alarmed to see a tiny trickle of blood running from the tiefling's nose.

"Truly, you are my path out of the mazes," said the bariaur. "No matter what wickedness my mind contrives to block the way, you will defeat it."

"Well . . . done." Tessali cringed as the giant let out a particularly loud and anguished moan. "Though . . . a more . . . merciful . . . death . . ."

The Amnesian Hero replied with a long string of hacking coughs, then followed it with a strangled rasp nearly as pitiable as that of the giant.

Silverwind's bushy eyebrows rose in alarm. "What's wrong? Are you injured?"

The Thrasson shook his head, then clutched at his throat.

"Something is lodged?"

Again, the Amnesian Hero shook his head. He curled his hand as though holding a cup, then raised it to his lips and tipped his chin back.

"Of course, you are thirsty!" Silverwind was relieved. "I imagine I have something in my saddlebags to take care of that."

Tessali began to fumble with the straps, but the Amnesian Hero was in no mood to wait for the clumsy fingers of the wounded elf. He sheathed his sword, then tore the knots free with his own hands. Inside, he found a bulging waterskin. The Thrasson grabbed the bag and jerked the stopper from its mouth, then tipped his head back and began to pour. The fluid that gushed out, red and warm and thick, was not water.

Wine, sweet wine.

FEVER VISION

The wine, warm and bland to the ash-coated tongue of the Amnesian Hero, muddied the dross in his mouth. He spat the slurry out and drank again. This time he tasted the ambrosia instead of the ash; the drink was plum-sweet and rich with cinnamon, a honeyed nectar to soothe the rawness in his gullet. He drew a long rasping breath, and the darkness retreated from his vision. He soaked his parched throat with another gulp, then smiled as a certain exhilarating warmth filled his belly.

"Silverwind, that wine would do Dionysus himself proud." The Thrasson's voice remained gruff, and he still felt flushed, but he counted himself lucky to be speaking at all. "I cannot imagine how you came by it in these mazes."

"The same way I came by you, of course. I—"

A tremendous groan rumbled down the passage, drowning out the rest of the bariaur's reply. The Amnesian Hero turned to see Periphetes slumping forward; the giant's head smashed into the labyrinth wall, loosing an avalanche of powdery dross. A raucous snort jetted from his gaping nostrils and stirred the airborne ash into a boiling gray cloud. He toppled on his side and lay in a fetal curl, blocking the corridor so completely that the howling wind faded to stillness. His skin began to grow coarse and grainy. A dark pallor blossomed over his entire body, quickly deepening to a drab, lusterless black. His anguished expression assumed the fixed, eternal character of a statue, and any hint that he had ever been alive vanished from his eyes.

"Good . . . riddance." So weak was Tessali's voice that the words sounded as though they might be the elf's last.

The Amnesian Hero turned back to his companions. The blood was flowing from Jayk's ears and nose more strongly now, and there was an alarming slackness in the way her limbs dangled over Silverwind's cradling arms. Tessali looked better only because he remained conscious; his face had paled from blood loss, and his eyes had that far-off look of someone mad with pain.

"Silverwind, the time has come to care for our wounded." The Amnesian Hero slung the wineskin over his shoulder, then lifted Tessali off the bariaur's back. Despite the lightness of the elf, the Thrasson flushed at the effort. "I trust this place is quiet enough to work your magic."

Silverwind nodded, then kneeled and laid Jayk on her cape. "Which one first?"

Tessali raised his hand and lifted a finger toward the tiefling. Though Jayk might well have considered the gesture an impediment to her progress toward the One Death, the Amnesian Hero approved of the elf's charity.

"You are noble for a Sigilite."

The Thrasson offered the wineskin to Tessali. Too weak to decline with even a modest shake of the head, the elf merely closed his eyes.

Already working on Jayk, Silverwind rolled the tiefling onto her stomach and ran his fingers lightly over the back of her head. He began mumbling to himself, at the same time tracing the star-shaped pattern of a skull fracture. After a time, he grunted, apparently satisfied that he had found the extent of her injuries. Then, to the Thrasson's astonishment, the old bariaur leaned forward and started to dribble spittle onto his patient's bloody head.

Though the Amnesian Hero was beginning to fear he had trusted Jayk's care to a senile charlatan, he restrained the urge to push the old fellow away. Things worked differently here in the mazes, and, strange as Silverwind's behavior appeared, it did not seem dangerous. Besides, Tessali had opened his eyes again, and he showed no sign of surprise at the method of treatment.

Once Jayk's head had been thoroughly wetted, Silverwind placed his palm over the tiefling's wound and uttered what sounded like a magical incantation. The bariaur grimaced, as though suffering a terrible pain, but there were no shimmering glows, no wondrous tinkling, no smoking brimstone. The tiefling's blood continued to drip from her nose and ears, and, as far as the Thrasson could tell, that was all that happened.

"What's wrong?" The Amnesian Hero wiped his brow; he was sweating harder now than he had during the battle with Periphetes. "She looks as bad as before."

Silverwind opened his eyes, then grimaced at his patient's condition. "It's my fault," he sighed, shaking his head. "I should never have given them free will. They're always straying off in strange directions."

"What are you talking about? Who's always straying off?"

Silverwind scowled. "You, of course: my thoughts."

The Thrasson was ready to take the old bariaur by the throat and choke him sane. "Jayk is not straying. She is injured."

"But she doesn't want to come back," said Silverwind. "She is content to fade into oblivion."

"You can't let her!" the Amnesian Hero commanded. "Try something else; cast another spell!"

A sudden spark lit Silverwind's old eyes. "Right you are–I am! Why didn't I think of that before?" He leaned close to Jayk's ear, then began to yell, "Tiefling, I have anointed you with my water, the water of life; I have seen your injury, I have felt your pain, and I have thought them gone–and still you think yourself dead; who are you to deny my reality? You are alive; I command you to believe me!"

It was the most absurd nonsense the Amnesian Hero had ever

heard, yet the blood immediately stopped running from Jayk's nose and ears. A single rasping gurgle spilled from her lips. Her torso began to expand and contract in the steady, deep rhythm of sleep-breathing, and the Thrasson found himself holding his own breath as he waited for her to groan or lift her head.

Jayk continued to breathe, but did nothing more.

Silverwind turned the tiefling onto her back. The murky pallor was returning to her complexion, while the blood runnels below her nostrils and ears had already dried into ash-crusted stripes. The bariaur thumbed open her eyes, displaying a pair of large, round pupils.

"My focus is returning." Silverwind smiled proudly. "I'll imagine my way out of here yet!"

"You're being hasty," said the Amnesian Hero. "Before we make another run for the exit, Jayk must be ready for a fight—and Tessali, too."

Silverwind's eyebrows came together. "That's impossible. Even I can't restore their full health in the flash of a thought! It will take meditation."

The Amnesian Hero groaned. "How long?"

"As long as necessary." The bariaur's answer was curt. "What does it matter? We have as long as we need—after all, time is only a concoction of my imagination."

"As is the monster of the labyrinth, which is surely looking for us by now." The Thrasson allowed his gaze to roam from Periphetes, blocking the way ahead, back along the passage to the entrance conjunction. There were no side corridors between the black square and the giant. "Sooner or later, the beast will find our conjunction. If we don't want to be trapped, we'll have to climb over Periphetes."

The Amnesian Hero hung the wineskin around his neck and started toward the boulder.

"No!" Silverwind danced forward to block the Thrasson's way. "Have you had too much wine, or are you the dumbest thought I've ever had?"

"You have split hooves," the Amnesian Hero retorted. "With a little help, you can make the climb."

"I know I can make the climb!" Silverwind retorted. "But to where? Don't you know anything about the mazes? If we try to climb out of this one, we'll fall into another—and it's not like going through a conjunction. There's no telling where we'll end up. Then how will I return to where I found the string?"

The Amnesian Hero scowled, recalling what Tessali had reported seeing—nothing—after he scaled the wall back at the entrance of their own labyrinth. The Thrasson was not convinced that clambering over a boulder was the same thing as climbing a wall, but the consequences of being wrong were more than he cared to risk. He would prefer a quick death at the monster's hands to spending eternity lost in the scorching passages of the Lady's mazes.

"What of moving the boulder?" the Thrasson asked. "Would that be the same as climbing over?"

Silverwind scowled at Periphetes's stony corpse. "I don't see that it matters. I can't imagine moving a boulder that size."

The Amnesian Hero glanced at the iron club that had fallen from Periphetes's severed hand. "But I can."

Silverwind thought for a moment, then shrugged. "Go ahead and try, but take that off first." The bariaur pointed at the Thrasson's amphora. "It won't do to shake that thing up. We don't want any more giants materializing here."

As the Amnesian Hero slipped the amphora's sling off his shoulders, Silverwind scowled and stooped over to peer at the Thrasson's flank.

"How long have you had this?"

"Had what?"

The Amnesian Hero raised his elbow and looked under his arm. He could barely see a short cut running down the side of his chest. The wound was sealed by scorched blood and seared flesh, but beads of white pus were seeping from the jagged seam between its puffy red lips. Though the Thrasson did not remember receiving the scratch, he felt sure he had suffered it during the battle with the monster of the labyrinth.

"No wonder you look so flushed!" Silverwind reached for the wineskin hanging around the Thrasson's neck. "I've been letting you drink wine, and you have a fever!"

The Amnesian Hero pushed the bariaur's hand away. "I'm still thirsty!"

"Too much wine is dangerous for you. You shouldn't drink any more until I imagine some water into existence."

"I'm thirsty now." The Thrasson turned away before the bariaur could reach for the wineskin again. "Do what you can for Jayk and Tessali. I'll see to finding us a safe place to hide."

The Amnesian Hero stepped over to Periphetes's iron club. The weapon was half-again as long as Silverwind was tall. The diameter of a man's ankle at one end, it swelled along its length to the size of a bear's head at the other. So thickly scaled with rust was the weapon that the Thrasson feared it might break under the strain of what he had planned.

The Amnesian Hero squatted at the thick end and wrapped his arms around the club, then heaved it out of the ash and began dragging it toward the giant's legs. He had lifted heavier burdens—for instance, when he fetched the treasure chest of King Minaros from the lair of the Ragarian Thieves—but his footing had been more secure then, and the temperature much cooler than in these mazes. By the time he had dragged the unwieldy weapon to Periphetes's side, the Thrasson's sweaty body was coated with ash from all the times he had slipped and fallen.

The Amnesian Hero dropped the head of the club beside the giant's waist, then unstoppered the wine sack and washed the dross from his mouth. After quenching his thirst, he sealed the skin and dug a deep, pitlike tunnel under Periphetes's hip. By the time he finished, the sweat was pouring from his brow in runnels; he needed another drink.

After catching his breath, the Amnesian Hero shoved the thick end of the club into the hole he had excavated. Then he went to the narrow end and hoisted the rod up. At first, as the head rocked into the pit, it rose easily. That changed, however, when the shaft reached the height of the Thrasson's waist and the other end made contact with the giant's belly.

Taking a deep breath, the Amnesian Hero squatted down and slipped his shoulders under the rod. He stood, using the strength of his thighs to raise the lever, and Periphetes's enormous body began to roll. The Thrasson drove forward, his feet slipping in the ash as though he were trying to push a wagon through a bog. The giant rolled a little farther, and the weight on the Amnesian Hero's shoulders seemed to double. His sweat poured from his brow in curtains; again his throat began to close, but the thought of giving up never crossed his mind. Men of renown did not falter; they succeeded or they died, but never did they give up.

There was a tremendous sucking sound. All at once Periphetes rolled onto his back, and the weight vanished from the Amnesian Hero's shoulder. A blast of howling wind filled the passage. The Thrasson looked over to see a cloud of ash boiling from beneath the giant's stone legs, still bent in the kneeling position as they rose into the air. Coughing and choking, he shoved the club off his shoulder and spun away from the billowing dross, and that was when he noticed the sword and the sandals.

Glowing with that yellow aura peculiar to enchanted gold, they lay pressed into the ash where Periphetes's huge belly had rested. The sword, both shorter and broader than the Amnesian Hero's own star-forged blade, had a golden hilt and a golden scabbard decorated by a single stripe of sapphires. The sandals had soles cut from the finest crocodile hide and legging straps woven from threads of pure gold.

Periphetes had no doubt stolen the magnificent booty from some unfortunate wayfarer. By right of victory, the spoils were the Amnesian Hero's, yet he hesitated to claim them. The giant had been created by Poseidon's magic—magic intended for the Lady of Pain. After hearing Tessali's account of the relationship between the Lady and the gods, the Thrasson feared the King of Seas had trapped the prizes with some disabling enchantment.

Still, the Amnesian Hero had no choice except to pick them up. He had promised to deliver the amphora to the Lady of Pain, and he did not think Poseidon likely to excuse him for leaving part of its contents to vanish beneath the ash. He quaffed another mouthful of wine, then stooped down and gingerly pinched the legging strap of one sandal between two fingers.

Nothing happened.

The Amnesian Hero plucked the sandal out of the ash. Nothing flashed or banged or gave off foul odors. He sighed in relief, guessing the shoe had to be worn to activate the enchantment. Being careful to avoid touching the sole, he fastened the legging strap to his sword belt. He retrieved the other sandal and tied it beside the first.

The sword he grasped by the scabbard.

The magic glow blinked out of the gold and a strange prickling shot up his arm. He screamed and tried to drop the weapon and found he could not. A yellow fog was forming behind his eyes, filling his head as a cloud fills a mountain valley; the smell of ash was yielding to the fragrant tang of salt pine, the parched air was growing moist on his skin, and a voice was speaking to him over the rumble of distant waves.

"One of your fathers left those for you." The figure of a tall, handsome woman appears in the fog; her honey-brown tresses are bound by a princess's circlet, and her sad face stirs the Thrasson in a way that the face of no other woman ever has. "How I have prayed you would not find them; Hera help me, now I must send you away!"

"To where?" the Thrasson gasps. The woman is all he can see, and it is more than he can do to tell whether she stands within his mind or without. "Who are you?"

Tears well in the woman's eyes. She spreads her palms and embraces the Amnesian Hero. "Is it possible? Can a son forget his mother?"

This cannot be; that woman is no memory of mine. What is she doing in the amphora Poseidon sends to me?

The Amnesian Hero stole her from me, that is what. Periphetes was to be mine, but the Thrasson stole him and killed him, that is what. The memory became his, that is what, and now it is forever lost to me, and might that memory be of the one who paid the bride's price for my heart?

Would I be lost then, or safe?

No bride can long stand fast against he who holds her heart; let him come softly in the night, and surely she will open herself to him, whoever he may be, to be ravished or sacked as he pleases.

And afterward, what then? An eternity of drudgery and servitude, if he is wicked; oblivion, sure and quick, if not.

Better to know the beast now, to prepare my defenses before he comes pounding at my gates. There may be time to change what is done; there may be time, if I dare, to steal what has been bought, to shut what has been opened, to save what is lost.

And what of the Thrasson, standing there in his mother's embrace? His strength will tell. He knows what is right and what is wrong; he will choose his own punishment.

"Mother, who am I?" the Thrasson asks. The yellow fog that filled his mind earlier is now swirling about outside his head; it has lost its color and changed into a haze of windblown dross. The ash has coated his body, glued there by the sweat of his fever, and the air has grown parched with heat and acrid bitterness. "Tell me my name; I have been lost and cannot remember."

"I am not your mother, Zoombee." The voice was weak and raspy. "My head, she hurts too much for this."

Still clutching the sword he found beneath the massive stone corpse of Periphetes, the Thrasson pushed the woman back to arm's length. In place of the regal face of his mother, he saw the twilight visage of Jayk the Snake.

"What became of her?" The Amnesian Hero released the tiefling and pivoted in a circle, desperately searching for his mother's silhouette. He saw Silverwind kneeling over Tessali's crooked knee, but no sign of the woman who had told him about the sandals and sword. "Where did she go?"

"Who?" Jayk asked.

"My mother!" The Thrasson shook the golden sword at her. "She came to me when I touched this!"

"You are scaring me, Zoombee." Jayk backed away, her hands pressed to the sides of her head. Her legs were shaky, and she seemed in danger of falling. "*I* came to you. You awakened me with your scream."

"Forgive me. I don't mean to yell."

Still feeling flushed, the Amnesian Hero opened the wineskin and took a long drink. His hands were quivering, his heart pounding, his thoughts whirling. He knew the woman who had come to him; whether or not she had actually been standing there before him, he recognized the smell of her honey-brown hair, the warmth of her arms enfolding his body, the smack of her lips kissing his cheek. He *remembered* her.

"Perhaps she wasn't here in the passage," the Thrasson said, "but I did see my mother."

Jayk rolled her eyes up under her brow and, without taking her hands from her aching head, gave the Thrasson a skeptical look. "I thought you could not remember your past, Zoombee."

"It was a vision—or a memory." The Amnesian Hero thrust the golden sword into his belt, then pointed at the amphora, still lying near Silverwind and Tessali. "It came from there, along with the giant."

"How can that be?" demanded the tiefling. "Poseidon would not send your memories to the Lady of Pain. It must be intended for her, yes?"

"No! I remembered the woman. She was my mother."

From up the passage came the sharp crackle of Silverwind straightening Tessali's injured knee. The screech that followed drowned out even the howling wind, prompting the Amnesian Hero to worry that it would reverberate through the conjunction. He clumped over to the bariaur's side.

"We should move on, if it is safe for Tessali."

"I'm feeling . . . better already." The elf sounded a little stronger, but his face remained pale with anguish. "And moving is safer than waiting here for the monster."

Silverwind gathered Tessali up. "I imagine this one will survive a short move."

The Amnesian Hero nodded, then stooped down to pick up the amphora.

"We need no more . . . giants," gasped Tessali. "Leave it!"

"That I cannot do. Poseidon charged me deliver this amphora to the Lady of Pain." The Thrasson lifted the jar and slipped the sling over his shoulders. Even that effort seemed to make him hotter and thirstier. "And, just as importantly, I think it has my lost memories."

"Pah! Those memories, they are the Lady's." Jayk tottered over to join them, reeling as though she might fall unconscious any moment. "You only think they are yours."

The Amnesian Hero steadied her. "I know my own mother."

"Then you tell us about her, yes?"

"Of course." Still supporting the wobbly tiefling, the Thrasson led the way toward the archway beneath Periphetes's bent knees. "She is a beautiful princess, with olive skin and honey-brown hair."

"And?"

"And what? I only saw her for a moment."

"I fear Jayk . . . could be right." Tessali, still being carried in Silverwind's arms, was close behind the Amnesian Hero. "If this is truly your own memory, you should recall more. Her name, perhaps."

They reached Periphetes. The wind was squeezing under the giant's bent legs with a chugging roar, blasting ash into their faces and threatening to sweep them from their feet. The Thrasson scooped Jayk into his arms, then pinched his eyes shut against the stinging dross and ducked through the archway. Hard as he tried, he could not drag his mother's name from the depths of his mind. He recalled only what he had learned during his vision.

A few steps later, the gale diminished to a bluster. The Thrasson opened his eyes, blinked away a flood of sweat, and, through the billowing haze ahead, saw the dark mouth of a side passage. He still could not remember his mother's name.

"What of . . . the name?" asked Tessali.

"If I say I saw my mother, then I saw my mother!" The Amnesian Hero scowled over his shoulder. "And even if I am wrong, I am still bound to deliver this amphora to the Lady of Pain!"

Tessali could only shake his head. "It is no wonder . . . we are in the mazes."

"I would not wish anguish on anyone, elf, but I liked you better when you were too pained to speak."

Too hot and drained to continue carrying Jayk, the Amnesian Hero returned her to the ground and, still supporting her with an arm, clumped into the side passage. This corridor looked much the same as the one from which they had come, with high, powdery walls and a whirling ash haze that at times reduced visibility to an arm's length. Being careful to stay within Silverwind's sight, the Thrasson worked his way along the wall, taking first two right turns, then shifting to the opposite side of the passage and taking three lefts. At last, they stopped to rest in a short dead-end blind where, with no wind howling down the passage, the ash remained on the ground.

The Thrasson wiped the sweat off his face, only to find fresh runnels pouring down it before he finished. He took a long drink of wine–it tasted cooler than before–then offered the skin to his companions. "Does anyone want some before I go?"

"Go?" Jayk clutched his arm. "Where?"

The Amnesian Hero pointed up the short passage, to where a curtain of blowing ash marked the corridor from which they had just come. "Someone's got to keep watch."

"No wine . . . for me," said Tessali. "And you shouldn't–"

"I've told him so." Silverwind, already examining one of the elf's wounds, did not look up as he spoke. "But he is a stubborn one. No need to worry, though; I imagine that fever of his will knock him out soon."

"You imagine wrong, Silverwind." The Thrasson turned to clump toward the intersection. "When you finish with Tessali, I will be waiting."

"And I will be with him," said Jayk. "Maybe some wine will take the bite off this headache."

"It would be better to wait until I can imagine some water." Silverwind looked up from Tessali's wound. "With that head injury, I fear wine could undo you."

Jayk whirled on the bariaur. "Life is an illusion, but this pain is not!" She pursed her lips and spewed a plume of damp ash in the general direction of the bariaur's hooves. "I spit on your water!"

The Amnesian Hero passed the wineskin to the tiefling. "Jayk, it is good to have you with us again."

They went to the intersection together. The Thrasson slipped the amphora off his back and leaned it against the ash wall, then sat down amidst the eddies of dross swirling in from the main corridor. He felt more overheated than feverish, and it seemed to him that the weakness in his muscles resulted more from thirst than illness. Nevertheless, when he reached around to touch the scratch on his side, he was surprised to feel how sore it was, and how hot it seemed under his fingertips.

The tiefling settled in beside him, and they sat quietly for a time, passing the wine back and forth, washing the dross down with long sips of sweet ambrosia. When they had both drank their fill, Jayk pushed the stopper into the mouth of the wineskin. She placed the sack between them, then braced her elbows on her knees and held her head between her hands.

After a time, the tiefling said, "Tessali, maybe he is right." She picked up an ash clod and tossed it at the amphora. "You should throw that jar over the wall."

The Thrasson was glad he was not drinking at the moment, for he would have spewed a mouthful of good wine onto the ground. "Jayk, what's wrong with you? Better than anyone, you know why I can never do that."

The tiefling shot the amphora a black look. "You are so simple, Zoombee. Poseidon, he tricked you."

"Nevertheless, I promised to deliver the amphora to the Lady of Pain, not to cast it away in the mazes."

"What does your promise mean here?" Jayk thrust a hand skyward. "The Lady of Pain does not want the jar, and it is only trouble to us."

"It is more than that to me."

"Pah! That vision was meant for the Lady. Why would Poseidon put *your* memories in a gift to someone else?"

"I don't know—he promised to restore my memories after I delivered the amphora." The Thrasson found himself staring at the jar and, through an act of will, looked back to the main corridor. "Perhaps he wanted them to return to me when the Lady of Pain opened the jar. The gods enjoy spectacles like that, you know."

Jayk rolled her dark eyes, then winced at the pain it caused her. "If Poseidon wishes to impress someone, I think it is the Lady, not you."

Unable to argue with the tiefling's point, the Thrasson snatched the wineskin. "I can't explain why the vision came from the amphora, but I *know* it was my mother." He swallowed a mouthful of wine, then said, "Maybe what the amphora holds aren't memories, but spells that summon lost memories."

"Or maybe they are spells that make you think you remember what you don't, or maybe they are djinn tricksters, or maybe they are what could be but isn't," Jayk scoffed. "We don't know. You must throw that jar away before another giant gets loose. We have enough trouble."

"I would never think to hear you sound like Tessali." The Amnesian Hero raised his sweaty brow, unleashing a cascade of salty drips that had been gathering above his eyes. "You're *scared!*"

Jayk began to rub her forehead with the heels of her hands, but not quickly enough to hide the flash in her eyes. "Scared? Of what, Zoombee?"

"You tell me—I know you're not afraid of dying." The Amnesian Hero pointed at the amphora. "It's something in there."

The tiefling pulled her hands away from her face, and, a little too steadily, she locked gazes with the Thrasson.

"What is in the jar makes no difference to me; if you think it has your memories, why don't you open it?" She stood and stepped over to the amphora. "I will do it for you, yes?"

"No!" The Thrasson jumped to his feet. Jayk was scared; he knew that, though not as certainly as he knew she would pull the stopper just to prove him wrong. He grabbed her arms and drew her away. "You mustn't open it!"

"Why not, Zoombee?" Jayk's smirk was just broad enough to betray her relief. "I thought you wanted to know who you are."

"You know why you can't open it," the Thrasson growled. "No matter what the amphora contains, it's not mine to open."

"Too bad." Jayk thrust out her lip in an exaggerated pout, and that gesture was what betrayed her secret fear to the Amnesian Hero. "I know how important it is for you find out who you are."

"And why should that frighten you?" the Thrasson demanded. "Are you afraid that if I remember who I am, I'll forget about you?"

Jayk could not hide the force with which the question struck.

Her pupils instantly took the shape of diamonds, and the tips of her fangs dropped into view. Her murky face grew even darker, though it was impossible to say whether in anger or sorrow, and she slumped to the ground.

"Jayk, you have nothing to worry about. I have promised to return you to Sigil." Had the Amnesian Hero not witnessed the deadly effects of her bite, he would have squatted down to embrace her. "By now, you must know I am a man of my word."

"Zoombee, I am not afraid of being forgotten; before we reach the One Death, we must forget all." The tiefling looked up; there were emerald tears welling in her eyes. "I am sad because you are going the wrong way!"

DREAM GIRL

I thought him stronger than to sit ruby-faced with his salt-damp back to the ashen wall, wound fever burning in his eyes and a thief's craving smoldering in his soul. For an hour (or a day or a week or a minute, for all it matters to us or him) he has been sitting there, staring at those crocodile sandals and that golden sword, wondering: do I dare, and do I dare? He has walked the narrow streets and breathed the yellow fog; he has cracked the jar of memories and split the gates of Sigil and dared disturb the multiverse, and now he frets over a giant's booty?

Call him honorable, call him ethical if you like; it makes no difference to me. The Thrasson has taken himself to a place where there is only desire and action and consequence, and now he has gone off into the blinds to search for right and wrong and lost his way. There are no commandments or codes in the mazes; the madman who looks for guidance is more lost than the fool who does not; he imagines reasons to turn one way and not the other; he waits upon signs that have no meaning; he does not act for fear of offending deities that cannot see him and would not care if they could.

I call him a coward.

In the end, the Amnesian Hero will lace those sandals on his feet, and he will learn the name of his parent—but first he must agonize over his scruples. He must consider his honor and ask his gods for guidance, he must weigh the killing of the giant against his oath to deliver the amphora, and he must find sanction to claim the plunder. Until then, we are expected to wait while he deliberates, to watch through a mind clouded with fever and wine as he sits and thinks and argues—and I won't abide that kind of drivel.

So I will tell you now what will happen. The Thrasson will put the sandals on the ground, then he will bare one foot and set it upon a rugged sole. He will feel an uncomfortable sizzling in the arch of his foot. A pair of ashen arms will sprout beside his ankle; they will take up the legging thews and wrap them about his calves, and a wispy voice will come on the wind:

"I offer you this advice, my son: when you reach the palace of King Aegeus, do not tell him at once whose blood flows in your veins. Say instead that you bear greetings and news from his friend in Troezen, King Pittheus. When he sees the sandals you wear and the sword that hangs at your side, he will ask where you came by them; if King Aegeus strikes you as a good and honorable man, you may tell him how you found them. In that manner, he will discover for himself that you are his son and will not doubt your claim to his city. But if King Aegeus seems a jealous and selfish man, you must tell him they are a betrothal gift from a granddaughter of King Pittheus; he will think I bore him a daughter and bear you no malice, and then you will be free to return home without fear of treachery or harm."

Thus will the Thrasson discover the name of one father. He will cry out in joy. He will shake so hard that when he sets his brick foot upon the second sandal, he will almost lose his balance—but you will have to wait to learn what happens then. Now, the Amnesian Hero still sits against the ashen wall, seeking consent to do what we all know he will surely do; Jayk rests warm against his flank, as idle and silent as a corpse; Tessali is limping up the passage, one swollen knee as red and round as a blood melon.

"Go ahead." The elf has hung his shredded cloak over his shoulders, though the monster did not leave enough of the garment to conceal the stitch lines striping his slender torso. "There's nothing stopping you."

"Stopping me from what?" The Amnesian Hero's voice had finally returned to normal, and if his tongue sounded a little thick, he felt sure that it had more to do with his fever than with the wine he had drunk. He swung his gaze back toward the adjacent passage and stared into the swirling cloud of ash. "I am only keeping watch."

"Yes—on those." Tessali raised his arm and—wincing at the pain it caused him—pointed at the sandals in the Thrasson's lap. "You want to put them on and see what happens."

"How do you know that?" The Amnesian Hero sounded less contradictory than irritated. "Can a man have no privacy even in his own thoughts?"

"Not when he wears them on his face for everyone to see. Besides, if you think it was your mother you saw—"

"I *did* see my mother."

"Of course." Tessali nodded as though he had never doubted it. "So it's only natural that you should want to see what happens if you wear the sandals. I don't see any reason you shouldn't."

"Except that the sandals are not mine to wear."

"How do you know that unless you try them on?"

The Amnesian Hero narrowed his eyes. "You seem anxious for me to wear them."

Tessali shrugged. "We will not solve this mystery until you do." The elf cast a wary glance at the amphora, which the Thrasson had tried to patch with a coating of wine-soaked ash. "And it would be better to know the truth before we start out again. Assuming the exit is close to where Silverwind found the thread—"

"It is."

The Thrasson's conviction did not seem to reassure Tessali. "Yes—well, in that case, the last thing we'll want is another surprise from your jar."

The Amnesian Hero smirked. "I know what you're thinking, elf."

"So, I'm not the only one who reads minds?"

Ignoring the sarcasm, the Amnesian Hero said, "Your plan won't work." He wiped a bead of fever sweat from his eyes, then looked at Tessali. "Even if I put the sandals on and remember nothing more of my mother, I would not be disappointed enough to throw the amphora over a wall—nor would I allow you to."

Tessali raised his arched eyebrows just enough to make the Amnesian Hero wonder if he had guessed wrong. "So, what are you afraid of?"

"Nothing!" Even as the Amnesian Hero snapped the word, he realized the very quickness of his answer had betrayed him. Addled as his thoughts were by fever and fatigue—and by wine as well—perhaps now was not the best time to match wits with Tessali. "But I have sworn an oath, and I do not take oaths lightly."

"I can see you don't." Tessali sighed, sounding more relieved than disappointed. "If there's no convincing you, I guess I'd better just have a look at Jayk."

"Perhaps we should let Silverwind do it." It was growing increasingly difficult to guess Tessali's game, and the Amnesian Hero did not want Jayk's condition to become part of the elf's manipulations. "He was the one who mended her skull."

"Sorry. The Imaginer of the Multiverse has worn himself out mending his creations." Tessali nodded toward the back of the passage, where Silverwind lay stretched out on his side. The old bariaur's eyes were closed, and his ribs were rising with the steady rhythm of someone deep in sleep. "Let's hope he's dreaming of us. I'd hate to vanish just because he fell asleep."

The Amnesian Hero would not let the elf's humor disarm him. "We can wait."

Tessali shook his head. "We don't want her to sleep too long. It's dangerous for people with head injuries."

With no further debate, the elf stepped around the Amnesian Hero and went to Jayk's side. As he squatted down beside her, he grimaced and dropped a hand to his ribs.

"I hope the monster does not find us soon. I won't be able to run," groaned Tessali. "Silverwind claims he healed the cracked ones, but they still feel broken to me."

"Good. I will know where to hit you if this is another ruse."

Tessali accepted the warning with a good-natured smile. "You are a peery one, aren't you?"

The elf turned back to Jayk, calling her name and gently jostling her shoulder. She did not stir. Tessali frowned and pulled her away from the Amnesian Hero's side, shaking her more violently.

The tiefling remained as limp as empty clothes.

"How long has she been asleep?" Tessali demanded.

"It may have been half an hour." The Amnesian Hero did not think Tessali was trying to manipulate him. As hard as the elf was shaking her, Jayk should have been awake. "What's wrong?"

"Abyss Sleep," said the elf. "On occasion, someone who's been hit on the head falls asleep so deeply that he is unable to awaken."

Tessali thumbed Jayk's eyes open and cursed, then shoved her at the Amnesian Hero. "Shake her, hard!"

The Thrasson sat the sandals and sword aside and obeyed.

Tessali astonished him by slapping the tiefling and yelling, *"Jayk!"* When she failed to respond, he slapped her again, then glanced up at the Amnesian Hero. "Shake her!"

The Thrasson, who had not realized he had stopped, renewed his efforts–then nearly lost his hold as Jayk lunged for Tessali's throat. The astonished elf fell backward into the ash and scrambled away, his eyes round as coins. The sudden tension drained from the tiefling's body; she groaned once and grabbed her head.

"Ah, Zoombee! She hurts so much."

Jayk had barely uttered the words before her chin slumped to her chest. The Amnesian Hero began to shake her again.

"That's enough." Tessali crawled forward and carefully raised an eyelid. "We only needed to wake her briefly."

"Is she well?"

"She'll survive, but she won't be well until she spends some time in the Gatehouse. You know that."

The Amnesian Hero fell silent and leaned back against the ashen wall. Even through his fever-clouded, wine-hazed mind, he could see Tessali was right. Jayk's peculiar beliefs about her relationship to death made her a danger to herself and others—especially to others. And perhaps the Thrasson would have admitted that, had his own experience not proven the Bleak Cabal's penchant for caging people of perfectly sound mind. As it was, he thought the tiefling justified in charging that the only way those confined in the Gatehouse ever left was by becoming Bleakers themselves.

The Amnesian Hero pulled Jayk close and wrapped her in his arm. "I suppose you'll give us adjoining cells?"

Tessali was quick to shake his head. "You're well enough—or you will be, once I help you remember who you are."

The Amnesian Hero gave Tessali a wary gaze. "I have not asked your help, elf."

"There's nothing to fear. The hardest part will be figuring out how to administer to your loss. There are many ways to lose one's memory."

The Amnesian Hero could not prevent himself from being interested. "There are?"

Tessali nodded. "A blow to the head, an impairment of the emotions, an event too frightening to recall, drinking from the River Styx . . . " The elf paused and pointed to the flattened wineskin. "Or, more likely in your case, being too fond of wine."

"I am not too fond of wine." The Amnesian Hero looked toward the adjacent passage and stared into the blowing ash. "I was thirsty."

Tessali laid a hand across the Thrasson's forehead. "It's no wonder, as hot as you are." He reached into the pocket of his shredded cloak and extracted two holly leaves. They were both smeared with blood from his injuries. "I am not as skilled as Silverwind, but I can break your fever and mend your wound."

The Amnesian Hero continued to stare into the ash. The last time he had allowed Tessali to cast a spell on him, he had ended up with a brick foot. The elf had claimed it was the only thing he could do to save his life, but it had since occurred to the Thrasson that it was also a good way to keep an escaped patient from fleeing again.

"It would be best to let me do what I can," said Tessali. "Healing wounds is tiring work, and Silverwind will have plenty to do before any of us are ready to run again. Whatever I can do to spare him may make the difference between going to where he found the thread or waiting here until the monster finds us."

Tessali's warning did not go unheeded. The Amnesian Hero was already surprised at how long it was taking the monster to find them; part of him feared the beast was in the adjacent passage at that moment, standing camouflaged amidst the swirling ash, watching and waiting until the Thrasson nodded off. Only the steady roar of the ashen gale reassured him this was not the case; a creature that large could not come down the corridor without causing a sudden change of pitch in the howling wind.

Reluctantly, the Amnesian Hero nodded. "Do what you can for me. But if this is one of your tricks–"

"Truly, you have no reason to worry. I will even keep watch while you sleep."

"Sleep?"

"Of course. We are all in need of rest, and, after your long run, you more than any of us." Tessali picked up the wineskin and shook it. There was little fluid left to slosh in the bottom of the bag. "Besides, given your fever and how much of this you have had, it is a wonder you have not passed out already."

"If it's going to make me sleep, you can put that holly back in your pocket. I am no fool. As soon as I close my eyes, you'll throw my amphora over the wall."

"And follow it over when you wake? You must think *I'm* barmy."

"I am no murderer," the Amnesian Hero bristled. "No matter how angry–"

Tessali waved the Thrasson silent. "I'm sorry. I know you would never do such a thing–any more than I would throw away what belongs to you–but I don't know why you're so distrustful of me." The elf paused a moment, then said, "Let us agree on this: if the amphora isn't here when you awake, I'll accept any punishment you mete out."

The Amnesian Hero asked, "Why are you so concerned with my health?"

"Pure self-preservation. You're as much my way out of the mazes as you are Silverwind's. If we run into that monster again—and I don't doubt we will—you're the only one who seems capable of slaying it."

"Have you forgotten the last time?" The Thrasson gestured at the elf's wounds. "I didn't do very well."

"We're alive, aren't we? And you felled that giant nicely," Tessali pointed out. "When the monster comes the next time, perhaps Jayk and I can be ready with some magic. We all stand a better chance of getting out of here if we work together."

"That is the truest thing I have ever heard you say." The Amnesian Hero paused, glancing at the sword and sandals lying by his side. "Now that you are in a more truthful mood, tell me why you want me to put the sandals on."

"I don't want you to; I think you must," the elf answered. "To me, it makes no difference whether you put the sandals on or throw them over the wall. But *you* won't be happy until you try them on, and it would be better for all of us if that wasn't distracting you right now."

The explanation seemed both practical enough and adequately lacking in principle to convince the Amnesian Hero that Tessali was being honest. "What you say is true enough, but you forget they may not be mine."

"Bar that!" said Tessali. "You are the one who felled Periphetes, not the Lady. That makes them yours by right of combat."

"Perhaps, but the issue is not clear." As much as the Amnesian Hero wanted to accept the elf's reasoning, he feared even more the possibility that doing so would be a breach of honor. "If my neighbor's bull breaks free and wanders onto my lands, I may certainly kill it to spare my cows. But then do I have the right to slaughter it and eat it?"

"Better that than to leave it rotting because he is away," countered Tessali. "And if you can give him some extra meat later because of what you ate from his bull, then he will be better off than had you dragged the beast back to rot on his land. Certainly, it would have been better for all had the bull stayed at home, but it did not and now it is your duty to do as well by your neighbor as you can."

The Amnesian Hero knitted his brow, trying in vain to clearly see the analogy through the haze in his head. "I fail to see what this bull has to do with my sandals."

"If you don't put the sandals on, you'll remain distracted and we'll all be killed," Tessali explained. "The Lady's bull will rot in the field."

"That's true." The Amnesian Hero began to unlace his own sandal. "I am doing good for her, am I not?"

What a pointless thing is the mortal mind; with its snaking walls and untold conjunctions and endless looping passages, it is a maze that builds itself–a maze where every path always leads wherever the captive wishes. Where is the challenge in that? Was there ever any doubt that the Thrasson would step into the sandal? I said he would, and even now his bare foot is settling upon the insole.

You recall what comes next: the ashen arms rising to lace the thews, the voice on the wind offering advice, the mention of King Aegeus, one of his two fathers. So you will not be surprised to see the joyful tears streaming down his flushed cheeks, or to hear him bellowing, "I am the son of Aegeus! I am the grandson of Pittheus! I am the son of . . ."

Here, it will occur to the Amnesian Hero that he does not know the name of his mother. He will look down and realize that he cannot remove the sandal from his brick foot, and a cry of despair will rise from his throat. Tessali will place the new sandal on the ground and suggest it still might work its magic. The Thrasson's legs will start to tremble so hard that he can hardly stand. He will support himself by grasping the Bleaker's shoulder–a poignant touch, that–and begin to lower his foot.

All that could have happened by now, had the Amnesian Hero not spent so long fretting over what is right and what is wrong. But he pondered and brooded and wasted a precious hour seeking to justify what he already knew he would do. And so he has not yet heard the voice on the wind or learned his father's name or realized that he still does not know his mother's; only now are the ashen arms rising to lace the sandal thews about his leg. We must wait for the woman to speak, and for the Thrasson to bellow his joy and realize what he does not know, and all the while there is a figure in the adjacent passage skulking through the gray, howling haze.

To be certain, matters would be different had the Amnesian Hero no fear of dishonor (I called him a coward, and every coward fears something), had he not squandered priceless time in pointless debate, had he acted without awaiting the permission of an eel-tongued elf. But it is the Thrasson's nature to act when he should ponder and ponder when he should act, and to deny him his quandary would have been violence to his character. Better to let him grapple with his honor, to let him reluctantly forsake his morals and slide unwittingly into the abyss of iniquity; better to leave him to his palter, no matter the consequence, than to let him come off a high-talking fraud.

And now the Thrasson has caught his story: his brick foot is quaking upon the crocodile sole, his hand is clamping the elf's shoulder, his eyes are waiting for the arms to rise from the ash. I hope you will not be disappointed by what follows next:

Nothing.

On trembling legs, the Amnesian Hero stood waiting for the second sandal to work its sorcery. In his mind, he could almost hear his mother's voice, whispering both her name and his in words too wind-garbled to comprehend. But no magic sizzled into his foot, no arms rose from the ash to lace the thews about his leg, no words of motherly advice came to him on the roaring wind. His brick foot remained stone-numb in its brick sandal. His stomach seemed heavy and cold, and his knees felt ready to buckle. The Thrasson twisted his foot against the insole, as though grinding the sandal into the dross might summon forth the ashen arms. Nothing happened, except that he grew even more despairing and frustrated.

"It's this damned brick foot!" The Amnesian Hero tried not to sound as though he were blaming the elf for the problem, though of course he was. He could not help himself. "The magic will not work through brick."

"I doubt it would have worked through ooze, either." Tessali kneeled at the feet of the Amnesian Hero. "But you have flesh above the ankle. Perhaps if I lace the thews . . ."

The elf crossed two laces over the Amnesian Hero's shin, wrapping the thews in a half square-knot so they would not slip, then ran them behind his calf. This time, as Tessali tied the half-knot, the Thrasson felt the thongs biting into his leg. He resisted the temptation to look down, knowing he would only be disappointed by the sight of the straps still glowing with their magic.

The elf crossed the laces once more and made a third half-knot before the Amnesian Hero noticed the slight rise in the pitch of the wind. Even as he turned to see what was coming down the adjacent passage, the Thrasson was unsheathing that star-forged blade of his. Tessali, rising too fast, nearly lost an ear as the sword flashed past his head.

"What is it?" the elf whispered.

"Trouble most untimely." The Thrasson saw nothing save ash whirling down the adjacent corridor, but the *pop-pop, pop-pop-pop* of shaggy mats of fur came loud to his ears. "Wake Jayk and Silverwind–and have no fear of drawing that." He pointed at the golden sword he had left lying beside the tiefling.

"We'll come back once I've roused them." Tessali scooped up the sword and Jayk–with an anguished groan–then limped toward the back of the blind. "Try to hold the fight until we return."

The Amnesian Hero did not say so, but he doubted he would have much choice in the matter. The monster of the labyrinth had already proven itself to be a cunning hunter. Certainly, it would see the advantage in attacking while its foes were lethargic and trapped in a dead-end blind. The company's best chance, whether for victory or flight, lay in stalling the beast until Tessali roused the others. The Thrasson stepped into the adjacent passage, then, staying close to the wall where he would prove more difficult to see, started forward to ambush the beast.

The wine and fever had taken a heavier toll on his body than he realized. Within a few clumping steps, he was dizzy and coated with sweat-moistened ash. His breath came ragged and hot, and his star-forged sword felt as heavy as the iron blades of the githyanki bounty hunters. In no condition for a long battle, he knew that his best tactic would be to lop off one of the creature's feet and flee back to his companions.

The Amnesian Hero dropped to his belly, then crawled to the center of the passage. He scooped out a shallow pit to lie in, then swept a coating of ash over his back. With any luck, the monster would not see him until he raised himself to attack, and by then it would be too late. The Thrasson closed his eyes against the stinging ash–this close to the ground it was so thick that it clung to his eyeballs like flour to wet grapes–and trusted his ears to tell him when the beast arrived.

It required only a moment for the flapping sounds to grow loud enough for him to tell the creature was creeping down one side of the passage. The Amnesian Hero reoriented himself slightly. Then, wishing he had some wine to wash a mounting cough from his throat, he raised himself to his knees and hefted his sword.

Instead of the hulking, half-visible silhouette of the shaggy monster, the Amnesian Hero found himself staring at the ghostly shape of a beautiful woman. So blurred by blowing ash and the flapping of her white gown was her statuesque figure that the Thrasson thought he was imagining her–which, as Silverwind would have hastened to point out, made her no less real–and he began to think he had fallen into a fever dream.

Then the wind lifted her silky jet hair away from her cheek, revealing smooth olive skin and a regal nose, and the Amnesian Hero knew that his fever had nothing to do with her appearance. It was the same woman he had seen in Rivergate and a hundred other inns, his wine woman; even in the Lady's mazes, she had come to him.

Her emerald eyes swung in the Thrasson's direction, and it was then that, if illusion she was, he lost control of his own imagination. A cry of surprise broke from her lips. Her gaze flickered briefly to the sword raised in his hand, then she turned and fled the way she had come.

"Hold!" The Amnesian Hero sprang—or rather lurched—to his feet. "I mean you no harm!"

The woman did not slow. The Thrasson clumped after her as best he could, rasping for breath and raining sweat into the ash. He had to run with blade in hand, for he had not a spare moment to sheathe his sword. Already, his quarry was a mere white blur in the howling gray ahead, and he hardly dared to blink for fear of losing her. More times than he could count, she had vanished in a mere instant of inattentiveness, and he knew she would be gone the instant he glanced at his scabbard. The woman turned down a side passage. The Amnesian Hero staggered after her, certain she would be gone when he rounded the corner.

She was there, a white blur standing in the center of the passage.

"Wait!"

The woman turned and darted down another corridor, which the Thrasson had not seen through the blowing ash. He felt something pop on his leg above the brick foot and recalled that Tessali had not finished lacing the magic sandals. The highest half-knot had come unfastened. He continued to run. She would vanish soon enough, and then he would worry about the sandal.

The Amnesian Hero's vision blurred, and it seemed to him that the hot sweat pouring off his body was melting flesh. His lungs ached and his muscles burned and his head spun, and still he hobbled after the woman. She rounded another corner, and he found himself struggling to remember whether this was her third turn or fourth, and whether one had been left and the rest right. He stumbled and almost allowed himself to fall, confident she would be gone when he rounded the corner.

Just make the turn, he told himself, and she will be gone. Then it will be time to rest.

A second half-knot popped. One more, and he would lose the sandal—and this time he would not feel the thews slacken.

The Thrasson rounded the corner and knew by the sudden stillness that he had entered a blind. He stumbled out of the ash wind, coughing and choking and dizzy; there, a dozen paces ahead, stood his wine woman, staring into the hovering black square of a maze conjunction. She was facing away, hands clasped before her torso as though wringing them. The Amnesian Hero stopped where he stood and, without taking his eyes off the woman's back, found his scabbard and sheathed his sword.

Only then did he speak, and only in his softest, calmest rasp. "Please, you have . . . nothing to fear . . . from me."

The woman turned and, to the surprise of the Amnesian Hero, did not flee. Her mouth fell open and her hands rose to her cheeks. She stumbled a single step forward, staring at the Thrasson as though she were looking at a dead man, which he suspected was exactly what he resembled.

"Can it be?" she gasped. "I have been searching for you for so long!"

The Thrasson's trembling legs chose that moment to buckle, and he dropped to his knees in the ash. He opened his mouth, but when he tried to speak, he found his heart had risen into his throat. He could not force the words out.

The woman slowly came forward, her hands reaching uncertainly toward him. "I thought you would come back for me."

The Amnesian Hero swallowed his heart down to where it belonged, then touched his fingers to his cheeks. "So you know this face?" he asked. "And this voice? You know who I am?"

The woman stopped, her emerald eyes now growing wary. "Of course I know you! You stole me from my cruel father and carried me across the sea! Don't you remember?"

"I do not." The Amnesian Hero forgot himself then and closed his eyes. "My memory is lost. I awoke on a beach in Thrassos, and I recall nothing of the time before–not even my name."

The Thrasson's only answer was a long silence. He cursed himself for a fool, and open flew his eyes.

The woman was still there. "How could you forget me?"

Tears began to stream down her cheeks, and she turned away. Thinking she was about to flee, the Amnesian Hero raised one knee and started to rise. The woman buried her face in her hands.

"Don't!" she cried. It was more a plea than a command. "How could you forget? We loved each other once!"

"And I love you still, I am sure. Help me remember!"

The Amnesian Hero braced his hands on his knee and pushed himself up. Then, as he started to step forward, his brick foot caught on something and snagged. The Thrasson stumbled and, in his weakened state, fell back to his knees. He looked down and saw that the second sandal's loose thews had gotten caught beneath his good foot.

Cursing himself for a buffoon, he started to rise again, this time bringing his good foot forward first. "Beautiful lady, if you loved me and love me still, then truly I am the man most blessed by the gods," he said. "When we return to Arborea, the citizens of Thrassos will shower us with rose petals."

When the Amnesian Hero raised his gaze, he found that he was speaking only to himself. The wine woman had vanished again.

PAINS OF THE HEART

Like pillars they stand, there among the ash-eddies—demented bariaur, bombastic elf, blood-loving tiefling—all peering into the roaring drabness of the adjacent passage, all searching for the absent Thrasson, all sure they will see the monster instead. They carry spells primed on their tongues and weapons ready in their hands, and they know better than to think they will survive without the Amnesian Hero. He is their way out, their strength, their confidence, and, though they know it not, their curse.

The Thrasson has nourished well his deep-rooted Pains, and some have grown round and heavy and rubbed off on his companions. The pods hang fat and firm on their bodies; already, some have ruptured upon Jayk and Tessali, and more are ready. They have stopped throbbing, and their skins are thin and tight and transparent. It will not take much to split them—a careless gesture or a callous word—so we must be watchful, vigilant even. As ripe as they are, the Pains might burst all at once, and that would not be something to miss.

You must not call me cruel—never cruel! The suffering of others brings me no joy—or remorse—I do only what must be done. If, knowing the Pains they bear, you fear for the Amnesian Hero and his friends, do not despair. Think on this: it is only by trial that we learn resolve, by ordeal that we earn strength, by tribulation that we grow brave, by turmoil that we win wisdom. Yes, they will suffer torment unimaginable, they will endure anguish enough to crush a giant, they will bear grief to shatter a god—and yet, when the last blow is struck and the last word spoken, all will end well; they will be together, alive, triumphant, stronger than before—I promise you this.

But now the time has come to see the face beneath the black hood and look into the eyes that would rule me, to learn the name of the one who bought my heart. I lift one foot off the ground, then the other, and the Lady of Pain is there before them, standing among the ashen eddies, the hem of her gown floating just above the dross, the blades of her halo chiming in the wind.

Their spells melt like salt on their tongues; their weapon hands fall to their sides. Jayk, wisest of all, flees to the back of the blind. Silverwind steps forward, daring to think that he has imagined me. I flick my hand; he slams flank to ground, the breath shooting from his huge bariaur lungs in a single bleat. Tessali recovers from his shock and turns to flee, but a Pain picks that instant to burst; the elf remembers the amphora. He shoves the golden sword into his belt and turns to the vessel. I slash a fingernail through the air, and the hands that have offended me drop into the ash.

The elf does not scream. He is too stunned, or perhaps too frightened of affronting me further; he simply turns, both stumps trailing red, and runs after Jayk. I start to float toward the amphora, which takes me nearer gasping Silverwind. Though he has not recovered his wind, the old bariaur scrambles to his hooves and gallops away. A Pain bursts, spilling green ichor down his withers, and he does not break stride as he comes to the back of the blind. Instead, he springs into the air and disappears over the wall, his rear hooves clipping the crest as he passes out of sight, and only then does he realize what he has abandoned.

Jayk looks from the wall to me. Her murky complexion pales to pearl, then she grabs Tessali by the elbow and drags him to the two plumes of ash that mark where Silverwind left the blind. She laces her fingers together to boost the elf, who, aside from a forlorn glance at the hands he leaves behind, hesitates not at all to step into her palms. The tiefling heaves him over the wall and scrambles after, and then I am alone with the amphora.

How long I stare at the jar, I cannot say. In Sigil, mortals enter their little inns walking and come out crawling; the iron is poured hot into the mold and pulled out cold; the fingersmith is caught and judged and locked tight away, and still I stare. I have a churning coldness deep down inside. I feel myself quivering, and I ache with the weakness of mortals. The amphora can hold only ill for me, else the King of Seas would never have sent it, yet open it I must. Whether the net inside be twined from strands genuine or false, the truth remains of the void within my breast, and, no matter how unlikely, that a god might have what belongs in my chest is a threat to Sigil too great to allow.

I go to the amphora, but do not pull the stopper. That is what Poseidon would want. The memories would come swirling out all at once, overwhelming in number and power, and then would I be lost. Better to let them come singly, to sort and judge and to learn the extent of the Sea King's deceit in my own time.

I wipe the ashen patch from the jar's neck, then hold it on its side until a golden thread writhes from the crack. The strand is as yellow and fine as my wind-blown hair when I stood with Poseidon and my mother. Even now, I cannot say what magic this is, whether illusion or conjuration or healing, but it can be no happenstance the amphora looses golden filaments for me and black tatters for the Thrasson, and that is knowledge in itself.

I return the jar to its resting place, then step back. The strand writhes free and floats over to me. It circles my head once. My breath quickens, and a low, hissing wind gusts through the streets of the Lower Ward. The fiber circles twice, and an acrid drizzle falls in the Hive. Thus does the Lady of Pain betray her worry; we are one, Sigil and I.

A third time the strand circles, and from the emptiness in my chest rises a feathery effusion, an airy gush that flutters and ripples and grows ever more compelling. I feel my feet moving and my body spinning, and the lilt of a satyr's gay-hearted pipes tickles my ears. The smell of roast swine fills my nostrils. I find myself clasped in the brutish arms of a great bull-headed ogre, my golden hair flying about us as we whirl through a dance.

"Nay, marry not that foul one." His whispering voice is low and rumbling, his breath sweet with wine. "Come away with me, and I will spare you eternity in misery."

We whirl past the high table where sits Poseidon, an entire swine and a cask of wine before him. Seated with him is my groom, the black-cloaked helmsman of the black-sailed dhow. Save for two yellow eyes burning in the stygian depths beneath his hood, his face remains shadowed from view. In the center of the table sits my heart, still pulsing inside green-tinted glass; next to it, the bride's price, still locked away in four ebony boxes.

"Have no fear," whispers my bull-headed dance partner. "I will steal your heart, that Set will have no power over you, and I will steal the Pains, and make them a betrothal gift to you."

Set slams his fist down, and a thunderclap peals through the hall. The dark god rises from his seat and leans far over the table, and by the light of a candle I have my first glimpse of my groom. He has the hideous face of a jackal, with a long pointed snout and enormous ears and a coward's spiteful eyes.

"Have done with your whispering, and your dancing, Baphomet!" His voice yowls like steel upon the whetstone. "I will not have you soiling my bride with your filthy bull's tongue."

The music stops at once, yet Baphomet whirls me around one last time. "Be ready," he whispers. "Tonight."

He releases me, and again I am in the maze, hovering before the amphora with the bitter ash burning my nostrils and the roaring wind chugging in my ears and a thousand questions whirling in my mind. Well has Poseidon twined his net, that one question answered raises two even greater. Again, I must take up the jar. Another fiber snakes from the crack; I step back and wait as it circles me once; my dread wells, and claps of thunder roll through the Clerk's Ward. The strand rounds me again, and the Market Ward shudders with my trepidation.

The golden filament circles a third time, and from the void in my chest trickles a chill swirling, a numbing current that runs and purls and grows ever more cold. A foul, swampy stink hangs thick in the air, and a stinging wind bites at my flesh. I am kneeling at the brink of a vast salt plain, staring into the inky shallows of a broad, torpid river. The black sky is booming and yowling with my father's bellowing and Set's yelping.

"Drink and be safe." Baphomet stands at my side, a black satchel slung over his shoulder. I have not seen what is inside, but the bottom hangs low with something round and heavy. "Drink, and none will have power over you."

But I do not drink. Though I carry the four ebony boxes in my own satchel, Baphomet has not returned my heart to me. Though he denies it still, I suspect that is what he carries in his black sack, and I know that this is the River Lethe—some call it by another term, but they who have drunk from it can never recall its true name. If I swallow those dark waters, I will not remember Set, or my father, and then only he who holds my stolen heart will have power over me.

"Thieves!" booms Poseidon. "Return what you have stolen!"

"Wife-stealer!" Set howls.

Baphomet's eyes widen, for he is no match for my father's fury. "Drink!"

While I recall my father's name, ever will Poseidon have the power to find me. Still, I refuse. Why should I trade one master for another? Better that they should kill each other upon the salt plain, and by their blood that I should be free.

Now does Baphomet mark my plan. "Scheming woman!" With a circle of his wrist, he gathers my hair in his great hand and drags me forward. "You *will* drink!"

Quick is my hand to my dagger. Quicker still my dagger to my golden hair, and with a single slash the sharp blade cuts my bunched tresses. I fall back on my haunches. Baphomet screams and plunges headlong into the river, the dark waters closing fast over his body.

With Poseidon's bellow thundering in my ears and Set's yowling grating down my back, I watch the inky currents many moments before Baphomet surfaces far down the river. He is choking and gagging and spewing black water from his bull's nostrils. His arms are pounding the surface. The black satchel no longer hangs from his shoulder, and when his eyes turn in my direction, there is only emptiness and confusion in his gaze.

I rise and run along the bank. At last I glimpse the dark sack, floating a hundred paces ahead and drifting faster than I can run.

From the black sky booms my father's voice. "There, Foul One, upon the shores of the Styx! Hurry, or she is lost!"

I turn to face the river, but instead of black waters, I am staring at the amphora. The wind is roaring out of the adjacent passage, stirring up eddies of gray ash, and my mouth is parched with despair. Where now, my heart: Carceri, Avalas, Malbolge? Must I pull another strand to learn the answer, then another to discover hence from there?

From that void beneath my breast rises a fierce, tumultuous boiling; it matters not whether I pull the strands one at a time or all at once, I will never know the answer until I have emptied the jar—and, now I realize, not even then! If I did jump after the satchel, I would have forgotten the reason I leapt! A ferocious storm rises in Sigil: hailstones fall as large as fists, pounding roofs into rubble and striking men dead where they stand; gales blast through the lanes, smashing sedan chairs into walls and walls into each other; chains of lightning dance from fountain to fountain, shattering catch basins and choking deep-dug wells with rubble. The ground itself trembles beneath my rage, and fissures run down the streets side-by-side, racing to see which one can topple the most buildings. Thus does rapacious Poseidon hope to bring Sigil low: by stirring me to such a state that I destroy the city myself, so that he might stroll among the ruins and make a slave of me with nary a fight.

Perhaps, had I been fool enough to pull the stopper, the plan would have worked. The memories would have rushed from the jar and seized me one after another. In the fervor of the moment, I might have believed that I had jumped into the River Lethe after my heart, that I had drunk of its dark waters to escape Set my betrothed and Poseidon my father.

But if I drank then, how can I call the river now by its true name? Lethe.

Thus is Poseidon's treachery defeated, and now does the ground in Sigil stop quaking; the lightning fades to crackling forks, the hail blanches to cold rain, the wind but moans. The city is safe again, and so it will remain as long as the King of Seas' vile tricks remain safe inside the amphora.

And who can make that so, if not the Lady of Pain?

I fill my palm with ash, then wet it with blood squeezed from Tessali's severed hands. The patching paste is brown and coppery smelling, and sure to attract the monster of the labyrinth.

KARFHUD

There had been no choice, really, except to enter the conjunction. The only place for the wine woman to go had been through the black square, and so the Amnesian Hero had tucked the wayward sandal into his belt and followed. Unlike the first time he had entered one of the strange portals, he had experienced no sensation of falling, heard no great roaring, felt no wind tearing at his hair or ash scouring his face. He had merely stepped into the darkness and stood there waiting—forever it seemed—to emerge on the other side.

That was when the Amnesian Hero recalled the gout of flame that had nearly incinerated him earlier, as Silverwind stepped from the iron maze into the ashen one. The fireball had erupted the instant the bariaur passed through the conjunction: large, bright, and too hot to miss. And later, on the other side, he had cautioned the Thrasson about standing too close to the black square, for fear that it would "torch up" and draw the monster's attention.

There had been no fireball when the wine woman disappeared.

The Amnesian Hero stood pondering in the darkness, his mind spinning with fever and his sweaty body trembling with weakness. The wine woman could have gone no other place; the conjunction had been the only route out of the blind—at least that he had noticed. He considered going back to see if he had missed something, then found himself wondering if he *could* return. Presumably, the black square hung directly behind him, but what if he was moving? There was no fluttering in his stomach, no air stirring against his skin, no sensations at all suggesting motion—yet he had been standing there in the gloom quite some time. He had to be moving. He could imagine no other reason for the delay.

Better, then, to continue waiting. He could only guess what might happen if he tried to step one way or another while passing through a conjunction—would he come out someplace different than he should? Stay lost in the darkness forever? Vanish into oblivion? All these possibilities seemed disastrous. Moreover, even if the wine woman had disappeared down a side passage, she would be long gone by now. He could only hope that, just as this conjunction differed from the first in duration of crossing, it also differed in not expelling gouts of flame when someone stepped through.

Still, the Amnesian Hero saw no need to stand about in tomblike darkness. He pulled that star-forged sword from its scabbard and held the blade aloft.

"Starlight cleave the night," he commanded.

A brilliant blue radiance burst from the tip, creating a small globe that bathed the area in an eerie sapphire light. After the long darkness, the sudden illumination hurt the Thrasson's eyes, and he was still trying to blink away his blindness when he perceived a woman-sized shape slipping from the brightened circle.

"Wait, I beg you!"

Eyes half shut, the Amnesian Hero started after the fleeing figure and found himself clumping down a narrow dirt lane. A row of windowless mud brick tenements bordered the street on each side, their open doorways as still and black as a conjunction square. The Thrasson cursed himself for a berk, wondering how long he had been standing about in the dark thinking himself caught between mazes. It was a wonder the wine woman had still been near when he lit his sword.

"Please . . . wait!" he gasped. "I'm too . . . sick to keep this . . . up."

The Amnesian Hero clumped past an intersection and saw, out of the corner of his eye, the woman's figure turning to flee. In the blue light, her gown looked more gray than white, and her shoulders seemed somewhat more hunched than he remembered, but there was no time to ponder the differences. The Thrasson lurched into the alley and lunged out to catch hold of her.

Her shoulder seemed soft and spongy, and the cloth covering it had the dusty, brittle feel of ancient linen. The gown was no longer belted at the waist, but hung like a sack, dingy and stained, down past her knees. In the sword's blue light, her hair looked colorless and drab; it was also stiff as straw, and so thin it barely concealed her red-blotched scalp.

"Lady? Is that . . . you?"

The woman's only reply was to lean forward and try to pull away. The Amnesian Hero squeezed her shoulder—then groaned in disgust as her flesh erupted beneath his grasp. A foul, too-sweet stench filled the air, and a warm, slimy fluid coated his fingertips. He pulled his arm away, still holding a handful of moldering cloth and some brownish stuff that had probably once been flesh.

The Amnesian Hero gawked at his hand. "I . . ." He could not think of the words to apologize. "Lady, please forgive my clumsiness! I meant no harm."

"What did you mean?" The woman's voice was haggard. She spun on the Thrasson, raising a lumpy, gnarled mass at the end of a scaly arm. She extended her index finger, all that remained on the hand, and pointed at her head. "To look on this? Is that what you meant?"

The Amnesian Hero struggled not to retch. The woman's face was a sagging mass of folded flesh and festering boils, so grotesquely misshapen that it scarcely looked human. A pair of black marbles peered out from beneath a puffy brow, while her nose had vanished—nostrils and all—into an enormous dark nodule that had taken over the middle of her face. Only her mouth, an enormous gash rimmed by red, cracked lips, remotely resembled its original form.

"I . . . I beg your . . . pardon." The Amnesian Hero suddenly felt very weak and braced his ichor-covered hand against a wall. Twice had he braved the Leper Cities of Acheron to rescue the Virgins of Marmara, and never had he set eyes on such a gruesome, pitiable visage. "I thought you were . . . I was looking for a young woman in white. . . . Perhaps you saw her . . . come this way?"

"How do you know you haven't found her?" So deep and rumbling was this new voice that the Thrasson seemed to hear it in the pit of his stomach. "In this place, we all wish we were someone else."

Behind the woman appeared an enormous darkness, not creeping into the sapphire light so much as forcing back the radiance. The gloomy figure stood easily half again as tall as a man, with a torso so broad it filled most of the narrow lane. As the Amnesian Hero's eyes grew more accustomed to looking at what was essentially a darker shadow standing in the murk, he saw—or imagined he saw—two maroon eyes flashing somewhere beneath a set of wickedly curved horns. Behind the creature's broad shoulders, there seemed to be a pair of folded wings that rose a good six feet above its head and ended there in two bony hooks.

The newcomer leaned over the woman, bringing his head toward the glowing sword and highlighting the curved horns and maroon eyes the Amnesian Hero had noticed earlier. Even so, it was not until the dark visage actually entered the globe of light that the sapphire glow brightened its features. Hidden beneath sagging folds and black nodules similar to those covering the woman's face were the venom-dripping fangs and vaguely apelike muzzle of a great tanar'ri.

The Amnesian Hero grew suddenly as hot as steam. A distant ringing filled his ears, his vision blackened around the edges, and he felt too frail to stand. The fiend pushed his face closer, and the Thrasson had to pull back to keep from touching the brute's inflamed black lips.

"This girl you have lost, by what name is she called?" The fiend's breath reeked of cinders and rancid flesh. "Karfhud is a favorite of all the girls! Is that not so, Do—?"

The Amnesian Hero did not hear the woman's name, for the ringing in his ears had grown too loud. The darkness rushed in, sweltering and thick, then his legs went limp, and he felt himself fall.

Down he falls, down to the boundless, eternal dark, down to the black cold void where monsters hatch and slither, down to the stale hissing murk that churns like slow-boiling pitch inside us all. Were Jayk there to catch him, the fall would not feel so endless. But she is somewhere beneath a low, copper sky, lost upon a sandy path, beset by thorn brambles left and right, keeping watch on the hedge crest—with fear for me, with hope for the Thrasson—her cape hem hanging ragged where the old bariaur has torn away strips to swaddle Tessali's wrists.

And the elf: he stares, glassy-eyed and confused, at the emptiness at the ends of his wrists; his arms throb up to his shoulders, his bones ache to the core and out again—but not his hands. Those hurt not at all. He still feels them hanging from his wrists, still feels his fingers moving when he tries to make a fist, still feels his knuckles brushing the bariaur's chest as the old fellow works—but does not see them. For some reason he does not understand, they have turned invisible. He is like the ghosts who, by hiding in the shadows of things past, slip the Unbearable Moment.

He should know better.

The Bleak Cabal calls it the Grim Retreat, this taking of refuge in dark places. With every breath, Tessali draws that murk down into himself; with every breath, the gray light grows a little dimmer to his eyes. If he stays too long in the shadows, the darkness will fill him completely; he will lose himself to his blindness as surely as Jayk has—or as I might have, had I not seen the treachery of Poseidon's gift.

Before Silverwind has finished swaddling Tessali's stumps, the black bandages are soaked with blood. The weary bariaur can do nothing about it. He has already cast spells to ease the elf's pain and slow the bleeding, but he has no more healing magic until he has rested.

Tessali spreads his stumps, looks between them. "I can't see my hands." He frowns at the red drops falling from the ragged bandages; his eyes grow vacant, he looks back to Silverwind and asks, "Why can't I see my hands?"

"The Lady took them." Silverwind's reply is weary, impatient, even gruff. "It'll do you no good to confuse the issue now; I saw what I saw, and you can't change it. They're gone."

The elf shakes his head, frantic. "I feel them!"

"You *imagine* you feel them. But I imagine they're gone, and since I am the One, they are gone." Silverwind palms both stumps, rubs them hard enough to draw a gasp of pain. "You see?"

Tessali squints, leans forward and stares at Silverwind's palms covering his wrists where still he feels his own hands. Slowly, the elf struggles up through the darkness, back to the gray light; the glassy sheen vanishes from his eyes. His mouth gapes open.

"The Lady took my hands!" He jerks the stumps from Silverwind's grasp, crosses them over his breast. "What am I to do? Without hands, I cannot heal!"

Jayk kneels next to the elf, wraps a consolatory arm around his shoulder. Her head is pounding, but she knows when she has been called. "Do not fear, my friend. I can help you, yes?"

"You can?" Tessali looks more hopeful—even relieved—than wary. "How?"

Jayk smiles. Her pupils elongate into diamonds. She presses close to the elf. "We make kiss, yes?"

Tessali leaps to his feet, tears free of her embrace. "No!"

Jayk pouts, fangs dripping venom on her lower lip. "There is no need to be afraid; you are already dead. If you admit this, nothing will trouble you."

"I'm not ready to admit anything—especially that!"

Tessali eases from the tiefling, fixes his gaze on Silverwind, who is looking down the thorn-walled corridor. The passage continues about thirty paces before rounding a sharp corner. Behind them, it joins a cross passage.

"Silverwind?"

The bariaur turns, but says nothing.

Tessali holds his stumps before Silverwind's face. "You're the One Creator. You can make me a new pair of hands."

Silverwind shakes his head. "No, I cannot."

"Of course you can." Tessali's expression has grown sly. "If you're truly the One Creator, you can make whatever you want."

The old bariaur gives him a reproachful sneer. "By that logic, I would create *only* what I want—which, since I had never intended to create you or your friends, would hardly be good for you." He pushes away Tessali's stumps. "Count yourself lucky I have limitations. It is better to lack hands than not to exist at all."

Again, the elf thrusts his stumps toward Silverwind. "You don't understand. Without my hands, I can't cast spells. I can't restrain the barmies, or protect myself from the Menaces. I'm nothing!"

"Then you are nothing." Silverwind shrugs. "If I had something to work with, perhaps I could restore what you have lost—but even I cannot create something from nothing."

Tessali's eyes grow wide. He glances up the hedge, sees the two divots where Silverwind's hooves scraped the top. "Jayk," he says, turning to the tiefling, "if you go back and fetch my hands, no one will ever try to lock you in the Gatehouse again. I'll see to that."

The tiefling narrows her eyes, suspicious. "How?"

"It doesn't matter," interrupts Silverwind. "You can't go back—not by climbing. There's no telling where you'll end up, but it won't be in the ash maze."

With that, the bariaur snorts and turns down the passage.

"Wait!" Tessali calls. "Where are you going?"

"If you are so determined to have your hands back, we'll have to go and look for them, won't we?"

"You know the way?"

"I'm as lost as you are." Silverwind continues toward the corner.

"But now that the Thrasson is gone, what else is there to do?"

"We must wait here!" Jayk stamps her foot, brings the bariaur to a stop. "If we are gone when Zoombee jumps over the wall, what will he think? That we have left him, yes?"

"Jayk, come along." Tessali arches his brow. "The Amnesian Hero won't be jumping over the wall. He's dead."

"So are you." She glares at the elf's wrists. "And did I leave you behind? No!"

"You know that's different." Tessali has assumed his patient mind-healer's voice. "The Lady only maimed me. She kill—er, annihilated—the Amnesian Hero."

"How do you know? Did you see this?"

"What else could have happened?" The elf stretches a stump toward her, as if he still had a hand to extend. "The Amnesian Hero wouldn't want this; he sacrificed himself so we could escape."

Jayk folds her arms. "That is why we will wait. He deserves that from us, yes?"

"He would, if he were coming. But—"

"Tessali, the mazes do have their scavengers," Silverwind interrupts. "Do you want to find your hands or not?"

"Jayk, let's go." The elf cannot keep his head from pivoting down the passage. "There's no use waiting here."

"You only worry about your hands." Jayk looks away. "I wait for Zoombee."

"You may do as you wish, but you do understand that once we're gone, you'll be alone? We may never see each other again."

"I did not ask to see you the first time."

"As you wish, Jayk." After restoring a thousand madmen to their senses, Tessali knows a bluff when he sees one—or so he thinks. He turns and, with Silverwind's help, climbs on the bariaur's back. "I will miss you."

Confident Jayk will follow once she sees he is serious, Tessali nods, and Silverwind turns and trots down the passage. When they round the corner, Jayk is still standing where they left her, arms folded across her chest and gaze locked atop the hedge.

It will be some time before she sees the Thrasson come leaping over the crest. At the moment, he is still falling through the sweltering darkness, his heart rising into his throat, his stomach light as air. There is a woman's voice, keen and high, ringing in his ears; she is trilling a single name over and over, the syllables tumbling and gurgling over each other like the lilting aria of a waterfall. The Amnesian Hero keeps trying to understand what she is singing, as though catching hold of her voice might spare him the crash at the end of his plunge, but it will take more than that to save him.

The Thrasson is still falling when he opens his eyes and finds himself lying in the dirt street. He does not remember hitting the ground, and his insides remain squeamish and unsettled, but either he has stopped moving or everyone is moving with him—he cannot decide. He is staring up at a ring of sagging, rumpled faces illuminated in the sapphire light of his star-forged sword, which the tanar'ri Karfhud has picked up and raised high aloft, like a fog-haloed moon in the darkness.

The Amnesian Hero could not pick out the woman he had seen first. The faces above him were all round festering masses of folded flesh and dark nodules. Some, those in the earliest stages of the disease, retained something of their original shapes; brows and cheeks and jawlines still manifested themselves beneath flakes of dead white skin. Other visages, unbearable to look upon, were mere ooze-glistening blobs that made the Thrasson feel guilty for his own good fortune.

A peal of deep laughter boomed from Karfhud's round muzzle. "Stranger, you are not so fortunate! The star that guided you here was a foul one indeed." The fiend turned to the others. "My friends, we have here a noble one. He truly feels for us!"

"Then leave him be, Karfhud." The rasping words slipped from the lips of a blob-face. "He means us no harm."

"Truly, I do not!" The Amnesian Hero propped himself on his elbow, at once surprised by the plumes of darkness that this small exertion sent shooting through his head and how well the fiend had read his thoughts. "And I will do . . . whatever I can . . . to aid you."

The blob shook his head. "You can do nothing, stranger."

"Do not be . . . hasty. I am a man of renown . . . the slayer of the Hydra of Thrassos . . . the tamer of the Hebron Crocodile . . . the bane of Abudrian Dragons . . ." The Amnesian Hero felt more feverish and parched with each declaration. For once he wished his listeners would interrupt, but the villagers had all the time in the multiverse to listen. "The champion of Ilyrian Kings . . . the killer of the Chalcedon Lion . . . the scourge of foes too numerous to name . . . and always have I done as I promised."

"Then you have never promised what cannot be done." The blob-face raised his chin and swiveled his head toward his fellows. "It'll be best to leave him where he lies."

The speaker stepped back and vanished into the darkness. The other villagers followed, squeezing past Karfhud and disappearing down the gloomy lane.

"Wait!" The Thrasson knew better than to think he could cure their disease, but Tessali or Silverwind might well be able to help. "I'm not alone–"

"You should save your strength," Karfhud rumbled. "Yelling will not change their minds."

"But there are–"

"Maze Blight cannot be cured," the fiend interrupted. "The magic of your healers is of no use."

The Amnesian Hero scowled. "Do you hear everything I think?"

Karfhud nodded. "I do. And you must not be angry with my companions."

The Thrasson raised his brow. It had not yet occurred to him that he was angry at being abandoned, but, of course, the fiend was right. Despite his obvious need of water and rest, the villagers had left him to die in the street.

"They are doing you a kindness. Better to die of fever, quickly, than to linger here. It would take a century for someone of your health to rot away."

"All the same . . . I prefer to take my chances . . . In a century . . . I'll be dead . . . anyway."

The fiend's black lip twitched upward. "You will certainly wish you were."

Without awaiting a reply, Karfhud dropped his gaze to the

Amnesian Hero's flank, where the infected scratch had grown so puffy and inflamed it was about to split. A chill tickled down the Thrasson's spine. He caught himself gawking at the sagging brow beneath the fiend's wicked horns, wondering if the tanar'ri meant to imply he had already contracted the Maze Blight. Surely, the disease could not be so catching that one acquired it simply by walking into the village.

"Do you forget what happened when you grabbed Dorat's shoulder?" asked Karfhud, again intruding on the Thrasson's thoughts. "But truly, not one of us can say how he acquired the disease. There is a certain beast—"

The monster of the labyrinth! thought the Thrasson.

A little more of Karfhud's fangs seemed to show beneath his lips. He lowered the Thrasson's sword and began to inspect the glowing blade. The blue light reflected off his maroon eyes, filling the lane with brown flashes.

"A most wonderful weapon." The fiend scraped his thumb across the blade, grating off a cascade of tiny black flakes. "Starforged, is it not?"

"You know your weapons." The Amnesian Hero had no doubt the fiend intended to steal it from him—

"On the contrary!" Karfhud kneeled, his enormous legs straddling the Thrasson's chest, and flipped the weapon around so that he was holding it by the naked blade. "I was hoping you would make me a gift of it—after you die, of course."

"I—I have no intention of . . . dying."

"No? More the pity for you, then." The fiend laid the hilt in the Amnesian Hero's hand, then stood. "Still—and I hope you do not find me rude for noting this—you don't look well. In case you happen to expire, would it be too much to ask the command words that activate the magic?"

Of course, even as he thought not to think it, the phrase flashed through the Thrasson's mind: Starlight cleave the night.

"One spell!" Karfhud growled. "For such a magnificent weapon, that hardly seems enough!"

"It is all . . . you will discover!"

Knowing what Karfhud would surely do next, the Amnesian

Hero lashed out at the fiend's belly with a vicious backhand slash.

Karfhud, of course, had realized the Thrasson's intentions even as he formed them. The fiend was already out of reach when the blade flashed past.

"Because you are sick and confused, I forgive you that mistake." There were little tongues of fire flickering in the tanar'ri's dark pupils. "But I warn you, I will not abide such an insult again."

"I care . . . nothing for your warnings. I know better than to trust . . . a tanar'ri lord."

The Amnesian Hero clambered to his feet, deliberately exaggerating his clumsiness in an attempt to lure the fiend into attacking. The ruse failed as miserably as the first, and the Thrasson found himself facing an extremely large tanar'ri lord in very cramped quarters. Given his condition, the mere fact that he was still alive suggested he had badly misjudged Karfhud's intentions.

"Now you are being sensible." The fiend stepped forward. He extended his wrist and, using his own claw, opened a vein. "Give me your hand."

The Amnesian Hero began to retreat. "What for?"

"My blood is my bond." Karfhud caught up with a single step. "I pledge not to steal your sword, to cause you no harm while you live, and to aid you any way I can."

Seeing that retreating would do him no good, the Thrasson stopped. "And in return?"

"I ask less than I pledge." Karfhud seemed unconcerned about the steady stream of dark, hissing blood spilling from his opened wrist. "Only that you cause me no harm while you live, and that when you die, your sword and all your possessions shall be mine."

As badly as he needed aid, the Amnesian Hero knew better than to trust a fiend—especially one of the tanar'ri, who believed less in the rule of law than they did in the rule of evil.

"And if I refuse?"

The tanar'ri's wings rose behind him, filling the alley and

making the fiend seem even larger than he was. "You do not want to refuse."

"If I have no choice but death, then I agree."

The Thrasson lowered his sword and extended his free hand. He had no misgivings, for it was no dishonor to exchange such an oath under threat of death—nor, in the eyes of his gods, was it binding.

The tanar'ri caught the proffered wrist in a movement as fast as lightning. The fiend wrinkled his muzzle into a gruesome parody of a smile, then held his bleeding wrist over the Amnesian Hero's hand. A single drop of black blood landed in the center of the Thrasson's palm.

There was a loud sizzle. The smell of acid and fire and melting flesh filled the air. The Thrasson's arm felt as though he had plunged it into boiling oil. He screamed and, thinking the fiend had betrayed him already, tried to raise his sword to attack. No sooner had the thought flashed through his mind than the weapon slipped from his grasp and dropped to the ground. The Amnesian Hero stared at the glowing blade and tried to ignore his searing pain and the terrible, sinking feeling that he had just made a mistake worse than dying.

At last, the sizzling died away, and the sick acid stench faded from the Thrasson's nostrils. The burning agony drained from his arm, and Karfhud released his wrist. The Amnesian Hero turned his hand into the light and, tattooed onto his palm, he saw the ruby-eyed semblance of a slender, wicked-horned tanar'ri.

"That was before the blight." Karfhud sounded almost wistful. "But that was many centuries ago—and we have more immediate concerns, do we not? Gather up your sword, and let us be on our way."

Seeing nothing else to do, the Amnesian Hero did as the fiend instructed. "And where are we going?"

"To collect our supplies, of course!" Karfhud seemed genuinely surprised by the Thrasson's question. "And then we shall return you to your friends!"

"My friends?" The Thrasson did not relish the thought of returning to his companions in the company of a Maze-Blighted tanar'ri. "It might be better if I returned alone."

"In your condition? You would never succeed!" Karfhud swept the Amnesian Hero up in a single arm. "And did I not swear to aid you any way I can?"

HANDS

She stalks the mazes like a bloodblade on the prowl, shambling around corners, skulking along walls, squinting into the windblown ash. Faint as it is, the smell of wine and sour sweat and crusted blood grows more distinct with every step. She stops, sucks down a chest full of gritty air, turns her maw skyward; from her throat rumbles a low growl that rises to a deep rolling bellow and spreads like thunder across the dark sky. The winds grow still in the fury of the roar. Cascades of ash boil down the walls, the ground goes soft with trembling—and the echoes boom back to her bland and hollow, with no resonance of terror. She is alone in this maze; the prey has abandoned her to its spoor. Her matted fur bristles with cold ire, and her craving grows worse for its denial.

We have the same dark hungers, you and I and the monster. We all ache to sate the same appetites we dare not name. It is the same emptiness inside us all; we stare into that same darkness, we fling our treasures into that same unfathomable pit, and, in the end, we all come to that same scant solace: the comfort of warm blood, the fellowship of a groaning voice, the intimacy of the death rattle. Do not damn the monster; until we look to ourselves, we do not dare.

She is only searching, and no matter that she will never find what she seeks in Poseidon's amphora; it suits me that she thinks she might. She is kneeling before the jar now, her flat and shaggy face pressed close to the neck, her cavernous nostrils flaring as she sniffs at the ashen patch. It smells of blood and fear and pain, which sate her appetites as well as anything, but also of something more, pride and hope and even, well-masked beneath the rest, treachery. The amphora is not likely to flail or shriek or dash away when she begins to play, but it may offer some new kind of fun—if not, she will return later for the prey. They cannot roam far.

The monster tucks the amphora under her arm—the same one that was lopped off earlier—then steps into the billowing dross, and by the time the Amnesian Hero directs Karfhud into the blind, she has left the ashen maze and turned toward her lair.

The Thrasson was sitting in the crook of the tanar'ri's elbow, with one arm wrapped around the fiend's spongy neck and the other pinned against the brute's enormous biceps. The fever had not broken, but the Amnesian Hero felt well enough now. Shortly after allowing his palm to be marked with Karfhud's blood, his dizziness had faded, the fog had evaporated from his mind, even his fatigue had vanished. Save for his unrelenting thirst and the throbbing of his infected scratch—and the uneasy suspicion that he owed his fitness to the fiend's mark—he had no complaints whatsoever. In fact, he was allowing himself to be carried only because his brick foot made it impossible to keep pace with the tanar'ri's ground-swallowing stride.

Karfhud turned the corner and stopped in the mouth of the blind. The dead-end passage ahead looked like the place where the Thrasson had left his companions. The same ash eddies swirled about the entrance, it was the same thirty paces deep, and it had the same ash walls rising along its sides. The only difference was its emptiness; Jayk and Tessali and Silverwind were missing, and so was the amphora.

"Put . . . put me down!" The Thrasson's gasping tone had less to do with thirst than with shock.

Karfhud straightened his arm, allowing the Amnesian Hero to drop to the ground. "You're certain this is where you left them? In the mazes, many places can look the same."

"I am no stranger to mazes!"

Karfhud narrowed his eyes, hiding his maroon pupils between the folds of his sagging face, and made no reply. Tanar'ri lords were not known for their forbearance, but the Amnesian Hero was more worried about his missing companions than angering the fiend. He clumped over to the wall where he had left the amphora. In the powdery ground, he found the shallow basin where he had worked the bottom into the dross. In front of this depression, a pair of hollows had been pressed into the ash. The craters were the size of a man's chest, slightly elongated, and almost two paces apart. Something had kneeled there–something larger than Karfhud.

"The monster was here," said the tanar'ri, voicing the Thrasson's conclusion even as he reached it. "And she took your amphora."

"She?"

Karfhud nodded. "The monster is female–is that not always the way? I wonder what your jar contained to interest her?"

"So do I." For once, the Amnesian Hero had no answer for the tanar'ri to pluck from his mind.

The ground was not churned up, as was to be expected after a fight, and, while the eddies had dusted the entire area with ash, the two depressions where the Amnesian Hero and Jayk had sat talking were completely filled, yet the basins where the amphora had rested and the monster's knees had pressed down were covered by only a light coating.

"You are right, Thrasson." Karfhud gazed up and down the blind. "This battle site makes no sense."

"Will you allow me the privacy of my own thoughts?"

"Why do you need privacy–unless you're trying to hide something?" Karfhud hung his sagging face over the Thrasson, curling the swollen black lips of his muzzle just enough to bare the tips of his yellow fangs. "Certainly, you do not concern yourself with proprieties. The thought has not crossed a human mind that could offend tanar'ri sensibilities."

"I doubt the tanar'ri have sensibilities," grumbled the Thrasson. "And I certainly have nothing to hide. You can read minds. You must know my opinion of you by now."

The Amnesian Hero turned away to see if he could learn more about what had happened to his companions. Given how often eddies spun into the blind to coat everything with a fresh layer of ash, he knew better than to think he would find many hints on the ground. Instead, he walked along the wall in both directions, searching for anything to suggest there had been a battle: stray weapon marks, blood-soaked clods, indentations left by hurled bodies.

The Amnesian Hero found nothing, which, he decided, meant nothing. The battle could easily have been fought without leaving its mark on the wall. His companions might have escaped without a fight. Or, when they reached the mouth of the blind and found him missing, they might have fled before the monster arrived.

"No, that cannot be what happened."

Karfhud's intrusion startled the Amnesian Hero so badly he jumped. He landed with his sword half-drawn and spun on the fiend, angry enough that he felt flames licking in his eyes.

Karfhud showed no sign that he noticed the Thrasson's fury. "Your friends were in a hurry, or they would have taken the amphora with them."

"Not necessarily." The Amnesian Hero did not know why he bothered speaking, except that it made him feel a little less like a fiend in the making. "To them, the amphora was nothing but trouble."

Although the Thrasson did not bother to elaborate, Karfhud nodded. "Ah, yes: the giant."

The Amnesian Hero grated his teeth, but dropped to his hands and knees near the place he and Jayk had been sitting. Karfhud had given him an idea. He began to sweep his hands through the ash, searching for the wineskin he had left lying on the ground. Presumably, the skin would still be there if his companions had left in a hurry.

The Thrasson brushed something cold and much too smooth to be Silverwind's wineskin. He lost contact with it, then spread his fingers and raked both hands deeply through the ash. This time, he caught the thing squarely. His pulse raced in his ears. He half-expected whatever it was to bite him and squirm away, but the object remained dead in his grasp. It had a strange texture, with a soft exterior wrapped over a hard, lumpy core. From one side protruded several long, flexible appendages . . .

The Amnesian Hero's stomach went hollow and qualmish, then he found himself shouting in revulsion as he pulled a rather fine-boned hand from deep beneath the ash.

"Foul Hades!" The Thrasson dangled the thing by its thumb. "There *was* a fight!"

A sick, guilty feeling welled up inside him; while he was off chasing his wine woman, the monster had come and devoured his companions.

"Do you have to be so maudlin? It is only a hand!"

The tanar'ri snatched the thing from the Thrasson's grasp, then wiped the ash off the severed wrist and raised it to his muzzle. From the fiend's mouth snaked a long, pointed tongue coated in white fungus. The tip flickered over the stump several times and when Karfhud began to rub it back and forth over his taste buds, the Amnesian Hero forced himself not to look away. The cut was uncommonly clean; even his star-forged blade could not have cleaved the bone so smoothly.

Several nauseating moments later, Karfhud lowered the hand and sighed, deeply satisfied. "Elf—a little old, but elf nonetheless."

The Amnesian Hero nodded. "Tessali. One of our party."

Karfhud dropped to all fours and snuffled along the ground, allowing the Thrasson his first good look at the enormous back-satchel the fiend had fetched after their exchange of oaths. Secured snugly by heavy leather straps buckled around the tanar'ri's powerful wing joints, the sack was fashioned of some smooth, lightly colored hide that might have once belonged to either a pig or a man. It was large enough that the Amnesian Hero could have stood inside with Tessali at his side, although they would have been covered only to their chests. The top was drawn closed by a sturdy cinch strap, but several open pockets had been sewn onto the side to hold odds and ends.

"If you find my rucksack interesting, you would do well to remember that it is *my* rucksack." Karfhud pushed himself into a kneeling position and, before the Amnesian Hero could ask the reason for the threat, displayed Tessali's second hand. "This is not the doing of the monster."

The Amnesian Hero had already reached the same conclusion. The cut was far too clean, and, cunning as the beast was, the Thrasson could not imagine why she would leave both hands behind. "Then who?"

Karfhud shrugged, then lowered his face into the ash again. Still carrying Tessali's hands, he began to snuffle toward the back of the blind, raising a great cloud of gray dross each time he exhaled. The Amnesian Hero limped along behind, trying to puzzle out what had happened. Something–he could not even guess what–had come along and cut off Tessali's hands, then chased away the elf and the others. Sometime later–and not long ago, judging by the thin coating of dust in the knee depressions–something else, probably the monster, had come along and taken the amphora.

Karfhud reached the back of the blind and started to sniff up the wall, then suddenly stopped and cocked his head, nearly hooking the Thrasson's cheek with a black horn. "You have a marilith in your party?"

"Marilith?"

"Female tanar'ri! Six arms, serpent's tail." Karfhud cupped his hands beneath his chest. "Three or four big–"

"No! Not among my companions."

Karfhud managed a real smile. "Well then, I think we know who cut off these." He displayed Tessali's hands, then reached around behind his wing, bent his arm in a direction it should not have bent, and slipped the appendages into one of his rucksack's exterior pockets. "I am fortunate indeed."

"Fortunate?"

Karfhud attempted a wink, momentarily hiding one maroon eye between the folds of his blighted face. "You cannot imagine the centuries that have passed since last I did the fray upon a female tanar'ri!"

With that, the fiend grabbed the crest of the wall and pulled himself up. The Amnesian Hero looked back toward the mouth of the blind, torn between following Karfhud and going back to search for the amphora. His promise to Poseidon—and, in truth, his curiosity about his own past—obliged him to pursue the jar; his duty to his companions obligated him to go after them. He could not do both. Once he climbed over the wall, it would prove difficult to find his way back here, and every minute that passed before he started hunting the amphora slashed his chances of success.

"I may have misjudged you, Thrasson. I took you for the sort of fool who might regard the lives of his companions more highly than his own desires." Karfhud, already sitting atop the wall, swung his legs to the other side. "Make your decision soon. I won't wait for you."

The fiend pushed off and, even before he dropped down the other side, vanished from sight. The Amnesian Hero snorted his frustration, then jumped up, caught hold of the crest of the wall, and pulled himself to the top. As much as he relished the thought of being free of Karfhud—though he suspected that could not truly be while the tanar'ri's heinous face remained tattooed on his palm—the Thrasson knew the fiend had judged him correctly. No man of renown could abandon his companions in a time of such dire need—even if it meant breaking his word to a god. He pulled his chest atop the wall, then swung his legs to the other side and pushed off.

It is not like passing through a conjunction.

The Thrasson's stomach does a flip. His body rotates, his feet drifting up over his head. He is falling, he thinks; then no, he realizes, he is floating; an instant later, he decides he is suspended like a beetle in amber, in the syrup of nothingness. In his nostrils, there is nothing, not even the reek of his own unwashed body. His ears roar with silence, his skin prickles with the touch of emptiness, his tongue craves the taste of his own teeth. He sees what dead men see: not darkness, but an ocean of endless, colorless depths. Something goes slack, and the Thrasson feels himself uncoiling inside; his spirit and his mind and his body all drift toward their own separate peace.

Then a terrific jolt drives his knees up to his chin. He finds himself squatting on his heels, his ears ringing as though someone had boxed them, his bones shuddering from the impact. It would be wrong to say the Thrasson has landed; that would imply falling in the first place. It is closer to the truth to say his paradigm has shifted. Now he sees himself crouching between two rows of brambly hedges with dagger-length thorns, watching in morbid astonishment as Karfhud snuffles about searching for the marilith, harrowing the sandy floor with his blighted face.

It is clever, is it not, how the Amnesian Hero avoids thinking, even to himself, what a buffoon is that lust-struck tanar'ri? The Thrasson knows, better than any of us, that there is no marilith; would not his Hunter's nose have scented her spoor back in the blind? Would not those special eyes have seen beneath the top layer of ash to pick out her slithering trail, or those fingers have sensed the slimy dampness of her passing? The blood that has so roused Karfhud's passions belongs to Jayk, who was conceived at death and spawned from a marilith's leathery egg, but the Amnesian Hero is careful to think of none of this. He watches the tanar'ri sniff, his thoughts full of concern for his companions and strategies for fighting snake-women. Wiser to play the fool, to hide his nature until the time comes to betray his new keeper and make the fiend his.

A dangerous game, to be certain—and the only way to defeat the monster of the labyrinth—but how does the Thrasson know all this? Certainly, I did not tell him. And who else could, but you? Someone has a loose tongue, I fear, and they will pay.

But do not trouble yourself now. It will change nothing in the end, and what good is punishment if it comes expected? Even now, Karfhud has changed directions. The fiend is sniffing back toward the Amnesian Hero, who stands in the middle of the passage, somehow not thinking about the faint rasp of Jayk's breath whispering down the passage from the intersection, somehow pretending that his Hunter's ears don't hear a thing. What happens when Karfhud stops at the Thrasson's feet, it would not do to miss.

"This cannot be right!" The fiend has jerked his face from the sand and pointed down the passage, away from the intersection. "The blood trail leads around that corner, but the marilith went the other way—with a human!"

The Amnesian Hero scowled. "That can't be. I was the only human in our party."

"My nose may look blighted, Thrasson, but it does not lie."

Karfhud turned to stomp up the passage, leaving the Amnesian Hero to clump behind as best he could. Though it was only a short distance to the intersection, the tanar'ri reached it several paces ahead of the Thrasson. The fiend stopped and looked first left, then right. His great wings flared, drawing a curtain of darkness across the corridor; from his throat rumbled a sonorous growl, so low it felt like an earth tremor.

"Tiefling!"

Jayk's voice came around the corner high and shrill, cracking with fear as she uttered her incantation. A tremendous crackling bounced down the passage, and Karfhud's huge wings folded over his back satchel just as a cloud of fire boiled out of the side corridor to swallow him. The passage filled with a yellow smoke that stank of brimstone and charred flesh. The Thrasson stopped and turned away, shielding his face, daring to hope the tiefling had freed him from the fiend.

The heat of the flames continued to build. The Amnesian Hero flattened himself on the sand and tried to hold his breath. The foul smoke had already filled his lungs, and he could not keep from coughing; with each gasp, he swallowed more of the fiery fumes, which caused more convulsions, and he thought he would suffocate.

Though a lifetime seemed to pass, it did not take more than a few seconds for the flames to die down. Still coughing, the Amnesian Hero pushed himself off the scorching sands and peered up the passage. Karfhud looked a little blacker than usual, as if that were possible, but stood exactly as he had before the fireball engulfed him.

"Now will you have reason to lament, tiefling!" The fiend unfolded his great wings, revealing the blackened exterior of his back-satchel. There was a wisp of brownish smoke rising from the pockets where he had stored Tessali's hands, but otherwise the sack appeared intact. "For that fireball, and for raising my appetites with that false smell of yours!"

"Karfhud, wait!" The Amnesian Hero started up the passage, but the fiend was already rounding the corner. "It's not her fault!"

"Zoombee?" cried Jayk. "Help me!"

The Amnesian Hero drew his sword and clumped around the corner. Karfhud's wings blocked the passage from one side to the other. Between the fiend's feet, the Thrasson could see Jayk lying on her back, frantically trying to push herself up the passage. She flung a handful of sand toward the fiend's face and ran her fingers through the gestures of a spell, but she was so badly frightened that she could not choke out the incantation.

"Karfhud, stop!" When the fiend did not obey, the Amnesian Hero rushed forward, sword raised to strike.

As soon as the Thrasson started to bring the blade down, the weapon slipped from his grasp. He could not violate his oath to the tanar'ri.

Karfhud stooped down to grasp Jayk in his clawed hands. She shot a frightened glance through the fiend's legs, then tried to call out to the Thrasson. She managed little more than a croak.

The Amnesian Hero dropped to his knees and snatched up his sword. Then, hoping he had guessed correctly about how to free himself from the fiend, laid his tattooed hand in the sand. He raised the star-forged blade above the wrist, took a deep breath, and started to bring the weapon down.

A huge, black-taloned hand caught the Thrasson's wrist.

The Amnesian Hero looked up to see Karfhud's massive horned head sitting backward on the fiend's hulking shoulders. The tanar'ri's maroon eyes, smoldering with suppressed fury, were glaring down over his scorched back-satchel.

"She is yours?"

"She is my friend." The Amnesian Hero twisted his sword arm free, still determined to strike off his tattooed hand—if that was necessary to defend Jayk. "But harm to her is harm to me."

"So you have proven." Karfhud reeled the rest of his body around to match the direction he was looking. "You could have mentioned this before I became so . . . fervent."

"You hardly gave me the chance! Besides, you should have known—unless Jayk's smell interferes with your thought-reading as well as your judgment." The Amnesian Hero hoped it did.

"You should be so lucky," Karfhud remarked.

Resigning himself to disappointment, the tanar'ri bent his arm around in that impossible manner and plucked one of Tessali's hands from his back satchel. Jayk's fireball had left the appendage dark and crispy, but the charring did not bother the fiend, who bit off a blackened finger and began to crunch.

"It is just as well." The fiend spoke around his snack. "As small as she is, the fray would not have lasted long."

Though he had managed an indifferent tone, Karfhud's tense bearing betrayed his true feelings. He shouldered past the Amnesian Hero, nearly shoving the Thrasson into a thorn hedge, then disappeared around the corner. He was still chewing Tessali's charred finger.

As soon as the fiend was gone, Jayk spread her hands and flung herself at the Amnesian Hero. "Zoombee! You saved my life!"

The Thrasson caught a glimpse of her diamond-shaped pupils, then dropped his sword and caught her at arm's length. Her broad smile was ruined, for him at least, by the two curved fangs hanging over her lower lip.

"I may look bad, Jayk, but I'm hardly ready for your kiss."

"Zoombee, you are never ready!" The tiefling pushed her lip into an exaggerated pout, which quickly converted itself back to a sly smile. "And you are wrong to be afraid. You are already—"

"Already dead—I know." The Amnesian Hero released Jayk,

then retrieved his sword. "But it seems to me I'm not the only one who fears death. Did you not just thank me for saving your life?"

Jayk's face grew as dark as Karfhud's. "It was only an expression, Zoombee." She raised her chin. "I think he meant to steal my spirit, yes? That is why I thanked you."

"I have not met the tiefling yet that is not a liar." Karfhud's voice rumbled around the corner, putting an end to the Amnesian Hero's vague hope that the fiend needed to see a person to read his thoughts. "You thought I was going to kill you, and you were afraid of dying."

The Amnesian Hero cocked an eyebrow. "Karfhud *does* read minds, Jayk."

The Thrasson regretted the comment the instant it left his mouth. The tiefling's jaw worked silently, trying to find the words to deny what they all knew to be true. Finally, she gave up and spun away, burying her face in her hands.

"No, don't cry, Jayk." The Amnesian Hero sheathed his sword, then took her in his arms. "It is not wrong to love life."

The tiefling tried to pull away, but the Amnesian Hero held tight.

"If I were you, Thrasson, I would release her," warned Karfhud. "You are very near to discovering the truth about the One Death."

The Amnesian Hero continued to hold Jayk, confident that even for her, there was a difference between thought and action. "Jayk, you were terrified—and with good reason. Don't blame yourself for one moment of doubt."

Karfhud leaned around the corner, his folded brow lifted as far above his maroon eyes as the Amnesian Hero had seen. The fiend was holding his charred back-satchel in hand, cinching the top strap after having checked on the contents. Given that his face looked no angrier than usual, it appeared the sack's load had survived Jayk's firestorm intact.

"Thrasson," Karfhud rumbled. "I warn you, she—"

A whimper of terror tumbled from Jayk's lips, then she slipped around behind the Amnesian Hero.

The Thrasson reached around to pat her hand. "There is no reason to hide now, Jayk. He won't hurt you while I am here."

"That is true, tiefling." Karfhud knotted the satchel drawstring, then heaved the sack between his wings and bent his arms back at those impossible angles to buckle it in place. "As long as the Thrasson lives, you are safe enough."

Jayk slipped from behind her shield. "He . . . Zoombee is dead already . . . as we all are." The tiefling's voice had the desperate, soft quality of words that had misplaced their meaning. "But why should it matter to me? I . . . I do not fear death—or you."

"Good, as it appears we are to wander together." Karfhud pulled his cracked lips back in a gruesome smirk. A few tendrils of Tessali's charred hand had gotten stuck between his fangs. "Let us leave on this instant; catching the bariaur will prove difficult enough without giving him more of a start."

DREAM

Karfhud has led them back to the city of iron. Though thunder rolls somewhere in the distant sky, there is no hail to allay the scorching heat that pours off the rusty walls, nor steam to dampen the parching air that whispers down the crooked passages. The searing dryness draws beads of inky dew to the surface of the tiefling's dark complexion; the Thrasson's skin burns and itches and stays dry as salt; he has not lost a drop of fluid since striking his bargain with the fiend. That should worry him, but in truth he is relieved at this new harmony with heat. No longer does it sap his strength or make his joints ache, nor fill his mind with clouding steam; now it nourishes him, burns away his pain, even gorges his weary muscles with vigor long spent.

Thus does the defilement begin, not with the terrible act itself, but with a gift, freely given, and the offer of more. There is no coercion, no force, no one to blame; the victim makes her choice, thinks she will be the smart one, the strong one, the lucky one who sees the brink looming ahead and . . . But another time, perhaps. This has nothing to do with the Thrasson, and he has come to a crossroads. One branch leads into a warren of narrow, crooked alleyways where the heat bends and blurs the air like poorly blown glass; the other runs only a few paces before intersecting an avenue so broad and inviting that the far wall seems but a mirage.

Karfhud has stopped in the passage leading to the broad avenue, squatted down to scrape a circle of crusty brown mucilage off the paving bricks, licked the stuff from his black talon.

"Elf." The fiend smacked his lips and, not rising, turned his head backward to stare at Jayk. "Did you not say Silverwind was returning to the ash maze?"

Jayk nodded and stumbled one step back. "Silverwind, he says he needs Tessali's hands to fix things right. So they go back."

The Amnesian Hero did not know whether Jayk had noticed Karfhud eating the charred hand earlier—or if she connected it with the elf—but he saw no use in pointing out the relationship now. She still seemed shocked by the fiend's near-assault, and he did not want to do anything to make her more fearful of their new companion.

Karfhud's maroon eyes continued to glare at Jayk from beneath his sagging brow, but he said nothing. The Amnesian Hero stepped forward, blocking the fiend's line of sight.

"Stop staring. She answered your question."

"I beg her forgiveness; it was not my intention to seem menacing." The shadow of a sneer flashed across Karfhud's muzzle. "I was only wondering why, if they wanted to return to the ash maze, they turned away from the entrance."

"Silverwind, he does not know how to find it!" The quickness of Jayk's explanation betrayed her anxiety. "He said they could only—"

"Turn around." Karfhud rose and bent his arms back to undo his satchel straps. "You, too, Thrasson."

Jayk's hand dropped toward her dagger, her fear broadcast by a sharp intake of breath. The Amnesian Hero caught her wrist, then wrapped an arm around her shoulders and turned her around.

"Don't worry. Karfhud's not going to hurt us."

"How can you know that, Zoombee?"

"Because if that was what he wanted, we would be—" The Thrasson almost said 'dead', then caught himself. Given Jayk's crisis of faith, it might be better not to talk about death. "Because if Karfhud wanted to hurt us, he would have done it by now."

Behind them, there was a sharp thump as Karfhud dropped his satchel to the ground. Jayk flinched and would probably have taken off running, had the Thrasson's hand not been grasping her shoulder.

"Zoombee, what is it he wants from us?" Jayk whispered, apparently forgetting that the fiend could hear every thought that flashed through her head. "It is not natural, this friendship he has made with you."

"I'd hardly call it friendship!" It affronted the Amnesian Hero that Jayk could even think he would be friends with something so wicked as a tanar'ri. "It's more of an arrangement. He claims that all he wants is my sword."

"And you believe him?"

The Thrasson cringed, for that was the one question he had tried to avoid asking himself until he could figure out how to shield his thoughts from Karfhud. Still, there was no use dodging it now; the answer had already flashed through his mind.

"Only a fool would trust anything a tanar'ri says."

The Amnesian Hero heard a soft shuffling sound, as though Karfhud were paging through a stack of parchment sheets.

"Thrasson, you would be wise to keep your thoughts on the tiefling's question. I have warned you about my satchel."

"I can't figure out what Karfhud really wants." The Amnesian Hero spoke rapidly, attempting to keep his curious mind from speculating about the shuffling sound. "If it was my sword, he could have had it easily enough. As weak as I was, he would not have had to trouble himself with killing me."

"Then what he wants is something from you, Zoombee."

From behind them came the soft rustle of a parchment being unrolled. Without even trying, the Amnesian Hero realized what the fiend had in his satchel: maps. A chill tickled down the

Thrasson's spine, and he wondered if the realization would provoke Karfhud into attacking. He would have reached for his sword, save that he knew it would only slip from his hand.

When no assault came, the Amnesian Hero dared to glance over his shoulder. As expected, he saw Karfhud kneeling over an unrolled parchment. The fiend had tongues of white flame flickering in the pupils of his maroon eyes, and he was glaring at the Thrasson. They locked gazes for an instant, then the tanar'ri returned his attention to his map.

The Amnesian Hero looked back to Jayk. "Whatever Karfhud wants, I think it is from *us*. He seems rather determined to track down Silverwind and Tessali."

"Yes, and is that not your fault as well?" Jayk pushed his arm off her shoulder. "Or maybe you think they deserve to have a fiend hunting them, yes?"

"No!" he said. "Why would I think that?"

"Because they abandoned your amphora, of course!" Jayk's voice became more shrill with each word. "What happened to Tessali, that does not matter to you! You only wanted him to save your amphora, even if it cost him his hands!"

This was the first the Amnesian Hero had heard about how the elf lost his hands or what had happened to the amphora. The Thrasson had avoided asking about the matter, fearing his questions would further disrupt Jayk's fragile state. He took no comfort in knowing he had been right.

"Jayk, I don't blame Tessali for losing the amphora." He clasped the tiefling by the shoulders and spun her around to face him. "I don't blame you, either. When the monster came—"

"What monster? It was the Lady! You go off to chase your wine woman and leave us to save your amphora from the Lady of Pain!" Jayk spat at his feet. "I spit on your amphora; it is your own fault if you lose it!"

Though the tiefling's version of events did not match the evidence the Amnesian Hero had found in the blind, he thought it wisest not to press the matter. "Jayk, if the Lady came while I was gone, I'm sorry—but I don't blame anyone for leaving the amphora. I came to Sigil to deliver it to her. Don't you remember?"

The tiefling's jaw dropped, then she took a sharp breath and allowed her eyes to roll up. "Yes—I forget!"

"Be that as it may, Thrasson," said Karfhud, still speaking from behind them, "it surprises me to hear *you* lying. You and I both know the amphora was—"

"That's enough!" The Amnesian Hero released Jayk and turned to glare at the fiend. "Jayk's right. No matter what happened to the amphora, I have no one to blame but myself."

A deep chuckle rumbled from Karfhud's throat. "Come now, Thrasson. You know it is no good to swallow your feelings! The amphora was your best hope of learning who you are, and now you feel betrayed because your companions abandoned it."

"Zoombee! This is true?" Jayk's pupils were elongating into diamonds, and her fangs were folding down from the roof of her mouth. "When you reach the One Death, you will have no use for memories!"

"Calm yourself, Jayk," said the Amnesian Hero.

He began to back away, casting an angry glance past the tiefling toward Karfhud, who was laughing so hard that his face had melted into an undulating mass of wrinkles.

"There is a difference between sentiment and reason," the Thrasson continued. "I am disappointed, but—"

Jayk leapt, fangs bared and hands clawing at his face.

The Thrasson sidestepped her rush, at the same time curling his hands into fists. He was spared the necessity of knocking the tiefling unconscious when Karfhud caught her from behind.

"That is enough, Little Shadow!" The fiend lifted her off the ground, still cackling in delight. "I cannot let you bite the Thrasson! He and I have sworn an oath of blood."

Instantly, Jayk went as still as a statue—save for her trembling muscles and her quivering lip.

"There," said Karfhud. "It always helps to understand the situation completely, does it not?"

Saying nothing more, the tanar'ri put Jayk down and returned to his maps.

The tiefling remained very still until her pupils had become round again, then fixed an angry glare on the Thrasson's face.

"What were you thinking, Zoombee, to lead a tanar'ri back to us?" She jerked her chin back over her shoulder, though she was careful to avoid actually looking in the fiend's direction. "You will discover what he wants before he finds it, yes?"

"What I want is to save your friends." Karfhud's parchment rattled as he rolled it up. "And, at the moment, the reason is not so important as the need to hurry. If Sheba–"

"Who?" the Amnesian Hero asked.

"The queen of the labyrinth–the one who attacked you and your companions," Karfhud said. "If Sheba took the amphora–"

"No, I told you!" Jayk whirled around. "It was the Lady who came for it!"

The Amnesian Hero turned to see Karfhud stuffing the rolled parchment down among the many dozens in his satchel. The tanar'ri had apparently resigned himself to letting the pair in on his secret, for he showed no irritation at having the contents viewed–which worried the Thrasson more than any fiendish glowering would have. The tanar'ri would not take them into his confidence unless he meant to kill them later.

If Karfhud was aware of the Thrasson's thoughts, his disfigured face did not betray it as he fixed his attention on Jayk. "It may have been the Lady who chased you and the others away from the amphora, but it was someone much larger who took it." The fiend pulled the satchel drawstrings tight and, with a clumsy flutter of his blight-gnarled talons, knotted them closed. "We found a pair of large depressions where someone had kneeled to pick up the amphora–and, as I'm sure you know, the Lady of Pain leaves no sign of her passing."

When Jayk made no further protests, Karfhud hoisted his satchel onto his back and began buckling the straps. "If I am guessing correctly, this Silverwind intends to follow the Great Way down to the alley of the ash window–"

"Ash window?" asked the Thrasson.

"Surely, you remember it? You had to go through it to reach the maze of ash!"

The Amnesian Hero nodded. "Silverwind called it a conjunction "

"That is a peculiar way to describe it." Karfhud's folded brow dipped in the middle, then he shook his head. "But it matters not; it is more important that they are likely to meet Sheba coming the other way. You must catch up to them before she does–then stop her."

"Why us?" Jayk demanded. The prospect of confronting the monster again seemed to make her less afraid of the fiend. "What about you?"

The tanar'ri bared a long row of fangs. "I will be behind her." He pointed up the short alley toward the broad avenue. "When you reach the Great Way, you must see it as a straight line. Ignore the corners, whichever way they turn, and count only the intersections. Go down twenty-eight alleys, counting only those on your right, and turn into the twenty-ninth–which will be on your left. Go down this lane until you reach a 'T' and turn to the left, then go eleven more intersections, counting only those on the left, and turn into the twelfth, which will be on the right. The fourth window on the left leads to the ash maze, but by then you will meet either Sheba or me."

"What if we lose our way?" asked Jayk.

"Then I will be very angry–but you may always summon me by speaking my name." The tanar'ri looked to the Amnesian Hero. "Repeat my directions."

"Count twenty-eight alleys on the right and enter the twenty-ninth, which will be on the left. Follow it to a 'T' and turn left, then count eleven passages on the left and turn into the twelfth, which will be on the right. The fourth window on the left leads to the ash maze, but we don't really need to know that. By then, we will either be dead or reunited with you."

Karfhud nodded approvingly. "For a man who cannot recall his own name, you have a most excellent memory."

"I suppose that is because it is not cluttered," the Thrasson said. "But I do have a question."

"You may ask."

The Amnesian Hero looked up the passage toward the broad avenue. "Do we turn left or right onto the Great Way?"

Karfhud scowled. "Which way do you think?" He turned away,

entering the hot, crooked alleys that opened beside them. "Left!"

The fiend departed at a lope, leaving the Amnesian Hero alone with Jayk and his instructions. The Thrasson started up the alley, clumping half a dozen paces before he noticed the tiefling was not following. He stopped and looked back to see her studying the direction from which they had just come.

"Jayk?"

The tiefling glanced at him only briefly, her eyes filled with fear, then looked back the way she had been staring. For a moment, the Thrasson thought she would bolt, but then her shoulders slumped and she started up the alley toward him.

"Zoombee, how does he know?"

"Know what, Jayk?"

"That we will do what he orders." She passed the Amnesian Hero without stopping, then stepped into the Great Way. "I think we will never be free of him."

Her name is not Sheba, of course. Karfhud calls her that because she reminds him of a succubus who once bested him in the fray. But the monster of the labyrinth has no name; she would not even understand what a name is, for it is beyond her to think of others apart from herself. She is like Silverwind that way—or any of us, if we look deeply enough—except that she never despairs, and that makes her ever so much stronger—strong enough, even, to defeat a tanar'ri lord.

That is what the Amnesian Hero is thinking as he clumps down the Great Way, trying to keep pace with Jayk. Unlike the tiefling, he is losing his fear of Karfhud, for he has begun to understand what the tanar'ri wants from them. For centuries—it has been millennia, but no mortal can truly conceive of such a time—for countless ages, the fiend has been lost in the labyrinths. The Thrasson is no tanar'ri, but he knows enough about the wicked race to understand that to a powerful lord like Karfhud, being trapped is less an abuse than not being master of the prison.

What the fiend wants is to kill the monster. The Thrasson begins to form his plan; he is thinking of the amphora, of course, and of Karfhud's maps, and he is wise enough to know that the tanar'ri knows what he is thinking. But there will be a battle, and battles breed confusion, and when the confusion passes, it will be the one who still stands that has the amphora and the maps and his life.

And so, leaving it to Jayk to ignore the corners and see the Great Way as a straight line and count the alleys on the right and guide them into the twenty-ninth on the left, the Amnesian Hero plots and schemes and falls so deeply into thought that he does not notice as Jayk guides them to the left at the "T" intersection, and he does not mark the growing rumble of thunder or the rising steam-laden breeze, and he does not hear the clatter of galloping hooves reverberating off the iron walls, or heed even the monster's sonorous roar until it breaks over the maze like Hephaestus's mighty hammer knelling upon its anvil.

By the time the Amnesian Hero has realized what is happening and draws his sword, Silverwind has rounded the corner ahead at a full gallop. With Tessali's gruesome stumps wrapped around his waist and the roar of a hailstorm echoing close on his tail, the bariaur glances at Jayk and the Thrasson only briefly, as though he has expected all along to meet them in precisely that spot, and continues on.

"Flee for your lives!" Silverwind veered toward one side of the passage. "Oh, I have recalled you at a bad time!"

"The monster's hard behind us!" Tessali looked far too frightened to be surprised by the Amnesian Hero's return. "Run!"

Seeing that there was no time to convince his companions to stay and fight, the Amnesian Hero extended his brick foot and caught Silverwind's front hooves. The bariaur bleated and pitched forward, then he and Tessali bounced off the hot iron wall and went tumbling across the bricks together.

"Zoombee?" Jayk sounded more curious than alarmed. "Why do you—"

The Amnesian Hero pushed her behind him. "Prepare your spells—and tell Silverwind to do the same." A cloud of rust-colored steam boiled around the corner ahead, followed closely by a wall of driving hail. "Maybe you have something to clear the storm?"

Behind him rose Tessali's voice, groaning and cursing the

Thrasson for a menace and a berk. The Amnesian Hero ignored the insults and clumped forward, veering toward the inside wall of the corner. He knew better than to think he would surprise the monster—Sheba was much too cunning to round a blind corner on the inside—but he only needed to stall her long enough for Karfhud to arrive.

The Amnesian Hero stopped two paces shy of the corner. He took his sword in both hands and pressed as close to the scorching iron as he could bear. Behind him, his companions, mere silhouettes in the curtain of hail, were standing close together. Both Jayk and Silverwind were fumbling for spell components, but their attention seemed alarmingly divided. Tessali was leaning across the bariaur's back, gesturing wildly with his wrist stumps and hurling questions at Jayk. The tiefling shrugged and shook her head in disavowal, less concerned with the coming battle than with appeasing the elf. She was still in shock from Karfhud's attack; certainly, she would never have worried about such a thing before.

The Amnesian Hero felt a cold prickle between his shoulder blades. He looked across the passage to see an ice-gray blur rounding the corner. Her long mats of fur rendered her almost invisible in the driving hail; she seemed a mere deepening of the storm, a ghostly mass drifting slowly forward through the orange steam. Only the neck of the amphora, protruding on the far side of her body, looked at all solid.

The Thrasson cursed his bad luck that the jar was on the other side of the monster, then sprang across the passage to slash at Sheba's leg. If he could strike her lame, he would be free to stall until Karfhud arrived to finish the kill. After that, surviving—and laying claim to the fiend's maps—would become a simple matter of keeping his head while the tanar'ri and the monster killed each other.

The Amnesian Hero thumped down beside Sheba, his star-forged blade already biting into her leg. In the next instant, a deafening bellow reverberated down the iron passage, then a huge hand came from nowhere to crash into the Thrasson's shoulder. He lost his sword and went tumbling across the bricks and, three somersaults later, slammed into a scorching wall. There was a loud sizzle and the smell of burnt flesh, yet the Amnesian Hero felt only a faint nettling where his bare flesh touched the blistering metal. He pushed off the wall and tumbled to his knees, then found himself staring up at a curtain of matted fur. A huge, black-taloned mitt was reaching down to clutch him.

The Amnesian Hero ducked his shoulder and rolled, only to have Sheba pivot around before he could get his feet under him. He glimpsed a stripe of oozing black sap where his star-forged blade had bit into the knee, but the limb appeared discouragingly whole. He saw no sign of his weapon; the sword lay lost somewhere in the steam. The monster reached for him again, and the Thrasson began to wonder if his companions had abandoned him.

"Jayk?"

His scream was answered by the hail-muffled syllables of the tiefling's incantation. A pair of yellow streaks flashed through the orange steam, pulsing into the monster's shoulder, then bursting in a spray of golden light and silver fur. Sheba grunted and stumbled a single step back.

The Amnesian Hero crab-scrambled around behind the monster, frantically sweeping his hands across the bricks in search of his sword—and hoping he would not find it by slicing his fingers off. Sheba gave a baffled growl, then her head began to pendulum back and forth as she searched for him.

Silverwind cast his spell, filling the passage with a booming incantation even louder than the pounding hail. A roaring wind came blasting down the corridor to sweep the steam around the corner and blow the hailstorm back the way it had come.

When the tempest cleared, Sheba was staring directly at the Thrasson's sword, which lay less than three paces in front of her foot. The Amnesian Hero, slightly behind her and off to one side, found himself well beyond the limit of her peripheral vision—at least that was what he hoped. The amphora was tucked beneath the monster's arm on his side of her body. He considered trying to knock it free and dive for his sword, but decided that he had a better chance of getting stuck in her gummy fur than coming up with either his weapon or the jar.

The monster pivoted, her head tipped forward to search for her foe. The Amnesian Hero started to crab-walk around behind her, hoping to complete the circle and grab his sword—and that was when he noticed a huge black shadow slipping around the corner.

At last.

The Amnesian Hero let his brick foot clatter on the ground behind the monster, then he threw himself in the opposite direction, diving for his sword. Sheba was already spinning; her talons raked furrows of cold pain down his spine, but he was much lower than she had expected and going in the opposite direction. He belly-flopped onto the bricks and crawled to his sword, then whirled onto his mangled back, bringing the blade around just in case she attacked him instead of switching to Karfhud.

Sheba was nowhere in sight.

The Thrasson found himself staring directly up at the fiend, whose smoldering eyes were focused somewhere up the passage. The Amnesian Hero rolled once more and saw the monster, with the amphora tucked beneath her arm, loping past his companions. They were so terrified that they did not seem to notice their backs pressed tight against the scorching iron walls. The Thrasson hoisted himself to his feet and clumped up the corridor in his best imitation of a sprint.

Karfhud's massive hand caught him by the shoulder. "It is too late." The evenness of the fiend's tone was surprising; certainly, the mind-reading tanar'ri knew how the Thrasson had tried to play Sheba off against him, yet his voice betrayed no ill will. "Now we must do this the hard way."

"Do what the hard way?" the Amnesian Hero asked.

"Only what we both wish to do—hunt down Sheba."

Karfhud watched the monster disappear around a corner, then turned his gaze upon Tessali and Silverwind. The pair were staring at him and looking even more frightened than they had when Sheba was chasing them.

"But first, Thrasson, we must do something about your brick foot," said Karfhud. "We will both need to be at our best. Call your friends; they will be of use."

"You won't hurt them?"

Karfhud shook his head. "I told you, they will be of use."

Thus reassured, more or less, the Amnesian Hero waved his companions down the passage. Led by Jayk, they approached to within a few paces and stopped. Silverwind promptly began to chastise himself for failing to retain better control over his evil side.

"We are all tired." Karfhud spoke over Silverwind's rantings, at once silencing the old cleric and taking command of the little company. "We will rest here."

Always one to challenge another's authority, Tessali shook his head. "We must reach the ash maze as quickly as possible." He raised his arms, displaying the bandaged wrist stumps. "My hands were cut off, and we must–"

"Your hands are not there. I have already eaten one." Karfhud reached into his back satchel and produced the elf's remaining hand. "And I fear your tiefling friend overcooked the other one."

Tessali stared at the charred hand for a full twenty heartbeats before uttering a sound. Then he let out such a shriek that it sounded as though he was dying of shock. At length, it became clear that he was actually screeching a question.

"You what?"

Karfhud shrugged. "It was a mistake–but I warn you, I will eat the other one if you do not quiet yourself."

Tessali fell silent, but made the mistake of reaching for the charred hand. Karfhud pushed the elf to the ground, then stuffed the appendage back into his satchel.

"I will keep this one, to insure your cooperation–and your silence." Without awaiting a reply, the fiend turned to Silverwind. "Bariaur, you will prepare your healing magic."

The fiend's command seemed to jolt Silverwind out of his confusion, at least for the moment. "Healing magic–for what?"

"We must change the Thrasson's brick foot for a flesh one." Karfhud removed his back satchel, then opened it and pulled an enormous wineskin from inside. This he held out to the Amnesian Hero. "You may drink your fill."

Jayk quickly intercepted the skin. "That idea, she is a very bad one. When he drinks–"

"I know what happens." Karfhud jerked the wineskin away, then thrust it into the Thrasson's hands. "Drink. I will clean your sword for you."

The Amnesian Hero accepted the skin and yielded his sword, which was still coated with Sheba's saplike blood. The Thrasson pulled the stopper from the wine sack and took a long swallow. The stuff tasted like stump water, but it was powerful, and it quenched his thirst. Without asking the fiend's permission, he poured a long draught into Tessali's mouth, then passed the sack to Jayk and Silverwind.

Karfhud made no comment on the Amnesian Hero's generosity. Instead, the fiend slashed open one of his own veins, then dribbled his blood over the Thrasson's star-forged sword. The foul-smelling stuff hissed and bubbled and instantly dissolved the sticky black gunk that Sheba's wound had left smeared over the blade.

"Tanar'ri blood: the best cleansing agent in the multiverse." Karfhud dried the star-forged blade, then took the wineskin from Jayk's hands and passed it back to the Amnesian Hero. "Drink; this will hurt."

"What?" The Thrasson demanded.

Karfhud ignored him, instead motioning Jayk to sit down in the middle of the passage. "Tiefling, you will hold the Thrasson—and no biting."

The Amnesian Hero was beginning to understand the fiend's plan. "Karfhud, I am not going to—"

The fiend whirled on him. "Did I not swear I would cause you no harm?"

"Yes, but—"

"I warn you, if you are lame when you enter Sheba's lair, you will not leave again." Karfhud let out a long breath, then calmed himself and stepped back. "But the choice is yours. I will not force you."

The Amnesian Hero thought for a moment, then lifted the wineskin and began to drink.

"Good." Karfhud turned to Silverwind. "Are you ready?"

The bariaur nodded, then kneeled close to Jayk and began to

lay out the components of his healing spells.

"Is there anything I can do?" Tessali cast a glum look at his wrist stumps, then added, "I used to be a healer."

Karfhud studied the elf for a moment, then motioned him over. "Perhaps you would do me the honor of standing at my side. I may have need of advice."

The fiend spoke with such compassion that, had he not been a tanar'ri, the Amnesian Hero would have sworn he was trying to make Tessali feel better. As it was, Karfhud's kind words only puzzled—and worried—the Thrasson.

"Karfhud, I'm sure you know—"

"Drink up, Thrasson!" Karfhud's eyes flashed like forge flames. "And do not worry about Tessali. Helping will do him good."

"Indeed it will." The elf went to the fiend's side. "I am glad to offer what little I can."

The Amnesian Hero raised the skin and took another drink. The wine had already filled his head with sweet clouds, but not so thickly that it had befuddled him as much as the fiend's flattery seemed to befuddle the elf. Karfhud kneeled beside the Thrasson. Then, when Tessali had come over to stand at his side, he grabbed the brick foot and, without ceremony, brought the sword down.

The Amnesian Hero had not expected it to hurt—not really—but he had never been so wrong in his life. Even before his brick foot had clattered to the ground, a ferocious ache was shooting up his leg to his very heart, so paralyzingly painful he could not even scream. He noticed Jayk's fingernails digging into his shoulders, then felt his own fingernails clawing at the ground, then began to yell for more wine.

Silverwind picked up the skin and poured a long draught down his throat, and that was when Karfhud grabbed Tessali's ankle. With a quick yank, the fiend jerked the elf off his legs, then raised the Thrasson's star-forged sword to strike off a foot.

The Amnesian Hero pushed the wineskin aside. "No!"

Karfhud's head snapped around. "You must have a foot!"

"Not . . . not someone else's!" The Thrasson shook himself free of Jayk's grasp and sat up—then nearly blacked out when he saw the muddy slime oozing from his ankle stump. "Not . . . Tessali's!"

"But he will be no use in Sheba's lair!" Karfhud objected. "He cannot fight. He can cast no spells. He cannot even carry our weapons."

Tessali, lying on the ground very still, said nothing.

"I won't . . . have it!" The Thrasson turned his tattooed palm toward the fiend. "I . . . will . . . die first."

For once, Jayk did not inform the Amnesian Hero that he was already dead. Instead, she leaned forward and placed her lips upon the Thrasson's throat, then whispered, "We die together, Zoombee."

"That won't be necessary." Karfhud released his terrified captive, then pulled his back-satchel over and removed the elf's blackened hand from a side pocket. "We can make do with this."

"A hand?" gasped Silverwind.

"It seems to be all we have." Karfhud tossed the appendage to the bariaur. "I suppose you have a spell of enlargement?"

NAME

In the Thrasson's sleep, two disembodied hands—charred hands, with long black talons and black flakes peeling off to expose the mottled pink flesh beneath—brush along his naked body. They are cold against his skin, and scaly, and they leave a trail of moldering reek wherever they touch: his cheeks, his neck and shoulders, his armpits, down to his stomach, over his hips and back again to that area of dark tangles and darker cravings, along his thighs, past his knees to his feet, even to his toes; wherever they roam, he feels his flesh rising up in welts, swelling into thumb-shaped lumps that sprout tiny hooked spines and start to pulse. The blisters grow large as melons. They turn emerald and gold and ruby and jet, and ooze ichor, and throb like hearts, and so heavily do they weigh upon the Amnesian Hero that he cannot rise. He cannot sit upright to look at his pod-palled body; he cannot lift so much as his finger to flick the fetid husks away.

It is the beauty of dreams to reveal what is true without betraying what is real—or so I have heard. In truth, unless this endless watching is a nightmare, I cannot say. It has been so long since I dared to sleep that I have forgotten what it is to dream, or even to rest. Always must I be on guard, lest some god think to storm my ramparts; always must I survey those who come and those who go, lest one is the spy who leaves open the gate. To slumber is to surrender, for then my enemies will surely come and prevail.

And it is the same for the Thrasson. As he slept away the wine and the pain, Ruin has come stealing along, to hold his head in her lap and tickle her soft touch over his body high and low; she has folded him gently in her arms and hugged him close, and it is her hands that he dreams of even now, each caress drawing forth another of the heaving pods that have been slowly ripening since first he entered Sigil.

In his dream, the disembodied black hands sprout a pair of ivory arms from their severed wrists; the arms begin to grow, slowly stretching up to connect with the shoulders and torso of a naked woman. This is all the Thrasson can see, for he remains pinned beneath the heavy, throbbing husks—but it is enough. The woman has the full figure of a goddess and the smooth skin of a statue, and her humming voice is as sweet as a trilling flute.

Slowly, it returns to him: the terrible shock of Karfhud lopping away his brick foot, the horrid searing of Silverwind melting the huge blackened hand onto his ankle, the dark sick tide rising up to swallow him, the shadowy fingers digging into his shoulders as Jayk struggles to hold him down.

"J—Jayk." He tries to crane his neck back to see her face, but the bloated throbbing husks hold him down. Still, through the lingering haze of wine and pain, it seems to him something is wrong with the color of her skin. "Jayk? It's me—Zoombee."

"Zombie? You mustn't say such things." The voice is female and familiar, but it does not belong to the tiefling. "You're far from dead, my love."

His wine woman!

She lays her palms upon the Thrasson's cheeks; her hands still feel scaly and charred. Her lap shifts beneath his head. She leans down, bringing her face close to his, her bosom flattening the bloated pods that cover his chest. The Amnesian Hero sees a visage classic and narrow, an aquiline nose, a cold, callous gaze—a halo of many-styled blades.

He dreams the woman is me.

An emerald husk, squeezed too tightly between their close-pressed bodies, bursts; green ichor oozes down his flank, oily and full of bitter stink. Wherever the stuff touches, he bristles with a chill nettling; cold needles of agony pierce his skin, then drive deeper with agonizing languor. So slowly do they sink that he suffers before he suffers. His dread deepens faster than the anguish itself.

The Thrasson tries to push the woman away, but he cannot raise his arms. He screams, frightened by his immobility. All of the green pods burst, and the ichor paints him emerald head to foot; he burns with that slow, terrible scalding and shrieks and wails, anguished more by what he fears than by what he feels. The Amnesian Hero has succumbed to the first Pain.

"*Sssshhhh!* You mustn't draw the others to us! I have waited too long for this." The voice remains that of his wine woman. She smothers his cries with a kiss, then whispers a trio of soft syllables: "Theseus."

The word plucks a harp string inside the Thrasson's breast, sets his whole being to thrumming. Suddenly, he stops dreaming. Theseus was somebody's name, he remembers.

It was *his* name.

His eyes snapped open, and the Thrasson found himself lying on the hard brick pavement, looking up not at the Lady of Pain's face, but at that of his wine woman. She was beautiful as ever, with olive skin and emerald eyes and high, proud cheeks.

"Theseus?" he croaked. "I am Theseus?"

"You remember!"

The wine woman gave him a moon-bright smile and hugged him close to her breast, and that was when the Thrasson—no, Theseus—that was when Theseus remembered the throbbing husks of ichor clinging to his breast.

"No, wait—"

A trio of yellow pods burst, filling the air with the stench of spoiled meat. A pasty yellow ichor spread down the Thrasson's breast. Belts of crushing agony tightened around his chest; the pain began to sink, dropping through his sternum and slipping down between his ribs, settling deep into his torso. A blanket of grim wet pain fell over his lungs, and Theseus found himself fighting to draw every anguished breath. He felt cold fingers around his heart, not squeezing so much as holding, thwarting the swell of each beat so that his entire chest cramped with every pulse.

As the pain deepened, the reek of the yellow ichor grew stronger and more bitter, until the smell grew so overwhelming that Theseus could not prevent himself from gagging. The convulsion caused more yellow pods to burst; more golden ichor spilled over his body, and crushing bands of agony began to tighten around his stomach, his legs, even his throat. The rancid rotten-meat stench grew overwhelming, and he knew he could not keep himself from retching.

The wine woman barely had time to push Theseus's head off her lap. She jumped up and glared down at him, her mouth twisted into an expression of distaste.

"Is the scent of my bosom so sickening to you, Theseus?" Her emerald eyes betrayed no hint that she smelled the stench of the awful ichor that covered his body, nor that she saw the bloated pods clinging to it. "Has our love grown so repulsive to you?"

Theseus shook his head, and a painful ringing echoed through his skull. "No. Our love is well—I am sure."

"Then prove it." The woman raised her chin. "Tell me."

Now that the green and yellow pods had burst, Theseus was not so heavily burdened. He managed to raise his head so that he could look his wine woman directly in the face. "I love you."

Tears welled in her eyes. "You're lying! How can you declare your love without even knowing my name?" She began to back away, her lips trembling. "I thought you would remember if I told you your name—but you've forgotten me!"

"No!" Theseus stretched a hand toward her, causing the last yellow husk to burst. His arm went limp and dropped to the ground, feeling as though Karfhud had stomped on his elbow. "Can't you see? I'm in pain!"

"So am I!"

With that, the woman spun and ran out of sight.

"Wait!"

Theseus gathered his strength and rolled onto his side, intending to rise and go after her. Instead, he smashed two red pods clinging to his flank. The husks burst, filling the air with a smell so cloying and sweet it dizzied him. The red ichor did not spill over the ground, but spread upward over his body, drawn into his flesh as lamp oil is drawn into the wick. His skin began to burn, then went strangely numb. He suddenly felt hollow and broken inside. A vague nausea welled up someplace deep in his belly, and what little strength he had been able to muster abruptly drained from his limbs. He rolled onto his back, crushing more red pods; he felt the ruby ichor rising into his flesh, stinging his skin with that strange burning numbness.

Theseus thought the hollow feeling would start expanding again; he expected to grow weaker, to feel even more broken within. Instead, he experienced a fierce longing to hold the wine woman in his arms, to fill the emptiness inside him and feel her lips pressed to his, her bosom crushed against his chest, her loins grinding into his own. He could think of nothing but her, of his desire for her and how unfair she was to desert him. He would have her; he would hunt her down and seize her and make her understand that he had forgotten her through no fault of his own.

The Thrasson's strength rushed back to his limbs. He pushed himself upright and saw that the wine woman had dragged him away from his companions. The passage was flanked by the rusty red walls of the iron maze and paved with the same dark bricks, but he was sitting in a small dogleg passage he did not recognize, and there were no signs of his four companions.

It did not matter; nothing mattered except catching his wine woman. Theseus started to draw his legs up, and that was when he saw the hand.

The thing was flopping there at the end of his leg, just below the inflamed, crudely stitched seam where it joined his ankle. About twice the size of a normal hand, the appendage was still ugly and charred and covered with scaly black flakes and mottled patches of bare skin. The pinky was where his big toe should have been, and the thumb was on the outside where the little toe should have been. The long fingers, seared and slender as they were, made the thing look more like a fiend's claw than a man's foot.

Theseus tried to bend his big toe. The blackened pinky started to curl, and that was when his last red pod burst. He had done nothing to squeeze the husk or jar it. The thing had just grown too full and split, spilling ruby ichor down his breast.

Again, there was that cloying sweet smell and the strange numbness sinking into his skin. Something shattered inside, and a terrible, overwhelming grief filled Theseus. He would never catch the wine woman with that ghastly thing on his foot! And, even if he did, how could she ever return his love? If not a monster, he had become at least a monstrosity–hardly worthy of the adoration of someone so beautiful as his wine woman!

Theseus let his body slam back to the ground, barely noticing as his skull smashed onto the hard bricks.

"Karfhud," he cried, "what have you done to me?"

The Thrasson had barely uttered the fiend's name before a blocky, horned shadow fell over his face.

"There you are. I was beginning to fear you would not think to call my name." The ground shuddered beneath the fiend's steps, then Karfhud's yellow-fanged muzzle appeared over Theseus. "I cannot imagine how you wandered this far. Silverwind said you would be in too much pain to walk."

"It was my beloved," the Thrasson explained. "She brought me here."

"That cannot be. Jayk is still–" Karfhud stopped in mid sentence, reading the Thrasson's next thought even as it formed itself. "I shall have to keep a careful watch for this wine woman. It is a rare kidnapper who can steal a cap–er–comrade while my back is turned."

"She did not steal me." As the Thrasson stared up at Karfhud's face, he was surprised to notice a thick coating of yellow ichor and a golden, goiterlike pod throbbing on the fiend's neck. "Had I been awake, I would certainly have gone willingly. I would do it now."

"And miss the battle with Sheba?" Karfhud scoffed. "I thought you wanted to recover your amphora and steal my maps—or have you lost your ambition, now that you recall your name?"

"There is still enough I do not recall." Theseus was surprised to notice another yellow pod, much smaller, dangling beneath the fiend's pointed ear. He wondered if Karfhud was aware of the two husks. "And whether I recover the amphora or not, I will never lose interest in finding the exit to this place."

"Then let us return to the others; Silverwind must ready you for battle, and then we will attack."

Karfhud stepped around to Theseus's side and kneeled down to pick him up. The fiend's body was coated in yellow ichor, and there were at least ten golden pods, ranging in size from no larger than a thumb to as big as Sheba's head, dangling from his body. The Thrasson saw no husks of any other color hanging on the tanar'ri.

Before taking Theseus into his arms, Karfhud hesitated and glanced down at his body. "What are you looking at? I see no pods!"

"Here."

Theseus tried to pluck a husk off the fiend's body. He might as well have tried to grab a bubble; the pod burst the instant his fingers touched it, and a fresh wave of golden ichor spilled down the tanar'ri's chest.

Karfhud hissed in pain, then glared at the Thrasson with yellow flames licking in the pupils of his maroon eyes. "Whatever you did, do not do it again!"

With that, the tanar'ri snatched the Thrasson into his arms and turned up the passage. Theseus smiled at his newfound weapon, then glanced over his own body and frowned. He still had twice as many pods as Karfhud, and all of them were black.

PAINS OF THE SPIRIT

The fog drags across my face, coarse and sour as damp wool, heavy with the smell of blood and cleaved bone and entrails strewn across gray waters. The streets murmur with the sound of whimpering children and the rasp of tiny claws scraping raw bone, with the disbelieving groans of the slow and the foolish and the unlucky. The night air is cold for Sigil; my breath shoots yellow and steamy from my mouth, and from the tips of my steel halo depend crimson icicles.

I am disappointed—I admit that, and freely—but only in myself, only in my failure to see what is obvious. The wine woman has been helping him all along: it was she who lured Tessali and his guards out of Rivergate, it was she who led him to Karfhud, and—though I need not tell *you*—it can only be the wine woman who revealed the pods to him. Wine has that power over men, I know; it makes clear to them what they otherwise do not see at all.

Still, I must ask you why.

Sympathy for the Thrasson, I understand. He is the Amnesian Hero, and ever are you mortals searching for heroes. But what of Poseidon? Is not aid to this battered castaway—

(Do not think me fool enough to call him Theseus, for well do I know the legend: how he was gotten on Aethra by two fathers at once, King Aegeus and the god Poseidon; how he found Aegeus's sandals and sword beneath a boulder and cleared the road of robbers as he walked to Athens to claim his birthright; how he narrowly escaped death at the poisoning hands of his father's jealous queen; how he sailed to the land of King Minos and, with the aid of the king's own daughter Ariadne, entered the labyrinth and slew the terrible Minotaur; how he forgot Ariadne on the isle of Naxos and in his distress neglected to signal his safe return, so grieving his father that the king threw himself off a cliff—a clever way to usurp a throne, was it not? How he bequeathed democracy upon his city. . . . I know the whole legend, this and much more, so do not think to fool me into calling this addle-brained, hand-footed castaway Theseus!)

—aid to the King of Seas? If the Amnesian Hero and Theseus are the same, then is his mother not Aethra? Are the memories in the amphora not true, and if true for him, then not also true for me? You must see where that will lead: back to the banks of the River Lethe, to the dark thieving waters and the question that must not be answered.

So I must ask again, did *you* send her, and *why?*

GRAY WATERS

Bruised palm slapping stony ground and leg still throbbing from ankle to hip, the Thrasson hobbles through the rocky gorge as best he can, hissing his breath between clenched teeth and clutching his star-forged sword tightly in his hand. On all his companions he sees pods and ichor: green ooze dripping from Tessali's stumps, emerald and ruby husks throbbing on Jayk's shadowy breast, ebony slime and white blisters clinging everywhere to Silverwind, yellow hulls squeezing out beneath Karfhud's back-satchel, black burrs cleaving to his own breast. Despite his pain, despite all the pain clinging to his companions, he thinks of nothing but the fiend's bitter wine, of the wine woman's return, of folding her into his arms and . . .

First, there is a battle to win, an amphora to recover, memories to reclaim, a woman's name to recall, a fiend to fell, and maps to steal. After the victory, there will time for drinking and celebrating and lovemaking, the Thrasson is quite certain. To best a tanar'ri lord, to rescue a lost love, to escape the Lady's mazes, all in one day, all with a hand for a foot and only cripples and barmies for a war party, will be his greatest feat yet. The gods themselves will sing praises to the name of Theseus!

A hero's spirit, they say, never breaks.

But will it shatter?

Karfhud's pace has been slowing for some time, and now he has stopped before an irregular circle of darkness hanging on the side of the gorge. The blackened area could have been a cave, save for the scorch marks on the opposite wall of the passage. The fiend has furled his map, bent his arm around at that impossible angle and stuffed the roll into his satchel.

"Prepare yourselves," he said, pulling out an unmarked parchment. "We are entering Sheba's lair."

With that, the tanar'ri stepped into the mouth of the blackness. A tongue of flame lashed out to lick briefly at the gorge's opposite wall, then died away. Theseus moved forward, blocking the conjunction, and faced his remaining companions.

"This is your chance to escape the tanar'ri, my friends." Theseus ran an uneasy gaze over the pods on his companions' bodies, wondering if he could prevent the husks from bursting by sparing his friends the battle to come. "The fighting will begin soon, and then Karfhud will be too busy to come back for you."

"What about you, Zoombee?"

The question took Theseus by surprise. Since departing the iron maze, Jayk and Tessali had been hanging back together, quietly whispering back and forth so intensely they had nearly gotten lost several times. The Thrasson had assumed—perhaps even hoped—that the tiefling's crisis of faith had caused a transfer of affections. Apparently, the conversation had been less romantic than he imagined.

"For my own reasons, I'm as eager as the tanar'ri to kill the monster." Theseus raised his hand, displaying the gruesome face tattooed on his palm. "Besides, as long as I have this, the choice is not truly in my . . . hands."

Jayk stepped forward. "Then I am going too, Zoombee."

"It would be sa—" The Thrasson caught himself and did not say "safe," unsure how Jayk might react to the suggestion that she feared for her life. "It might be better to wait here."

The tiefling shook her head stubbornly. "My place is with you."

"And I certainly have no intention of letting you slip my thoughts again," said Silverwind. "You are the thread that will lead me out of here."

Theseus looked to Tessali, who now stood at the back of the line looking disgruntled and more than a little frightened.

"I have no intention of staying here alone, if that's what you're hoping. You'll just have to keep an eye out for me." The elf glanced at the Thrasson's feet. "After all, that's my hand you have there."

"As you wish." Theseus was addressing all three of his companions. "But don't be afraid to turn and run. It will be easier to kill the monster if I know you are safe."

Theseus raised his sword to a middle guard, then turned and leapt through the conjunction. There was no splash, and no ripples spreading across the silvery surface away from where he stood. The Thrasson simply found himself standing chest-deep in the cloudy gray waters of a narrow swamp channel, the fingers of his new foot curling into the silky mud bottom. A pearly fog lay upon the water like smoke, so thick that he could barely make out tangled webs of prop roots rising along the banks to support impenetrable thickets of vine-choked bog trees.

About four paces down the passage stood Karfhud, a black silhouette rising from the water like a great cypress. He was looking down one of the passages of a four-way intersection, holding his map in one hand and tracing a line upon its surface with a talon of the other. The air was still and hot, and so quiet Theseus could hear the rasp of the fiend's claw on the parchment.

"The others did not want to wait." Karfhud was not asking a question. "They think you will be their salvation, but you must not let them distract you. In the mazes, each must look out for himself."

"I expect you to protect them as you would me." Theseus remained near the conjunction, so that the flames shooting from the other side would prevent his companions from coming through until he was more familiar with the area. "If you fail, don't expect any help from me."

"What makes you think I expect help now?" Karfhud dipped his talon into the wound he had opened on his opposite wrist, then used the blood to draw a line on his parchment. "You will find it necessary to defend yourself, and that is enough."

"Enough for what?"

Instead of answering, Karfhud motioned the Thrasson forward. "Let your friends in. The longer we tarry, the less I map before Sheba attacks."

Theseus remained where he stood, wondering if he could force the fiend to tell him what was so important about mapping the monster's lair.

"I would tell you," Karfhud said, reading his thoughts. "But then I would have to kill you, and I have already sworn not to do that."

"We both know the value of that oath."

Karfhud's head snapped around, his maroon eyes flashing so hotly that little beams of scarlet seemed to shoot through the fog. "That is the trouble with you honorable types. In your arrogance, you presume to know the tanar'ri mind. You know nothing. If you did, you would think less highly of yourselves."

"Perhaps—but it does not change our circumstance. We both know that one of us, at least, will perish before this battle is done."

A low rumble began to echo out of the sky, quickly building to a tremendous bellow that set the tree leaves to quivering and the surface of the water to shuddering. Karfhud cast a nervous glance down each of the passages around him, then looked back to Theseus.

"There is no need for matters to end as you say. My maps will not lead you out of the mazes."

"Perhaps I would believe you if you told me why you're making them."

The fog began to thicken, and Karfhud hissed a curse. "Release me from my oath, and I will tell you."

Theseus raised his brow, shocked by the fiend's demand. Why would the tanar'ri want his oath released, unless he was bound to keep it?

"Or unless I wanted you to think I was bound." Karfhud peered into the thickening fog, pretending to study a side passage. "Your arrogance is a pity, really. Once you know what I am doing, you will lose interest."

"That is for me to decide."

Another bellow rumbled over the swamp, this time shaking the trees so hard that several dead branches cracked and fell. Karfhud glanced up at the leafy canopy, which was nearly concealed in the dense fog, then shrugged.

"I will tell you this much: this is the last one."

"The last what?"

"Labyrinth," the fiend replied. "I have plotted all the others. Once I have done with this one, my maps will be complete."

"That's not possible. You're lying."

Karfhud dipped his horned head in the Thrasson's direction. "Your arrogance is beyond imagining."

"You can't map all of the mazes. Silverwind says that a new one is created for every person who—"

"Silverwind is correct," Karfhud interrupted. "But you entered the mazes in the company of Tessali and Jayk, and you are all together. If Silverwind is right, should you not each be in a separate labyrinth?"

Theseus frowned, trying to find the string that would help him unravel this riddle.

"A millennium would not be time enough for you to solve this enigma," Karfhud said. "You honorable types have no grasp of the Plurality. The answer is simple: there is only one maze, and there are many mazes."

The Thrasson scowled. "Now you are talking nonsense."

"Am I?" Karfhud glanced down a side passage, then turned away and started to wade in the opposite direction. "I will explain as I work, if you wish, but I have done with waiting. You are no good to me if Sheba kills you here. I'll only have to retreat again."

The fiend vanished around the corner, leaving Theseus alone at the end of the channel. The Thrasson quickly waded forward, for he needed Karfhud's help as much as the tanar'ri needed his.

Only together could they hope to slay the monster of the labyrinth—or at least to keep her at bay long enough to recover the amphora and map the maze.

Theseus had barely reached the intersection before Silverwind came through the conjunction with Tessali on his back and Jayk in his arms. There was a loud splash as the bariaur dropped the tiefling's legs into the water. An instant later, another of Sheba's thunderous bellows reverberated through the swamp.

"Zoombee!" Jayk threw herself into the channel and began to swim after Theseus.

Silverwind, still carrying Tessali on his back, plowed through the water close behind. The Thrasson waited for the others to catch up, unsettled by the tiefling's uncharacteristic display of fear. As happy as he was to see that she valued her life, he had the uncomfortable feeling that she had attributed that value to him—and he had the wine woman to think of.

Jayk stopped at his side and set her feet on the bottom. "Zoombee, you stayed very long in front of the conjunction." She reached for his arm. "The fight, we thought she had already started!"

"Without you? Never!" Theseus freed his arm from the tiefling's grasp, then glanced at Silverwind and Tessali. "Prepare yourselves, and keep a sharp watch."

The Thrasson turned and led the way after Karfhud.

They caught the tanar'ri at the next intersection, where the fiend had stopped to make some more scratchings. Theseus quickly assigned each of his other companions to watch in a separate direction, taking forward for himself.

He slipped past the tanar'ri to assume his post. "Karfhud, you were going to explain?"

The fiend looked up and cocked his head. "Very quiet." He started down one of the passages he had just marked. "She is coming for us."

"Don't change the subject." Theseus glanced back to make certain the others were following, then positioned himself ahead of the fiend. "How can one maze—"

"What is it you seek?" Karfhud interrupted. "In the mazes, I mean to say."

"Only one thing: the exit."

"And that is why you will never find it." They waded around a gentle curve and entered a long, snaking channel where the bog trees hung so low that Karfhud's horns ticked against the boughs as they moved forward. "You are also seeking something else—something for which you are willing to fight Sheba. Think."

"That requires no thought." Craning his neck back so he could keep watch on the low-hanging canopy, Theseus relied on the charred hand sewn onto his ankle to feel his way through the water. "I want the amphora."

"Because?"

"Because I promised to deliver it to the Lady of Pain."

"I am done wasting my breath on you!" Karfhud growled. "I could give you my maps, and you would never find your exit!"

Theseus glared over his shoulder at the fiend's maze-blighted face. "If you are so wise, why are you still here? Why haven't you found your own way out?"

Karfhud's maroon eyes deepened to black. "What makes you think I want to?"

A distant sloshing sounded someplace ahead, eliciting a startled gasp from both Jayk and Tessali.

Theseus turned his attention forward. "Maybe we should try another passage."

"That is what she wants," said Karfhud. "Otherwise, we would have heard nothing. We are doing better than I had hoped."

"Better?"

Instead of replying, Karfhud slipped past the Thrasson and continued up the passage, using his own blood to carefully trace each bend and curve on the parchment. Happy to let the fiend assume the risk of leading the way, Theseus waded along behind, periodically glancing back to check on his companions. It was hardly necessary; Jayk and Silverwind did not look away from the channel banks for so much as a second, while Tessali, reverse-mounted on the bariaur's back, was gazing holes through the fog behind them.

Sheba was far too cunning to attack while the party remained so alert. Aside from the recurrent rumble of her bellowing and an occasional slosh in the distance, she did little to trouble the odd company. Karfhud was able to map more of the swamp than he had hoped, and Theseus had plenty of time to consider their earlier conversation. The Thrasson's true reason for wanting the amphora was to learn more about his past. Regardless of his promise to Poseidon, the memories in the jar were his, and by rights he should have them. Even if he were to happen upon the exit at that very moment, he doubted he would leave without the amphora's treasure.

See how gently the rot steals into the soul? How smoothly the wish unfulfilled becomes the right withheld? Show me the heart that is pure, and I will show you the heart that is stone. We all have our Karfhuds, our unquenchable thirsts, our secret treasons; we all have our reasonable excuses and our tempering cases, but that cannot change what we have done. We have all struck our bargains. Pretending that we had no choice does not make us tragic or noble or virtuous—it only makes us weak.

"Deeper."

Karfhud had stopped in the confluence of five channels, and he was carefully peering down each one and marking it with his own blood.

Theseus scanned the area. The silvery waters still rose only to Karfhud's waist, the channels ahead remained as placid and smooth as a mirror, and the tangled roots of bog-trees continued to flank the passages. He saw no signs at all that the swamp was deepening.

"Not the swamp—you." Karfhud selected one of the side passages, seemingly at random, and started forward again. "Look deeper."

Theseus frowned, reluctant to trust Karfhud, yet uncertain of how the tanar'ri's simple advice could be dangerous. "Why are you helping me?"

"Did I not swear to aid you in any way I can?"

"You can do that by finding the amphora."

"What do you suppose I am doing now?" Karfhud turned down a side passage the Thrasson had not even noticed. The fog was growing thicker. "But finding the amphora will do you no good if you do not know what you are looking for."

Theseus followed the fiend into the narrowing channel, then glanced over his shoulder to make certain his other companions also made the turn. Jayk rounded the corner less than three paces behind him, a shadowy head and shoulders plowing along the surface of the silvery water. A moment later came Silverwind's much larger silhouette, his fog-blurred torso looming almost as high above the channel as Karfhud. Tessali was a hazy blotch on the bariaur's back.

"Close up the line some more," Theseus ordered. "I can hardly see you back there."

He turned forward again, only to discover that Karfhud had nearly vanished into the mists ahead. The Thrasson sloshed ahead, the fingers of his makeshift foot digging deep into the canal's silky bottom.

When he caught the fiend, he said, "I'm looking for my memories. What else could it be?"

"Only you can determine the answer to that."

"Why don't you help me?" Theseus's voice was more bitter than challenging. "You can read minds."

"Even I cannot read what is not there. You have forgotten what it is you seek." Karfhud raised his muzzle, as though sniffing the air, then motioned the Thrasson closer. "Let me see your sword. I have something that will keep Sheba's fur from stealing it out of your hands."

Remembering how the tanar'ri had used his own blood to clean the monster's black sap off the blade earlier, Theseus waded to Karfhud's side. He did not yield the weapon, however, but simply raised it high enough so the fiend could swab the steel.

Karfhud clucked at the Thrasson's suspicions, but made no other complaint. He switched his map to his free hand, then ran his slashed wrist up and down the flat of the blade, smearing a thick coat of black, acrid-smelling blood over both sides.

"Dip the blade into the water now and then to slow the drying," the fiend advised. "But even so, it will not last long. Tell me if it begins to crust before Sheba attacks."

"Then she is close?"

Karfhud stared past Silverwind into the thickening mists. "She has never been far. But she has grown quiet."

Theseus cocked his brow, for the fiend was right. The monster had not bellowed, or even made any splashing sounds, since they had entered this narrow passage. He started to mention this, but Karfhud abruptly turned away and started down the passage, no longer bothering to trace its course on his parchment. Clearly, he expected Sheba's attack soon.

Karfhud lowered his hand and quietly waved Theseus up. "But perhaps I can be of some help to you, Thrasson. Knowing what the others seek may help you discover what you must find."

Theseus waded to the fiend's side. "I am listening." It was a half-truth; he was much more intent on searching the fog ahead, but he saw the wisdom in carrying on as they had been. A sudden silence would alert the monster to their vigilance, and he was anxious to have the battle done before the company grew even more weary than it was now. "Still, I fail to see how an exit can serve one person and not another."

"The Plurality." Karfhud answered. "Is it not a law of the multiverse that there are a thousand meanings for every fact?"

"No!" The answer came from the rear of the line, where Silverwind had apparently been paying more attention than Theseus realized. "That is not the way I imagined it, not at all! What you're talking about would be chaos—"

"Precisely. Chaos!" Karfhud stopped and turned around, rolling up his new map as he spoke. "That is the way of the multiverse! No one is right, and everyone is right."

Tessali groaned. "A Xaositect." The elf peered over Silverwind's shoulder at Theseus, then added, "I should have known better than to trust you to pick a guide."

"Keep your watch!" Theseus pointed his sword at the elf. "This is no time to get into an argument about—"

Karfhud's talons pinched the Thrasson's shoulder. "Did you not ask for my help, Theseus?"

"Yes, but—"

"Then listen—and learn." Karfhud slipped past Jayk and went

to Silverwind, who stood his ground and looked the fiend squarely in the eye. "Are you not the imaginer of the mazes?"

The bariaur nodded. "I am the imaginer of all things."

The haze had thickened to the point where the Thrasson could barely make out their two looming shapes. The bog trees flanking the channel were little more than dark, hulking shadows, and it was no longer possible to tell the surface of the water from the fog floating upon it. Karfhud's arm snaked back to stuff his map into his satchel, and Theseus thought he understood why the fiend had picked that moment to start a debate with Silverwind.

Sheba was coming up from the rear.

Karfhud continued to speak with the bariaur. "You made the mazes, and yet you cannot find a way out?"

Silverwind shook his head. "No. I am as lost as you."

Theseus slipped by Jayk, gently nudging her and fluttering his fingers in the semblance of a spellcasting. She grabbed his arm and refused to let him pass. He scowled, then pried his arm loose and waved his fingers again. The tiefling bit her lip, but reluctantly nodded and plunged her hands into the water to retrieve the necessary ingredients. The Thrasson continued toward the others.

Karfhud was continuing to debate Silverwind, as though the differences in their particular creeds were more important than any monster stalking the party. "You are the imaginer of the mazes, yet you are lost in them," the fiend was saying. "So, your search for an exit is really a search for the inner truth of your own being, is it not?"

Silverwind's eyes lit up. "Why–why, yes it is!" The bariaur suddenly looked half a century younger, but it did not escape Theseus's notice that a pair of the old fellow's pods had stopped throbbing and grown quite firm, like melons about to burst. "I have been looking at this all wrong–I'm not trapped in the mazes at all!"

Karfhud nodded gravely. "Then you are looking for–"

"The reality of my own being!"

So excited was Silverwind that he kicked his heels up, dumping Tessali into the water. Theseus eased his way close to the bariaur's flank and, doing his best to keep an unobtrusive watch down the channel, reached for the elf.

Tessali came up sputtering and glaring at Karfhud. "The barmies in my ward speak better sense than that!"

"No doubt," Karfhud agreed. "In your wisdom, you have already discovered the essential meaning of the multiverse, have you not—that it has no meaning?"

This seemed to calm Tessali, if not Theseus. The argument was just the distraction the monster had been waiting for.

"Try not to be so overwrought, Theseus," said the fiend. "Sometimes, the only thing we can do is be patient."

Karfhud cast a cautionary glance at the Thrasson, then looked back to Tessali, who, now that his wisdom had been acknowledged, seemed to regard the tanar'ri with newfound respect.

"Tessali," the fiend continued, "I can see that you are one of those rare elves who has a true understanding of himself—and I have read enough thoughts to know. Let us describe life as a maze, and your salvation as the exit; I am sure you can tell me what you are searching for."

"Certainly." Tessali's gaze grew uneasy and shifted away from Karfhud. "But I don't see what this has to do with the plurality of the multiverse."

Karfhud's voice grew stern. "I am not explaining chaos; I am honoring my oath to the Thrasson. Given your trade, I should think you would want to help."

The tanar'ri was acting more like a celestial seraphim than an Abyssal fiend, and that made Theseus's spine creep.

Karfhud's puffy lips began to twitch—no doubt with the effort of not smirking at the Thrasson's absurd thought—but the fiend kept his attention fixed firmly on Tessali.

"Well, elf? Will you help this man or not?"

"That won't be needed," Theseus interjected. "Whatever Karfhud is playing at, it can only lead to harm."

"No, he's right," said Tessali. "I should know myself well enough to answer his question."

Tessali fell deep into thought, leaving it to Theseus alone to watch for Sheba. Karfhud's maroon eyes remained fixed on the elf, as though he had completely forgotten about the monster. Silverwind was mumbling to himself about essential realities and knowing his own mind, and Jayk was off hiding in the fog somewhere. A disturbing thought occurred to the Thrasson, and he slowly turned in a circle, searching the channel's haze-shrouded surface for the dark silhouette of the tiefling's head and shoulders. He saw nothing but gray.

Theseus was about to call her name when Tessali looked up, raising the stumps at the ends of his arms. "For too long have I let my hands dictate the meaning of my life!" His eyes were flashing with excitement, and, as with Silverwind, one of the husks hanging from his body had stopped throbbing and looked ready to burst. "But there is no meaning outside ourselves! My healing hands have only been distracting me; without them I am free to look inward."

"Then you are better off without your hands than we are without Jayk," Theseus said. He dipped his sword into the water to wet Karfhud's blood, then called, "Jayk?"

"The tiefling knows how to find her exit," Karfhud said. "She has always known, but she doesn't want to leave yet."

Theseus whirled on the fiend. "What are you saying?"

"I think you know." Karfhud's eyes glimmered crimson. "What is it she's always saying? 'Life is an illusion'?"

As badly as he wished that he did not, the Thrasson understood Karfhud's meaning. As a Dustman, Jayk sought the path to the One Death.

"Yes." Karfhud was smiling now. "But she is afraid to reach the end, because she knows you won't go with her."

"Where is she?" Theseus glared into the fog. "If you've let anything happen to her—"

"Me?" scoffed Karfhud. "You are the one who turned his back on her."

Theseus pushed past the tanar'ri. "Jayk!"

"She will not answer. The monster is too close upon her."

Theseus rushed into the fog, pushing through the waters and making a great splashing—loud, but not so loud that it drowned out Karfhud's wheezy snickering. The Thrasson's chest tightened with anger, though less at the fiend than at himself for allowing Jayk and the others to come with him into Sheba's lair. It was one thing to strike bargains with tanar'ri on his own behalf, and quite another to drag his friends into the quagmire with him.

When he did not find the tiefling within a dozen steps, Theseus stopped to study the area. Although the channel was no more than four arm-spans wide, he could barely see the tangled banks; they were little more than a slight darkening in the fog. Behind him, the pearly haze had swallowed Karfhud and the others entirely. It was as if he had passed through a conjunction and entered a different maze.

"Jayk?"

His answer came from the channel behind him, in the form of a startled shout that instantly intensified to a shriek of anguish. Before Theseus could identify the voice, a deafening bellow crashed through the fog, drowning out the scream and driving spikes of pain through his eardrums. He whirled around and splashed down the passage, cursing Karfhud's treachery in not telling him from which direction the monster was approaching.

By the time the ringing in Theseus's ears began to die down, he could see the fiend's black, blurry silhouette in the center of the passage. The tanar'ri was writhing about madly, his claws flinging snarled tangles of fur through the haze, his wings beating the water into a silver froth. The Thrasson angled toward the bank so he would enter the fray on the monster's flank. Even after moving past the flailing black wall of Karfhud's wings, he had trouble finding Sheba herself. So closely did her color match the pearly fog that, save for the snarl of flailing arms and hooves tucked under her far arm, Theseus would not have seen the beast at all.

Was Karfhud fighting to save Silverwind? It could not be possible.

A sharp crackle hissed up the channel. A brilliant flash lit the fog behind the monster, creating a spectacular halo around her shaggy figure. A spray of smoking fur and black drops erupted from behind her shoulder. Sheba suddenly lurched forward, her face and chest slapping the water like the flat of a paddle. Karfhud leapt on her, tearing into the wound with both claws and burying his fangs deep into her collarbone.

Theseus brushed past Tessali, who was standing helpless and gape-mouthed several paces shy of the battle, and waded into a churning cloud of smoke that stank of scorched fur and rotten, charred meat. The Thrasson saw Silverwind's face and arms bob above the water, only to disappear an instant later as Karfhud pushed the monster's head beneath the surface. Jayk was nowhere to be seen; she was somewhere behind the monster, no doubt preparing more magic.

Theseus hoped the spell would not strike him by mistake. There was nothing but three paces of water between him and a clear strike at Sheba's head. He raised his sword, already imagining the gurgling pop it would cause as the blade cleaved the monster's neck.

Silverwind suddenly came out of the water, still tucked beneath Sheba's arm. The monster's head came up next, spewing a huge piece of Karfhud's wing from her mouth. Though Theseus was only two steps away, the monster did not even seem to see him as she spun half away. There was a sharp crackle, then her shoulder, now caught in the clutches of Karfhud's hands and teeth, slipped from its joint. Sheba threw her head back and loosed another deafening bellow, this one all the more terrifying because of the anguish in her voice.

Theseus sidestepped to avoid hitting Karfhud—he would not have bothered, save that experience had taught him that his sword would slip from his grasp—then pushed forward, drawing that star-forged blade down across the front of Sheba's shoulder. The steel, still black with Karfhud's blood, sliced through the monster's hide and thick gristle as though it were mere silk.

Sheba's bellow did not resound in Theseus's ears so much as pummel them. Everything went black, and something cool and wet splattered his face. The Thrasson ducked instinctively, but no crushing counterattack came. When his vision cleared, he saw the monster's arm floating in the water, with Karfhud, also stunned by the bellow, still clinging to it.

Sheba was a blurry gray shape retreating through the fog. Theseus drove forward after her, his eyes fixed on the black circle of sap oozing from her cleaved shoulder. Beneath her good arm, Silverwind's struggles were growing more feeble by the second—though, thankfully, the bariaur was trailing no red drops to match the black string of blood beads that the monster left bobbing on the channel surface.

To Theseus's surprise, the wall of bog trees ahead of his quarry seemed to be growing darker and more distinct with each step. Already, he could make out the shapes of individual limbs and, lower down, the web of tangle roots. The Thrasson hoped Sheba was heading for some hidden passage he could not yet see; if she climbed over the wall, he would have to choose between abandoning Silverwind or jumping into an unknown maze with no guarantee that Karfhud—or even Jayk—would follow.

Theseus's concerns changed when he heard the tiefling's frightened voice stuttering out an incantation. Sheba was not fleeing, he realized; she was only covering her flank.

The monster let out another bellow, then stopped before a snarl of vine-draped bog trees. Theseus pushed through the water as fast as he could, tempted to try swimming but knowing that, with his sword in hand, it would probably be even slower than wading. Jayk finished her spell. There was a sharp crackle, then a long spray of matted fur and black, sticky blood shot from Sheba's side to splash into the channel. She did not fall.

The monster raised one leg out of the water, then leaned slightly away from the bank, preparing to deliver a stomp kick. Theseus considered throwing his sword, but that was a desperation move, to be attempted only as a last resort, and only when the blow would be a killing one. If the monster could be killed at all, he knew a single strike would not do it. Besides, only two more steps . . .

Sheba lowered her foot, smashing through a tangle of prop roots. From somewhere distant, somewhere beyond the Thrasson's ringing ears, came a single, strangled cry—then he was on the monster. Theseus swung, burying his sword deep where a human's kidney would be. In the same motion, he drew the blade free and reversed his attack, striking upward into her ribs, trying to reach her lungs.

As Theseus wrenched his steel free to try for a third strike, Sheba spun, smashing Silverwind's rear quarters into his shoulder pauldron. The Thrasson's god-forged bronze absorbed the worst of the blow, but the impact still knocked him off his feet and sent him sinking toward the channel bottom. His first and only thought was of his sword. He still felt the hilt in his hand, and he concentrated on nothing except making certain it stayed there. No matter what else happened, he would be lost without his weapon.

When Theseus settled into the mud an instant later, the entire side of his body ached. His head throbbed, his chest was convulsing, and his lungs were burning for air—but the sword remained in his hand. He gathered his legs beneath him and pushed off the bottom, shoving his head above water.

Directly ahead of him lay a broken tangle of prop-roots, a hole the size of a man's chest smashed through the center. A small, shadowy hand had risen out of the great jumble to clutch at a low hanging vine, and a red slick was already spreading out into the channel. Still coughing up water, Theseus rushed over.

Jayk lay deep inside the snarl, her head propped against the bank and her shattered body half-submerged. The silvery water was smeared with green and red ichor from burst pods. Down near her hip, a single red husk was still bobbing just beneath the surface. The tiefling was bleeding from her nose, mouth, and half a dozen holes where broken ribs had pushed through her torso. Her pupils were narrow and shaped like diamonds, and the tips of her long fangs were dribbling blood onto her chin.

"Zoo . . . bee."

She released the vine and reached for Theseus, then slipped a little farther into the water. The Thrasson tried to make the stretch, but the tangle was too deep, and he did not want to crawl inside for fear of jostling her. He quickly used his sword to cut an opening into the snarl, then started to ease inside.

A huge taloned hand caught him by the shoulder. "Leave her," said Karfhud. "The tiefling has found what she seeks. You have not."

Theseus tried to pull free, but Karfhud held him tight.

"Tessali will stay with her," said the fiend. "We have a monster to track."

"Look at her!" Theseus hissed. "This won't take long."

"It would take longer than you know, Thrasson."

Karfhud forcibly pulled him back, then pointed at the string of black blood beads bobbing in the water. One of the globules sank as they watched.

"Besides, her blood trail will not last long," the fiend said. "Even if you do not care to save Silverwind, there is still your amphora to consider."

"Zoombee, you . . . stay with me . . . no?"

"No, Jayk–I can't."

When Theseus turned away, he did not see that last red husk burst. He felt it.

ISLE OF DESPAIR

Down the twining canals they push, the Thrasson and the fiend, down the purling alleys between leafy walls looming dark and nebulous in the fog, down the meandering silver ribbons where sticky strings of black beads lie bobbing upon the waters. Thick in the air hangs the monster's stench: the acrid reek of her dark blood and the musty fetor of her matted fur. All around, the white haze sizzles with her quick, shallow breath. They see her flight in the arrow of ripples spreading across the channel; her fear, they taste in the sour bile of their own growing thirst. The Thrasson's zeal pounds heavy and hard inside his skull; they will run the monster down and save Silverwind—if Silverwind can be saved—but what of Jayk? Her heart has stilled, her blood has grown purple and settled into her haunches, all her Pains have passed.

There is an anger down in the Thrasson's stomach, sour and boiling hot and black as pitch. He would have us believe he rages at Karfhud, or even at himself, but who is fooled by that? His wrath is a lie—a foul perjury, a stain upon his name so shameful he will not concede it even to himself—and I know the truth. The Lady always knows.

He is no man of renown, this Thrasson; he is too selfish, too jealous by far. Rather than begrudge Jayk her freedom, he should rejoice in her going; he should celebrate the unraveling of her labyrinth and be light of heart—and so should you. There is no reason to lament, no cause for outrage. I have not betrayed my pledge. It is true that the tiefling has suffered torment unimaginable and endured anguish enough to crush a giant and borne grief that would shatter a god, all as I promised she would, but has she not also run her maze and found her prize? If the One Death is not the triumph for which you hoped, I am not to blame. I said she was a Dustman, and it is no concern of mine if you harbor a secret taste for the dead.

Down a haze-crushed canal they turn, the Thrasson and the fiend, still following that floating string of black blood and that arrow of spreading ripples, still breathing the monster's stink and still searching the pearl-white fog for her gray shape. The looming bog-trees have given way to walls of ash-drab granite, hardly discernible from the hanging still mist, and the channel's silty bottom has grown hard and rugged beneath the palm of the Amnesian Hero's gruesome foot. A low rampart has appeared at the end of the passage, visible in the fog only because of the dark cracks between its great limestone blocks and the small archway at its center.

Without a moment's pause, Karfhud sloshed up the channel to the gate.

"A sinking palace." He ducked under the lintel and pushed forward. The silver waters drained from his battered wings as he ascended a submerged stairway. "How I wish we had time to map."

"There will be time later—after we slay Sheba." Silently, Theseus added, if you don't make me kill you, too.

"You are very confident of yourself." The tanar'ri reached the top of the stairway, where the water was only ankle deep, and stopped. "That is good—especially if we are to defeat her trap."

Karfhud flattened himself against the wall and motioned Theseus up beside him. Pressing tighter to the fiend's maze-blighted chest than he would have liked, the Thrasson squeezed into the opening and found himself staring down a narrow passage. The water was flowing away from him ever so gently, swirling over a layer of stone shards broken loose from the palace's ancient walls. The fog was thinner here. He could see a dozen paces down the corridor, to where a long pivoting gate stood edge-on in the center of a four-way junction. The Thrasson had stormed enough fortresses to recognize the ironclad gate as a manstile, designed to funnel attackers into a confusing labyrinth of side passages and deadly cross fire.

To one side of the manstile lay Silverwind, bloodied and motionless, save for his heaving ribs. Against the other side leaned the amphora. Sheba was lurking at the stile's far end, her matted bulk spilling past both sides of the thick gate. She was squirming restlessly, and she had a black-oozing circle where the Thrasson's blade had cleaved off her arm.

"She's trying to separate us."

Karfhud shook his head. "No doubt that would make her happy enough, but that is not what is in her mind. She is offering you a choice: the bariaur or the amphora." The fiend lowered his gaze and curled his muzzle up in a yellow-fanged sneer. "Now you must decide whether you are a hero. Will you choose your friend's life, or your lost memories?"

"Any man can choose; a hero takes both." Theseus scraped a handful of dark blood from one of the many scratches on Karfhud's body, then smeared it over his sword blade. "I'll rescue Silverwind. You retrieve the amphora."

A red gleam shot from Karfhud's beady eyes. "If you think to give me orders—"

Theseus squeezed past the fiend, at the same time striking a sharp blow to one of the golden husks dangling from the tanar'ri's blighted flank. The pod burst, spilling a stream of yellow ichor over the fiend's immense hip. Karfhud dropped to one knee, a long sizzle of pain hissing from between his lips.

"I don't want to waste time arguing." The Thrasson laid his hand on another of the yellow husks. "We are going—"

"Pain me all you wish," Karfhud growled. "If we separate, it will be as nothing to your suffering. Even lacking an arm, Sheba would flay you alive—and, were I to escape, I would do the same to your friends."

The fiend glared at the Thrasson's hand, but made no attempt to remove it. Theseus scowled. Could Sheba truly be so terrible that, even one-armed, she struck fear into the heart of a tanar'ri lord?

"Tanar'ri hearts do not fear." Karfhud slowly drew himself to his full height, then glanced down the passage. "If you have no care about your friend, then let us make use of him. If we do not retrieve the amphora before he dies, Sheba will change her mind about letting us take it."

"I *will* have both."

Theseus used his makeshift foot to feel under the water for a throwing stone, then shifted his sword to his left hand and took the rock in his right. Not so long ago, he would have wasted valuable time debating the honor of what he was about to do. He would have agonized over his obligation to Poseidon, asking himself if it had been discharged when the Lady of Pain chased his friends away from the amphora. He would have spent precious minutes wondering if she had meant to abandon the jar, and, if so, whether that gave him a right to its contents.

Now, the Thrasson simply assumed all those things.

"My friend, you are beginning to think like a tanar'ri," said Karfhud. If the fiend fostered any ill will over the pain Theseus had caused him earlier, his voice did not betray it. "I like that."

"Then I am certainly in danger of losing my honor."

Theseus turned and splashed down the corridor, Karfhud following close behind. They ran straight down the center of the passage, giving no hint as to which side of the stile they would choose.

As they drew near the gate, a bank of white fog began to rise about Sheba's ankles. She continued to squirm, but made no move to turn and watch them approach. Her restraint troubled the Thrasson; she was too cunning to think herself well hidden.

By the time Theseus closed to within a pace of the gate, the fog bank had risen as high as the monster's knees and was spilling into the rest of the passage. The Thrasson feigned a lunge for Silverwind, then abruptly danced back to the other side of the corridor. Karfhud, reading his mind as always, squeezed past to rush the bariaur's side of the stile. Sheba remained at the end of the gate.

The Thrasson whipped his throwing arm forward. The stone struck the amphora with a loud, hollow clunk, then disappeared through a jagged hole. A spray of tattered black ribbons and silky golden threads sprouted from the break, writhing and fluttering like a tangle of young snakes struggling from their brood den. Across the intersection, Sheba's matted flank still showed around the edge of the gate.

"By all the darkness!" Karfhud's curse was followed by a loud ripping sound, then a fiendish roar of pain. "She–"

The rest of the sentence was swallowed by a loud gurgling roar. Theseus gawked at the monster ahead, then saw that she still had not moved and began to realize what was happening. He started to round the gate to help Karfhud, then thought better of it and rushed forward into the intersection.

A tremendous knell reverberated through the gate as a heavy body slammed into it. Theseus reached the amphora, the bottom quarter now hidden in the rising fog. Tempted as he was to retrieve it and flee, he could not betray Karfhud. So far, the fiend had done exactly as he had pledged, and the Thrasson still had enough pride of honor that he would not lower himself beneath a tanar'ri. He settled for kicking the jar as he passed.

Instead of shattering, the sturdy vessel merely tipped over. A scrap of coarse black cloth rose from the new hole that Theseus's foot had opened and caught hold of his ankle. The Thrasson tried to shake the thing off, but the ribbon only tightened its hold and began to circle up his leg.

On the other side of the gate, the clamor of battle–the roaring and the hissing and the pounding–continued unabated. Theseus splashed out of the intersection, giving wide berth to the hulking gray shape writhing at the end of the stile. As he passed by, he saw that the figure was indeed Sheba–or rather, Sheba's snarled pelt. The hide was hanging from the gate, held in place by its own sticky fur, looking rather empty but still squirming. The eyes and mouth were empty voids, and the hole left by the loss of her arm had been carefully pinched shut.

Though the Thrasson knew what he would find inside, he did not pause to slice the thing open. Already, the air reeked with the brimstone stench of tanar'ri blood, and Karfhud's bellows sounded less angry than desperate. The last thing Theseus wanted was to battle the monster by himself.

The Thrasson rounded the stile at a sprint, then stumbled over a leathery mantle floating upon the water. He put a hand down to catch himself and saw that the thing was one of Karfhud's great wings. Save that it no longer hung upon the fiend's back, the appendage was remarkably intact.

A tremendous crash reverberated through the passage. Theseus looked up to see the huge tanar'ri lord being slammed into the gate by a slimy red . . . there was no way to describe the beast except as a *thing*. The creature had only one arm, was about the right size to be Sheba, and looked more or less bipedal—but any semblance to what they had been battling so far ended there. The thing was all raw tendon and muscle, with a web of black veins lacing its body and a skin of clear mucous membrane. Its entire figure pulsed with a rapid, strong-soft beat that seemed to set the air itself throbbing.

Theseus gathered himself up and charged across the floating wing, praying that Karfhud would survive long enough to hold their foe's attention until he attacked. The tanar'ri, as usual, knew exactly what the Thrasson was thinking. As Sheba slammed him into the gate yet again—the muffled crack of a breaking rib echoed down the passage—the fiend found the strength to bring his hands up and bury his talons into the monster's gristly head. She whipped her neck around. The motion tore long strips of red sinew from the sides of her face, but freed her head. She leaned forward and sank her maw into the tanar'ri's throat.

It was all the distraction Theseus needed. Had he been tall enough, he would have lopped the monster's head off her shoulders and been done with it. As it was, he had no choice except to go for a heart kill. He flipped his blade around for an overhand strike, then plunged it into the middle of Sheba's back, driving it clear to the hilt. A geyser of hot, gummy sap bubbled from the wound to coat his face. He barely managed to turn his head aside in time to keep from being blinded.

At a minimum, Sheba should have given a startled gurgle and fallen to her knees. Karfhud should have slipped free of her grasp and staggered away coughing and choking, one hand clutched to his bruised throat. The monster should have pitched forward and lain facedown in the shallow water, her spinal cord severed and her heart burst by the Thrasson's star-forged blade.

Instead, Theseus glimpsed her elbow swinging around toward his head. He had just enough time to wrap his second hand around his sword hilt and duck behind his shoulder pauldron. He felt the armor strap break, then his body exploded in pain, and he sensed that he was flying away from Sheba.

His arms were nearly jerked from their sockets, but he did not release his sword. He felt the star-forged blade pivoting on the edge of the wound, slashing through Sheba's chest, and he wondered how she could still be standing. By now, he had surely cut through half the breadth of her torso.

The Thrasson's sword slipped free of the monster. He slammed into the ironclad gate; the breath left his chest in a sharp cry. He crumpled into the water, groaning, too stunned to ache; then saw a tornado of flailing black talons driving Sheba away from the stile. The monster, oozing cascades of dark sap from the long gash Theseus had opened across her back, was hard pressed to defend herself. It was all her single arm could do to keep swinging back and forth between Karfhud's slashing claws and prevent her head from being swiped off her shoulders.

Sensing that any attack would overwhelm her defenses, Theseus rolled onto his knees—and that was when he noticed the black cloth from the amphora rounding his chest. He could not say how many times the ribbon had circled him already, but he did know that any distraction at the moment might well prove fatal. Still aching from the monster's first blow, he leapt to his feet—or rather, to his foot and his hand—and rushed into battle.

Sheba saw him coming and launched a lightning kick at Karfhud's midsection. When the fiend lowered his arms to block, she pulled her foot back and stepped toward the far end of the stile, keeping the tanar'ri neatly between herself and the Thrasson. She began to retreat out of the intersection.

The black ribbon circled Theseus a second time. He ignored it and, realizing what Sheba was trying to do, sprinted forward. On his mind was one thought: Dive for her legs!

It took Karfhud just an instant to realize the thought was directed at him, but by the time he threw himself at Sheba's legs, Theseus was already upon him. Before flinging himself into the air, the Thrasson had to hesitate a single heartbeat, and that was too much.

The monster jumped back, well out of Karfhud's reach. Then, when Theseus and his star-forged sword came flying over the fiend's back, she snapped a slimy red foot up from the shallow water. The blow caught the Thrasson square in the chest. He saw the black ribbon flash past one more time, and then he saw nothing at all.

WOEGATE

The growl of the surf is gentle in his ears, the touch of sea air cool upon his skin, the stars sweet upon his eyes; a woman—*the* woman, a tall beauty with olive skin and emerald eyes—lies youthful and naked in the crook of his arm. The world is as it should be for young heroes and their maidens: battles won, wine drunk, slumber taken—but they have erred, and grievously. They have lain naked beneath the craving eyes of the gods, and what the gods see, the gods will have.

Gentle as a kiss, a rivulet of wine tickles the Thrasson's lips, trickles sweet onto his tongue, runs warm and welcome as ambrosia down his throat; he dreams, and he does not dream: above him stands a handsome youth, pouring the sweet nectar upon his lips from a silver ewer. The young man's face is no mere flesh stretched over bone; it is chiseled from marble, with features balanced more perfectly than those of any mortal and skin that shines like pearls. The god's eyes are purple as grapes; upon his head he wears a laurel of growing vines, upon his lips a broad grin of flashing mischief.

"Great Theseus, know you who honors you with this libation?"

The Thrasson nods. "Dionysus." The god of vines, the embodiment of joy, mirth, camaraderie–also madness, delirium, and hallucination. "I do you praise."

The god's purple eyes sparkle. "As the gods will you, Theseus–if you do as I charge."

The Thrasson says nothing, for he knows the danger to those who follow the ways of Dionysus–as he also knows the folly of those who refuse the gods.

"Well have you done to rescue the daughters of King Minos." Dionysus glances into the distance, where a small ship sits beached upon the sand, its single black sail furled upon the spar. "Their father was a tyrant even to his children, and all we gods have longed to see them free."

"May I always please the gods."

"Then must you yield your prize, great Theseus." A crooked smile creeps across Dionysus's lips. He shifts his gaze to the beauty who sleeps secure in the crook of the Thrasson's arm. "Leave her on these shores, and I will watch over her. It is the younger princess, Phaedra, that we mean for you."

"Never! I will not abandon–"

"Take Phaedra, and my blessing with her." The god grabbed a handful of shore sand and held it before him. "Though you plant your vines on the salty beach, ever will they droop with the best fruit in the land. In wealth, your wine will buy you more palaces than you can number and fill them all with your treasures; in war, your treasures will buy you the finest weapons in the land and you will never know defeat; in fame, your name will be spoken upon the tongues of men as long as men have tongues to speak."

"And if I refuse?"

Dionysus let the sand trickle from his hand. "Then your vines will wither though you plant them on the hills of Olympus itself; your people will know thirst and starvation; your enemies will slay your hungry warriors; your name will be a curse upon the tongues of your people, to be gladly forgotten after they have dumped your naked corpse into the sea."

It is the last threat, I am sure, that makes the Thrasson abandon his princess. He loves nothing so much as fame—and for that, must we all suffer:

Have I not seen the broken amphora, the ribbons of black sail and the strands of my golden hair fluttering from the jagged hole? What choice now but to call them real?

Too much is explained, too many bricks stacked and mortared for me to deny the wall. Poseidon sends the memories, but Dionysus sends the woman, and those two would no sooner share a victory than a bed. There is a weight in the sky, a low rumbling beneath the streets like the growl of the leviathan. The air has the feel of an epoch grinding to an end, and I am all that stands before the crushing wheel.

Dionysus tips his silver ewer, and the wine falls again upon the Thrasson's lips. This time the taste is foul and moldy, but Theseus drinks; he knows better than to offend a deity, and he has a thirst as great as a lake. The god's purple eyes change to burning maroon; his brow grows wrinkled and heavy, his face dark as a shadow and brutal as a beast's. A pair of long curving horns sprouts from his head, and his mouth pushes out to form an apelike muzzle.

"This is no time for your dreams!" growled Karfhud's angry voice. "Wake yourself, or I swear I'll leave you to drown!"

The threat did not move Theseus, who was beginning to feel the cold serpent of guilt writhing in his stomach. No matter what Dionysus threatened, he could not have abandoned his beloved on that lonely shore! He was a man of renown, and men of renown always found the clever way to evade the dire choice. Surely, he had swum back ashore after dark, or bested the god in a drinking contest, or tried something to win her back!

"How will you ever know, Theseus?" The wine continued to pour, not from Dionysus's silver ewer, but from Karfhud's filthy wineskin. "If you will stop feeling guilty and rise, we can still recover the amphora. Sheba is on the run, and we have but to catch her."

"And then what?" Theseus pushed the wineskin away. He was

lying upon the fiend's dismembered wing, which was still floating in the junction where they had fought Sheba. The manstile had been pushed shut, creating a single angled passage where there had been a four-way intersection before. "If we couldn't kill her—"

"*Kill* her?" Karfhud stood, wincing in pain. His body was laced with gashes and covered in golden ichor, but several small husks of pain had somehow survived the battle without bursting; with each pulse of the fiend's heart, they grew a little larger. "How can we kill her? It would be easier to flatten the mazes themselves!"

Theseus scowled. If the fiend did not want to slay the monster, then why was he chasing her?

"I have my reasons, and so do you—or are you afraid to recall what you did on that island?" The fiend pulled Theseus to his feet, then thrust the Thrasson's star-forged sword into his hands. "Now help me with the gate. If we hurry, we will catch Sheba and end this thing."

As the tanar'ri turned toward the ironclad manstile, Theseus recalled Sheba's decoy. He had a sinking feeling, then turned and saw the matted pelt lying in the shallow water at the far end of the gate. It was no longer squirming.

"Karfhud, we've forgotten about Silverwind."

The fiend glanced down the length of the gate. "We have no time to waste on the dead. Minutes have passed already since she escaped."

"If Silverwind is truly dead, this won't take long." Theseus wetted his sword with the fiend's blood, then sloshed over to the sticky pelt and stuck the tip into the empty mouth hole. "Silverwind? Are you in there?"

When he received no answer and the pelt did not move, he carefully sliced it open. Inside, eyes closed and curled into a tight fetal ball, lay the old bariaur. His brief captivity had left him covered with slime and filth, but his chest was rising at regular intervals, his hooves were twitching as in a dream, and he was still covered with throbbing husks of pain.

"Silverwind, wake up." Theseus reached down and gently shook him. "We've got to hurry."

Silverwind's eyes snapped open, and he gave a start of surprise. "Theseus?" The old bariaur raised his head and took in his surroundings. "I thought I had imploded! Can you imagine? I would have had to imagine it all again—the whole thing!"

"You may yet," growled Karfhud, waiting at the far end of the gate. The fiend shifted his gaze to Theseus. "Have you done with this stalling?"

Theseus helped Silverwind out of the monster's empty hide, then the two of them joined Karfhud. Sometime earlier, no doubt before deciding that he still had need of the Thrasson's help, the fiend had tried to push aside the heavy gate and managed only to crack it open—this despite the fact that Sheba, sorely wounded and in a hurry, had closed the thing with only one arm. Theseus began to wonder who was hunting whom.

"Does it matter?" Karfhud laid his hands on the iron sheathing and leaned into the stile. "She has your amphora."

Theseus pressed his shoulder to the gate. "And what do you want from her, if you cannot hope to slay her?"

Karfhud gave him a sidelong glance. "I am surprised you have not guessed that by now, Thrasson."

From the gate's center pivot rose a loud grating noise. The heavy stile slowly started to open. A moment later, Silverwind butted into it at a full sprint; there was a loud bang, and Theseus and Karfhud nearly fell as the gate bucked forward. They pumped their legs to catch up, then smoothly pushed the stile back to its original position.

In the adjacent passage stood Tessali, Jayk's limp body resting across his handless arms. Theseus's heart jumped; for a moment, he thought she might still be alive—then he noticed how her spine bent in the wrong direction, and how the ends of her broken ribs formed a ring around the sunken hollow in the center of her chest. The Thrasson saw no ichor on her body; at least her pain was gone.

"Theseus, she died with your name on her lips." Tessali shuffled forward, his accusing gaze fixed on the Thrasson. "She asked that you burn her body and carry the ashes with you."

Theseus moved forward to take the corpse, but Karfhud shoved in front of him.

"We have no time for pyres, Thrasson. If we let Sheba put herself back together, more of us will die."

Theseus glared into the fiend's fiery eyes, knowing that he spoke the truth and silently cursing him for it.

"I am not to blame. You are the hero, Theseus; you must bear the burden: will you risk the lives of four to grant the wish of one?" Karfhud paused, gently scratching his broken talons along his chin. "It occurs to me that your choice is similar to the one Dionysus presented you; either way, you betray someone. How unfortunate that you cannot recall how you resolved *that* dilemma."

"Damn you, Karfhud!"

The fiend cocked a wrinkled brow and gazed around the narrow passage. "This? Hardly." He chuckled and shook his head. "The mazes are as nothing to the Abyss."

Theseus scowled at the tanar'ri's mocking snicker, but motioned to Tessali. "Come with me. We can wrap her in Karfhud's wing until after the battle."

The elf glanced at the dark wound where the fiend's wing had been ripped from his shoulder blade, then grimaced and looked back to the Thrasson.

"What if we don't–"

"Then we will rot with her!" Theseus snapped. "I don't suppose she could blame us for that."

The Thrasson paused just long enough to scan the area and make certain the monster had taken the amphora–she had–before leading the way back around the stile. He pulled Karfhud's tattered wing from the water and swaddled Jayk's body inside, then laid the bundle back in Tessali's arms and went to cut some long mats from Sheba's discarded pelt. The elf followed close behind, holding the cocoon as Theseus wrapped it in gummy tangles of fur.

"I would have cured her, you know," Tessali said. "Even without my hands and my spells, I was beginning to make her understand. I don't think she wanted to die, there at the last."

Theseus suspected that Jayk's change of heart had more to do with her close call with Karfhud than any Bleaker wisdom Tessali had imparted to her, but he held his tongue. The elf had lost enough already; if he found comfort in such delusions, it was not the Thrasson's place to disabuse him.

After encasing Jayk's cocoon in the monster's gummy fur, Theseus took the bundle and stuck it to the stile, affixing it as high as he could reach. Though he had seen no scavengers in the mazes, neither had he seen any untended carcasses or skeletons, and the dead bodies had to be going somewhere.

By the time Theseus and Tessali returned to the others, Karfhud had already taken a mapping parchment from his battered back-satchel and marked the locations of the adjoining passages. He motioned the Thrasson to follow close behind, then set off down the opposite corridor without a word.

Despite Karfhud's condition—he was limping badly and hunched over a broken rib—he moved through the crooked, narrow passages in near silence, sketching in junctions and side-corridors as he went. There was no fog, so they could see that the walls were lined by arrow loops and murder holes, all located well above the reach of even Karfhud. Every so often, they would glimpse a heavy wooden shutter or an oaken door guarding some portal far above their heads, but there were never any such entryways down in the bottom of the labyrinth.

As before, they had little trouble following the monster. Although there were ankle-deep streams in all the corridors, the currents were gentle and slow. Sheba's black blood marked her path as clearly as it had in the swamp; the companions found beads of the gummy stuff everywhere: clinging to the walls, bobbing in the corners, stuck on the jagged stones that littered the passage floors.

Sheba also seemed to be having trouble containing the contents of the broken amphora. Every now and then, they ran across strands of golden hair hovering in the damp air, and twice they met scraps of black sail cloth wafting up the passage. The first ribbon circled Theseus three times: he saw himself running a golden comb—the same one he had with him when he washed ashore near Thrassos—through the auburn hair of his dead wife Antiope, who had perished at the hands of her own people for loving him.

When the second ribbon circled him, the Thrasson saw himself, much older, holding a silver palm mirror—the same one that had been in his satchel with the golden comb—over the mouth and nose of another dead wife, Phaedra. This memory troubled him more than the first, for Phaedra was sister to . . . even now, Theseus could not remember the name of his beloved princess, only Dionysus's voice urging him to abandon her.

Theseus tried to calm himself, noting how much older he had been in that second memory than when the god had spoken to him. Many years had passed between the two events; because he had married Phaedra, it did not necessarily follow that he had abandoned her sister.

As they followed Sheba's dark trail deeper into the palace, a soft slurping sound, muffled by distance and the crooked passages of the labyrinth, began to echo off the stone walls. Karfhud cocked his head and waved Theseus into the lead, but the fiend continued to dip his talon into his own dark blood and trace the maze on his parchment. High up on the walls, they started to see more doors and shutters, many of them hanging half open and askew. The water began to flow more rapidly, making it more difficult to follow the monster. Several times, they had to stop at intersections while the Thrasson searched the side corridors for her blood trail. At least they were catching up; each dark bead seemed a little warmer and stickier.

The echoes of the slurping sound grew steadily louder, and the water flowed ever faster. Soon, the current was swirling around their ankles, tugging at their feet and making a hazard of each step over the rubble-strewn floor. Sheba's blood trail vanished, though it hardly mattered. Theseus had already realized that the monster was traveling with the water, which had become a gurgling stream gushing along a single course through the labyrinth.

After a time, they rounded a corner and entered a small vestibule where half a dozen smaller corridors came together. At one end of the enclosure, a pair of huge oaken gates hung cockeyed and half-open beneath a great stone arch. The bottom third of each gate had long since rotted away, allowing the waters to rush unimpeded into a large courtyard beyond. The slurping sound had ceased to be an echo; it was now a steady, half-muffled sucking noise just loud enough to drown out the purling of the stream. Karfhud slipped into the vestibule beside Theseus, and together they crept forward to peer past the oaken gates.

They found themselves looking across a flooded courtyard at an immense, dark-windowed palace with a flat roof and the vestiges of elaborate, brightly painted patterns flaking off the pale limestone walls. The courtyard itself had probably once been a magnificent sunken garden, for the surface of the water was broken everywhere by the heads of ancient statues and the spandrels of decorative arches. Near the center of the square pond swirled the cause of the slurping sound, a silvery whirlpool nearly as broad as the span of Karfhud's wings—had the fiend still had both of them to stretch.

It took Theseus a moment to notice Sheba, not far from the whirlpool's edge. She was lurking beneath the spandrel of a sunken arch, up to her neck in water and surrounded by a stringy slick of her black blood. Her red, sinewy head, laced with black veins and still gleaming with mucous slime, remained as motionless as that of a statue. The Thrasson groaned inwardly. The water would be above his head, and he truly hated having to swim while he fought.

Sheba backed out from beneath the arch. Then, keeping her dark eyes fixed on the gate where her hunters were hiding, she began to float on her back. She held the amphora in the crook of her arm, her massive hand covering both holes Theseus had made. For a moment, the Thrasson thought she was merely taunting them, then she began to kick her legs, pushing herself toward the whirlpool.

"I cannot believe what I am imagining!" gasped Silverwind.

"She knows she is defeated," said Tessali. "She's drowning herself."

"I should be so fortunate as you are foolish, elf." Karfhud rolled the parchment he had been working on. "She is escaping into another maze—and I am out of mapping skins."

The fiend bent his arm back to stuff his furled map into his satchel, at the same time running a sidelong glance over the elf's pale skin.

"Karfhud, you know better," Theseus warned.

"So now you too can read minds?"

Out in the pond, Sheba began to move in a circle as the currents at the edge of the whirlpool caught her. Karfhud stepped through the arch and began to wade down the submerged stairs. Theseus started to follow, then stopped and looked up at the heavy oaken gates. He rapped on the wood. It sounded solid enough, at least near the height of his chest.

"Karfhud, can you take one of these gates off?"

The fiend turned to glare at the rusty hinges, then bared his yellow fangs and came back up the stairs. He took hold of the one on the right, which was hanging by a single strap of twisted metal, and braced his foot against the wall.

"You're not thinking of riding that thing down the whirlpool!" Tessali gasped.

Theseus nodded. "I am." He backed away from Karfhud, who was struggling to pull the gate free and shaking the entire vestibule with his rumbling grunts. "In the past, I've found it easier than swimming."

"Don't you think we'll drown?" Silverwind's question was more of an inquiry than an objection.

Theseus glanced toward the center of the pond, where Sheba was disappearing into the heart of the whirlpool. "Only if the monster drowns first."

Karfhud gave a final sonorous groan, and, amidst a great crackling of wood, the gate came free. The fiend staggered under its weight, barely managing to face the pond before his heavy load began to tip away. He let go and stepped back, allowing the gate to splash down with a loud, cracking slap. Their new raft instantly started to drift away, so Theseus sheathed his sword and clambered down the submerged stairs to grab hold.

So heavy was the gate that it began to pull the Thrasson away from the shore. He managed to slow the raft by digging his fingernails into its ancient wood and jamming the fingers of his improvised foot into a silty crack in the step. Even then, he found himself inexorably drawn toward the center of the pond, until he was half-floating in the water, his pain pods bobbing around him like a swarm of spiny black sponges.

Theseus heard a sharp crackling behind him, then craned his neck around to see Karfhud ripping a long plank from the edge of the other gate. Silverwind and Tessali were standing a short distance up the passage, their eyes gaping at this demonstration of the fiend's strength.

"Perhaps a little help would not be too much to ask for?" the Thrasson called.

All three of Theseus's companions swung their heads around. Tessali stepped to the edge of the stairs, but seemed at a loss as to what he could do, while Silverwind galloped forward and jumped onto the gate—nearly dislodging the Thrasson as he landed. Karfhud simply jerked his plank the rest of the way off the gate, then tossed it onto the raft and waded into the water.

"Perhaps we should change places." The fiend reached past Theseus and sank his talons into the gate, then pulled it back toward shore. "You help the elf."

Tessali backed away. "You can't be serious. Riding a raft down a whirlpool is madness!"

"It's a small whirlpool." Theseus climbed out of the water, but did not reach for the elf's arm. "Still, you can wait here if you like."

"Of course!" Karfhud's voice contained only a hint of mockery. "We'll fetch you when we come back to burn the tiefling."

Tessali shot the fiend a look as sharp as an arrow, but shrugged and reluctantly stepped to the edge of the stairs. Theseus helped the elf leap onto the raft, then picked up the long plank Karfhud had tossed aboard and thrust the end into the water, holding the vessel in place while the fiend boarded. They arranged themselves to distribute the weight evenly—the massive tanar'ri had the front of the gate all to himself—and Theseus shoved off.

Karfhud pulled off his back satchel and busied himself cinching it tightly closed. The others simply waited, listening to the slurp of the whirlpool grow increasingly louder. Their wait was not a long one. The current caught the cumbersome raft and whisked it toward the center of the pond. When it became apparent that he would not need to do much pushing, Theseus laid the plank down on the back edge of the raft—where he could kick it away if need be—and drew his sword. Though he had no idea where the whirlpool would come out, he felt certain Sheba would be waiting for them on the other side. She wanted them to follow, or she would not have waited before going down the whirlpool.

The raft slid past the spandrel where the monster had been lurking, then picked up speed. It began to curve toward the whirlpool, and that was when, barely audible above the slurping din ahead, Theseus heard a faint, familiar cry from behind.

"Theseus, my love!" As muted as it was, he recognized the voice as that of his beloved wine woman. "Have you forgotten me?"

The Thrasson spun and looked toward the great entry arch. There, standing upon the submerged stairs, hip-deep in water, was the white-cloaked figure of his wine woman. Her dark hair hung loose about her shoulders, and, beneath her emerald eyes, he could just make out the tear-trails glistening down her cheeks.

Theseus sheathed his sword. "We must go back!"

"Good thought," gasped Tessali. "Blessed be the Great Meaninglessness!"

Theseus stooped down to reach for the plank, then felt the raft pitching as Karfhud started toward him.

"No—you made your decision," the fiend rumbled. "You cannot take it back now."

On the steps, the wine woman stretched out her arms. "My love, what have I done to offend you? Why do you abandon me?"

Theseus snatched the plank up and shoved the end into the water, leaning into it with all his weight. "We're going back."

The raft pivoted around the plank, then curved along the whirlpool's edge facing backward. Without the fiend's weight to hold down the front, the surface was pitching toward the Thrasson at a dangerously steep angle.

"The current has us." Karfhud eased back toward his end of the gate. "There is nothing you can do."

Theseus looked back to the stairs. The wine woman was growing smaller by the instant, but he could see her well enough to tell she was tearing her clothes and hair in grief.

"I must try."

Theseus plunged the plank into the water, pushing against the current with all his strength. This time, the raft pivoted away from him, swinging toward the heart of the whirlpool. The swirling waters fell away, curling downward in a wild, rushing spiral. The nose of the raft hung above the slope for a moment, then suddenly dipped and caught.

The deck bucked under Theseus's feet. He dropped the plank and threw himself down, trying to grab hold of the high side of the raft. The surface rose up to meet him, slamming into his face and flipping him onto his back. He started to slide into the whirlpool, then the fingers of his makeshift foot caught the edge of the gate. He clamped them down and held on for his life.

Theseus looked toward the front of the raft and saw Silverwind lying next to him, eyes closed and clinging to the edge of the gate with both hands. On the other side of the bariaur was Karfhud, the talons of one claw driven deep into the oaken deck, the other hand clamped tight around one of Tessali's wrist stumps.

The tanar'ri raised his chin and locked gazes with the Thrasson, then his maroon eyes flashed scarlet. He sneered and let go of the elf's wrist.

If Tessali screamed, Theseus never knew it. The elf simply vanished into the whirlpool, then the raft tipped onto its side and followed the Bleaker into the swirling waters.

THE HEART OF THE MATTER

Round and round and down they twirl, pressed flat as crabs to the raft, arching spandrels and half-sunken pillars and screeching wine woman flashing past: arch-pillar-woman arch-pillar-woman, hearts in their throats like throbbing stones, rushing gray funnel rising up past their heads, ears ringing with the whirlpool's roaring, gloomy maw below, yawning wide, wide, wider until in they go—where only the Lady knows.

She will be waiting, there in the darkness below.

There was never any sense of plunging. Theseus's stomach went qualmish with dizziness and rage, and his pulse drummed in his temples, but he never had that light, upside-down feeling in his belly. The raft only continued to whirl around and around until the vertigo became too much and he shut his eyes. An instant later, the waters bubbled up to swallow the raft and still they swirled, not through the currents, but with them. The Thrasson felt his body starting to float; he clamped the fingers on his foot more tightly onto the edge of the raft and dug the fingers of his own hands into the tiny fissures between the gate's oaken planks. His lungs began to burn for air. He opened his eyes and saw nothing but darkness.

The twirling seemed to slow, then they burst through the surface. Theseus felt the damp air spiralling past his face and his body longing to fly off the raft, but he could make no sense of what his senses told him. Now it felt like they were spinning on the outside of a swirling column of water, as though they had passed through the whirlpool and emerged in a waterspout. Thinking some light would help matters, he reached for his sword—and was nearly hurled from the raft the instant his fingers left their crevices. He dug in again and waited.

The air spiralled past his face more slowly, and the force threatening to hurl his body from the raft grew steadily less powerful. At length, the strange current slowed to the point where Theseus heard the purl of water echoing off stony walls he could not see. The sound seemed to be coming from all around, as though they were spinning through a long, dark tunnel. Finally, the Thrasson could draw his sword without being thrown from the raft. He raised the blade over his head and called upon its star-forged steel to light the darkness.

As the sapphire radiance burst from the tip, Theseus saw that they were indeed floating upon the surface of a swirling column of water, which was spinning like a carpenter's auger down the center of a dark round tunnel. There were no shores or banks; the stream was swirling through midair. At first, the Thrasson thought they must be spiralling straight down a pit, then he saw a side passage drift languidly past. They were moving far too slowly to be plunging straight down.

"Now what have I done?" Silverwind gasped. "I have envisioned certain principles, certain laws to govern the multiverse. This makes no sense!"

"It makes as much sense as anything. We have entered the heart of the mazes—the very birthplace of the Plurality!" Karfhud was staring around in wide-eyed amazement, peering longingly into each side tunnel they passed. "How I need a mapping skin!"

Theseus swung around just in time to see the fiend reaching

toward Silverwind. "Leave him alone," the Thrasson warned. "If you harm another of my friends, I swear on my life I'll find a way to kill you."

"Another?" Karfhud snorted. He expelled a cloud of red steam from one of his grotesque nostrils, but withdrew his hand. "I have done no harm to any of them."

"You let the whirlpool take Tessali!"

Karfhud shrugged and looked away. "I thought he no longer mattered to you."

Theseus scowled, too angered by the tanar'ri's obvious lie to reply.

"Truly!" Karfhud protested. "If you had been thinking of him—or any of us—you would not have tried to go back for the wine woman."

"You expected me to abandon her?"

Karfhud rolled his eyes. "We tanar'ri are wiser than to *expect*—especially from humans. I am only saying that you cannot have matters both ways, hero." He spoke this last word as though it were an obscenity. "You tried that back at the palace gate, and it cost me a wing. From this moment forward, you must choose whether you will please yourself, or do what is best for your companions. I have no care which, but I will have nothing to do with this trying to have things both ways."

"If that means you'll have no more to do with me, I welcome it," Theseus growled.

"Truly?" Karfhud glanced back up the tunnel. "Then you have no wish for my help against Sheba? Or have you decided to abandon Tessali, too?"

"He's alive?"

"Do you wish my help or not?" Karfhud spoke with an exaggerated air of impatience. "The longer it takes to decide, the more difficult it will be to track her. We are already quite far from where I saw them."

Theseus thought the fiend might be bluffing, but the claim did make a certain amount of sense. Without a raft to cling to, both the elf and the monster would have been hurled free of the stream soon after emerging from the whirlpool—long before he had managed to light his sword. Assuming Karfhud could see in the dark–

"I can," the fiend interrupted. "Just the warmth of bodies, of course–but Tessali and Sheba were almost fiery. The excitement of the hunt, I imagine."

"If this is a trick–"

"Theseus! Have I ever lied to you?"

Without awaiting a reply, Karfhud pushed off the raft and landed gently on what Theseus had at first taken to be a wall. Silverwind quickly followed, alighting opposite the fiend on what should have been the ceiling. With the bariaur standing upon it, the surface looked as much like a floor as where the tanar'ri stood. The Thrasson pushed off the raft and landed between them. The stone beneath his feet certainly felt like "down." By all appearances, both his companions were standing on the walls, while the stream was running through the air above his head–which made no sense at all. Even if "down" happened to be wherever one's feet were planted, the water should have been coursing along the walls instead of flowing through the center of the passage.

"Just accept what you see." Karfhud started up the tunnel, spiralling around the river as he walked. "If you try to figure out the Plurality, you will go as mad as–but I suppose that is not possible. You could never truly be as mad as a baatezu."

"I fear I already am," whispered Silverwind.

Theseus followed his companions up the tunnel, twining around the gaping side passages and trying to swallow his anger. Tanar'ri lord or not, Karfhud had no business making lectures. Had the fiend held onto Tessali, the attempt to turn back for the wine woman would have caused no harm to anyone. As far as the Thrasson was concerned, the blame for the elf's misfortune lay not on his own shoulders, but squarely on those of Karfhud.

Of course, Theseus did not expect the tanar'ri to repent his treachery. Karfhud had his own reasons for hunting Sheba, and no doubt releasing Tessali had somehow furthered the fiend's cause. That Theseus did not understand *how* only underscored his need to discover what the fiend was really doing: mapping the mazes, certainly, but why?

If Karfhud was eavesdropping, he neglected his usual admonition for Theseus to mind his own business. Instead, the fiend stopped at a side passage. A faint odor of rotting meat exuded from the dank tunnel, and there were strings of sticky black blood smeared just inside the mouth.

"I believe this is the one." Karfhud sat down on the edge of the passage and dangled his legs inside, then cast a wistful glance toward the swirling waters above his head. Although the stream was spinning past at breathtaking speed, it made only a soft gurgling and did not interfere with the fiend's voice. "How I wish I had a mapping skin!"

With that, he stepped onto the wall of the side passage—and promptly plunged headlong into the darkness. A short, gravelly curse rumbled up the shaft, then he was gone.

Theseus dropped to his belly, reaching down with his sword to illuminate the pit. Perhaps ten paces below, the shaft started to bend away, but he could not see where it went.

"Karfhud?"

When no answer came, Silverwind suggested, "Maybe he was killed."

Theseus shook his head. "We can't be that lucky."

The Thrasson tried again to call the fiend. When he received no answer, he dangled his own feet over the edge, then turned around and slowly lowered himself into the pit. The passage walls were as rough as those of any cavern; he had little trouble finding a foothold, and, having found it, even less difficulty clinging to it with the fingers of his borrowed foot. Although the stones were damp and slimy in his grasp, Tessali's hand made Theseus feel so secure that he did not even bother to pass his sword to Silverwind before descending the shaft.

With four split hooves and two hands, the bariaur was even more sure-footed than the Thrasson, and he followed close behind. The damp air grew thick with the reek of decay and spoiled meat. Theseus knew the stench well enough; he had smelled it in the lairs of more man-eating monsters than he could recall.

At the bottom of the shaft, they found Karfhud waiting just beyond the bend. The fiend's maze-blighted flesh looked rather scuffed and his remaining wing hung crumpled and broken on his back, but the fall seemed to have caused him no other harm.

"Why didn't you–"

The fiend spun around, one talon pressed to his black cracked lips. "I see a heat glimmer up ahead." So low was the tanar'ri's whisper that Theseus had trouble hearing it over the rush of blood in his ears. "About ten paces away. It's coming from around a corner."

"Then she's seen our light by now." Theseus twisted his sword hand back and forth, sending rays of sapphire radiance dancing across the entrances of half a dozen adjoining passages. "We may as well go."

Silverwind pulled a handful of white sand from his satchel. "I am ready."

Karfhud nodded and started up the passage, but the Thrasson caught hold of the fiend's shoulder and took the lead himself. In the cramped confines, it would be easier for the tanar'ri to reach over his head than for him to strike around the fiend's dark bulk. Theseus sprinted ten paces up the tunnel and turned down the first side corridor, where he stopped so suddenly that Karfhud slammed into his back and sent him tumbling across the floor straight toward what had caused him to stop.

Me.

I am standing, as I have been since Karfhud tumbled down the chute, waiting in the darkness as I promised to wait, my halo of blades scratching at the tunnel ceiling, my gown hanging limp and still in the damp air, my feet flat on the stone, invisible, a spider awaiting her prey. He should have rushed headlong into my arms, the smell of old death thick in his nose and worry for the elf pounding in his breast, his blood boiling with battle fervor, his nerves prickling with watchfulness–but when he rounded the corner, his mouth fell open, he stopped, and the tanar'ri hit him in the back. Now here he lies, upon my very feet, gaping up at my countenance and white with fear.

How he can see me, I wish to know.

The Thrasson's mouth starts to work, and he lifts himself on his foot and three hands and scrambles away backward. "The-the-the Lady!"

The tanar'ri and the bariaur scowl at his terror and look straight through me and show no sign of fear, and so I know they cannot see me.

"She's only in your mind." The bariaur pushes past Karfhud and goes to shake the Thrasson. "Stop imagining her—before we see her too!"

The tanar'ri pulls the old cleric back. The fiend cannot see me directly, but he knows what is in the Thrasson's mind, and so he supposes me to be some new trick of Sheba's.

We know better, do we not? Someone warned the Thrasson I would be waiting, just as someone also showed him how to see the Pains. For this second betrayal, I should kill him on the instant. The matter would be simple now, with his god-forged armor lying crumpled and useless back in the mazes, with him groveling on the ground before me like any common bloodblade vain enough to think I care—and what punishment more fitting than to rob you of your hero so close to victory or defeat? To never know whether he could have slain the monster, saved Tessali, won back his memories, and—doubtful though it seems—learned the meaning of his maze? That punishment you deserve, for betraying my trust, and for so much, much more.

I push a fingernail toward his torso, and a hole the size of an arrow shaft appears in his chest; dark blood spurts out in a great, throbbing arc, spattering the walls and imparting a faint, coppery tinge to the passage's fetor. The Thrasson does not scream or thrash about in agony; all his golden husks have long since ruptured, and only the black ones remain. I have been expecting them to burst for some time now, but in that, too, I have been disappointed. He only gasps in astonishment and stanches the flow by sticking a finger into the wound.

The insolence! No mere man of renown may refute my will. I drag a finger up through the air; a red seam opens along one side of his throat, pouring a curtain of blood down over his chest.

The astonished tanar'ri grabs him under the arms, thinking to pass him back to the bariaur for healing. I step forward, lifting first one foot, then the other off the ground, and I show myself to the Thrasson's would-be rescuers.

Karfhud allows a groan to slip his cracked lips. We have met once before, longer ago than I can count, when the Blood War spilled into Sigil and made the Slags, and I am the one thing in the multiverse he dreads more than he hates. He drops the Thrasson and sprints from the passage without looking back. What happened to the bariaur, I cannot say. He is gone even before the fiend.

The Thrasson is quick to his feet and turns to follow, but him I must show no mercy. I blink, and when he takes his first step after the fiend, it is into my arms he runs.

Angry as I am at your betrayal, I do not kill him. I have seen that the Thrasson is a man fated to carry the Pains, and it is not my place to rob destiny, only to punish you. I hug him close to my breast, as a mother would a child. He thinks to raise his star-forged sword, but he is too late; no mortal alive has the strength to free himself from my embrace. I hold him until I feel the Pains rising from that void in my chest; until my flesh tingles and flushes and shudders with delight; until my ecstasy fills me to glutting, sates me with honeyed rapture and bliss rolls into sweet agony; until my body nettles with scalding anguish; until I boil in my own sick regret, and still I hold him. The well pours forth, fills me with anguish as fire fills a forge, and still I hold him. I have but one chance, and now all Sigil's hope lies with the Amnesian Hero.

Yet, do not think I have forgiven your betrayal. You have made yourself a part of this, and so I give you the same privilege that I gave Karfhud: go and wander the mazes alone, never look upon the Thrasson again, leave him bleeding and friendless in my tender arms, the Pains rooting deep down in his soul—or remain loyal; continue along with him and suffer the same as all who call Theseus their friend. The choice belongs to you, and that is vengeance enough for me.

REPRISAL

Who can say how long the Thrasson has been cringing there in the fetid damp murk, his knees and his elbows and his face all cold upon the floor? Long enough for the stink of fear to fill the tunnel, long enough for the welts to become blisters, long enough for the blisters to swell into pods and the pods to start their throbbing, long enough for the husks to stretch out their black waving spines and curl their tips into barbed, man-catching hooks.

Check yourself. You know what to look for: a welt, a blister, a rising boil or red pimple, an abscess, a sore you wish you did not have. You're part of it now, one of the damned and the damning, one of the wayfarers who brings a little something extra back from his trip, one of Sigil's bright-shining angels of pain. You will ask yourself, when you happen on some glassy-eyed derelict wandering mad in the streets or hear an injured friend wailing in agony, if it was you who passed him the pod; you will suffer a little with each poor wretch; you will be quietly grateful the husk was not on you when it burst.

Blame me if you will, but these Pains you have earned. I hope you will bear your few better than the Thrasson his thousand.

Still he cringes there on the floor, a blob of spiny pulsing pods, looking more like the egg sack of a bebilith than a man. How long has it been? More than minutes, maybe more than hours, perhaps even days. He may mean to starve himself, though I doubt even he can say: never has a whirlpool spun so fast as the one in his mind is spinning now.

Because he keeps his head cold to the floor, he does not see the dark hand reaching into the tunnel. He does not behold the black ribbon slipping from between its fingers to flutter down the passage toward him, nor does he notice the scrap circling his body, passing through the mass of clinging pods like a spear through fog. He only remembers himself, hunched and weeping, staring out his palace window toward the distant seashore. There lies his son Hippolytus, crushed beneath the wheels of a chariot when a sea monster rose and frightened the horses.

"Your son's death is my doing, King." The servant's broken voice comes from behind Theseus's back. "Had I told you how angry Phaedra became when your son rebuked her advances, you would never have called Poseidon's curse down upon him."

In his hands, Theseus holds a message, found beneath his wife Phaedra's swinging feet, accusing her stepson Hippolytus of defiling her womanly honor. The Thrasson crumples the scroll, and he feels something shrivel inside.

"No!"

At last, Theseus has lifted his head off the tunnel's cold floor. The first black pod has burst, covering his chest with a glistening cascade of ebony ichor. "I cannot bear it!"

"My gift does not please you?" Karfhud stepped into the tunnel. He was furling a new mapping parchment, and there was dark blood dripping from his index talon. "Then I apologize. I thought you wanted to recover your memories."

Theseus rose and cast a wary eye at the parchment. It looked too damp and pink to have been forgotten someplace in Karfhud's satchel. The Thrasson waved at the thing with his sword's glowing tip.

"Where did you get that?"

"I doubt you really want to know," Karfhud said. "But have no fear. I did not kill either of your friends for it."

"Where else would it come from?" the Thrasson demanded. Perhaps Karfhud had not seen Sheba at all. "Is that what you were thinking of when you let Tessali drown?"

Karfhud shook his head. "Tessali is not drowned—and your friends are not the only prey in the mazes."

"But they are the only prey likely to be down here." Theseus sniffed at the rotten air, then added, "At least the only prey whose skin might still be usable."

"Now you are becoming like Silverwind. Your imagination has taken the place of your wits."

"Then put my imagination to rest." Theseus stretched his hand out. "Let me see the parchment."

Karfhud jerked the skin away, orange flames flickering in his maroon eyes. "No one may touch my maps!"

Theseus's rage welled up, burning like bile in his throat. Had he not known the hilt would slip from his grasp the instant he raised his sword, he would have rushed the fiend and attacked. The Thrasson fixed his eye on the two yellow pods still hanging from the fiend's body, contemplating whether to take what vengeance he could. When he looked down at his own body and saw the mass of husks hanging from it, however, he decided that it might be wiser to forego the reprisal. Simply hurting Karfhud would neither avenge Tessali nor bring him back.

"A wise choice." Karfhud stepped forward and glared down at the Thrasson. "I am certain we could cause each other a great deal of pain and never violate our oaths, but that would neither save Tessali nor help you recover your memories."

Theseus scowled. "Are you saying—"

"Yes." Karfhud raised his map. "I have found Sheba's den."

"And Tessali is inside? Alive?"

The fiend shrugged. "I would be lying if I claimed to have looked inside. But I saw no sign of him elsewhere—and this is not his." Karfhud waved his new parchment. "But I do feel certain the monster has your amphora. That memory I gave you slipped free of her den as she entered it."

Theseus regarded the tanar'ri cautiously. "How do I know this isn't a trick?"

"You are the only one who has ever thought of tricks between us," countered Karfhud.

"I have no way of knowing that." Theseus was silent for a moment, then said, "I'll go with you after you tell me why you want to attack Sheba."

Karfhud shook his parchment at Theseus. "Because I need time to complete these!" The fiend's voice was almost fanatical. "And, until she is scattered to the four corners of the mazes, I will not have it."

"That, I can see already. But surely you have found a way out of the mazes by now?"

"Of course. Do you think no one in the Abyss has called my name in these many thousand years?"

"Then why haven't you answered their summons?" Theseus asked. "What can be so important about completing the maps?"

The fiend looked away. "You would do better to worry about finding your own meaning." He folded his arms, then slumped to the floor. "But if you will not go until I answer that question, we will wait here. It makes no difference to me. Sheba will come for us eventually—when she has done with her other prey."

A cold tremor ran down Theseus's limbs, then he suddenly felt tight in the chest and more than a little sick to his stomach. He had experienced such sensations a few times before, often enough to recognize them as symptoms of a deep, visceral emotion few men could truly control.

"You are frightened?" Karfhud gasped. "Of the monster?"

"Terrified," Theseus admitted. It was the husks, he realized, that truly frightened him. He had faced death more times than he could recall without flinching, but the mere memory of the last time his pods had burst was enough to make him go weak in the knees. He clenched his teeth and motioned Karfhud to stand. "Let's get this done."

Battered as he was, the fiend leapt to his feet as gracefully as an acrobat. "I have always said the gods hate a coward." He glanced around the tunnel, then added, "Though I suppose that hardly matters here."

Karfhud unfurled his map and started down the corridor, his muzzle twisting into an anxious grin. As the tanar'ri pushed past, Theseus tried to sneak a closer look at the parchment. He saw nothing but a section of straight line and a string of fresh gristle.

"What about Silverwind?"

Karfhud did not even look up. "If you want to save Tessali, I suggest we waste no time looking for the bariaur."

Trying not to think about what he could not do if the fiend's reply meant what he thought it did, Theseus followed Karfhud through a long, winding array of cavern passages. Every now and again, the tanar'ri would stop at an intersection to twist his map this way and that and mutter to himself. Most of the time, he barely looked up as he rounded corner after corner and strode one dank tunnel after another. The Thrasson made little effort to keep track of where they were going; even if he somehow found his way back to the whirlpool later, he would have no way to climb up the water spout—and no idea where to go even if he reached the flooded garden.

Theseus spent much of the walk trying to puzzle out what Karfhud was looking for. The fiend wanted to complete the seemingly impossible task of mapping the ever-expanding mazes, yet he claimed his escape did not depend on success. Only one thing would elicit such devotion from a tanar'ri: power. But how? Was he trying to map a route for an invasion force? Were the mazes somehow tied to the countless number of portals that connected Sigil to the rest of the multiverse? The Thrasson puffed out a breath of exasperation; the mere fact that Karfhud had not complained about his line of thought meant he was not even close to the truth.

"Of course, my silence could also be misleading." Karfhud looked up from his map and sneered at the Thrasson. "But I doubt it. You would spend your time better worrying about yourself."

"My thanks for the advice." Theseus nearly gagged as he spoke. Though he had noticed the stench of rotten flesh growing steadily stronger as they advanced into the warren, he had not expected to actually taste the stuff when he opened his mouth. "But we both know what I'm looking for."

Karfhud raised his pleated brow. "Do we?"

The fiend turned down a crooked corridor, leaving Theseus to contemplate his question. The Thrasson could not imagine what he might possibly discover in the mazes that he would not stand a better chance of finding back in Arborea. Despite what Karfhud had said in the swamp, it seemed to him he could only be searching for his memories. Better than anyone, the Thrasson knew that someone without a past was a hollow crust, a brittle shell of habit laid over a skeleton of animal instinct.

Karfhud bent his arm back at that impossible angle, stuffing his map into his satchel, then pointed at the floor ahead. Across the gray stone lay a carpet of bones, some old and powdery, some with smears of blood and bits of sinew still clinging to the joints—though none looked fresh enough to have provided the fiend's new parchment. Theseus flushed, and his stomach began to writhe. The dank air grew unbearably close, whether because of the horrid stench or because of his own mounting fear, he could not say. To be rid of the clinging mass of husks, he would have peeled off his own skin. Only the thought that they would burst prevented him from trying.

"Can you do this thing?" Karfhud asked.

"If I can't, kill me here."

"If you cannot, I will not have the chance."

Carefully picking his way through the bones, the fiend led Theseus to where a small fissure opened into the wall. Taking the crooked gap to be the entrance to Sheba's lair, the Thrasson slipped forward and peered into the cramped passage—then Karfhud quietly grasped his head and redirected his gaze up the passage.

About three paces ahead, the tunnel opened into a large, serpentine chamber coiled around an immense pillar of natural stone. The column was square and nearly as broad as a house, the top so high that it was lost in the vaulted darkness above. Aside from a mat of tangled bones strewn about its base, the shaft's only adornment was a decorative post carved into each of its corners. There was no entrance, at least on the two sides the Thrasson could see.

After allowing the Thrasson to inspect the battle arena, Karfhud waved a claw at the fissure. "Wait in there—with your sword sheathed; it would not do for Sheba to notice its light before you strike."

Theseus peered again into the cramped passage. It was half filled with the powdering skeletons of those who had perished before in its tight confines, no doubt with the monster lurking just outside. The Thrasson could squeeze his body into the crack easily enough, but his bulky jacket of pods would never fit.

"What are you frightened of?" Karfhud growled, noticing his hesitation. "Just imagine these pods of yours are soft enough not to break. They are all in your mind anyway."

"If so, you have imagined them too—or have you forgotten their bite?"

The fiend snorted in disgust. "We could trade places, but you can hardly be the bait. Sheba would catch you in an instant."

Theseus glanced into the serpentine chamber and saw the wisdom of what Karfhud said. The fiend's legs, both longer and more powerful than those of any human, were more suitable to plowing through the jumble of bones.

The Thrasson took a deep breath, then gingerly squeezed into the fissure. Most of the pods, still pulsing in time to his heart, simply passed ghostlike through the stone. A few of the larger husks, squeezed like grapes between fingers, stopped throbbing and rolled along his body. But only one broke. It was a big emerald one that filled his mind with a nettling green fog; as the ichor spilled down his arm, his heart began to race, and his jaws ached with the urge to vomit. He clamped his mouth shut and tried to tell himself it was only the smell of moldy bones troubling him.

Karfhud stuck his dark head into the fissure and fixed his red eyes on Theseus's face. "It is a mystery to me, this insanity that has come over you—but know this, Thrasson: Karfhud delga' Talator does not give his blood bond to cowards or sods." Compared to the rancid fetor of the cavern, the brimstone stink of the fiend's breath was almost a relief. "When the time comes, you will act like what you are—or we both shall perish."

Theseus nodded—though not too much, as he did not want to burst any more of his pods. "You may count on it."

"Good." Karfhud pulled his head from the fissure, then glanced toward the pillar. "Stay hidden until you hear us pass this tunnel. I'll stop just beyond the mouth and drive Sheba back toward you. I am in no condition for a long battle, so take her legs from behind, and quickly. After that, we can scatter her at leisure."

Karfhud picked the scab on his wrist and offered his blood to dress the Thrasson's star-forged blade. Then, with one last exhortation to be ready, the fiend turned away. Though the bones lay knee-deep in the next chamber, the tanar'ri moved through them in utter silence. Theseus slipped his sword into its scabbard, plunging the fissure into utter darkness, and tried not to think about what would happen when he leapt from his cranny. Perhaps the tanar'ri was right; perhaps he was only imagining the husks—but if so, then he was also imagining the Lady of Pain, and nobody seemed to doubt her existence.

Theseus was careful to keep his mind off Karfhud until the battle began, which happened soon enough. It started softly, with a low, sonorous growl that rumbled through the cave like an earthquake, making the bones dance, filling the passages with the eerie chatter of a thousand ribs knocking together. Next, the tanar'ri let loose with a deafening bellow—it sounded as terrified as it did angry—and the Thrasson knew the time had come to make his plans.

There were a couple of muffled thuds somewhere deep in the serpentine chamber, then the distant crackling of Karfhud's heavy feet stomping through the bone pile. Theseus did not consider, even for a moment, the possibility that the fiend intended to let him live after the battle. As little as the Thrasson knew about the maps, he was sure the tanar'ri would have liked it better if he did not know anything—and lords of the Abyss had a habit of getting exactly what they liked.

A sharp tearing sound rasped up the passage, followed by a tanar'ri curse and a loud, wet slap. The monster roared, leaving Theseus's ears ringing and making it nearly impossible to hear the bones crackling under the feet of the two enormous brutes.

The Thrasson began to ease out of the fissure, praying he would not burst too many of the husks. He would not be much use lying on the ground writhing in pain. And, whatever Karfhud was planning for after the battle, the fiend was telling the truth about one thing, at least: if they did not destroy the monster together, they would perish together.

Karfhud's heavy steps splintered past the mouth of the passage, with Sheba's close behind. Theseus pushed a leg free of the fissure—and felt a pop. Something warm and sticky oozed down his thigh. He nearly bit his tongue in two to keep from screaming, then his leg went dead and useless, a scalding wave of anguish seething down its length. His knee buckled, and he tumbled out of the fissure onto the dark, bone-strewn floor.

How many pods burst, or which ones, Theseus could not say. He simply fell into a boiling ocean of pain. For an instant—it could have been no longer than that, though it seemed an hour to him—he lay there trying not to scream, not to writhe or beat his feet against the floor, or to do anything that would draw the monster's attention. Half a dozen paces away, he could hear the battle raging: growling, pounding, tearing, snorting, popping, snapping, splintering, and muffled shattering. Karfhud growled, Sheba roared, he screeched, she wailed. The smell of sulfur and ash, tanar'ri gore and monster blood, filled the passage.

Theseus pushed himself to his feet. The effort sent rivers of molten slag boiling through his veins, but he forced himself to stumble toward the din. He did not run; if he ran, he might fall. If he fell, more husks would spill their ichor, and then he would be done. As it was, every throbbing, raw nerve in his body was begging him to turn away from the maelstrom, to flee into the darkness; he kept them at bay only by concentrating on the pain he would feel if Sheba survived to catch him alone later.

Something wet and foul-smelling swept through the darkness, so close to Theseus's face that he felt the air stir across his cheeks. Karfhud let out a low, deep groan, then countered with a terrific, wet-sounding blow. Sheba's sticky blood spattered the Thrasson's brow.

As Theseus started to pull his bright-shining sword, he heard

Karfhud clatter a single step backward. The battle lapsed for just an instant. Sheba stood wheezing in the darkness, no doubt trying to puzzle out the cause of the strange lull, and then the Thrasson understood Karfhud's plan.

"Why do you wait?" the tanar'ri yelled. "Strike!"

And Sheba did, launching such a furious assault that it sent the tanar'ri crashing to the floor in a thundering din of old crackling skeletons and fiendish bones breaking anew. Karfhud shrieked in pain, and the monster roared in glee.

Theseus leapt into the darkness, whispering a single word as he drew his sword: "Darkstar."

The star-forged blade came out of its scabbard black as ebony, then slashed through something the thickness of an olive tree. Sheba howled and crashed to the ground. Theseus, attacking blindly, struck again. This time, his steel bit deep into the monster's thick midsection. She hissed in pain and rolled across the jumble of skeletons. The Thrasson followed by sound, swinging blindly into the darkness and cleaving nothing but bones. Still, he did not light his weapon; with the tip of his sword glowing bright as a moon, he would have drawn the monster's attention straight to himself, leaving Karfhud free to clean up the mess at his leisure.

Theseus, still chopping his way across the cavern floor, much preferred things as they were now—especially when he heard the clamor of rattling bones and snarling throats off to his left. He stumbled over and began hacking into the darkness, taking no care what he struck so long as the blow landed on something live. Three times, he felt that star-forged steel slice through something as big around as his waist, and three times he heard the monster roar. He heard Karfhud, too, but groaning, and that only softly. The Thrasson took no care; he continued to swing until, at last, a claw lashed out of the darkness to send him crashing to the cluttered floor.

Theseus felt the husks bursting one after the other, and now he could not stop himself from screaming. Still, he rolled to his feet, lost his legs and plunged through a vat of boiling, seething anguish. He began crawling back toward the battle.

It took Theseus a moment to realize he had no idea where he was going. His own screams were drowning out any cries he might have heard from Karfhud or the monster, and his nose was too full of his own blood to find them by scent. Slowly, he managed to thread the thought through his tormented mind that he needed to be silent, that if he kept screaming he would summon his enemies to him like scavengers to the battle dead. The Thrasson closed his mouth, and that was when he heard the awful stillness.

The chamber was quiet, but not quite silent. Somewhere ahead, there was Karfhud's groaning, low and steady. All around the fiend, there seemed to be a soft scrabble, as though the rats had already come out to gnaw at his fingers. There was a terrible, howling wheeze—it took Theseus a moment to identify it as his own labored breath.

"Star . . . light . . ." It seemed difficult to believe the frail voice struggling to issue the command belonged to Karfhud. "Cleave the . . . night."

The sapphire light glimmered to life on the tip of Theseus's sword, revealing a sight only slightly more gruesome than before the battle had begun. One of Sheba's black-veined legs lay at his feet, the toes still twitching, the ankle and the knees still working as the thing slowly inched its way toward the den. Scattered around the chamber, wherever they happened to have landed after the Thrasson's sword hacked them away, were other pieces of the monster: an ear, a wedge of torso, the matted hand from the arm that had been cleaved back in the swamp maze. Like the leg, they were all writhing back toward the central pillar.

A few paces away, Karfhud lay in a hollow of smashed bones, soaking in a pool of his own bubbling blood, his blighted face torn half off, and his black ribs shoving up through his chest in a dozen places. Though his maroon eyes had faded to mere orange embers, they looked no less hateful than ever, and they were fixed on Theseus's face.

"Coward."

Theseus shook his head. "Treacherous, perhaps."

The tanar'ri shook his head. "Can't . . . fool . . . me." The fiend raised a broken talon, beckoning the Thrasson closer. "Give me . . . a little blood."

Theseus stayed where he was.

"Last . . . request," Karfhud said. "I'll . . . tell . . ."

Theseus shook his head. Even in death, the tanar'ri was not likely to reveal the secret of his maps.

"Not . . . maps. You . . . will . . . never know . . . that—but what . . . of . . . friend? There is . . . secret . . ."

The Thrasson cursed. Tessali was probably dead by now, but Theseus could not leave here until he learned the truth.

"Of course . . . you can," Karfhud gasped. "Who is . . . to know? Your . . . fame . . . will not suffer . . ."

Theseus started toward the fiend. "My fame isn't what matters—Tessali is."

Had Karfhud not looked away and uttered a curse, Theseus might never have stopped to consider his own words. He had been a man of renown for so long that he had grown accustomed to considering his feats not in light of how they helped others, but merely in the glory they won him. He had lost sight of the quality that had made him a hero in the first place—his true concern for others—and focused his attention instead on the trappings of being a famous champion. Perhaps that was why he had lost his memories in the first place: he had lost himself.

"Don't . . . have much . . . time to waste . . . congratulating . . ." Karfhud gasped. "I . . . may not . . . last."

Theseus kneeled beside Karfhud's head, then he ran his own palm down the cutting edge of his sword. The blade opened a clean red gash. The Thrasson made a fist, but did not allow any of his blood to dribble on the tanar'ri's lips.

"Tell me."

Karfhud's only reply was a long, gurgling wheeze. The fiend licked his lips, but shook his head. "You . . . already peeled me . . . once."

Theseus swung his hand over the tanar'ri's lips and tightened his fist, squeezing a long red stream into Karfhud's mouth. He allowed the fiend to drink for several seconds, then pulled his hand away again.

"Now, tell me how to find Tessali."

Karfhud licked the blood off his cracked lips, then a raspy laugh rumbled up from deep in his chest, and the embers in his eyes went cold.

Theseus wasted no time trying to revive the fiend, for he knew well enough when he had been swindled. Instead, the Thrasson rolled the tanar'ri's heavy body onto its side and cut the fiend's battered back-satchel free. If there was a secret to entering the lair, Karfhud would certainly have marked it on his beloved maps. Theseus rifled through the parchments until he found the freshest one, then pulled it out and, as he unfurled the chart, found a clump of nappy white bariaur fur still clinging to one pink-tinged edge.

It is true, despite all I promised, that someone else is dead. It happened this way: while we were looking elsewhere, Karfhud jumped the bariaur from behind. Before Silverwind realized what was happening, all his legs and both his arms were broken, his skin was being peeled from his back, and he was already making plans for what he will imagine better the next time around.

I wish I could say the bariaur's multiverse ended quickly, but that is not how tanar'ri do things. They are masters of the slow death, with a thousand ways to prolong the torment, and each more agonizing than the last. Sometimes, the torture lasts even beyond death; the bariaur was spared that, at least, for the price of becoming a map.

A pity for Silverwind, of course, that he never found his way out of the mazes, but he was hardly a great loss to us: a boring, self-centered old fool, the likes of which you can find sleeping in any gutter in Sigil. And, really, what did you expect from a tanar'ri? Wisdom *and* goodwill? Consider yourself lucky the fiend settled for a bariaur's hide when he could have had prime, olive-skinned human.

The Thrasson, of course, was right about the map. It took him only a moment to find the pillar, a moment longer to see the three circles, no time at all to realize what he had to do. Already, he has hurled Sheba's writhing parts back into the adjoining passages; already, he has rounded the column twice; already, he has tossed aside the unfurled map and set himself to the task.

Staved ribs aching and bloody slashes throbbing, Theseus staggered the third time around the pillar and did not notice the peace gift in his path. He only saw the dark door opening before him, then heard his foot shattering the pottery, felt the broken shards crumbling beneath the palm of his borrowed foot, and looked down to see the black ribbons swirling round and round, rising up one after the other, circling his body once, twice, three times. He remembered, once before, standing in the mouth of a dark, fetor-filled cavern. His young wine woman had been there with him, pressing a ball of golden thread into his hands.

"I will hold the end, brave Theseus. After you have slain the minotaur, follow the string back to me."

"You may be certain I will, Princess." Theseus had kissed her long upon the lips. "And then will I carry you away from cruel Minos, across the sapphire sea to make you Ariadne, Queen of Athens."

Ariadne.

No sooner had the name come than the Thrasson felt the bursting of a husk; he looked down and saw the black ichor oozing down his breast. His chest went hollow, and inside he felt a cold, bitter wind scraping across his raw ribs.

"No more!" he cried. "I have remembered too much already!"

But the memories continued to come; with each, another black pod ruptured and spilled its dark purulence over his body. He saw clearly what he had only glimpsed before: his callous betrayal of Ariadne, how his neglect caused his own father's death, how his own prideful blindness cost the lives of two wives, how his fury destroyed his innocent son. From the moment of his first victory, he had lost the very thing that had made him a hero.

And now, here the monster was, offering the same terrible bargain that had brought him so much misery before: a life, a single life, in exchange for eternal fame and renown; Tessali for all his memories of glory and fame. This time, Theseus knew better than to accept. With the black ribbons still whirling about him and the black pods still spilling ichor down his chest, the Thrasson raised his sword and rushed through the black door.

He found himself in a dark, vaulted chamber thick with the smell of sweat and fear, where gloom clung like smoke to the ceiling and the rasp of anguished lungs echoed from every wall. The room was cluttered with iron cages of every size and shape, some square, some round, some shaped like pears, some big enough to hold Sheba herself and others barely large enough for a gnome. Dozens of manacles and shackles dangled from the support pillars; many of them still held the rotted remains of their latest prisoners.

In the center of the room, Tessali hung by the neck on a long rope, kicking his legs and rasping for breath. His arms were not bound, and he was rubbing his raw wrist stumps across the noose in a vain attempt to keep himself from strangling. The monster was nowhere in sight, though the Thrasson knew she would be lurking somewhere within easy reach of the elf.

Theseus took off at a sprint, taking no precaution other than to curve around so he could approach from the side. Though he was rushing into a certain ambush, he had no time to be prudent—not if he wanted to save Tessali.

As the Thrasson neared the rasping elf, he was nearly overcome by the mordant smell of ash. He dodged behind a pillar, narrowly avoiding a swiping claw, then pivoted around behind the column to sprint past Sheba's back.

Tessali's eyes were already bugging out and his face was contorted with suffocation, so Theseus could not say how surprised the elf was to see him charging to the rescue. The Thrasson crossed the last few paces of floor in a flying leap, his blue-glowing sword flashing like lightning as he slashed through the rope.

Theseus's blade had barely cut the line before a deafening roar exploded in his ear. He felt himself flying sideways through the air, then landed in a crumpled, aching heap beneath the beast. Pods of pain burst by the handful. He opened his mouth to scream and found his cry smothered by the monster's slimy red hide. She began to burrow her maw down toward his throat. The Thrasson tried to bring his shoulder up to protect himself, but she was too powerful to resist.

Then, suddenly, there was an opening between their bodies.

Theseus rolled onto his back and saw a length of rope looped about Sheba's throat, pulling her head up and away. Behind the monster, with one end of the line clamped between his teeth and the other threaded around his elbow, stood Tessali.

It was the perfect set. Theseus gave a great war cry and brought his sword arcing up toward Sheba's throat–but the monster of the labyrinth lives inside us all. She is the dark, devouring hunger that is never sated, the creeping shadow that ever plays the fiend to our seraphim, the secret rage hidden in our hearts; deny her, and we become her slaves; fight her, and we make her invincible. By now, you must know that no monster can ever be killed, not really–and so the Thrasson's star-forged steel slashes through the air in a perfect sapphire arc that nearly cleaves a githyanki in two.

"Watch it, berk!"

The fellow dances aside, delivering a swift kick to Theseus's head.

When the githyanki's foot comes away, he does not see the throbbing yellow pod clinging to his ankle. He only sees a battered, foul-smelling Thrasson seated on the bed of hard cobblestones, gaping at the cursing, bustling crowd, at the squalid, unmortared stone huts that flank the street, and, most of all, at the ragged, wild-eyed elf standing before him.

PAINS UNENDING

He thinks he has given me the slip, that sun-bronzed man of renown, but no one leaves the mazes, not really; they only turn a corner, cross a threshold, open a door, and forget they have walked the same path before. I see him there upon Lethe's black, barren shore: a quivering mass of husks, bloated and throbbing with ichor, bowing over the cold waters to look upon his own dark reflection. His eyes, sunken and rimmed with red, stare back from some murk-filled place as deep and brutal as the Abyss; his cheeks have gone gaunt and hollow with dusky hunger; his swollen and cracked lips bleed with that vile thirst he can never quite escape. Nothing has passed his lips since quitting the monster's den: not bread, not fruit, not sweet, cool wine; he squandered not a moment upon Sigil's wonders, nor took an hour's ease, nor even provisioned for his journey. He only rushed down Scab Way to burst through Rivergate's grim door and hurl himself through that purling portal in back.

The Thrasson kneels upon the cragged bank and cups a precious mouthful of the river's dark, soothing water in his hands. How many times before, he wonders, has he done this? How many times before has he been the Amnesian Hero, the man of renown searching out his legacy, only to discover it not worth the having? How many times has he knelt upon these same barren shores, taken these cold waters in his palms to drink the numbing bounty of the Lethe?

Lethe?

Those who have drunk of Lethe's waters cannot remember its name, yet that is the name I recall. If he has drunk, then have I also? What matter then that the monster has collected all Poseidon's lies, that she has strung them like golden tinsel safely inside her den? If the Thrasson has drunk, then so have I. The lies become truths forgotten. I become prodigal daughter to the King of Seas and bride of Set, obliged by blood and rite to honor them both.

Yet, it may be the Thrasson never drank, that he lost his memory through accident or god-curse, that even now the game has not run its course and cunning Poseidon plays at making a daughter of one to whom he is no father. Then would I know his golden gifts for lies; then would the cracked gate mend; then would this Theseus, this sunken-eyed drudge, return to Arborea just one more Hunter bearing gifts for his master.

Has he drunk before? You have the answer within, I am sure; is the river's true name Lethe or . . . some other?

I will know soon enough. The Thrasson is lifting his hands toward his face; the Pains have become too much. Already—as he battled the monster, as he pushed his way down Scab Way, even as he has been kneeling there on Lethe's cragged bank—a hundred husks have burst; but what is a hundred to a thousand? He cannot bear that broken emptiness inside, that cold, sick guilt gnawing at his belly, that eternal ache in his breast. He has only to drink and they will be gone; the spines will straighten, the husks will slip from his body and splash into the cold, swirling waters.

The Thrasson lowers his face to meet his rising palms, purses his lips to draw the soothing waters into his mouth . . . but if he drinks, he will forget Ariadne. Will she not return to torment him? Will he not start chasing her through the mazes, begging her to tell him his name? Will he not keep making the same mistakes, keep adding more Antiopes and Hippolytuses and Jayks to his long ledger of betrayals, keep adding to the terrible burden he must shoulder each time he seeks out his legacy?

The Thrasson looks deep into his cupped hands, studies those hollow cheeks and thirst-cracked lips on his glimmering likeness, stares many long moments into those red and sunken eyes, and he sees something of the fiend in them: a tinge of maroon around the irises, two tongues of orange flame flickering in the Abyssal darkness of his pupils. He does not look away; he opens his hands and lets the dark reflection drain away. Terrible as the Pains are, better to bear them forever than to turn his back on a tanar'ri.

O MISTRESS AND MOTHER OF PLEASURE,
THE ONE THING AS CERTAIN AS DEATH,
WE SHALL CHANGE AS THE THINGS THAT WE CHARISH,
SHALL FADE AS THEY FADED BEFORE,
AS FOAM UPON WATER SHALL PERISH,
AS SAND UPON THE SHORE.

WE SHALL KNOW WHAT THE DARKNESS DISCOVERS,
IF THE GRAVE-PIT BE SHALLOW OR DEEP;
AND OUR FATHERS OF OLD, AND OUR LOVERS,
WE SHALL KNOW IF THEY SLEEP OR NOT SLEEP.
WE SHALL SEE WHETHER HELL BE NOT HEAVEN,
FIND OUT WHETHER TARES BE NOT GRAIN,
AND THE JOYS OF THEE SEVENTY TIMES SEVEN,
OUR LADY OF PAIN.